MW00884085

SHOCK AND AWESOME

LEXI GRAVES MYSTERIES

CAMILLA CHAFER

A

Audacious

ISBN: 1497345235
ISBN-13: 978-1497345232

ALSO BY CAMILLA CHAFER

The Stella Mayweather Series:

Illicit Magic
Unruly Magic
Devious Magic
Magic Rising
Arcane Magic

Lexi Graves Mysteries:

Armed & Fabulous
Who Glares Wins
Command Indecision
Shock & Awesome
Weapons of Mass Distraction

CHAPTER ONE

The very last person I expected to see walking out of my boss's boardroom was my ex-boyfriend, Detective Adam Maddox. Okay, so he wasn't exactly the "last person," but he was definitely in the top ten. After all, it wasn't like I could think of a single thing they had in common, except me, and I was fairly sure neither was too happy about that. Not that there was anything doing in "that department." Nothing at all. Which made their handshake as they paused just outside of the doorway, as well as Maddox clapping Solomon on the shoulder, all the more strange. Now that their romances with me were over, had they moved onto — I swallowed hard — a bromance?

"I'll get the details to you this afternoon," Maddox said as they released hands. Solomon's right hand immediately dived into the pocket of his black chinos as he nodded in response. Okay, so maybe not a bromance. Solomon didn't seem as happy as he first appeared, not that he would ever make it obvious, of course, but after several months working with him, I got to know his

1

most subtle moves. Solomon was up to something with my ex-boyfriend, but he wasn't altogether thrilled about it. I wondered what got to him the most: my ex or whatever they were collaborating on. Most of all, I wondered when someone was going to tell me. If there was one thing that made me more uncomfortable than having two former lovers in the same room, it was being kept in the dark on work ops. Now, with Solomon's expansion of the agency still a big secret under wraps, I was doubly eager to uncover whatever this latest thing was. I swear it had nothing to do with personal issues. With either of them. No, not I. I was a professional, and a polished professional, albeit a snoop, at that.

Turning on his heel, Maddox barely blinked at the very moment he noticed me at my desk, but our eyes met and his softened slightly before his face hardened. Okay, someone was a cross bunny. With a curt incline of his chin towards me, he marched out of the large room that served as the private investigators' shared office, towards the exit.

I didn't realize I was watching him go until the door clicked shut behind him and I turned back to my laptop, briefly glancing up to see Solomon's eyes on me, his face blank. Without saying a word, he turned away, returning to the sanctum of his office next to the boardroom.

Well, that was weird. Solomon and Maddox once worked together, and that was how I met them, after pretty much tripping over a corpse and landing in one humdinger of a financial crime. Neither were friends at the time; indeed, Maddox seemed suspicious of Solomon, given his history, which was one of shades, rather than a clear-cut resume like Maddox. His rise through the ranks of Montgomery PD was as obvious as every serving police officer in my family.

Since that first case ended, Solomon decided to retire from whatever he did in national law enforcement — no one was ever totally sure what or who employed him — and stick around Montgomery to start up his own detective agency. He offered me a job and Maddox presented me with the top position of girlfriend. I was still a private investigator, and though I had a lot left to learn, I was definitely off the trainee rung, but the girlfriend spot was on hiatus. Not least because I suspected Maddox of cheating with his supremely pretty undercover partner, Detective Rebecca Blake, but also because I subsequently did the horizontal horror with Solomon in several moments of unconscionable madness.

Now I was single, but gainfully employed, and my two exes were shaking hands like they were simply agreeing to man the barbecue together at Montgomery's next town fair. It was baffling. Even worse, I was desperate to know what it was all about, and so would my best friend, Lily Shuler, the moment I told her. If I didn't have the answers, I would have to listen to a whole bunch of her theories. But how was I to get the information out of a man so shrewd, he would know what I was doing as soon as I eased out of my chair?

Simple. I would wait for him to tell me. He was probably dying to, I reasoned. After all, everyone loves to share a secret.

For the next hour, as I impatiently waited in desperation for Solomon to share, while it ate me up inside, I filled the time with less paperwork and more surreptitious texting of Lily. She was as intrigued as I.

"He's dying to tell you," she texted by return.

I looked up, narrowing my eyes at the blind-covered interior windows of Solomon's office. He gazed at his laptop screen, and only briefly did I notice his left eyebrow flicker, as if he were suddenly aware someone was watching him. I ducked my head, fully aware that he not only knew it was I, but also that he wasn't even remotely dying to tell me a thing.

How annoying.

"Nope," I typed, "his mouth is tighter than a clam."

"Bastard," pinged the reply.

Bit harsh, perhaps, but not far off the mark in the general scheme of my thoughts.

My phone vibrated again and I peered at the screen. "Do you think they want to share you?" asked Lily.

My eyes widened and I reached for my glass of water to quench my suddenly dry mouth. I doubted it, somehow. I wasn't even sure either of them wanted me solo, given the way things abruptly ended between Maddox and me, and then Solomon and me. Just my luck, really. Wait forever for a decent guy to show up, sweating my buns off in Anton's ass-kicker of a spin class, just to keep said butt looking peachy in the interim, and just when one hot guy turns up, so does his hotter pal. As for who was hot, and who was hotter, that was hard to say. What I did know was one cheated and the other seemed to have forgotten to call. Ever.

Having said that, the thought of them going two at a time gave me a hot flush before my brain became the consistency of the innards of a Twinkie.

"I'm having a hot flush," texted Lily.

"Get aircon," I messaged. "How do I find out why Maddox was here?"

"Ask. Or bug S's office."

Well, that was an idea, but somehow, I knew Solomon would find out, and when he did, I could imagine him firing my ass. What would I do then? The PI gig was my favorite job since I joined the world of the gainfully employed. Would I want to return to temping? Working the worst bits of a job to earn a measly paycheck along with the general disdain of the other employees? No. I wanted to crack cases, catch bad guys and make enough money to afford the butter yellow bungalow on Bonneville Avenue, which I had my eye on. A few months ago, it was for sale, but the sign disappeared within days. I wished it was for sale again, especially now that Lily's parents put our apartment building up for sale the moment the cast came off my arm. Having it broken while chasing the bad guys was one of the downsides of the job, but it managed to earn me several weeks of paid recuperation time.

Since getting my fill of the important goings-on in Hollywood via the E! Network, I returned to my job early and got stuck with desk duty. Now the cast was off, I was raring to go, but Solomon had yet to assign me any cases. It wasn't just that I was itching to get out there and do something productive, the bonus money was undeniably a delightful extra. My salary paid my basics, but the case completion bonus, paid by the clients, was an extra boost to my ebbing morale. I was bored. I might complain about a numb ass when I was sitting on it for hours during surveillance, in a cold car, watching an assortment of criminals, idiots, and cheats, but anything had to beat the humdrum of office work. After all, this was what I thought I escaped from when I took the job.

But aside from all that, asking was not an option. After all, I was cool and aloof! I cared not for the activities of the two men not all that in my life! If they wanted to be buddies, that was their business. Oh, whom was I kidding? I seethed with nosy desperation.

"Are you bugging S's office right now?" came Lily's next text, a few minutes later.

"No," I tapped into my cell phone's on-screen keypad. "I'm just going to wait for him to tell me."

"Ha-ha. Very funny. Seriously?"

I looked from the phone screen to the kit assembled on my desk. Digital camera, telescoping lens, listening bugs, miniature camera, my wire, my laptop, an array of programs and databases contained within, and I thought again. No, I decided, I had to be strong. I could not bug my boss's office. Today.

"Lexi?" I jumped at the sound of Solomon's voice and

looked up guiltily, as if he could tell I was seriously considering Lily's suggestion. He couldn't see the screen from his doorway, but that didn't stop me wrapping my palm over it anyway. "My office."

"Right away." I jumped to my feet, smashing my knee on the underside of the table in my haste and limped after Solomon, tucking my phone into the back pocket of my jeans. Today I was channeling every single female on *CSI Miami* by wearing white jeans, a chocolate brown shirt, the sleeves neatly rolled to elbows, and the sweetest pair of brown-and-cream pumps with the cutest leather bows. Smart, feminine, ready for anything. Well, except blood, because, let's be realistic, blood and white jeans? Just not okay.

Solomon waved a hand at the chair closest to the door and perched on the edge of the desk, my side, his long legs utterly distracting to anyone but a consummate professional like me. Instead, I focused on his chocolate brown eyes framed by skin the color of a licked peanut butter cup.

"I have a case for you," he told me without preamble.

"I'll do it."

His eyebrows edged together and the corners of his lips twitched upwards. He licked his lips, and I got the impression that he wanted to smile. Or laugh. "You don't know what it is yet," he pointed out.

I blinked. "Oh! it's optional?" Yeah, there might have been a touch of sarcasm in that, but if I didn't ask, I'd never know. Much like his meeting with Maddox. Argh! I really wanted to know!

"No. You're definitely doing it."

I wasn't going to let something like a cast-iron demand dampen my enthusiasm. "Great! I'll take it!"

"There isn't much by way of a bonus," he continued.

On second thought... not much of a bonus? I would soon be homeless. I needed money for a roof, along with walls and windows; and practically speaking, I needed a new purse too. "I'm sure it'll ease me back into work," I countered, wrinkling my nose a little.

"But it won't be too taxing, especially with your arm."

"My arm feels great. Never better!" I nearly added "Tax me!" but I wasn't that stupid. If it were an easy job with a little bit of a bonus, maybe Solomon would assign me a better case next time. I just had to show him that I was still made of awesome, even though my arm did still ache a little from the break.

"Okay, then." Solomon shrugged. "The agency has been asked to consult on a case for the MPD."

"Oh?" I kept my face still, impassive. In my eagerness for something to do, I forgot to connect the dots between work and Maddox's visit. Of course. MPD knew Maddox and Solomon were acquainted. It would make sense to send him to check the lay of the land. I bet they didn't give two hoots that I worked for Solomon either, though everyone in MPD knew I did. That was mostly because my family passed the information around faster than an unlabeled gift at Christmas.

"You may have noticed Maddox here earlier."

I shrugged, hoping it came off as "Nah, maybe, whatever," enough that Solomon didn't think it bothered me. "I saw him leave your office," I admitted, because we both knew I did. I didn't, however, know Maddox was here when I returned from my lunch break. although the partition blinds were shut, so seeing him was a surprise. That is, not exactly an "ooh, fifty percent off shoe sale!" surprise, but more the cotton-mouthed, dry palmed, heart skipping a beat surprise. Thing was, until then, I hadn't seen Maddox in a little over a month, not that my brothers — his fellow MPD officers — didn't keep me filled in on his movements. But it wasn't like I exactly asked them to. They just took it upon themselves to not shut up about it, though they did stop pranking him (to my relief), but I was sure they were still giving him a hard time. A part of me wanted to ignore it, but the hurt ran deep and I was glad my brothers cared more about me.

"Maddox will be our liaison with the department," Solomon explained as he ignored my inner crisis, which I disguised by inspecting my pearl pink manicure. "Will that be a problem?" he asked abruptly.

"Uh, no. No problem," I wheezed, looking up; it was only half a lie. Truth was, I had no idea if it would be a problem until we started the case; and once started, there would be no option, but to see it through. That's what professionals did. There would be no walking off this job and asking my temp manager for a new assignment. No, if Solomon wanted it done, I'd do it. If seeing Maddox every day was painful, or happy, or anything in between, I simply wouldn't know until it happened; but, I reasoned, Solomon wouldn't have taken the case if he didn't think it would be okay. He may not have called me on a personal level since the conclusion of our case at Fort Charles, but he wasn't an unkind man. I truly believed he would never cause me pain.

"The agency needs to develop its relationship with local law enforcement," Solomon added, effectively popping my optimistic bubble that this one case would be it. "This could be a good move for us."

"Right. And Maddox just happens to be point man." I tried to say it evenly, but honestly, there was a tinge of a whine in there.

"We've worked together before. It made sense for him to read me in."

I nodded. Yeah, but... hold on! That's what I initially thought, but something clicked inside me. Wasn't I related to a chunk of MPD? Any one of them could have pointed out their connection to me and taken point. Solomon must have thought of that too. The only logical explanation left was it must have something to do with Maddox's department and Maddox came because he wanted to. He worked both homicide and financial crimes; and as far as I knew, stuck with the latter. Although a smaller department, it was one that carried less risk of smelling like corpse and dumpster, but often was just as dangerous. The last job he worked undercover was the one that split us up. Since getting over the initial hurt, I still wasn't sure how I felt about it all. "Cross" probably covered it pretty well. Also, it was smart not to send Blake, in case I accidentally shot her.

"So, what's the case?" I asked, my voice sounding like a sigh. After all, murder was on my mind and I hadn't even read the brief yet.

"Theft."

I frowned. "What does that have to do with the financial crimes unit?"

"Fraud squad. Anyway, the case, at its most basic description, involves stealing. The thief, however, is creative and targeting Montgomery's super wealthy. Not only does he steal cash, but art and jewels too. He's also smart enough to make off with passwords that enable him to hack the bank accounts of his victims. Over the past few months, he's apparently made a fortune across the country. That's just for the cases we think we can join together. It's likely there are more, but I don't know how far back they go. Maybe ten years. This fraudster could have made off with millions."

I frowned as I connected the dots. "So, MPD know the target victim group and I'm guessing what's already been stolen but... they can't catch this guy?"

"That sums it up, Lexi. They just can't get close. He's too good."

I ignored that. There was no one too good, except, maybe Solomon. It was a good thing he was on the good side; I couldn't imagine how successful he would be as a criminal. "And they think we can?" I finished. "How?"

"For one, we aren't as bound by the book as they are. Two, we have resources at our disposal that they don't have, and a network that we can use to our advantage who might not be so keen to work with uniforms. Three, they have jurisdictional problems, as the crimes here have been linked to those in eight other states. The cross-jurisdiction taskforce they put together is co-operating so far, but it's only a matter of time. Plus, they just don't have the resources to devote to a ghost. If he turns to murder, that's another story, but so far, no one's gotten hurt. And four..." Solomon trailed off and smiled.

"What's four?"

Solomon's smile widened. "They don't know who the hell the guy is."

That didn't sound positive to me. That sounded like a problem. Way to go MPD dumping it on us. "Great. So we waltz in, solve it, and MPD is super happy?" I asked, sarcasm tainting my voice.

"That's the idea."

Numbers jumbled in my head beside flashing dollar signs. This sounded like a big, complicated case. "Can they afford us?"

"Not on this scale. I've agreed to a fixed fee; plus, if we do well on this case, they put out feelers to their partners, and we get more business." Solomon shrugged like it was no big deal, but it was. This wasn't the first time he hinted at expansion plans. The sudden clatter of hammering that started up directly above our heads was only another reminder that it had already begun. Solomon had big plans for his agency and I wasn't privy to them. Yet. I could still bug his office.

"I want you to co-lead on the case," Solomon continued after a minute, when the noise stopped. "I'll be working closely with you. All the guys will pull their weight on this one with surveillance. MPD will continue to work the case their end and we'll compare notes to close in."

"Okay, I get that. Hey, you keep saying this is a guy. How do they know that if they don't know who 'he' is?"

I asked, adding bunny ears in the air with my fingers.

"The profile gives the highest probability towards the perpetrator being a white male between the ages of thirty and forty. He's smart, charming, gives the impression of being successful, and women like him. This is based on all of his reported targets being women. Aside from all of these women being rich, there's only one other common denominator, which I'll get to in a minute."

I relaxed into my chair. Okay, I knew what the case was, and it intrigued me. "Why do I think asking them for a description of the man is a stupid idea?"

"It isn't; and several states have tried. However, every case we think is linked describes a different man. All we know is, according to the victims, he's white and aged somewhere between twenty-five and fifty-five. An FBI profiler friend of mine took a look and narrowed it down to give us a better lead."

I gave him skeptically raised eyebrows. "That narrows it down to, oh, only a matter of thousands in Montgomery."

"It's not much, I agree, but it's a start. Now, while each case describes a very different person, it's the crimes that indicate it's the same man. Evidence suggests he doesn't stay in town long, targets a few women, makes his move and disappears. MPD are scared that if they don't catch him within the next couple weeks, he'll go underground, move on, and the case will go cold. Once he moves across state lines, there's little we can do, but wait for another jurisdiction to get suspicious and raise concerns. Compounding that, there are bigger gaps between each time he appears, not to mention the women are often too embarrassed to come forward. They were duped and robbed. They might not get another opportunity to catch him. MPD are desperate."

"Why does he only target women?" I wanted to know.

"We don't know for certain that he doesn't target men, too. At least, none have come forward, but they could be embarrassed. Each case interview with a victim describes the perp as charming and dashing. He knows the psychology of women, how to get under their skin, and steal what he wants: their money. He knows how to disappear, and has an exit route planned from the moment he hits town. My profiler guy has yet to work up a full profile, but he's sure he's attractive, and can pass for different ages. He's also smart, knowledgeable of both people and technology, very comfortable in his own skin, and a terrific actor. He has no problem committing crimes. He's never hurt anyone that we know of, so we don't think he's violent, but then, he's never been cornered. We need to stay on alert."

"I don't suppose anyone thought to take a photo?"

"Not a single photo has come to light that is usable. We have a couple of the back of his head, but he's been blonde, brown-haired, and gray. Eyes described as brown, blue and green. Strong chin, weak chin, slim nose, fat nose... no description is identical. Digital photos disappear. He could be anyone."

"So how are we supposed to find this chameleon?"

"You're going to date him."

"Excuse me?" I gasped. Did I hear that right? Also, what?

"Here's the other common denominator. He meets his victims through high-end establishments. Previously, he posed as a realtor for exclusive properties, a hotel magnate, a playboy, and a Hollywood producer. In this case, we think he's operating via a dating website exclusively for matching millionaires. The website is co-operating fully. Actually, it was they who brought the case to MPD after two complaints were made, and MPD made the connection. It was a lucky break; and so far, he doesn't know that we know he's in town."

"So, he doesn't know we're onto him?" I surmised.

Solomon nodded. "That's what we think. Investigations have been highly covert so far, but that's not to say he doesn't smell a rat. The moment he does, he's gone, and the case collapses. Again. The dating agency wants to keep this as quiet as possible, or risk losing their clients, so they'll co-operate any way they can."

"And you want me to be the honeytrap?" I blew out the lungful of air I was holding in. "I hate to point out the obvious, but I'm not exactly a millionaire, and even if I were, who's to say he'd go after me?" He totally would though. Both Solomon and Maddox knew that. I was way more appealing than they to the kind of guy who could extract jewels from a rich woman by sleight of hand.

Solomon smiled, and really, that should have been enough to worry me. "You're going to be Montgomery's newest, most eligible, most loaded bachelorette, looking for love. We'll write your bio based on everything the profile suggests might appeal to him and..."

"Just wait for him to contact me," I finished, sucking the air right back in and puffing out my cheeks. Realizing I probably looked like Humpty Dumpty, I blew the air out again and pursed my lips. Seriously? Me, posing as a millionairess? Dating handsome, rich, eligible men in the hopes that one of them would turn out to be a master criminal? It didn't sound arduous; it sounded kind of fun.

It certainly beat working the dating websites, looking for The One amidst a punchbowl of nuts. All I had to do was find the most rotten one and have fun doing it.

No problem.

CHAPTER TWO

"It sounds like a dream come true!" squealed Lily after I finished telling her about Solomon's crazy idea to use me as bait. Rich bait, but bait all the same. I had the uncomfortable mental image of me as a worm, wriggling on a hook, waiting for a big, sharp-toothed fish to swallow me whole while simultaneously robbing me. It wasn't the nicest daydream I ever had. It certainly didn't beat the filthy one I accidentally had earlier while looking at Solomon's rear when he exited the office after our meeting.

"You think?" I asked, arching an eyebrow at Lily's delight.

"Yup."

I frowned, wondering if Lily fully grasped the concept of putting me in harm's way, or if she was just delighted at the idea of me working with two of Montgomery's hottest men, in my humble opinion anyway. "Which bit?"

"The being a fancy millionaire and going on dates with rich men bit."

"Ahh. I wasn't sure if you meant the working with both Solomon and Maddox bit."

Lily pulled a face and promptly shook her head before turning away to lift the tea kettle from the stove. "Oh, no. No, no, no. That bit sounds like a nightmare." She poured boiling water into a pair of matching mugs, and appeared to merely waft the teabags through the water before extracting them and depositing them in the trash. She handed me a cup and I followed her to the living room. Visiting Lily was great, for three important reasons. One: she lived right downstairs from me in the three-family building her parents owned. Two: she was my best friend. And three: since she hooked up with my brother, Jord, she was the embodiment of happiness, not to mention pregnant with my niece or nephew. She wasn't showing yet, not that the lack of a tummy stopped the constant stray hands of my extended family from attempting a fondle. I was pretty certain Lily would take out a restraining order against us soon.

"I know, right? I thought I'd have a heart attack when I saw them in the office together." I flopped onto the sofa and cradled the hot cup, raising it to my lips and trying not to shudder as I caught a whiff. It smelled, in a word, revolting. Lily's pregnancy triggered a health kick that was having serious repercussions on me. Gone was the wine, ice cream and, well, all the damn good stuff. Instead, she stocked the kitchen with teabags that smelled like dumpsters, cardboard crackers, and more fruit and vegetables than two people and a regular visitor could consume. I couldn't wait until she fully embraced the term "eating for two" and returned to normal.

"You don't like your tea?" Lily asked, taking a sip while beaming.

"Delicious," I replied, my inner voice adding, "if I didn't have taste buds."

"There's a new health food store near Monty's," Lily

informed me, namedropping our favorite pizza place and giving my stomach reason to grumble. A pizza with all the toppings would easily take away the foul stench of Lily's "health" tea. I resolved to order one the moment I escaped. If I had to spend the next couple weeks eating with fancy forks and knives, I planned on making the most of eating finger foods while I could. "I got you some organic bran. It keeps you regular."

"That's so thoughtful." I grimaced, wondering what else on earth was not going through Lily's head that made her worry about keeping me regular.

"That's what BFFs are for." She leaned in, fist-bumped me and then reclined, placing her feet on the coffee table. As I looked around, I saw evidence of my brother everywhere. He definitely planted his feet firmly under the table, and as far as I was concerned, it was about time too. He could do no better than Lily, who not-so-secretly crushed on him for years until one day, bam! They were in a relationship, expecting a baby and planning a wedding. I had to hand it to them: they really got on with things once their minds were made up. "Hey, listen, I'm dying to know more about this crazy scheme you kids are cooking up," she said, sounding suspiciously like a character from Scooby Doo, "but I have some news that I don't know how you're going to take."

"Twins?" I gasped.

Lily frowned. "No. Nothing baby-oriented. It's about the building." She waved her free hand in a large circle in the air, clearly indicating our home. "My parents accepted an offer on it last night."

"That's great, isn't it?" I asked, taking in Lily's reticence.

"Well, yeah. It's a cash offer, which is great in this market, and my parents got what they wanted, so Jord and I can go house hunting, which is really great." I sensed a "but" coming, so I waited for Lily to stop fidgeting. "So, um, we have to move in four weeks."

"Four weeks!"

"It's a condition of the sale."

"Can you even close an escrow in four weeks?"

"I have no idea. My parents are handling it all. They said Jord and I can stay at their house until we find a place, as they aren't using it. I'm sure you can come too. There's plenty of space."

It was a nice offer, but somehow the thought of sharing with Lily and Jord didn't thrill me. It's all very well having roomies, but I grew out of that a long time ago. I liked my own front door and knowing that no one but me judged the microwave food in my refrigerator. Plus, three weeks ago, I'm fairly certain I heard them having sex, and it wasn't an episode I looked forward to repeating. On the other hand, I could probably stay with my parents, although my parents would, no doubt, pester me some more about my unconventional job; and my mother would definitely try to sign me up in one of her night classes.

"Think about it, okay? I know it's all really sudden, but I wanted to make sure you had plenty of time to start looking for a place."

"No, it's fine," I assured her, remembering how excited she was just last week as we browsed properties on the Internet. Lily babbled on about square footage and whether to paint the nursery in neutrals, or wait until the baby was born. This was not my moment to be selfish. I swallowed, plastered a bright, reassuring smile on my lips, and dared a confident voice. "I'll be fine. Don't worry about me. I'll start looking for a place right away. No problem at all. Piece of cake."

~

Finding a place to live was *so* not a piece of cake. Not even a crumb. Not even a sniff of a crumb. It was appalling. There wasn't a single decent sounding place in the whole of Montgomery's rentals pages of the local newspaper. There were plenty in Frederickstown with good square footage, but the addresses didn't fill me with hope. Once upon a time, Frederickstown was built as a commuter suburb, but no one really thought about transport links, so the area went to seed. Amongst the poor, but nice folks who resided there, were definitely some undesirables. Out of the four apartments that looked the most promising, three were located in the don't-walk-at-night part of town, and the other was at the center of a recent gang shooting.

"What is the world coming to?" I asked myself, sounding eerily like my mother. I ran my finger down the rest of the column, over the second, and onto the third, moving away from apartments, to studios and finally, to room rentals. No thanks. I categorically didn't want to live with anybody, unless he was really hot and knew how to clean and had a lot of really hot friends, none of whom were in law enforcement. I'd so gone off the uniformed type. For now.

Reaching for the phone, I called one of the few women better informed than a longstanding police officer with a network of informants. "Mom, do you know any apartments for rent?"

"Let me think about it," said my mother. Cooking sounds clanged through the line and my nostrils flared as I imagined the aroma of whatever she had bubbling in the background. "Mrs. McIntyre went into a home. I heard her son was thinking about renting it."

"Is it in the same condition as when she lived there?" I asked, recalling the floral drapes and overstuffed chairs, not to mention the amazing collection of china birds and plates. It was a lot better than recalling the things Mrs. McIntyre was getting up to in the nursing home she recently moved into.

"Oh, yes."

"I'll pass."

"Why? It's so close. Your father and I could come to

your house for dinner."

"Compelling as your argument is, I think I need something closer to, uh, work."

My mother bashed something in the background, and I jumped before she came back on the line. "Of course you do, honey. How's the investigating going? Is there any career progression? Did you know your sister started her own business? We're so proud."

"It's going okay, I just got a new case." I paused, my forehead wrinkling as I thought about career progression. I really didn't think there was any. Solomon was the boss. The rest of us were merely minions. Right now, I was the lowest of the minions. Maybe one day, I would be top minion. Only if Delgado, Fletcher, Flaherty, and Lucas offed the job first, and the only way I saw any of them going was if they got an amazing offer elsewhere, retired, or were killed. Cheerful thoughts. "Maybe promotion one day," I told my mother.

"Oh, thank the Lord," sighed Mom, "I was getting worried. Your sister has her own business. Did I mention that? She's the boss."

"Yes, I..." I started before she cut me off.

"Maybe you'll start your own detective agency. Your father would probably want to join you. I wonder who would be boss? Maybe you could call yourselves Graves and Graves. Or Graves and Daughter."

No, thanks. "Solomon won't let me go. He really needs me," I told her, even though it was a semi lie. He needed me as much as a hippo needed a tutu; but I was good at the job, and he did need a woman on the team to get to the places the guys couldn't go... like the ladies' bathroom. That didn't necessarily mean he needed *this* woman, but I won't go into that.

"I'm glad it's going so well for you, honey. Have you asked for a raise yet?"

"I only just returned to work."

"Because you were hurt in the line of duty!"

19

"I still received my salary while my arm got better, and he paid my hospital bill, too."

"As he should. After he put you in danger."

"I think that was mostly my fault," I protested, since it was. I chose to go to a lonely warehouse on the outskirts of town, unarmed, and it ended badly. I was lucky to be rescued in time, although I did crack the case, helping to bring down a gang of drug smugglers. "So, about any rentals…"

"If I hear of any, I'll let you know. Janice Markowitz might be getting married to her young man. She has that nice condo two blocks over from you."

I didn't know Janice, as she was a few years older than I, and though she went to my school, we never socialized. I did see her kissing my brother, Daniel, once, when they were both seniors, and I pretended to puke, so I figured she didn't like me much. Her condo was pretty nice, I recalled. I wondered if she held a grudge.

"Let me know?" I asked. "Lily's parents sold the building and I need a new apartment in four weeks."

"No problem. I'll tell her mother you're going to be homeless soon and you're desperate. Perhaps she'll take pity on you."

I groaned. Janice would love that. She'd tell her friends and everyone would know I was the only Graves that couldn't find a home. "Please don't!"

"But…"

"Moooooom!" I whined. "She's mean and she'll make fun of me."

"Alexandra, how old are you?"

I garbled my age, covering it with a cough, which was pointless because I was pretty certain my mother was there on the day of my birth.

"That's right. Thirty in one month! No whining. Do you see your sister whine?"

"Not lately." Although she was a whiner, ever since she began humping Antonio Delgado, she cheered up considerably. That was an image I really didn't want in my head.

"Exactly. She had a baby, went through a divorce, and what happens? She pulled herself together, started a new business, and met that lovely Antonio. And she doesn't give a shit what Janice Markowitz thinks."

"Mom! You swore!"

"Everyone does these days. You should hear the swearing on the CD I bought your father for Christmas. These rappers are all at it."

I didn't know which was more shocking: that my mother swore for what I absolutely believed was the first time ever, or that she bought explicit-lyric rap CDs for my father, or that anyone still had CDs.

"You should try it, Lexi, it's liberating. Go on, say 'shit.'" My mother paused. After a moment, she hissed, "Say it."

"Shit," I said quietly, putting the phone down.

I called Lily next, even though she was only downstairs. The shock forced me into the kitchen and I was running my hands along the shelves in search of secret stashes of emergency chocolate. "My mother's gone mad," I yelled at my cell phone on the counter.

"What's new?" came Lily's voice via speakerphone.

"She swore."

"Get the fuck out!"

"Don't you start."

"I thought you were going to say she'd taken up some really crazy new hobby."

"Like belly dancing and Krav Maga aren't crazy enough?"

"When done together," mused Lily. "I'd like to see that."

"Call my mother. She loves you. Don't tell her about the bar though."

"Why not?"

"She'll really get on my case about running my own

business."

"Tell her it isn't the right economy."

"I told her Solomon needed me."

"Did you tell her you played the naked bump and grind with Solomon?"

I blushed, a rare reaction for me. Hot, followed by cold, raced through my body. Of course, that could have been because of my hand fastening on a bar of cooking chocolate. Good enough. I tore the wrapper open and jammed a square into my mouth. "No," I squeaked. "I have to go. I have to... do anything but think about this! Thanks for helping!"

"You're so not welcome," said Lily. "What are you eating?"

"Nothing. Chocolate. Cooking chocolate. Oh crap, I think I accidentally ate half of it already."

"That's okay. You're a PI. You're allowed to eat crap."

"What a cliché. I'd rather have a salad but I'm all out."

"Do you want to get a takeout cheeseburger? I think the baby wants one."

"Sure, why not? I'm hungry and I don't have anything in the fridge anyway."

"Plus, it'll stop you eating all that chocolate."

"Too late. Anyway, like a cheeseburger is better?"

"It has cheese," said Lily, but I wasn't sure if that was her argument. She sounded a little confused too. "And we can eat it at my bar."

"Is there alcohol?"

"No. Plus, I'm not drinking and out of solidarity with me, neither should you. Jord isn't drinking either."

"I'm pretty sure I saw him in O'Grady's three days ago having a beer with Garrett."

"That bastard! He put the baby in me so I can't drink. He has no right to enjoy himself!"

"Maybe it was a soda," I backtracked, wondering if I should point out that wasn't why Jord put a baby in her. I was pretty sure he didn't intend to leave a lifetime souvenir so early in their relationship at all; but I didn't think that would go over well.

"In O'Grady's? Hey, maybe we should go there instead and get their cheeseburger with a stack of fries and onion rings."

My mouth watered as I looked at the empty chocolate wrapper. Dessert first... how novel! "Okay," I agreed. "But only because I want to prove that I'm not a cliché."

"By eating a cheeseburger?"

"By not refusing it because I care about my weight, ergo, I am a normal woman, and um, because I do eat a lot of salad and maybe it's a healthy cheeseburger from cows that ate grass and, uh, nice things."

"And because you're totally hungry?"

That too. "I'll be at your door in five."

"Minutes?"

"Seconds."

I insisted on driving, partly because I was being nice, and partly because it meant Lily couldn't complain when I insisted on cruising past my favorite residence in Montgomery: the pretty, yellow bungalow with a neat yard. It was picture-perfect cute and today, as for many years, I was dying to look inside. I should have taken the opportunity while it was for sale months back.

"I'll always love this house," I told Lily. We were parked a little way down the road, and Lily filed her nails while I gazed lovingly at the bungalow.

"You're going to cheat on it with an ugly place, aren't you?"

I gave Lily a sharp look and sniffed. "Maybe," I said, "This place has never been sold and there's not another one like it in town. I know. I've been looking."

"Maybe you could get another bungalow and just paint it yellow. Paint on, paint off, or whatever Mr. Miyagi said," she added, flapping her right hand up and down with the nail file like a paintbrush.

"It won't be the same."

"You have to stop stalking this house."

"What's it gonna do? Call the police?"

An unearthly scream pierced the quiet air, long and haunting. All of a sudden it stopped. Lily and I looked at each other. A dog howled and Lily shivered.

"Please tell me we didn't just hear someone getting murdered."

"Nope, totally didn't."

"Oh, thank God. I really don't want to see any corpses. It would ruin my O'Grady's special and I'm really hungry. You think we should wait and see what happens?" Lily asked.

"Maybe." We waited. Lily finished filing her nails. I counted all the panes on the bungalow's windows, then took some photos with my cell phone camera. Lily tapped her feet; I tapped my fingers on the steering wheel. "I don't hear anything else," I said, at last. "It was probably nothing."

"Great! Can we go eat now?"

"Yeah. Thanks for coming with me."

"It was my idea to go out for dinner!"

"No, I meant to see the bungalow. It's my happy place."

"Not like I had any choice." Lily stroked her slightly protruding belly. It rumbled and we both looked at it. "Can you drive us to *my* happy place now? Please?"

Gunning the engine, we got there in record time. Not that it mattered. Lily called ahead and placed our orders, ensuring the food was on the table the moment we sat down since I didn't want to eat at her bar as the tables weren't in situ yet. I don't know if the pregnancy was making her extra hungry, or she was just generally hungry, but she ate faster than a woman on a diet, locked in a cake factory without security cameras. Setting her fork down, she wiped her hands on the paper napkin and scowled.

"What did I do?" I asked, glancing at my onion rings next to my half-eaten burger. I could give them to Lily. I didn't want to, but I could. She was my best friend and incubating my niece or nephew.

"Nothing. It's your brother."

"What did he do? Which one?" I had three brothers. It was hard to work out which one she was mad at, though I could take a guess as I stabbed an onion ring with my fork.

Lily didn't say anything. Instead, she whipped out her cell phone and hit the button, pressing it to her ear. "Are you drinking?" she said. "Hah! Liar. I can see you, you know. Turn around, buster."

I turned around, locking eyes with Jord, who was standing at the bar with our other brothers. Jord held a beer and looked sheepish. My brothers raised their glasses to us, and turned away, giggling into their beer mugs.

"You know, it's not so bad just having a beer," I told Lily. "Don't get irrational."

If steam could have come from Lily's ears and nose, it would have. Her eyes widened, and the vein at her left temple pulsed. Then, she slumped into the booth and stuck her bottom lip out. "I am, aren't I?" She dialed again. I glanced over my shoulder, and saw Jord contemplate not answering, before thinking better of it.

"Enjoy your drink, honey. I'm sorry. I love you," said Lily. "No, I love you more. No, I do love you more. I love you so..."

I grabbed the phone. "Can you order me a melon mojito and bring it over? Lily will take hers virgin. You suck. No, you suck more." I hung up and Lily giggled.

"I wish I had brothers and sisters."

"Sometimes, I wish I were an only child."

"It gets lonely," Lily told me, not for the first time. Ever since we met at school, she pretty much became an honorary Graves, hanging out at our houseful of people day and night, loud people; and going home to a quiet house with uptight parents who didn't have a lot of time for her. Sometimes, I enjoyed the peace and solitude of her home life, but I wouldn't have swapped my upbringing for the world. It was the same kind of life their child would have, exactly the one Lily wanted for him or her.

My brothers ended up sharing our booth before Lily and Jord headed home, probably to do something really gross. So hurrah for staying at the bar, only that meant Daniel had to drive my car home and help me upstairs, and, well, yeah, he made sure I got into bed too, before dropping my car keys on the nightstand. The last I heard was the apartment door clicking shut, and a minute or two later, the sound of Garrett's car leaving. Then I was off to Sleepyland in my best kitten pajamas, sleeping a dreamless sleep for the first time in a very long while.

CHAPTER THREE

"You ready for this?" Solomon gave me an imperceptible look as he pulled into a parking space in front of a dull, red brick building downtown. I kept my sunglasses on and hoped my queasiness didn't show. It hit me hard this morning that I drank one mojito too many; the most obvious clue being my green-hued skin, and waking up with my kitty pajamas on inside-out and a pillow atop my head.

I gave him a "humph" that could have meant anything from "raring to go" to "I really want to go back to bed — now" and looked up at the building. I don't know what I expected from Million Matches, but this didn't look like the kind of place rich folk came to find potential partners; but then, what did I know? I found my last boyfriend during a temp job and he was there undercover. I didn't know yet what to call Solomon? Ex? Fling? Former lover? None seemed appropriate. Friend, maybe. Boss, definitely. Anything else was yet to be defined. That lack of definition gave me a few sleepless nights, just as many, in fact, as whether Maddox was really playing an undercover role a few weeks ago, or having a little extra on the side with Detective Blake.

"Hello? Earth to Lexi."

"Here!" I plastered on a smile as I looked up to meet Solomon's beautiful brown eyes. I shoved my man problems into the corner of my mind that contained a big stick and a vault. If those distracting thoughts snuck out of that dark corner, I would mentally bash them. Twice.

"It's practically a done deal," Solomon continued with whatever I forgot to listen to. "All the director wants to do is check you over and make sure you'll fit in with their clientele. That's a nice dress. Pretty."

"Um, thank you. What exactly do you mean by 'fit'?" I had the uncomfortable feeling of being paraded about at a Miss World contest while being found a little closer to Near Miss. My dress was nice though: a pale pink shift that I got half-off on sale two years ago, with nude pumps, and a laser-cut, leather pouch bag that I found a huge discount for online. Heck, I was a sales ninja.

"Just that you're the kind of woman who would attract their kind of clientele," Solomon confirmed, glancing over me once more. His eyes lingered a moment too long and I gulped. "Or, more specifically, our unsub," he continued.

"I love it when you say 'unsub'. It's so *Criminal Minds*."

"I don't like the word 'perp'."

"It does sound like the noise a demented chick would make."

"Unsub it is." Solomon nodded, then fist-bumped me. Maybe I read it all wrong. Maybe he did just think I looked right for the meeting, because in that moment, I never felt less desirable. A fist-bump didn't exactly scream Solomon wanted me, and didn't want our fling-or-whatever-thing to be over. A fist-bump said "Hey buddy" and nothing sexy at all. What was wrong with him? That stream of jumbled thoughts reminded me, and I visualized my mental big stick bashing the stray thoughts involving my boss having the hots for me. Or not.

While I smoothed an imaginary crease from my skirt and wondered if my dress was suitable, Solomon exited the car, walked around and opened the door. "You look fine," he told me, without emphasis on "fine" not that it was important or anything. I slid my legs out, took a brief moment to see if Solomon was eyeing them — no — and grabbed my purse. It was really nice. I had seriously good taste.

The dating agency was accessed by a buzz-in entrance door with only a discreet black and gold label. It was sandwiched between an accountants' and a small fashion label. We took the elevator three floors up and stepped into a small lobby. It was exquisitely decorated with an antique desk, behind which perched a red-haired woman around my age, in a black suit and emerald blouse that matched her startlingly green eyes. She looked up and blinked with appreciation, then smiled as Solomon approached her and introduced us, only then noticing me. Great.

"I'm Madeleine, executive assistant. If you'll just take a seat," the redhead said, indicating the leather sofa under the window. "I'll let Ms. Callery know you're here." She stood and moved around the desk, revealing long slim legs, beneath a knee-length skirt, and super high heels. One look and I recognized Manolo Blahnik. Damn it! How high end was this place? Even the receptionist spent big bucks on fancy shoes! I had the uncomfortable feeling that my small wardrobe of fancy dresses and pantsuits would just not cut it with these people.

Moments later, the shoes returned - presumably the body in them did too, but I must admit being fixated on the elegant curve of the heels. She directed us towards the office of Solomon's contact, who awaited us at the door.

Million Matches' director was around fifty, although with some artfully placed Botox, she could definitely pass as ten years younger. She wore a pale blue skirt suit and had blonde hair that rested lightly on her shoulders. A Rolex adorned her wrist and a neat pair of gold earrings were her only other jewelry. Her bright red lipstick was most definitely not discreet, but perfectly applied. She reminded me a lot of Lily's mother. Discreet, elegant, yet slightly aloof. However, Lily's mother was a lot aloof. My entire family found it puzzling how so distant woman could produce such a bubbly, warm-hearted child. I found myself wondering if Ms. Callery had children, even though it was entirely irrelevant to the case. She was wearing a gold wedding band, so I guess she successfully made her own marriage, always a plus in her game, I decided.

"Helen Callery. Good to see you again, John. This is your protégé?" she asked, directing the question to Solomon as she shook his hand.

"Yes. Lexi Graves," he replied for me as I blinked at her use of his first name. Except for hearing it from him, and occasionally from me, I don't think I ever heard anyone call him anything but his last name.

Nevertheless, I smiled. Protégé sounded nice. Better than trainee anyway, although I assumed I graduated from that position a couple of solved crimes ago. "Pleased to meet you." I offered my hand and she gave it a firm shake, her eyes quickly running over my dress. Seeming to approve of my attire, she indicated we should sit in the blue upholstered chairs opposite her desk. Closing the door behind her, she moved to sit in her chair. As we made ourselves comfortable, I looked around. The office was sparse, but elegantly appointed. The furniture was nice, slightly more modern than the reception through which we entered, and there were a cluster of framed black and white photographs of happy, smiling couples crowding one wall. "Satisfied customers?" I asked, nodding towards them.

"Yes, indeed." Helen smiled as she ran her eyes over the montage of couples she managed to unite. "Here at Million Matches we do exactly what we say we do. We match wealthy clients with their perfect partners. These are just a few of them, and we've had seventeen marriages in the past two years."

"They're all wealthy?" I asked, my obvious curiosity getting the better of me.

"Oh yes. This is no Sugar Daddy agency. All our ladies and gentlemen are... independently wealthy, shall we say? It's very important for our clients not to feel like... targets." She took a breath at that as Solomon and I exchanged glances. Targets, indeed. Helen obviously had the same thought as we. Clearing her throat, she continued, "Poor choice of words, perhaps now that we suspect one of our male clients is targeting the ladies here. Solomon tells me you'll pose as a client to gain access to our clientele."

"It seems the best way to accomplish it," I agreed, filling the sudden silence as Helen clearly expected me to say something. "A hands-on approach."

"We'll build a profile for Lexi, itemizing what makes her the most attractive prospect, based on what has attracted the thief so far. All you have to do is supply those details to your male clients and we'll take it from there," Solomon told her. "There will be minimal involvement from you, and none from your staff. It will be very discreet."

She leaned forwards, placing her hands on the desk, and sighed. "That's very important to us. To me. Like you, I prefer the hands-on approach. Madeleine is my only staff member and I haven't informed her of my suspicions. If word gets out that our clients are being targeted by thieves, our subscription base will disappear. In short, we'll be ruined. No one wants a date with a gold-digging thief."

Everyone, that is, except me. Yippee. Being single never seemed so appealing as right now.

"Are you ready for this, Ms. Graves?"

"You bet."

"Lexi's cover story will be ready to go within the next twenty-four hours," Solomon told her. He stood up, extending his hand for a parting handshake. I followed suit. "The thief won't see her coming."

"You have no idea how glad I am to hear that," said Helen. "Let's get the ball rolling. You'll see to it that Ms. Graves is suitably briefed about the requirements of the job?"

"Of course." Solomon nodded as he looked towards me. "She's Montgomery's newest, most eligible millionaire, and everything about her will reflect just that."

Everything? Gulp.

~

There was only one closet I knew of that was consistently better stocked than mine. Actually, there were probably an awful lot of closets with better clothing than mine, but only one belonged to my sister, Serena. And by one, I mean she had one hell of a closet. Working in my favor was all the baby fat she still had to lose. As I handed Victoria back to my sister, I mentally thanked my baby niece for fattening my sister up. Most of her clothes hung unworn and pristine while Serena sported a shirt that had a suspicious looking glob dried midway down the front. Serena caught my eye, raised one eyebrow the barest fraction, daring me to mention it. I bit the insides of my cheeks, watching as her eyebrow edged upwards a hair's depth before thinking better of it. No point antagonizing the beast, especially when I still had a favor to ask.

"Please can I borrow a really nice dress?" I asked

between blowing kissy faces at Victoria. Victoria wriggled in her mother's arms, puffed out her chest, and let rip an enormous belch, then smiled lazily, her cheeks pinking with delight.

"Don't you dare high five her," snipped Serena as my hand began to rise on its own accord. I let it drop. "What do you need a dress for? You have a whole bunch of dresses."

"Yes, but you have really nice dresses and I only have moderately nice." She was also a total clothes horse and had really good taste, but I didn't want that to go to her head. We'd only recently started getting on and I wanted to keep a sense of equality in the relationship somewhere.

Serena nodded as if to agree that was perfectly reasonable, then persisted, "Why?"

"I have to do this undercover thing and I have to dress..."

I searched for the word, but Serena beat me to the punch with "Better?"

I shrugged. "Yup."

"I guess so," Serena agreed, turning and striding from the family room of her big house towards her bedroom. Victoria rested her chin on Serena's shoulder and watched me as I followed them. I blew more kisses and Victoria answered with a raspberry. She was definitely my favorite niece. I couldn't wait until she started speaking. "So what's the undercover thing?" Serena asked, glancing at me over her shoulder.

"It's an, um..." I mumbled, coming to a stop and glancing around the bedroom. Serena was in the process of getting a divorce from Ted Whitman-the-boring-Third and while she got to keep the house, he most definitely had a field day removing all the furniture. Her bedroom looked particularly sparse.

"He's taking the bed too, but he's welcome to it," said Serena, watching me noticing. "I have a new one on order."

"Good?"

"You bet," she replied cheerfully. "And I'm turning the guest bedroom into my office. The business is going well so far. I have clients! Actually, thanks to your suggestion, I'll be able to work from home *and* look after Victoria."

"Good for you! Mom's really pleased that you started the business."

"Thank you." Serena passed Victoria to me, who wriggled around until she found a comfortable space in my arms, settling down as we entered the large walk-in closet. I looked at the glass racks of jewelry suspended on the walls, purchased during Serena's more affluent days. I considered draping them over Victoria. I caught Serena looking. Maybe not. "What's the occasion? Business? Date? Really, who knows what your boss has you cooking up? Did you know he had Antonio doing surveillance dressed as a homeless man for a whole week? He couldn't even shower. Day four, I told him not to come over until the job was in the can."

"I'm definitely allowed to shower." Come to think of it, I probably should smell really nice. I wondered what perfumes Serena might have lying around. "It's for a meeting with a..." I made a noise that sounded like "Burble Burble Agency" and hoped it would be left at that.

"At a dating agency?" Serena gaped. "What for? Is this really work? Or are you trying to find a boyfriend? You should, you know. I've never been happier."

"It's for work!"

Serena gave me a suspicious look. "Are you sure?" she asked, pursing her lips like she caught me in a lie.

"Yes!"

"I really don't think you need a dating agency. What about your boss? Solomon?"

While I was fully prepared to accept Serena's

34

assumption, I didn't need a dating agency, was a compliment of sorts, I couldn't help pulling a face at the thought of my boss. Solomon and I always had chemistry, but only recently had that chemistry gotten naked while doing an undercover job, posing as husband and wife. It was a cover Solomon clearly took very seriously and our faux-marriage was most definitely consummated. Even as I thought about it now, my heartbeat sped up and my hands got clammy. Since then? Nada. Zip. Zero. And as for my ex-boyfriend, from whom I was on the rebound when the Solomon thing happened (several times), he was definitely a no-go subject. Nope, I was as single as single could be, and as long as I didn't think about it too much, I felt perfectly fine with that.

"Huh," said Serena. "I'm glad I'm not telepathic. Your face just went through twenty emotions."

I checked my reflection in the floor-length mirror. "And I'm still damn pretty!"

"Bright side. Okay, 'meeting,'" she said, making skeptical bunny ears, "with a dating agency. How about this... this... and this...?" She pulled out three dresses, one after the other, turning the hanger hooks around and looping them over the rail so I could see them. One was a plain navy shift with a demure cowl neck. The second had a slightly flared skirt with a delicate floral print; and the third was a pale blue shift with matching cropped jacket.

"No to number one, maybe to number two, though I'm not sure it's warm enough yet, and yes to number three if it fits."

"It'll fit. Try them on." Serena held her hands out for Victoria, who gave a tremendous wriggle and pretty much launched herself from my arms. "There's matching shoes, but I don't think they'll fit you. Fortunately bags fit anyone, and they're on the shelf above. I have to feed this one, but call me if you need anything," she said, while Victoria tried to latch on through Serena's shirt.

"Thanks. I really appreciate it."

"Don't mention it. Just dry clean and return everything when you're done." With that, Serena swept from the room, leaving me like a kid in a candy shop in her closet. It was all I could do not to rub my hands together in glee, before throwing all her belts and scarves on the floor and rolling on them.

~

Solomon and I stood looking at my VW in the Solomon Agency parking lot. Fortunately, the interior was clean, and all the traces of my last surveillance job were gone. However, the trunk was crammed with borrowed items from Serena's closet. Most were actually job-appropriate, while a couple I just really, really liked, including several purses. There was only a small chance she wouldn't get them back. Okay, a big chance. Eventually, I knew, she would hunt me down and force a return.

"Nope," he said, after several long moments of silence. "That won't do."

"Could have told you that without all the quiet contemplation," I murmured. Really, I could have told him via text if he told me why I was summoned to the office, and saved us both the bother. That would have given me extra time to go home to bed and catch up on my beauty sleep.

Solomon gave me an arched eyebrow in response. He looked so hot when he did that, not that I meant to think about it at all. No. My boss had to remain off limits. Not least because he hadn't given me any intimation that he was, er, available, in recent weeks. Or even interested. What was it with him? And me? The less interested he seemed in me, the more I wanted to know why. It was so annoying.

"I know a guy," he said.

"And there I was, thinking you were the Lone

Ranger. All cool, but no friends." Actually, even though I was joking, it wasn't far from the truth. I wasn't sure I'd ever seen Solomon socialize with anyone outside the office. Even with my colleagues, I never got the impression they all hung out after work. That is, except with me. I'd been to dinner before at his smart Chilton townhouse, and that evening had a distinctly date night feel. Of course, we hung out during our undercover case at Fort Charles when we posed as a married couple, but that was work, really. Except for the sex stuff. That was definitely off the clock... and off the charts.

"You think I'm cool?" The corner of Solomon's mouth edged upwards and his eyes sparkled. I probably made the last bit up, but whatever, he had really nice eyes.

I shrugged. "Nah."

He smiled then. "You think I have no friends?"

"I know Captain McAuley is your friend," I said, recalling how Solomon was drafted by his old buddy to solve the murder at Fort Charles, a local army base.

"Anyone else?"

"Ummmm..." I paused.

"I have friends." He turned to look at my car again. "We'll get you wheels to suit your new heiress status. You have any more of those dresses?" He gave my pink dress another appreciative glance, one that left me thoroughly confused. I could have been making that glance bit up too. Nevertheless, I intended to go with it because it gave me a tingly little boost. I thought of Serena's closet and the many expensive garments she no longer wore, now that she was a work-from-home mom. It seemed such a shame to waste. Thank heavens, several of them were in my trunk. "I have access," I told him.

"The dating agency will cover any reasonable costs," Solomon continued. "You'll have to go deep cover to make this work. You okay with leaving your life behind for a couple weeks?"

I thought about what might happen over the next

month. Oh, wait, nothing. "I'll make it work... hold on... deep cover?" Last time I went deep cover, it was at the aforementioned Fort Charles case. This time, at least I knew that I was posing as a single woman, and could rule out any Solomon-sexy-times, so what did that leave? No friends, no family, no life? Maybe this case wasn't as cool as it first appeared.

"The thief is being careful. He's only targeting rich women from whom he can steal high value items and cash. He's a pro. It stands to reason he's back-checking the stories of anyone he might potentially date. If he sees your apartment and car, he's going to smell a rat. They are not millionaire accoutrements. So, we set you up with a new home and car while you're on the case, both of which say *money*."

"Okay, makes sense. I can manage the wardrobe, but where am I going to get a new house at such short notice?"

"My neighbors are taking an extended vacation in Europe and they need a house-sitter. I volunteered you. You'll say you're renting it, as you haven't found a place yet, so it won't matter that your name doesn't come up in any searches."

"Your neighbors know why I'm really house-sitting?"

"They know you're my employee so you're vouched for. Plus, it's the ideal set-up. I can wire the house and monitor it from mine so there will always be someone on hand if there's any trouble."

My newly knitted broken arm, received in the line of duty, twinged, although it could have been psychological. "Should I expect trouble?"

"So far, nothing indicates that the thief is violent, but you never know if he will get desperate and escalate, so we can assume nothing. The homes are burglarized while the women are out, so I think you'll be safe, but we need to monitor the house at all times."

"Okay, but no cameras in the bedroom."

Solomon inclined his head and smiled, making me wonder if the thought crossed his mind. "You'll know where all cameras are and I'll give you a remote to shut them off." He turned away, but not before I heard him say, "Besides, I've already seen you naked."

I shivered. "You have. But Delgado, Fletcher, and Lucas haven't, and I'd like to keep it that way. Flaherty, too."

"Me too," agreed Solomon as he turned on his heel, walking towards the stairwell.

I didn't watch him leave, mostly because I found the way he walked mesmerizing and I didn't want to start getting any funny ideas in the lot. Instead, I mostly pouted at my VW. It might not be the most awesome car in the world, but it blended in and got me from A to Z, and all the stores in between. I wondered what kind of vehicle Solomon would provide for my cover story, as images of an Aston Martin Vanquish, or a sleek Viper flashed through my mind. I should be so lucky! All the same, as far as assignments went, this could be a fun one. I wouldn't have to stay at the Chilton house the *whole* time, surely?

I imagined I'd spend some days and nights acting as a wealthy woman, living in a super cool neighborhood for a couple weeks, driving a fancy car, dressing up in nice clothes that wouldn't get dirty from hiding in bushes and trawling through trash, and dating an array of rich, handsome, albeit possibly criminal, men. As my arm ached some more, I had to remind myself there were worse jobs in the world... and I'd done most of them in my previous career as a serial temp.

CHAPTER FOUR

"For how long?" Lily's face crumpled as soon as I told her of Solomon's plan to install me in the house next to his. "Ohh!" Her face lit up. "Do you think he plans to tunnel from his house and ravage you in the night?"

I pondered that. I pondered it for a whole one million minutes at light speed.

"You live in hope, right?" Lily pressed.

"No!" I pulled a face. Okay, it wasn't like it didn't cross my mind, but Solomon was the consummate professional. Plus, he already consummated this professional. Arf.

"Not even a little bit?"

"Not even. It's just convenient that his neighbors are vacationing and he can monitor the house from his, right next door."

Lily gave me her skeptical face, but I ignored it as I returned to the rentals section of the current edition of the newspaper. Since Lily waylaid me the moment I opened our front door, a half hour ago, I scoured the section, hoping for an improvement on the previous edition's offerings; but, so far, very little caught my eye. Only the thought of having to move in with my parents while I searched for a new home, or begging Janice Markowitz to lease me her place, motivated me to circle some of the properties.

"Besides," I said, returning to the original topic of the duration I'd be away while working the case, "it's not for too long, and we're moving soon anyway, and I don't know where I'll be. Think of it as training wheels for when we don't share the same building."

Lily pouted. "You could still move in with Jord and me."

"Nope. You need your couple time in the months before the baby arrives. Not couple time plus Lexi, third wheel."

"Sometimes third wheels are good things. I mean, look at tricycles!"

"And how many of them do you see on the mean streets of Montgomery?"

"Not many," Lily conceded.

"Exactly. Listen to this one. Apartment with access to garden and reserved parking. Large living room, separate bedroom, bath, kitchen with dining nook, video camera entry system. Harbridge. I know the building. It's near Maddox."

"You want to live near Maddox?"

I didn't particularly want to live near my ex-boyfriend, but it *was* a great neighborhood. Not that it was a viable option. I told Lily the price and her jaw dropped. "That's insane!"

"I know. And that's a nice one. I just circled a place in Chilton. It costs the same as here."

Lily leaned over and looked to where I tapped the newspaper with my forefinger. "That's not so... Oh. It's a studio. Its kitchen is a closet! There must be somewhere better." She took the newspaper from me and I reclined against the couch's pink pillows while she scanned the columns. "Maybe not," she decided a few minutes later as she returned the gazette.

"If it's affordable, it's a pit. If it's nice, it's not affordable," I told her.

"Maybe we should look at some anyway. Make friends with the rental agents. They might tell you if something better comes up."

"It's either that or the bench in Fairmount Park." I shrugged.

"It'll never come to that, Lex. Besides, we all know those benches are taken. Jord patrolled there last night. He said it was like a hobo sleepover with a gin tea party."

"Maybe I could house-sit in Chilton a little longer," I mused. "How long are rich people's vacations?"

"I bet proximity to Solomon has nothing to do with that little idea," Lily snorted. "Get calling those agents. I love house snooping. Even better when the chance of finding a corpse is zero."

"Are you ever going to let me forget that?" I asked, recalling, with a shudder, the day we found my ex-boss's corpse. Except for me, it was the second time.

"One day." She laughed, then pulled a face. "Unless we find anymore. Let's not, okay, Lexi? Promise me?"

I hated to say it, but I thought the chances of us not finding more bodies were low, seeing as we seemed to attract them. On the plus side, no one had been murdered on this case. Yet. All the same, I refused to make any promises I couldn't keep.

~

I declined Lily's offer of dinner with Jord and her, and retired to bed early. When I awoke, there was a thick envelope pushed under my door with a note from Solomon, simply saying "Read." Over breakfast, I opened the envelope and spread its contents across the coffee table. I played Eeny-Meeny-Miny-Mo to decide which rich dating dude's case file or police report I should read about first. Of course, none of the suspects were a sure thing, but Helen Callery had already done some of our work by narrowing down the likeliest suspects. Aside from being millionaires - which they stated and Helen assured us they most definitely were - the one other thing each man had in common was dating each of the complainants. That made our pool of suspects much smaller, against a surprisingly long list of rich singles.

My finger landed on the middle file, and with a sigh, I snapped it up, opening the manila cover to reveal a few loose sheets of paper and a sheaf of photographs. The top paper was obviously the application filled out prior to joining the agency.

David Markham was thirty-nine, a self-made man of indeterminate software expertise. He owned a house in the exclusive hamlet of Bedford Hills, never married and didn't have kids. He claimed to enjoy tennis, fine wine, hiking, and art galleries. I decided not to write him off as a total bore, just yet. Besides, he wanted to get married and have two kids; and if he were hot, after seeing his bank account, I most definitely would consider dating him.

I turned the application over and laid it face down on the empty side of the file. A bank statement confirmed his income to an eye-watering degree. Personal references attested how nice he was and what a catch he would be for the right woman. As I warmed to him, I turned the page and my stomach flopped. It didn't matter how nice this guy was on paper, he couldn't float my ocean-going yacht. Paunchy around the middle with a shirt a size too small and slicked-back, oily hair, he had a nice smile on otherwise plain features. He did not look like a suave operator. Or, sadly, my future husband. Not that I was looking for one anyway, but it never hurt to keep one's eyes open.

"*C'est la vie*," I muttered, closing the file.

File number two revealed the jackpot of dating: an English man with a title.

"Holy crap, my mother would love this," I squealed, scanning the application. Then I thought about English oppression, Independence Day, and Prince William's lack of availability. "Nope. She'll still love a lord," I decided.

Lord Justin Camberwell hailed from somewhere in England with a name that probably wasn't pronounced anything like it looked. Apparently, he spent a fair portion of his youth in the States and decided to return last year to oversee some family business dealings before taking up management of the family estate back home. His bank statement was missing, but there was a printout of a Wikipedia page and a dozen shots of Lord Justin playing polo, in his graduation gown with the towering spires of Oxford as a backdrop, and as a guest at a couple of royal weddings. I'm pretty certain one of the couples was Wills and Kate. He had blonde hair, sparkling eyes and a terrific complexion with a toned physique, assuming the tennis snap was recent. I put down ten bucks on a mental bet that he was top of every single one of Million Matches' millionairess's dating list. After all, titles were cool. "Lady Lexi," I tried, then, "Lady Alexandra Camberwell. Lady Alexandra Camberwell Graves. It could work."

His address was listed as "care of" a house in Chilton, just a few blocks from Solomon's house. It made sense that a visitor on foreign shores would stay with a friend, I guessed, and wouldn't have his own place if he didn't plan to settle here. His future plans for heading home, however, did make me wonder what he was doing searching for a woman in Montgomery. Was he dating for keeps? Or playing for now? And did playboys make good thieves?

I added Lord Justin's file to that of David Markham's as I opened the third file and wondered who else might be in the same league as a self-made software millionaire and an English lord.

Marty Tookey was a lottery winner. A big winner. Oodles of winnings. In fact, his bank account sniffed at most other winners, he had so much money. He was a local guy, born and raised in Montgomery, with a career in accounting until his big win. I recognized the firm as one with offices a couple blocks from the Solomon Agency. His application stated he wanted to be married with a family, and not see someone who wanted him for his money, which seemed like a no-brainer for me since this was a bags-of-money dating agency. I figured he thought it wouldn't hurt to state it. I wondered how much the winnings changed his life. Flicking past his references, I picked up a couple of photographs of an attractive man with sandy hair. He appeared in his early thirties. One shot showed him in tennis whites, and another on holiday, with a beach and palm trees in the background.

Reaching for my cell phone, I called Lily. "Does everyone rich play tennis?" I asked.

"Why are you asking me? What time is it?"

"Eight. You're rich."

"My parents are rich."

"Do they play tennis?"

"Yes."

"Do you?"

"Uh... yes," Lily admitted.

"Damn. I don't know how to play tennis. All my suspects so far play tennis. What if they want to play?"

"We were in the tennis club in school!" Lily reminded me.

I forgot about that and struggled to remember. I vaguely recalled looking super cute in my whites. "I only joined to look at the boys' legs," I admitted. "And to show them mine."

"Me too. I didn't learn much. My mother enrolled me

in tennis camp one summer. Do you remember?"

"Vaguely. Did you learn much?"

"Only that the camp counselors at tennis camp are easy. And despite having a weak backhand, I can definitely grip a..."

"Don't tell me! At least you learned something."

"True. It's a lesson that served me well. Boom. Tennis joke!" Lily giggled.

"Ha-ha. Do you have tennis whites?"

"Somewhere."

"Can I borrow them if I need to?"

"Sure. Plus the skirt is incredibly short, so if you need to distract your opponent, you could just bend over a lot and play with the balls."

I grimaced, though, come to think of it, that would be distracting. "I'll make sure to wear my best underpants."

"Or none at all."

"I don't think they'll need that much distracting."

"You never know. It'll be a fast way to find out where the jewels are hidden." Lily giggled and I sighed. Pregnancy brought out her filthy mind. Come to think of it, having a filthy mind probably helped her get pregnant in the first place. I preferred not to think of my brother having anything to do with it.

"I'll call you later. I have apartments to see this afternoon and another file to read first. Hope the next one doesn't play tennis too."

"Hope he's hot."

Suspect number four wasn't just hot. Ben Rafferty was smokin' hot. He hailed from New York, a trust fund baby who had access to the best schools, homes in the Hamptons, Aspen, and a family duplex on the upper east side. His family also had roots in Boston, and while he was there recuperating after a skiing accident, he visited Montgomery and liked our town. He planned on staying, maybe investing in local business, while also volunteering at community aid organizations. His references portrayed him as funny, charming, but not without foibles. In short, his friends didn't say he was a saint, but one of life's good guys, which seemed like a reasonable description for someone who wanted an honest representation. There were two headshots, one looked posed, and a little formal in an old class tie, though I couldn't guess where from. The other was a relaxed, candid shot of him sitting in the park, a soft breeze ruffling his hair, smiling broadly as he petted a small dog. I bet if his family money wasn't enough to sucker the women in, the image of the big guy being so sweet to a cute pup finished them off. It certainly worked for me. Best of all, he didn't mention tennis. Hurrah!

"Hello, date number four," I cooed, giving his puppy photo a stroke. "Two hotties, two notties. This job officially does not suck. Yet," I added, just to err on the side of caution, because, well, you never know.

There was one thing that bothered me about the case as I stacked the files and headed for the coffee pot and my second cup. Why would any one of these rich men be stealing? Surely they had enough money of their own? Even as I thought about it, the answer was clear. We assumed the motive for theft was the money, but what if it was theft for the sheer sake of thievery? Perhaps it was some rich man's game to stave off the boredom of a perfect life. A gentleman thief. We either had a penniless thief and a liar... or a real life Thomas Crown in our midst.

~

I arrived at my first appointment five minutes early, and four coffees into the day. While parking, I took a good, long look around the neighborhood, which was pretty easy as I was five minutes from my house. The West Montgomery apartment was the best of a bad bunch I booked to see this morning. The realtor told me it only just came on the rental market after the homeowner decided to move to Hong Kong. I really couldn't see how someone could just decide to move to Hong Kong, but that wasn't the point. This was a Holy Grail apartment; it was designed for an owner to live in, not for a money-sucking landlord to abandon. That meant it was probably pretty nice. And cockroach-free. The bathroom was new. Even better, it was in my budget.

As I slid out of my VW and approached the building, another couple strolled to the entrance. They looked young and smart. She wore ankle-length pants and a chic mac in lipstick red. He wore chinos and a navy blazer. They were holding hands. Perhaps they were my neighbors-to-be? My hopes of making friends with the happy-looking couple diminished as we both waited for the other to approach the keypad entrance.

We didn't move.

That meant one thing: they weren't my new buddies. They wanted my apartment.

I hated them. And her perfect mac.

"Cute mac," I said as we eyed each other suspiciously.

"Banana Republic," she replied, even though I didn't ask, while scanning my jeans and hip-length, mustard yellow, wool coat. I thought I looked awesome when I left my apartment, but felt a bunch less awesome under her stylish scrutiny. I hated when women managed to do that. It was a weird skill.

"Sale?"

"I don't shop sale," she shot back. That said it. On the plus side, she didn't know what she was missing when it came to sales shopping.

"Don't I know you?" Chic's husband looked me up and down with a little frown that half-turned into a smile as he tried to decide whether he recognized me from somewhere. I was pretty sure he didn't, but before I could answer, he nudged his wife. "Honey, here's the realtor." Mr. Chic, as I dubbed him, raised a hand to wave and I checked over my shoulder. Yup. Same realtor... and he double-booked us. What an ass! Even as I mentally added donkey ears to his white-blonde head, I saw an eager-looking third couple trotting along behind him. What were the odds of being triple-booked? Apparently, pretty good as the realtor beamed over his assembled crowd of apartment-seeking desperadoes.

"Great day for apartment hunting, huh? I'm Rick Taylor, and I'm your realtor today," he said with all the enthusiasm of a game show host. Grinning as he clapped his hands together, he might as well have just announced we were going to save lives! Today! "You can call me Rick. It's my name!"

Jerk, I thought.

"Awesome," said Mr Chic. Inexplicably, he and Rick high-fived.

"Let's head inside and see this place. You're going to love it," Rick promised to no one in particular. He gave his tie a quick adjustment, and punched a number into the keypad. As he held the door open and the Chics shot ahead, I caught him giving me an odd once-over before wrinkling his eyebrows. Perhaps he'd never seen a single woman before, I decided, while chastising him under my breath for being so judgmental.

The apartment was one of a rare breed and exactly as advertised. Light. Spacious. The furniture was modern, but comfortable, and showed off the great original features like the crown molding and fireplace. The galley kitchen was compact, but cleverly designed with plenty of storage, while the bathroom was neat and orderly with an equally surprising amount of storage. The bedroom was, in a word, dreamy. The whole place was a little smaller than my current home, and the view just as dull. It was also slightly more expensive, but I was used to the give-Lily's-friend-a-discount rate.

"We'll take it," said the Chics.

The third couple and I looked at each other. "I want it," I said at the same time the other husband blurted, "We'll sign the lease today."

"Way to go on the bargaining power," I muttered as the first couple rolled their eyes at each other. With all three of us wanting the apartment, it would surely come down to one thing now: money. Just the thing I wasn't exactly rolling in on my single income.

"It's just the right size for one," I murmured, loud enough for the couples to hear as I walked around. Perhaps a little reverse psychology would work? "I'd hate to share such a little apartment." I crossed to the window overlooking the street. "Oh my! Is that man breaking into that car?" I exclaimed in a shocked voice. "Is he taking the stereo?"

The realtor was beside me in a second, his worried eyes searching the street for the phantom thief. "I don't think so," he said, unconvincingly. "Probably just fixing it."

"Riiiight," I agreed, nudging him in the ribs and giving him a big wink that the second couple saw. "Definitely fixing it. Sure. Absolutely. Did you say it's unsecured street parking?"

"Uh... yes."

"So, uh, we have some other places to see." The door shut behind the second couple, cutting off their excuses as they exited. One down, one to go.

"I know what you're doing," hissed Mrs. Chic. "I use reverse psychology on my kindergartners. You aren't going to get rid of us that easily. We want this apartment."

"I want it too."

"So... when are you all looking to move?" asked Rick, nervously looking from the Chics to me, his commission suddenly uncertain.

"Straightaway," the three of us chimed in unison. Except, obviously, none of us wanted to move in with each other. Well, Mr. Chic might have liked sharing with his wife and an extra, but I was pretty sure Mrs. Chic wouldn't want to share her closet with me. Also: no way.

"Okay, great." Rick beamed. "Let me get some details from both of you and, um, you," he nodded at me, like I was an afterthought, adding "and we'll proceed."

"So... what happens next?" I asked as he extracted clipboards from his leather shoulder bag and handed us one each.

"Well, we'll run your credit history and then the landlord will make a decision as to who gets the place. You can submit your offers at the end of the form."

Huh? What? Offers?

"We're clearly the best bet," said Mrs. Chic, grabbing the pen and squinting her eyes at the small type.

"Says who?" I gave her my best "Are you kidding me?" frown. After all, it wasn't a fair observation after knowing me for oh, five minutes.

"I know you from somewhere," said the husband again. His mouth wrinkled with thought as he tried to place me. He tapped one finger against his mouth and frowned.

"I really don't think so."

"Yeah, you do look kind of familiar," agreed Rick. Great, now the guys were ganging up on me too? On the plus side, maybe their familiarity would help me out.

"Maybe it's through my volunteer work," I lied. Everyone likes a volunteer, right? I was sure I volunteered at something. Sometime. Somewhere.

"No, that's not it," said Mr. Chic.

"Are you sure? I volunteer a lot." I nodded to Rick. Rick frowned. So much for giving myself a good reference.

"Nope." Mr. Chic shook his head. "Can't think of it yet, but it'll come to me."

Hopefully, I'd be at home with a lease agreement in my pocket by then because if I slept with him and forgot

— although I was pretty sure that didn't happen — I wasn't sure it was a story I could confess to Lily. Also, fairly certain I'd never been into blondes of any shade, I was sure that couldn't be it. Not one hundred percent sure, but, you know, fairly certain.

"I know!" blurted Mrs. Chic, looking up, "You're the private investigator. I saw you in the newspaper!"

"Who? Me? No, I don't think so." I stepped back, shaking my head vigorously.

"Yes! It was you! You shoot people!"

"I do not!" Well, not often. Sometimes I just stab them, but only when my life is in danger, which justifies it just fine for me.

"That sounds dangerous," mused the realtor, edging away from me and closer to the Chics. "I think I've read about you. You were at that hotel convention. The one with all the weirdoes killing each other."

"I'm not dangerous," I assured him, with my best ditzy smile. Also, exaggeration. Much?

"She's really dangerous," Mrs. Chic insisted to no one in particular. She focused on the clipboard and began to scribble furiously, as if submitting the form first would definitely give her an edge. "Guns. Murderers. Snooping."

"I don't think the landlord will like that," Mr. Chic said, cottoning on to his wife's massive hints that I would not make a good tenant. He sidled next to the realtor, adding in a low voice, "I work in IT and my wife's a kindergarten teacher. Two very safe professions."

The realtor looked from me to them, clearly weighing up who was more likely to blow up the apartment and his commission. With a sinking heart, I realized I could not come out on top in the race for this apartment.

Whatever. It was too small anyway.

"We'll pay more than she can offer too. We have two salaries," added Mr. Chic, emphasizing my single status in the most charming way. Not.

"Done," said Rick, accepting their paperwork and smiling broadly. The men pumped hands and grinned at each other.

I looked at my clipboard. I hadn't even filled in my name. "Shame. I was going to offer an extra five hundred bucks a month for the next two years," I said with a shrug as I returned the clipboard. Rick's smug face dropped a little. "Enjoy your new place. See ya." I turned on my heel and strode out of the pretty little apartment, leaving the happy couple to negotiate their way out of paying too much, just as Rick repeated the figure I dropped.

Climbing into my car, I told myself it just wasn't meant to be. Getting the first apartment I saw was too easy, and there were more to see. Even if they didn't work out, it wasn't like I'd be homeless at the end of the month. I still had options. Sure, one option was hearing my best friend and brother humping, or I could stay with my parents and get roped into whatever my mother's latest obsession was. Admittedly, they weren't great options, but options all the same, and that was a lot more than some people had. Another thought occurred to me. I had the Lexi-is-a-millionaire-for-two-minutes house to look after while I continued the assignment. What were the odds that the owners would let me stay on a while longer while I pursued my house search? Possibly about as high as my ever owning the perfect, yellow bungalow that had long been the object of my house porn obsession. That thought cheered me as I drove to my next viewing. I wouldn't mind extending my stay in Chilton if it were anything like Solomon's house.

Frederickstown it was fair to say, was not at the top of my "really want to live here" list, but the apartment sounded nice in the listings and was on the nicer side of town. Or, at least, the listing seemed nice. But as I pulled up to the curb and surveyed the building, my heart just couldn't get excited. It wasn't because the building wasn't nice. It was actually pretty good, judging by the run-down neighborhood's standards. But I knew I didn't want to live miles away from my family and friends and work, not to mention decent coffee shops. Even if I had to be practical when it came to my future habitat, I still wanted to live well and not spend extra money on cab fares or never having a drink again just so I could drive home.

The realtor met me at the door. She was young, fresh-faced and eager to please. Or eager to get the apartment rented. Either way, she was a lot nicer than the last guy.

"I'm Renata. This your first place?" she asked with a hopeful smile.

"Nope." I shook her soft hand. "Just got to move."

"Oh." She shrugged and didn't ask anymore, choosing instead to fiddle with her keychain until she found the right key for the door. Opening it, she indicated that I follow. "It's top floor," she told me, over her shoulder. "So no upstairs neighbor noise."

"Great." I tried to sound enthusiastic, but failed as I plodded after her. We didn't see any other residents until the third floor when a man hurled past us, forcing Renata and me to plaster ourselves against the wall. With his jacket collar turned up, and a Yankees cap pulled low over his head, he bulldozed past us without so much as a "Sorry."

"Excuse us," snipped Renata, not too subtly or quietly. The man paused for a fraction of a second on the landing below. His chin turned upwards, revealing a stubbled, square jaw, and from what I could see, the lower half of a handsome face. Then he plowed on, casually flipping us the finger.

Nice neighbor.

"You're going to love the apartment," Renata continued as we made our way to the top. "It's freshly painted and the furniture is all included. You can move in right away."

I decided not to move in thirty seconds after she opened the triple-locked door and showed me a beige space. Sure, it was light and someone had clearly made an effort, but the fresh paint job didn't take away the lingering smell of cigarettes and the faint scent of something rotten. The laminate floor was cheap looking, and I'm pretty certain Renata got an electric shock when she flicked the kitchen light switch to show off clean, but desperately old units.

All the same, I checked the price with her as we made our way from tiny kitchen to tiny bathroom, which had no bath. On to the bedroom, the window of which showcased a panoramic view of the brick exterior of the building next door. A building less than two yards away. "It's really the best I have," Renata confirmed when I asked. "A lot of buildings here are going owner-occupied. People want to get on the property ladder while they still can. Frederickstown is very up and coming. It might well become unaffordable in a couple of years after the area renovation is completed."

What a depressing thought. Then a mouse ran across my foot. Renata screamed, concluding the apartment's plus points (i.e., affordable, no human roommates), which failed to outweigh the negatives that were too numerous to count.

My final appointment of the day looked promising. On paper. Seriously, what was it with realtors? Why did they have to waste my time by giving a glowing description for a less than average apartment? Why couldn't they just be brutally honest? The big plus for this one was that it wasn't far from the agency. Close enough, in fact, that I could walk there daily and thus save money on gas. Gas money to offset the super high rent. But when coupled with the location - within easy walking distance of stores, coffee bars and one of several of my favorite bars - there was a certain lure to it. Unfortunately, it took me thirty minutes of driving in circles before I found a parking spot; time spent that only dropped my mood lower. It was also time enough to see one attempted mugging; but the thief was unceremoniously lambasted by an old lady's purse and ran away limping. "You go, girl!" I cheered from the safety of my VW.

I knew I wasn't taking it before I ever stepped inside the building, even with a parking space I grabbed with one quick swing of the steering wheel, minutes from the door. I don't know what did it for me - the screaming couple in the lobby, or the Rottweiler slobbering at the doorman's desk, or the open dealing of narcotics - I really couldn't decide.

"It's not for me," I told the grumpy realtor. Unlike Rick and Renata, he clearly lost all enthusiasm for his job.

"No kidding," he replied, with a wry smile. "I just can't find a renter for this place."

"Can't think of why."

We both looked at the drug-dealing doorman. "Me neither," said the realtor. "Maybe the lobby needs a palm tree. Make it look classy."

"Yep, that should do it," I agreed, although I suspected he might not be joking. We took one last look at the dealer and left. My phone rang as soon as I climbed into my car, and Solomon flashed on the screen. Well, not flashed. That would be *awesome*. His name flashed on the screen. Even so, I had a hot flush just thinking about him.

Naked.

Him. Not me.

"I need you," said Solomon.

Holy cow, said a little voice inside me.

"Okay," I squeaked.

"Now."

Yes! Though... "Uh, what for?"

"I need a ride home."

Typical. "Don't you have a car?" I knew he had a car. When I parked my car next to it, the VW looked like his Lexus LX's baby.

"I do. But it won't move."

"So... fix it?"

"I have many talents, but fixing cars isn't one of them. My mechanic can't pick it up until tomorrow morning. So, I need a ride home from the office."

I tried not to think about his many talents. He was right though. He had many talents. "You're leaving kind of early."

"I have plans."

It was and wasn't news to me. No one really knew what Solomon did in his free time, though I had the opportunity to enjoy his free time on more than one occasion. I knew he could cook and he liked sports and was in the process of redecorating his house. But unless I was part of the plans - not recently - he never elaborated on what he did in his free time. Apparently, he wasn't going to now either. Not that I cared or anything.

"So..." he prompted.

"I'm near the office. I'll be by in ten," I told him. I pondered what plans were so important that he couldn't miss them and had to beg me for a ride. Of course, I still didn't care.

"I'll wait out front," said Solomon before clicking off.

It occurred to me as I pulled up outside the agency, that Solomon must have known I was nearby, otherwise why call when time was essential? Though now I thought about it, he did know I wasn't actively on a job yet, so he wouldn't be waiting hours. All the same, it would have been easier for him to call a car service. I said as much to him when he climbed in, folding his long legs under the dashboard, and sighing as he pushed the seat as far back as it would to go to give him some extra room. I'm fairly certain I didn't gasp audibly at the sight, but if I did, I would blame it on a backfiring tailpipe.

"I knew you weren't on a job," he explained. "Since I only assigned you one case and you haven't started yet."

"I have. I've been reading the background information you left this morning."

Solomon arched a brow as if to say I proved his point. "You weren't performing surveillance," he replied, which was pointless because, well, I already knew that. "What were you doing on Tenth Street?"

"How did you know I was on Tenth?"

"Fletcher saw you."

"And he called to tell you that? What a snitch." I feigned mock shock, but seriously, what a snitch.

Solomon grinned. "No. We were talking on the phone already and he mentioned he saw you go into a building and come out again two minutes later. You don't know anyone on Tenth." It wasn't a question. He knew too much. How annoying.

"How do you know?" I asked and Solomon raised his eyebrow again. "You're such a stalker. I was apartment hunting."

"What's wrong with your place?"

"It's sold. I have to be out in a month."

"Ah."

"More like 'argh!' Do you know how hard apartment hunting in Montgomery is right now? I saw a mouse."

"Did you shoot it?" Solomon smiled broadly.

Weird idea of a good time, but to each his own. I rolled my eyes as I pulled out into an open gap in the traffic. "I didn't have my gun because I didn't think I'd need it apartment hunting. Besides, I don't think that's the best pest control."

"But effective," Solomon countered. When I thought about apartment number three, I wondered what kind of pests I'd have to shoot to get a peaceful home life.

Since we were too early for rush hour traffic, we made it to Solomon's house in half the usual time. I parked outside his house, not bothering to pull into the vacant parking spaces, when he apparently didn't intend to make any moves to invite me in.

"You read up on all the suspects?" he asked, his hand lingering on the door catch.

"Yep. And I scanned the files of the previously linked crimes and read the witness statements too."

"Anything stand out?"

"Not a thing. You?"

"Not yet."

"Actually..." I paused, pursing my lips as I thought about not what was in the files, but what wasn't. "Actually, I can't see an obvious motive for any of these four guys to be the thief. Are you sure the suspect pool isn't wider?"

"I asked the same thing. Helen Callery assures me the criteria she narrowed the suspects down to was stringent. I had Lucas double-check and he agrees, but if we don't get any leads, we'll start on the next pool." He must have seen me pull a face. "Look on the bright side," he told me, amusement in his eyes. "Free dinner. No washing up."

"Yeah, can hardly wait. Just me, a millionaire, oh, and you listening at the end of the wire. How romantic."

"Sounds a lot better than some dates."

"I'll think of it as practice."

Solomon paused. "What for?"

"For real dating."

Solomon's eyes darkened for the briefest of moments, then he gave me a puzzled look and shook his head. "I left the keys for my neighbors' place at the office. I should have given them to you earlier so you could check it out. Thanks for the ride, Lexi."

A car honked behind me and I pulled in towards the sidewalk to allow it to pass. "Anytime, boss," I replied although I hoped he wouldn't take me too literally. Solomon climbed out and by the time the other car passed, Solomon had ascended the steps to his house and was pulling keys from his jacket pocket. Not that he needed them. As I watched, the door to his home flew open and a startlingly beautiful young woman stepped into the doorway. She was nearly as tall as he, with straight black hair that hung to her elbows, and a perfect, hourglass figure. She was wearing a dark brown pencil dress only a few shades darker than her flawless skin. She threw her arms around Solomon and drew him inside.

The door shut behind them without a backward glance, leaving me to wonder just what Solomon's plans were that made him hurry home, and did those plans include the glamazon who was waiting for his arrival?

CHAPTER FIVE

After three days of failed and uninspired apartment hunting, combined with frustrated lurking and monotonous thumb-twiddling at the office, I scored my first date with a millionaire.

"It's on," said Solomon, his head suddenly emerging from the office. We'd barely spoken since the night I dropped him off, and honestly, I wasn't sure if I were sulking or not. Seriously, just how beautiful was that woman who opened the door? She was clearly younger than I too. Did I wait so long for him to make a move that I forfeited the opportunity to make one of my own? Not that I even planned to make a move. I was still a big, old pile of confusion when it came to the men in my life. "Go home and change. I sent the details to your phone and there's a Ferrari Italia in the lot downstairs. Enjoy." He tossed me the keys and I caught them, quick as a flash. It surprised the hell out of me. Catching something, that is, not the cool car. "What color is it?" I asked breathlessly.

"Like there's a whole bunch of Ferraris to choose

from," laughed Solomon. "Go!"

I was out of there as fast as my four-inch heels could carry me, and minutes later, I made excited, squeaking noises as I slid into the cool leather interior of the cherry red Ferrari.

If this was how millionaires felt, I wanted to do it every day. I exited the Ferrari and planted my hard-earned Louboutin heels on the sidewalk, handing the keys to the valet before strutting towards the glass facade of the art gallery to meet suspect number one, David Markham. The gallery took up the first floor of what was once clearly an industrial building of some kind. On first glance, not a lot of work was evident, but after a double-take, I noticed the polished concrete floors, and sandblasted-bare brick walls and blinked at the clearly loaded clientele. The exhibition featured a visiting New York artist with a reputation for being edgy and raw. I knew that because Solomon made me search the Internet prior to the date so I would have some conversation topics. So far, all I'd come up with was, "My nephew, Sam, is an artist of similar methods", "The stripes are cute," and "Really? How much?"

Like the rest of the clientele, I was dressed up, but my dress was borrowed and last season - though damn nice. I had to give Serena plenty of credit for excellent fashion taste - but the wire attached to the inside of the dress was brand new. I doubt if many dates brought a bunch of guys to listen in either. According to Solomon, Flaherty was recording everything nearby outside, and Maddox was in close proximity. Oh, how I looked forward to this. As for Solomon's whereabouts, who knew?

"Lexi?" The man who approached me resembled his photo. Unfortunately, for him, that was a bad thing, although I had to give him props for not using an old snap or a professional headshot. His face was pudgier than his photos, visibly losing the fight against jowls that would undoubtedly fully develop over the next couple of years, and his skin pasty. Considering that he worked in IT, and we didn't live in sunny climes like Florida, that wasn't surprising. What surprised me was the quantity of pomade that slicked back his thick dark hair. He clearly decided more was more. And then some. It gave it the appearance of wet glue. When I imagined running my hands through it, I had a mental vomit. "Lexi?" he said again, smiling nervously.

Snapping out of my hair angst, I smiled. "Yes, hi. David?"

"That's me." David held his hand out. I slipped mine into it and he pumped it enthusiastically, giving me a bicep workout that neither of us appreciated. "I've looked forward to meeting you ever since I saw your photo. Wow. Just wow." His eyes roamed my dress, fixing on my cleavage for a moment, before traveling down... and back up. Cleavage again. He smiled.

To be fair, I think my face took on the same glazed, gormless expression when I looked at his hair. All at once, I remembered what his hair reminded me of: a licorice swirl. I don't like licorice.

"Pleased to meet you," I said, keeping my voice pleasant even as the idea of an evening with David made me break into a cold sweat. "Do you like the artist?" I asked to prompt the conversation.

"One of my favorites," David replied, finally averting his eyes from my cleavage, which was showcased in the vee cut neckline of a fabulous little dress. He held out his arm for me to hook mine around. "I might buy a new canvas this evening. Why don't you help me?"

Well, who wouldn't admire a man who lets his date pick out a pricey piece of art only minutes after meeting her? It was just a shame I knew nothing about art. I hated to think of selecting a lemon, but I figured he would probably take responsibility for his own decisions. Much as I do when shoe shopping. If I make a mistake, I return them and buy another pair, along with a coordinating purse.

David seemed happy to talk, and not in a must-fill-the-silence kind of way. David *loved* to talk. Specifically, David loved to talk about David: how smart, successful and rich he was. He also referred to himself in the third person, which was most disconcerting. I couldn't work out whether he was pompous or nervous, but I suspected the balance favored the former.

"Champagne?" David swiped two flutes from a passing waitress and handed me one without waiting for my response.

"Mmm." I sipped it. Bubbles slipped over my tongue. Something told me this wasn't supermarket champagne, but the real deal. "Delicious."

"So... when did you join the agency?" David asked after awhile, looking over his shoulder to see who was within earshot. At first, my heart thumped before I realized he meant the *dating* agency, and I hadn't been rumbled. "Recently," I said. "Actually, this is my first date."

"Maybe it'll be your last." David winked.

I gulped. "And... um... you? Have you been a member very long?"

"A year. I've been on a few dates. I had to join, you see," he said, leaning in to whisper conspiratorially, "too many gold-diggers. I want to meet a woman who doesn't see me as a walking ATM. Is it the same for you?"

"Absolutely," I agreed. "Not women, though. I want to meet a guy who doesn't care how loaded I am, or that I have diamonds and rubies in the home safe and drive a Ferrari," I added, checking David's reaction to see what he thought of that. He didn't blink. He didn't even seem very interested in my wheels. Instead, he just nodded as if that was perfectly reasonable. I guess to some people, it is. I just didn't move in those circles. At least, not until today. "You can never be too careful about whom you meet," I added.

"So true. Shall we look around?" David guided me through the gallery, pointing out this painting and that, stopping to chat with the gallery owner, as well as a local artist or two, and greeting everyone by name. Watching him pumping hands, I could see he was clearly enjoying himself. I barely had to say anything, just nod and appear interested when he asked me a question before interrupting my answer. Just as I tried to say something witty after a comment he made, he cut me off, while pointing to a large painting on the rear wall, which he guided me toward. I politely say guided; it was closer to being yanked. "What do you think of this one?" he asked as we approached. The painting, several feet in height and width, was a garish mix of neon oils that appeared to have been hurled at the canvas, then left to drip. The bottom half of the work dried into a mixture of colorful streaks, blobs and peaks. Yet there was something insanely attractive about it.

"I like it," I told him.

"Then I'll buy it." David turned, raising a hand to someone I couldn't see, and leaving me a moment to check the price tag. My eyes widened at the price. Holy guacamole! More than I earned in a year. Much, much more. And David planned to buy it because I said I liked it. "My date says this is the one to buy," he told someone behind us and I turned around. My gaze flew past the woman in the smart, black sheath dress to the couple standing a few feet away. A very familiar couple.

"Craptastic," I muttered under my breath.

"Pardon?" said David.

"I said, it's fantastic!"

"Perhaps you would like to see it when it's delivered. I think I'll put it in the family room," he told me, suddenly sounding as bashful as a little boy asking a girl if she wanted to see his new toy.

"Maybe," I muttered, my eyes fixed elsewhere.

I waited while David signed some paperwork and exchanged pleasantries with the gallery owner. He was promised an introduction to the artist later in the evening, and all the time, I tried to ignore Maddox and Detective Blake hovering. What the hell were they doing here? As far as I knew, Maddox's salary didn't include this kind of art, and I had to assume neither did Blake's. I was pretty sure Maddox wasn't even an art lover. Maybe Blake was? And that's when the horrifying thought entered my head: were they on a date? Was Solomon being sarcastic about Maddox being nearby?

David looped my arm through his again and started babbling about the artist. How excited he was to have another of his paintings and some other stuff that I forgot to pay attention to when Maddox's eyes met mine. He raised his glass with a nod to me. Then Blake gave me a little wave. I waggled my fingers in return and offered them a weak smile. Unfortunately, they mistook that as their cue to approach. Damn it.

"Lexi, how nice to see you." Blake stepped forward and air kissed me from approximately four inches away on both cheeks. Gone was her plain clothes uniform; replaced by a cocktail dress in deep purple with a flared skirt and cinched waist. Her glossy hair was pulled into a neat chignon. She kept her jewelry to simple gold studs in her lobes. I couldn't fault her. Annoying.

"So nice!" I faux-gleefully exclaimed. "Are you enjoying the exhibit?"

"Oh yes." Blake nodded, waving her full glass around. "So much to see."

"Adam," said Maddox, holding his hand out to David. He took it and gave it a firm shake. "And Rebecca. Are you a friend of Lexi's?" As if he didn't know.

"We're on a date," said David with a grin at me. It was all I could do not to roll my eyes. Poor guy just seemed too pleased. Really, I should have been flattered, and if he were my type, I would have been, but sometimes, being too grateful just isn't sexy. Compounding the problem, since Maddox and I broke up, I hadn't been on a date. If I had wanted him to see me on a date, it would have been with someone who could have at least made him jealous. Someone the male equivalent of Blake: glam, sexy, confident. Not licorice blob-haired David Markham, even if he was a millionaire. Damn it. What were Maddox and Blake doing here anyway?

"David, why don't you show Bl... er... Rebecca the painting you just bought?" I said, unlinking my arm and nodding towards the canvas. "I'm sure she'd love to see it. Huge fan."

David's eyes widened. "Would you really?" he asked. It was probably the first time two hotties showed any interest in him, or something to do with him. His chest puffed out. I'm fairly certain he would later tell his friends what a "player" he'd become. I hoped he would take a shine to Blake.

"Please," said Blake, stepping forward.

"What are you doing here?" I hissed to Maddox, after turning to watch David and Blake step away, and out of earshot.

"Same as you. Suspect surveillance."

"No. That's what I'm doing. You guys are supposed to back off so the thief doesn't get spooked. That was the plan. MPD stays in the background. If he's the thief and he guesses you're PD, the jig's up."

Maddox raised both eyebrows. "The jig's up?"

"You told Solomon that you needed someone on the outside to get close." I pointed to my chest and Maddox's eyes lingered on it. *Men.* I raised my finger to my chin. "Me. Outside."

"You really think this guy could be the one?"

"The one?" I was momentarily confused. Like hell did

I think he was The One.

"The thief," Maddox stage-whispered. Inexplicably, he added jazz hands.

"I don't get that vibe," I told him, relieved that the conversation was still on track. "I've only known him an hour-and-a-half and the few minutes it took to read his file. He doesn't have any motive, and I don't think he's the kind of man who could get under a woman's skin, make her totally trust him, then betray her."

"We're still talking about this case?"

"Of course," I huffed. Like, what else? A professional such as myself wouldn't dare comment on the kind of men I dated. "Thing is, David likes David a whole lot. He's more interested in what he's got to say than what I have to say, so I don't see him getting a lot of second dates; and I figure the thief needs to go on a few dates with the women he targets. He must build up a profile so he knows who to rob and what to steal and when to do it."

"I agree. And David doesn't fit that bill?"

"Not unless he's confident enough to wheedle the details on the first date, then simply watch his dates after that, but that's pretty time-consuming. I guess he would have the skills..." I thought about how David made his money and pursed my lips.

"They're coming back. What skills?"

"David's a software expert. Maybe he simply gets enough details to hack his date's computer and discovers the assets that way."

"Smart. Keep at it, Lex."

"I will and don't crash anymore of my dates."

"How do you know I'm not actually here on a date that happened to coincide with work?"

I glanced at Blake, my heart sinking as a tear threatened to drop from my left eye. Rubbing his affair in my face was just mean. "With her?"

Maddox opened his mouth to say something, but

David and Blake returned. David was talking about the kind of art he invested in and how he loved adding to his collection. He said he hoped his passion would turn into philanthropy one day while Blake just nodded and agreed with everything he uttered. She was exactly the kind of woman he liked and it showed. Shame he didn't see the eye roll she gave me as she stepped away to take Maddox's hand. The bitch.

"Let's go to dinner, David?" I suggested, sidling away from Maddox towards my target. I gave him a brilliant smile. What did I care if Maddox wanted to schmooze with Blake? I had a date! A millionaire! With hair like nasty candy! Woo!

"Okay, I know a great French place just around the corner. They do an amazing steak that you must try..." With that, David babbled on about food and how he aced a Cordon Bleu class in Paris. He also said something about wine tasting in the Italian countryside. I had just enough time to narrow my eyes at Maddox before David whisked me away to the cloakroom to retrieve our coats.

David insisted on walking to the restaurant and I refused to moan about the height of my heels — though internally, I let that whine unleash. By the time we were seated, I knew he loved to cook, eat, drink wine and had a wine cellar in his home, a newly built house in Bedford Hills. I discovered he put a lot of pride in the restaurants he frequented and how many chefs knew him by name. Oh yeah... he always got the best tables and often ordered off-menu. Honestly, I knew he wanted to impress me by the way he waited for my reactions occasionally, but it all just made him sound desperately annoying.

"Are you nervous?" I asked him after he spoke in broken French to the waiter. He managed to order another bottle of champagne and call himself something rude that the waiter politely ignored.

David's cheeks pinked. "Maybe a little," he admitted. "It's not often I get to go on a date with a beautiful woman who really knows how to listen. Some women are so self-absorbed. I really want a selfless mother for my future children."

Holy crap. Was that ever not going to happen. I wondered what Flaherty, on the other end of the wire, thought of that. Maybe he was thinking about going home to a beautiful woman. Maybe Maddox was thinking about going home with Blake on his maybe/maybe not date. Maybe Solomon was on a date with the gorgeous younger woman. All of a sudden, I wanted to go home, kick off my heels, pull on my pajamas and crawl into bed. Dating suspected criminals was hard work.

"I'm sorry, what did you say?" I asked as David paused, waiting expectantly.

"I asked if you were happy to be a stay-at-home mom? Are you still fertile? You don't want to wait too long." he said with a silly grin.

"Oh, well, I uh... oh the candle blew out. Let me light it. The table needs some ambiance, don't you think? Uh, romantic..." I babbled, trying not to think about being a stay-at-home mom. It wasn't that I didn't want to be a mother one day, but it was way too soon to discuss my fertility and potential motherhood with a first date. Also: it was kind of crazy. And: no. Just no.

"Good idea," agreed David, momentarily distracted from the thought of impregnating me by the wisp of smoke winding its way upwards from the blown-out tea light on our table.

I don't know what happened next, but it was a disaster. Somehow, as I reached over for the gently flickering tea light on the empty table next to us, intending to bring it to ours, the waiter approached with the ice bucket, and David leaned forward, causing all three of us to collide. Instead of lighting the candle, the flame caught the essence of David's volatile hair product and I watched in horror as his sideburns ignited, the flames licking upwards.

A most unholy wail emanated from someone, and pretty soon, the three of us were also shrieking in cacophonous protests.

~

Lily had one look at me standing on her welcome mat, water dripping from my hem, a bottle of champagne in hand, and raised her eyebrows. "Good date?"

"Interesting."

She sniffed the air suspiciously as Eau de Singe wafted from me. "Go on."

"The gallery was nice, and we bumped into Maddox and Blake, so I suggested we go to dinner. David and me, that is. Not me, Maddox and Blake, because that would be really weird, then he got all nervous and..."

"Who got nervous? Maddox?"

"No. David. He started talking about my declining fertility and I thought maybe a little candlelight would put him at ease, so I went to light a candle, only he leaned forward and I kind of set fire to him..." I took a deep breath as Lily mashed her lips together and her eyes widened. "He had so much pomade in his hair, it kind of caught fire."

"Kind of?" asked Lily, opening the door wider so I could step into the safety and serenity of her apartment. I did, but my legs didn't seem to want to move any further so I just stood there, inside the door, whimpering.

"At first, it was just the sides, then the whole lot went. Woomph!" I threw one hand in the air dramatically and waggled my fingers. "It was like a Christmas plum pudding with flames dancing all around."

"Don't stop now. This is even better than I expected.

71

This has to be a first." Lily paused and gave me a suspicious questioning look. "Lexi... it was a first, right?"

I gave her a shocked look. Seriously? "Absolutely. Never set a date's head on fire before."

"Oh, well, good. So..." She prompted.

"So I grabbed the champagne and threw the ice bucket over his head to put him out."

"Good thinking. Very brave."

"I know, right?" I heaved a breath and smoothed my damp dress with my free hand. "He didn't seem too thrilled, so I just ran."

Lily pointed with her index finger. "With the champagne?"

My shoulders slumped as I looked down, spying the bottle and the dead wire I pulled from my bosom, which it was wrapped around. "I forgot I was holding it." I also forgot that I was sticking David with the bill, but my date was a millionaire; and really, it would be the worst date story he could ever tell, which made it worth it. Plus, we hadn't even ordered before he caught fire. He would totally get sympathy dates after this. He might even catch a nurse. A fertile one.

"That's a good vintage," Lily decided, peering at the label. "Dom Perignon. Nice. Want me to get you a glass?"

"No. It's still corked. We should have it when the baby is born."

"Frickin' A! I love a silver lining."

"Can I cry now?"

"Sure. Why not? And maybe we should call the hospital and see what happened to your date?"

"He's not burned, just damp... and pissed... and a little bald."

"A little?"

I slumped onto the couch after Lily guided me to it with a little push. I thought about my last sight of David, drenched and hairless. "Completely bald. Maybe a little crispy."

"Worst dating story ever."

"Thank you." My stomach gave a rumble. "I'm hungry. We didn't even get dinner. Probably a good thing. David wanted to order rare steak."

Lily reached for the sheaf of takeout menus she kept under the coffee table. "Yuck. What are you in the mood for?"

"Is it bad if I say barbecue?" I winced, but my mouth watered all the same.

"Creepy munchies, Lexi. Remind me to never watch *Silence of the Lambs* with you."

"I can't eat lamb. They're too cute."

"But the smell of burning head puts you in the mood for a little barbecue?"

Hearing her put it that way, I had to admit she had a point. "Let's order pizza. Vegetarian," I suggested and Lily resisted a laugh.

~

I left the champagne with Lily. After all, the less reminders of David Markham, the better. "Great date," snorted Flaherty when I called him back after checking my phone and finding two voicemails and three texts asking me to get in touch. In my haste to leave, I forgot about him listening in nearby. I mentally thanked the heavens and stars I disconnected my wire before I got to Lily's.

"The best," I agreed. "So glad you could make it."

"You should have seen your date after you left. A catastrophe. A freakin' catastrophe!"

"Want to rub it in some more?"

"Like salve on a wound?" asked Flaherty with a snigger.

I winced. "Do you have to tell Solomon?"

"You can."

I thought about it, how mortifying it would be. "No, that's okay. You do it. Hey, how much did you record?"

My heart thumped in the silence as I waited for his answer.

"Everything." With a peal of laughter, Flaherty hung up, before I even got a chance to ask if David was okay.

The aftermath, being alone again, and the enormous feeling of being let down, reminded me of the time right after I was attacked by Somper the Stomper, a psychotic soldier and murderer behind a drug smuggling ring. I'd just gotten home from the hospital for a short time when my door buzzer rang one night, only weeks ago.

I let Solomon in and we talked for more than an hour, sitting cozily on my couch like old friends, like lovers, and not at all like colleagues. He held both my hands in his and told me he loved me, but couldn't be with me right now, not while we both needed to get our heads straight. I knew he was right - I needed time to get over Maddox and make sense of what happened: whether Montgomery's hottest detective betrayed me or told me the truth about being undercover while kissing his undercover partner. It still choked me a little to hear Solomon lay out our current situation, sensibly and plain. He didn't explain what he needed to get his head straight about, and I was too choked up to ask or listen, the emotions of the past weeks finally registering. I certainly wasn't ready for the declaration of undying love that part of me wanted to hear from Solomon, but it was an amazing declaration nonetheless. And one I would never forget.

It wasn't until later, after Solomon left, when I was all sore and alone, that I realized I didn't tell him I loved him too. Truth was, I didn't know, so I said nothing. And I still didn't know how I felt. So, he was absolutely right that I needed to get my head straight.

One thing was undeniable though. I was butt-ugly jealous of the beautiful woman who answered his door; and that alone told me one thing: that I wasn't over Solomon at all.

CHAPTER SIX

I would rather have slunk into work unobtrusively, but someone helpfully left a copy of the Montgomery Gazette on my desk. The headline read GREAT HAIRBALLS OF FIRE.

"Jeez," I muttered, tossing it to one side as I imagined the Chics reading the article over breakfast at their new apartment. "News travels fast."

"Heard you had a hot date last night," sniggered Fletcher as he walked by, a thick brown file in his hand. I stuck my tongue out at him. Okay, sticking my tongue out wasn't the smartest thing to do, but it gave me a brief surge of satisfaction. So I did it again when he passed by me again, this time fileless. He ignored me as he knocked on Solomon's door and stuck his head into the small office. I didn't catch what he said, but a moment later, Fletcher was out the door, grabbing his jacket and camera from where it lay atop his desk. "Later, hot stuff," he said, clicking his fingers at me.

Pulling my laptop from my shoulder bag, I leaned back onto one of the leather desk chairs Solomon finally furnished the office with. I began powering the machine up so I could write my report of last night's events. Before I could even enter my password, Solomon called my name. This may or may not have been a good thing, because so far the only thing I decided to write was "Oops."

"How you doing?" asked Solomon as I entered. He signaled for me to close the door behind me. I didn't think I was about to get fired for... well, setting someone on fire, given that Solomon usually liked the door closed during private meetings. He didn't mind whether the lights were on or off though. Wink-wink.

"David Markham was discharged from the hospital this morning," he told me. "Minor burns, but nothing too serious. He won't need surgery."

I let out the breath I was holding in. "That's good news."

Solomon gave me a skeptical look and I sucked the breath back in, waiting for whatever else he had to tell me. "That's the good news," he confirmed. "The bad news is David Markham's not our guy."

"I guess it was too much to hope we would be looking for a bald, angry thief in the near future." Solomon clearly struggled not to give me an eye roll, so I blustered on, latching onto the key point he just revealed. "Hey, how do you know he's not our guy?"

"There was a theft last night while Markham was getting treatment at the hospital. A big jewelry haul. I haven't seen the itemized list or photographs yet, but Maddox said it amounted to around a hundred thousand dollars."

"Wow."

"There's more bad news. We checked on the victim's recent dates and they included each of the three remaining suspects. There're a few others, but these are the only ones she has in common with all the other victims, so I'd say we're on the right track."

I brightened. I wouldn't have to date David again. My fertility was safe. Phew! "That sounds like good news!"

"It gets worse."

"It would, wouldn't it?" I sighed. I leaned against the doorjamb and waited for whatever bad news Solomon was going to unleash. Couldn't he just give me a list to peruse in my own time? Like over cocktails.

"Markham could press charges for assault."

I gasped. "Who assaulted him?"

Solomon gave me a pointed look. His nostrils flared and he nipped the corner of his bottom lip. Mmmm. "You."

Wait. What? "Oh yeah. No. Wait. I did not! If anything, he should sue the manufacturers of his hair product. Nothing so flammable should be allowed near an open flame. What a doofus! Is he really going to press charges? I'm so not going on a second date with him now! It's over. Um, can you tell him that? Please."

"You won't have to since he's in the clear now. Don't worry about the charges. I doubt they'll stick. Between MPD, Million Matches, and me, we'll make them go away."

"Thank you." I slumped in my seat and took a moment to admire my hot pink nail polish. No chips. I decided to take it as a sign that today would be awesome. Well, after this hiccup, it would be. "You know Maddox and Blake were at the gallery last night?" I asked, dropping the information casually.

"I heard the conversation on Flaherty's audio tape."

Of course he did. I struggled to remember if I said anything embarrassing. There was that bit about dating Blake, so... probably. "I thought we were doing this investigation low key. If MPD keep turning up on my dates, the suspect might get suspicious. I think the fewer eyeballs, the better."

"I agree. I didn't like the idea that they were going to

be there."

"So... it was prearranged? Thanks for telling me." Thanks oodles. If there was anything I hated, it was being kept in the dark. Especially when it came to Maddox, work, dating, Solomon, oh, everything really. I was nosy and it was one of my best qualities.

"It was a last minute decision," Solomon told me, looking entirely nonplussed.

"Huh." I snorted. Clearly, I wasn't party to the last minute decision, even if I were lead investigator, so I'd better up my game and make sure I didn't get left out again. There was no time for hurt feelings. I looked great and I had a thief to catch! Shame I was unlikely to close the deal before dinner with my family later. Shame. They would have been thrilled. "So, what's next?"

"Like I said, the suspect pool is down to three. You have a date with suspect number two for lunch."

"Lunch? On a first date?"

"It was the agency's idea. They thought it would be..." Solomon paused.

"What? Nice? Relaxed? Pleasant?" I prompted.

"Safer," decided Solomon.

Charming.

"Apparently, Lord Justin Camberwell likes dresses so... do your thing. Don't look hot, look..."

"Safe?" I huffed.

"Sweet."

"I can do sweet. It's my third best look."

"Dare I ask what your first two are?"

I smiled. "Since you ask. Smokin' hot and hot." That earned a smile out of Solomon, and for a moment, we just looked at each other. I thought Solomon might say something, something about us; then he turned away, the moment vanished, and I realized I was officially dismissed as his attention turned to the open file on his desk.

"Want me to wire up?" I asked, rising from my chair.

"Yes. I'll be in range," he told me, passing me a sheet of paper without looking up. "Details here. Don't be late."

"Am I ever? Don't answer that."

My cell phone rang as I returned to my desk, with my sister-in-law's name flashing on the screen. "Hey, Alice. How's life?" I asked, happy to hear from her. Luck had given me two great sisters-in-law, one not-so-great ex-sister-in-law, one future-sister-in-law-slash-BFF, and that was notwithstanding my brothers-in-law. Oh heck, this family was getting complicated. I wondered if we were close to being the biggest family in Montgomery yet, and if there was a prize.

"I heard you set a guy on fire," she gushed. Alice was a nurse at Montgomery General, so it wasn't exactly surprising that she knew. It would be just my luck that she was working ER last night and caught David as a patient. Not that she confirmed it, nor did I ask. "What did he do?" she wanted to know.

"Nothing! We were on a date."

"Huh. No wonder you're single. Hey, did he try to feel you up?"

"No!"

"I couldn't think of any other reason why you'd set him on fire."

"Ugh! Is this why you called?"

"Nope. Your mom was just here and she said to remind you about dinner later. The whole family is going."

"I'll be there. She sent a text this morning. Who taught her how to text? I thought we all agreed that would be a bad idea. What's for dinner?"

"Don't know, but your mom suggested flambé for dessert," said Alice, laughing as she hung up.

"Ha-ha," I said, pulling a face at the screen.

"Hey, Lexi..." said Lucas, behind me. I whipped around in my chair to face his uncharacteristically tidy desk, situated right behind mine. His desk, however, was twice the size and had an array of monitors. A large box sat on the floor beside it, serving as a reminder that our resident geek and cyber expert was moving to the floor upstairs, where Solomon was expanding the agency. Every time I thought about it, I felt put out that I wasn't in the know. I wondered if Fletcher, Flaherty, and Delgado felt the same, or if they did know. I couldn't ask them without showing I knew nothing. Damn it.

"Yes," I said, pre-empting him, "yes, I was on a date as part of a case and a man's hair caught on fire, but it was an accident. An accident!" My voice ended on an hysterical note and my lower jaw quivered. Though that could have been caused by sugar withdrawal, thanks to my current healthy eating phase, last night's pizza excluded.

"I only wanted to know if you wanted a coffee because I'm going to get one, but... really?" Lucas peered at me, and whispered, "On fire?"

I made a strangled noise and turned away. A moment later, I looked over my shoulder and said in my meekest voice, "Yes, please. Two sugars."

An hour, one coffee, and one filed report that didn't tell Solomon anything he didn't already know, later, and I was out of there. As I jogged down the steps to the underground garage, I wondered what it would be like to meet a real live English lord. Would I have to call him "Lord"? I could see that getting old really fast. I was pretty certain I didn't have to curtsy, but the rules around that one confused me. Plus, this country was a republic so... in his face! I thought about my experiences of Englishmen and aristocracy, while realizing that all my knowledge came from *Downton Abbey*, which probably didn't help.

Arriving at the parking garage, I ignored my VW and headed straight for the Ferrari. After all, it was there to give a good impression -- one that said "wealthy, please steal from me" — and there was a good chance Lord Camberwell might see me arrive at the restaurant, so my little car would just not cut it. Plus, the Ferrari was awesome to drive.

I slipped behind the wheel and took a moment to smell the delicious leather interior, while stroking the wheel. "My baby," I cooed at it. "Mommy loves you so much already." With a throaty purr, the engine fired up and I reversed on a curve, throwing it into drive and accelerating towards the exit.

There was no need to head to the Chilton house — that would only become a necessity if I were being picked up or returned "home," or if I invited someone back. There was no way I would invite a stranger and potential thief "home" for "coffee" until I was sure they were going to try something more exciting and illegal than putting the moves on me. Instead, I headed to my real home, parking the Ferrari in my usual spot next to Lily's Mini.

After unlocking the communal front door, I found it only opened a fraction of the way so I had to suck it in, bump it, and edge through sideways, only to be confronted with a stack of packing boxes. An attractive man made his way down the stairs, another box in hand, which he stacked on top of the rest.

"Hi," I said, sizing up the stranger and wondering who he was. Were most movers this cute? "Who are you?"

He gave me an equally puzzled look. "Jake. I live upstairs."

"Upstairs, upstairs?" I pointed upstairs, just to clarify. Also: where? The apartment above me had been empty since the last tenant left ages ago.

"Yup. Third floor."

"Huh." Perhaps it hadn't been so empty. Strange. I never heard a thing. "Have you lived here long?" I checked his feet. Big feet.

"Two months. You?"

Huge feet. Wow. Dainty walker. "Years."

"Well, great to meet you. I'm moving out, so I guess this is goodbye."

"I assumed so. I'd throw you a party, but that would be weird."

"See ya," said Jake, my new and now ex-neighbor. I waited until I heard him reach the top of the stairs before knocking on Lily's door.

"Did you know we had an upstairs neighbor?" I asked.

"Sure. Jake. He's such a nice guy."

"He's lived here two months and you never once mentioned him! I thought the apartment upstairs was empty."

"I never mentioned him? Odd. Anyway, he's moving out today. Such a shame. He's single, you know."

"I'm only dating thieves currently."

"Perhaps he could steal your heart?" Lily quipped, crossing her hands over hers.

"It's the only thing I have of value."

"You're home early. Want to talk while I pack? Jake had some spare boxes so I'm getting started. I need to send things to Goodwill too. Do you think Jord needs any of his stuff?"

"No can do and he probably doesn't need anything if it's taking up your closet space," I justified. "I've got to get ready for a date with suspect number two of the top secret case I'm not telling you anything about." I checked upstairs in case the light-footed Jake sneaked down and was listening. He wasn't. "He's a lord," I added.

"A real one? Not like a guy just named Lord. Like Earl isn't really an earl."

"A real one," I confirmed. "From England. We're having lunch at Alessandro's."

"Nice. Try not to do anything horrible to him."

"Can't guarantee it. I'll let you know after." I gave

Lily a wave and hightailed it upstairs, narrowly missing getting squashed by Jake lugging another box downstairs when I paused to stick the key in the lock. Inside, I shed my jeans and blouse and rummaged through Serena's clothes, finally selecting a very pretty, pale green shift in a boxy shape. I added my trusty, black, pointy-toed pumps and grabbed a cute Marc Jacobs bag.

Turning to check my reflection in the mirror, I couldn't help dropping into a curtsy. Was this the kind of thing a future lady would wear? It was neat, demure... definitely safe. Sweet, even, but not sugary-sweet. Sophisticated. And if Lord Justin knew his labels, he'd clearly know he was looking at an expensive little outfit. Shame I couldn't flash a few jewels, but it was lunch. I added an antique sapphire ring, which I inherited from a great aunt, and went to land myself a gentleman thief.

CHAPTER SEVEN

I'm pretty certain the vibrations from the Ferrari's engine were the most exciting thing to happen to me in weeks, given my current dry spell when it came to men. Although getting a spot right outside Alessandro's, coupled with the appreciative glances I got as I slid my legs out of the car, certainly gave me a thrill. Which was just as well because I was trying really hard not to turn around and shoot daggers at the restaurant across the street. That was where I once saw Maddox smooching Blake. I purposefully avoided the place ever since despite their reputation that the food was amazing. Even my parents liked it.

On the plus side. Date. English lord. Possible jewel thief. International jewel thief, given his European status. Cute accent. My life was so much better now that I quit temping and found my calling in private investigating. In fact, so long as I didn't think about my impending homelessness, single status, the fact that I slept with my boss and my conflicted feelings about my ex... my life was wonderful! But all that was irrelevant as

I entered the restaurant and gave my name to Alessandro's maitre d'.

"The other party has already arrived," he informed me, discreetly taking in my attire. I may have done sweet as requested, but I added a dose of va-va-voom! at the last minute by switching my low-heeled pumps for a sky high pair that made my calves look super toned. Raiding the accessories Serena loaned me, I also added a gold Chanel watch, a gift from her ex that she no longer wore, along with gold studs of my own. I was aiming for the less-is-more option when it came to jewelry. Mostly because I had less, rather than more, but that was beside the point, which was: I looked on the hot side of sophisticated. Lord Justin would have to be a dead fish not to like what he saw. It was just a good job he couldn't see my discreet wire, pinned to the inside of my dress, or my boss parked not far down the street.

The lord stood as I approached the table, smiling down at me from his full six feet. He was every bit as yummy as his photos suggested. Very smart in a cream lounge suit with an open-necked collar, and hair that was trimmed short and, thankfully, without a hint of gel or spray. There were also no candles anywhere, thanks to sunlight streaming through the windows.

"Lexi, what a pleasure." He held his hand out to me, taking mine, then folding his other over the top in a very familiar way. They were warm, dry, and strong. I gave his hand a little squeeze and he smiled. "I've so looked forward to meeting you."

"Likewise, Lord Justin."

"Justin, please. The lord thing gets so tiring," he informed me.

"Have you been one long?" I asked, mentally wincing. I knew I should have read up on that. Was one born into the title? Or did one earn it? Was inheriting a title as easy as buying it on the Internet?

Justin laughed while they seated us and passed out

the menus. My lack of protocol knowledge was brushed over as we made polite small talk. After a while, and some gentle prodding, Justin began reminiscing about his childhood in England and his travels, making me laugh with tales of his adventures. He gave me the impression that money was no object and he could travel on a whim, that he was well educated, and well connected by the way he dropped the names of younger European royals, and "Honorable this" and "Lady that." While he was charming, effusive, and definitely pleasing to the eye, there was one thing that puzzled me.

Why didn't I fancy him?

He had everything. Money, history, looks, charm, derring-do. He was a catch. He just wasn't the catch I wanted to reel in. I needed chemistry. Could I live on chemistry and none of the other things was another question, but I was pretty sure the answer was yes. After all, I didn't need a man to keep me. I could look after myself, and I would.

"Here I am talking about myself and I've barely let you get a word in edgewise," he laughed as the waiter placed our appetizers in front of us. Justin ordered soup, I opted for bruschetta. Looking at it, I wondered about the issue of crumbs in teeth. There was no classy way to avoid that, but maybe he'd like seeing me running my tongue across my teeth after every bite? If he had a tongue fetish.

"I like hearing about you," I told him, which wasn't untrue.

"Tell me about you instead. How long have you lived in this delightful town?"

"All my life. I was born here, though my family has an Irish background."

"Ireland, a delightful country. Have you been?"

"Once, when I was little, but not recently. I have some cousins there."

"I once partied at a castle on the coast. Terrific bash."

"Oh. Cool..." I wanted to party at a castle. Not necessarily with Justin, but I wouldn't say no. "Any dragons?"

"If there were, I'd gladly slay them for a fair lady such as you," Justin said with a wink. I laughed. "That's a very pretty ring. Family?"

"Yes, a great aunt. She left it to me when she passed," I replied, rubbing my thumb over the stone.

"How thoughtful of her. Do you have many family jewels?"

I suppressed the urge to giggle at "family jewels" since Justin might not have the lowdown on the dual meaning. I gave a half shake, half nod while I decided what to say. "Yes," I decided, "I have a few inherited pieces in my collection."

"You collect jewels?" Justin dipped his spoon into the soup and raised it to his mouth, seemingly making polite conversation.

"It's my passion. I'm a magpie when it comes to sparkly things."

"Tiffany's? Cartier? Chopard? Harry Winston? All of the above?"

"All of the above, and a few more," I lied.

"You must have a very happy allowance."

"Unlimited." I watched Justin carefully for a reaction, but there was nothing. Perhaps this was natural to him. "I like to shop. It gives me something to do."

"You don't work?"

"Oh no!" I exclaimed in mock horror. "Do you?"

"I suppose you made your millions?" Justin set down his spoon and appraised me as I nibbled the bruschetta. "No. I believe you have family money. Am I right?"

"Spot on."

"Do you mind if I ask how you like to invest? I'm here studying several businesses and I have a little cash to play with. What would you do with half a mil, Lexi?"

"Oh, well, I'm no financial advisor." I chomped down

on the bruschetta and chewed, then chewed some more. "It depends if you're staying or going. Home, that is."

"I do plan to return to England. It's my home," Justin admitted. He dabbed his lips with his napkin, a faraway smile lingering there. "All I need is the perfect lady to accompany me."

"In that case, something small, like art," I suggested, thinking back to the previous evening's art gallery and the eye-watering prices. "Easy to transport, with good return if you pick the right artist."

"Terrific idea. Perhaps you'll introduce me to your dealer?"

"Perhaps," I consented. "I'm sure he'll be glad to meet you." Not that he even exists! The further we got into dinner, the more Justin gently inquired about my wealth: my investments, my recent purchases, was I into cars and fashion, where did I go to school? and where did I vacation? Fortunately, Solomon and Helen Callery created a profile for me and I used it now, answering his questions as they arose, portraying myself as a rich young woman, with too much time and money on her hands.

"Shall we do dessert?" Justin asked as our plates were cleared, "or coffee?"

"I wish I could stay," I told him, the lying now glibly smooth, "but I have an appointment with my jeweler that I mustn't miss."

"I'd love to join you. Perhaps I could find a gift for my mother."

"It's a girls only thing," I said quickly, adding "just a few friends and me having a little tea party. Buying a few diamonds." I shrugged, like it was no big deal. Sneaking a look at Justin to see if he believed it, I was pleased at my apparent success. He nodded, and turned to look for a waiter, signaling with one raised finger.

"May I escort you to your car?" he asked as we left. "Or can my chauffeur take you anywhere?" He pointed to the town car drawing up to the sidewalk. Well, I wondered what Solomon would say about that. Also, I wondered if he would spring for a chauffeur. Probably not, I decided. Odds were probably as likely as letting me keep the Ferrari.

"I'm just here," I told him, pointing to the car. "I like to drive."

"You American women. So independent." Justin caught my hand and raised it to his lips, dropping a gentle kiss on my knuckles. "Exactly the quality I'm seeking in a wife."

I couldn't help giggling, and with a blush, I stepped backwards, careful to avoid planting my heel in a crack of the sidewalk. I checked over my shoulder as I walked towards my car, and sure enough, Justin was eyeing me as I retreated. He waved one hand and I waggled my fingers at him as I beeped the car open.

Solomon called me a few minutes after I joined the downtown traffic. "I hope you didn't fall for that crap," he said.

"Like an anvil," I teased, straight-faced. "I'm going to be a lady."

"America needs you, honey. You aren't going anywhere."

"Well, if you and America insist..."

"What's your impression?"

"Of America?"

"Justin."

"Right. Obviously, that's what you meant. Duh! He's charming, good looking, I bet the girls fall all over him." He just didn't set me on fire. Fortunately for him, I didn't set him on fire either. The date actually went pretty well. It definitely wasn't in my growing worst list.

"And?"

"He didn't do it for me; sorry. You?"

Solomon choked on whatever he just swallowed. "Me neither. I meant your impression of him generally.

89

Could he be our thief?"

"Maybe. He was too interested in what kind of money and things I had access to. He set my alarm bells ringing. It was a little... too much," I decided.

"He's also following you."

"No shit?"

"No shit."

I checked my rearview mirror and sure enough, the town car was three cars behind me. "Maybe he's going somewhere?"

"In case he's not, head to Chilton and go into the house. I don't like that he's following you."

I patted my purse. Yes, I grabbed the Chilton house keys earlier. "Okay, but he's not exactly being secretive about it. Where are you?"

"Two cars behind Camberwell."

"Cool. If I make a right, then right again, then another right, I'll end up behind you. We could all drive in a circle!"

"Drive to Chilton, Lexi," instructed Solomon before hanging up.

I did just that, checking my mirrors every few minutes. The town car stayed on me the whole way home and drew up as I exited the Ferrari. The window rolled down and I feigned surprise at seeing him again. Further down the street, I saw Solomon pull over.

"Justin!" I leaned forward in what I hoped was a demure way.

"I had to make sure you got home safely," said Justin. "Is this where you live?"

I pointed to the house next to Solomon's. "That one. Just a rental while I look for another place."

"Do you intend to buy?" Justin waited for me to nod. "Call me if you need company house hunting."

"I will," I replied, stepping back. "Bye, Justin."

Justin nodded, tapped his chauffeur's shoulder and leaned back, giving me a quick wave before the car sped away. I waited on the sidewalk until he rounded the corner, which happily coincided with Solomon rolling up. "Your neighbors will think I'm a hooker," I told him. "And I look like I can't even catch a date. I'm a failed hooker."

Solomon laughed. "Good to fail at something. I'm gonna follow his highness, and see where he goes."

"Have fun. I have a hot date waiting for me." I don't know what made me say that, but Solomon's eyes darkened and he gave me a most imperceptible look. I gulped. He had that effect on me. He made my hands clammy, my knees weak. He made me say stupid things and shoot my mouth off, and he made me breathe hard when he looked at me that way. "With my mom," I added after a few long seconds of mutual staring.

"Have fun," was all Solomon said before rolling his window up and driving off, leaving me cringing and alone.

CHAPTER EIGHT

Since I had some time to kill between my date with Justin and dinner, I decided to arrive early and spend some quality moments with my parents. It was the only way I would be able to get a word in edgewise before the rest of my loud and boisterous family arrived.

The evening promised to be a full night, not least because Serena was bringing Delgado to dinner for the first time. The last man she brought home was her cheating, scumbag ex-husband and, boy, were we all grateful she kicked him to the curb. Delgado was an infinite improvement. He might not be rich or smart like Ted, but he was affectionate, loyal, built like a tank, and worshipped the ground my sister and her baby Victoria walked on. Or in Victoria's case, rolled on. That Delgado was also my colleague was only a minor point, really. I grew to like him a lot more since he started dating my sister. It may have had something to do with her mellowing out and becoming a nicer person after they started dating. When I thought about it, I wondered if I had to start liking Ted too, since she became a lot nicer once she ditched him. Or maybe it was simply motherhood. I decided to like Victoria the most. She was cute as a button.

"You're still a private investigator?" asked Mom, looking over my clothing curiously as I joined them on the living room couch. My mother had a tub of potatoes on her lap and was busy peeling them while watching the end of a rerun of *Ellen*. "You look very nice. You keep it up and you'll get a boyfriend in no time." She leaned in and whispered, "So long as you're not hooking."

"Whaaaat? No!"

"What's wrong?" asked Dad, looking up at my shriek.

"Mom just asked if I was hooking!"

Dad blinked. "Are you?"

Ugh. Parents! "No."

"You look nice anyway," grunted Dad. "Chic. That's the word, isn't it?"

"Thanks, Dad. I just came from a job." My mother raised both eyebrows. "Not that kind of job. It was a date. Jeez, not that kind of date! C'mon! I'm doing some undercover work and I can't talk about it, but it's all legal and I don't have sex with anyone."

"Poor thing. You must be bored," said Mom. She took another look at my dress. "Is that Serena's?"

"Yeah. The watch too. Do you think she'll let me keep them?"

"Not a chance."

I sighed. "That's what I thought. At least the shoes are mine."

"And the car?"

The Ferrari was outside. "Not mine. Solomon's."

"What *does* belong to you?"

I thought about it. "My hair," I said, stroking it self-consciously.

The doorbell rang, but we all knew better than to get up. I don't know how many keys to my parent's house circulated in Montgomery. It was largely pointless as the door never seemed to be locked anyway. I wondered if my parents worried about crime, but having at least nineteen serving police officers in the family, I figured any criminal who decided to break in would probably get a standing ovation for sheer audacity. And then live to regret it.

Jord and Lily entered and my mother set the potatoes aside — on my lap — so she could fuss over Lily and sneak a stroke or two on her non-protruding belly. Nearing the end of her first trimester, Lily was the object of Graves' excitement. It wasn't that we just wanted another baby in the family — I had a bunch of nieces and nephews already — but getting Lily as an actual member of our clan, and not just an honorary one. The baby was the icing on the cake.

On Jord's and Lily's heels came Daniel and Alice with their children, Ben and Rachel, in tow, both kids eager to tell my parents about school and the general injustice of siblings, like none of us knew anything about that.

Delgado and Serena walked in thirty minutes later. It didn't surprise me that Delgado wore his standard leather jacket and black jeans, paired with a striped blue shirt that my mother took pains to admire. I was just relieved the undercover homeless gig was over. What did surprise me was Serena didn't bound in with her usual over-the-top style. Instead of attempting to bulldoze her way to the center of conversation, she simply greeted everyone pleasantly as she fought to hold a giggling, wriggling, Victoria in her arms. I blew a raspberry at Victoria from behind my sister's back and Victoria blew one back before wriggling some more. With one powerful kick from her legs, and one equally powerful "Parp!" she launched herself at Delgado who caught her with barely a blink. She nestled in his arms and reached for his earlobe, stroking it between her tiny thumb and forefinger. I think Delgado blissed out.

"Thought you said he was scary," said Lily quietly.

"He is. But not anymore. He's losing it."

"Heard that," said Delgado, staring at Victoria as she beamed her gummy smile at him. "Don't close your eyes when you go to sleep later."

"Back to scary," I mock whispered to Lily.

"Don't worry," she told me, linking arms. "This room is full of police officers who heard that."

"Yeah," I told Delgado. "You'll never get away with it."

He gave me a smile that said, "Watch me" before relaxing as he looked around at the many assembled Graves with a mix of wonder and appreciation. It occurred to me that I couldn't remember if Delgado ever mentioned his family. I wasn't even sure he had one. That was okay though; we Graves liked to collect strays and keep them forever. Plus, also in Delgado's favor, he had the Victoria seal of approval, and who could say no to that kind of recommendation?

By the time Garrett arrived with his wife, surly teenage son, and two younger kids, Lily and I had set the table, and my mother was putting out the food. My dad busied himself pouring drinks, which, given that seventeen of us were squashed around the table, was no mean feat. A retirement career as a barman was calling him. Unfortunately, he was too busy trying to get out of adult education classes with my mother to actually take up a second career.

As we ate, the conversation never once abated. If anything, it just got louder and more garbled as we simultaneously ate and yelled at each other. Even Delgado relaxed into the chaos. Watching him with my sister, I had to wonder if he was going to be my future brother-in-law and... I liked the idea. I would never have guessed he'd be the kind of man Serena would go for, but I was glad to be wrong. He may have been the absolute opposite of her ex-husband, but he was one hundred percent better for her. Also, he'd have to be on my team at the office. I wondered how Solomon would like that. And then I wondered what Solomon was doing. Was he with the beautiful woman right now? Was Maddox with Blake? Ugh. I shoved all thoughts of both of them from my head.

Of course, that, and seeing my sister so happy, and my brothers, too, with their families, was a reminder of my own single status. Would the day ever come when it was natural for me to arrive at a family dinner with a husband and children in tow? For the first time in my life, I felt a niggling pain deep in my chest. No, it wasn't pain: it was *want*. I wanted what they had.

Not that I was desperate, but I wanted a family too someday. A someday that wasn't too far away. I just didn't know with whom.

My mother gained our attention by clapping loudly and at length. That was surprising in itself because she could be pretty vocal, having raised five children, and Irish ones at that. She flapped her hands about and waited expectantly. I stole a look at the blank expressions around me with relief. Oh good, I totally didn't miss something. Mom flapped her hands again.

"What's she doing?" asked Jord to no one in particular.

"It's her latest hobby," said Dad, reaching for the gravy and drowning his plate.

"What is it?" asked Garrett. "Mime origami?"

"Shadow puppetry?" suggested Lily.

"Some form of dance?" asked Serena. "Like belly dancing, but with hands. Hand dancing?"

Mom rolled her eyes and moved her hands slowly.

"I think she's making a butterfly," said my niece, Chloe, linking her fingers together and making them flap.

"Or spiders," added her brother, Sam. He linked his

hands together and crawled them over to her plate. Chloe squealed and thumped him on the shoulder. No one chastised her. We all thought spiders were gross.

"Maybe she's going to be a hand model," suggested Delgado, getting in on the act. In his arms, Victoria snored softly. I was pretty certain she had no intention of ever letting him go. She just loved scary dude cuddles. I hated to think what kind of adult she would grow up to be. On the plus side, the whole of Montgomery would be looking out for her. Finally, someone else in the family would be arriving home in a police car. It was about time someone bore my mantle.

"Ugh," said Mom. "I'm learning American sign language. It's a very useful way to communicate."

"I know sign language," said Sam, flipping the finger at the entire table.

"Oh, God," said his mother, Traci, as she folded his finger back into his palm and tucked the offending hand under the table. She turned to Garrett. "I blame you."

"You taught him the 'F' word!" rebounded Garrett.

"Not deliberately!"

"Jesus!" said Sam. "Parents!"

"And now my grandson's blaspheming!" said Mom. I bet she was thinking of a few choice signs for us all. She sighed and carried on. "I thought I'd try something new."

"What about Krav Maga? And survival skills?" I asked, remembering the last new classes my mother tried dragging me to. In the case of the latter, I was bullied into it after my mother gloated that her gift of an army knife saved my life. We ended up doing a practical assessment in Fairmount Park and it was... interesting. Sign language sounded — no pun intended — much safer.

Mom shrugged and circled her finger around her ear. "Some of the Krav Maga folk were crazy. I just thought I'd try something new. You should come too, Lexi.

Maybe you'll meet someone. A man," Mom added loudly, just in case I, and everyone else, didn't catch her point.

Typical. "I'm too busy. I have a big case, and besides, I'm meeting lots of new people."

Delgado snorted. I guess he heard about the incident. It looked like I had to close this case if I were to redeem myself in the eyes of my colleague-slash-future-brother-in-law. Again. So much for him being on my team.

"You can do it, Lexi," said Serena, smiling at me and not in a patronizing way. "Whatever case you're working, I know you'll crack it."

Just as I was about to thank her for her support, Dad raised his glass. "Or die trying," he said.

Charming.

CHAPTER NINE

According to Solomon's text message the next day, Ben Rafferty insisted on picking me up from my "home" for our early evening date.

"I don't think so. What if he kills me?" I texted by return.

"Eyes on you the whole time," sent Solomon.

"Whose?"

"Mine. Open the package. Wear it tonight. Return tomorrow."

What package? I shivered, got out of bed, and opened the door, wondering what I would find inside a small padded envelope with my name on it. Not a dress. Boo-hoo.

Over coffee, I opened the envelope to find a gorgeous bracelet that sparkled in the late morning sun. It sure tempted me and I wasn't even a thief. Throughout the afternoon, I re-read Ben's file. I looked through his photos a few times and wondered what he'd be like in person, as well as what he expected of me. Not knowing where we were going for dinner, mid-afternoon, I pulled on a black dress and kitten-heeled patent pumps, adding the Chanel watch, earrings, and a gold pendant ready for the evening. I fastened the borrowed diamond bracelet on last.

Downstairs, Jack's boxes were all gone, but Lily was home and ready to do my hair, teasing and setting it while telling me the latest news of the bar and how her builders managed to cut through a section of pipe work and flood the place only that morning.

I dropped Lily off at the bar, waiting as she kissed the Ferrari goodbye, and drove to Chilton just as the rush hour began to pick up. By the time I got there, I had precisely thirty minutes to poke around my new "home" and get used to the space so my deep cover looked natural. After all, this was where Ben thought I lived, so I'd better act like it. Parking the Ferrari outside, I took a long look around for Solomon's car, but it was missing and his house appeared empty. Not that it mattered; he would turn up, ready for watching over me like a guardian angel.

Solomon's neighbors' home was gorgeously decorated, like it was lifted from the pages of a magazine. I dropped the keys onto the hall console and slipped off my shoes, feeling quite at home as I moved around the elegant house. Everything was just right and discreetly expensive. If I had to live here for real, I wouldn't object. However, I would probably remove the tiny video cameras Solomon and the crew had installed around the house, the live feeds of which were streaming straight to the bank of screens Solomon told me he set up in his spare bedroom. Not that he invited me in to see it. The niggling anxiety in the pit of my stomach couldn't help feed the wonder that maybe, just maybe, Solomon's beautiful house guest had something to do with my lack of invite.

Was she watching me poke around this house? I wondered. Did she know that not so long ago, I'd been more to Solomon than just an employee? And did she care? Biggest question: when did Solomon have a chance to meet her? As far as I was aware, he was no social butterfly. He worked, worked, and worked some more. Did he know her before he met me? Before we shared intimate moments? Or was he so bowled over by her beauty that she used it to her advantage and moved in on my...

"Whoa!" I said to the empty pristine, black granite and oak kitchen. "Don't go there!" Solomon was most definitely *not* my man.

Before I could analyze my thought processes any further, the doorbell rang, sending chimes tinkling through the house. I took my time walking to the door, after stepping into my patent leather black pumps, smoothing my hair, and giving my reflection an appreciative look. I looked damn fine and I wasn't even being vain. My hair hung loose and glossy about my shoulders, the mid-lengths in a gentle curl that looked natural and not like it took Lily forty minutes and a truckload of swearing at the heated brush. My dress was short, black, and perfectly fitted; and, on this occasion, from my own closet. I did, however, borrow the diamond ear studs from my sister, and Solomon, clearly calling in a favor with the bracelet. I didn't know from whom or where, but I could tell the diamonds was the real deal. Like the house, it was discreet, classy, and very expensive. I bet it cost more than a year's salary. Maybe even two.

My cell phone trilled so I plucked it from my purse. The text was from Solomon. "Stop preening and answer the door," it read. *Jerk.* He didn't even issue a compliment. I'd obviously paled into insignificance next to his supermodel girlfriend, I thought, pouting sulkily in the mirror. I turned in the general vicinity of the nearest camera, stuck out my tongue, and prepared to answer the door, remembering to stand straight, with my shoulders back.

My date-slash-suspect-number-three was even better than his photographs. By "better," I mean my tongue flopped out of my mouth and licked the door frame before I rolled it back up. He was hot. Hottie McHoterson hot. Tall, athletic. Dark brown hair, short on top. Clean-shaven with a strong, square jaw and the most mesmerizing brown eyes. He smelled delicious. If there were a catalog of men I could date, I would pick him first, no problem.

"Wow," he said, casting an appreciative glance from my top to my toes. "Looks like I struck the big time."

A blush crept over my cheeks. Now *that* was a comment I liked hearing. I hoped Solomon was taking notes, not that it would do me any good. Come to think of it, I don't even know why I thought about him so much. And now was most definitely not the time. Hello, Hottie!

"Great to meet you," I said, holding out my hand. Ben took it in his, leaning closer, and kissing me on the cheek. Then I died and went to heaven. Not really. Actually, we got into the back of his chauffeur-driver town car and went to dinner.

Ben chose Riverside for our date, a very fancy fish restaurant that, funnily enough, was located next to a river. So, it wasn't a marina with yachts bobbing on soft waves, but the owners had plenty of boating memorabilia. Lifejackets and oars decorated the white walls along with a large, black and white photo triptych of a catamaran leaping waves.

"Which interests you most? Sailing or art?" Ben asked as we were led past a cluster of other diners to our window table.

"Art," I said, because I excelled at looking at stuff. "You?"

"Sailing's my passion," Ben admitted as he took his chair opposite mine. "I have a yacht that I like to take out when the weather is good."

"Is it moored locally? Well, not locally since we're not exactly close to the sea but..." I struggled for the words.

"New York. I keep an apartment in Manhattan."

"So what pulled you away from Manhattan and the yacht to Montgomery? Aren't we a little sleepy for you?"

"Not hardly. I find Montgomery a very refreshing town; plus, it's close enough to Boston if I want some city life. I feel I can relax here. Is that what drew you here too?"

I shook my head. "I grew up here."

"In Chilton?"

"No. I moved there recently." Yeah, like an hour ago. Ben smiled politely at that and didn't probe any further. Instead, he looked up as the waiter approached with the wine menu, and browsed it for a moment. "Shall we have white?" he asked. "Any preference?"

"Why don't you order after we've chosen our meals?" I suggested. "Wine says a lot about a man." Okay, so I made that up. Really, it said a lot about this woman. It said I didn't know much about ordering wine and I was pretty certain the wine stashed in my apartment's kitchen wouldn't meet Ben's expectations. It was a lot closer to an "Oops, my paycheck ran out" budget than my fake heiress status; but then, how did I know if Ben wasn't a fraud too?

With such a handsome, attractive man giving me interest, it was at times, a little hard to remember why I was there: to catch him out in a lie, if not entice him to commit a crime. He was in no way an actual date because even if he were bonafide, I wasn't. Yet as we talked, I found myself liking him, his easy personality, the way he could turn anything into humor, along with the casual comments he made about his life and hopes. Even the indiscreet moments where we swapped stories of our worst dates (I left out David's) were funny. As he insisted on taking care of the bill, then escorting me hand-in-hand to the waiting car, I found myself hoping he wasn't the guy we were looking for. Yet, all the attributes I found so attractive about him were all the ones that would gain him the confidence of any healthy woman.

"Allow me," said Ben, exiting the car first and extending his hand. I took it, allowing him to help me out of the car. My heel caught the curb and I stumbled into him, pressing my hands against his firm chest. I looked up, my heart beating faster as he dipped his head. Instead of setting me to rights, his lips landed softly on mine with the most delicate kiss. When he stepped away, I was breathless. "Good night, Lexi. Until we meet again." He disappeared into the town car and blew me a kiss, speeding away as I stood on the sidewalk watching him leave.

"Get a grip," I told myself, "It was just a kiss." I gave myself a mental shake before turning to walk up the steps of the house, and letting myself in. Almost as soon as I entered, my cell phone rang.

"Debrief," said Solomon.

"Okay, Snappy. I was just gathering my thoughts."

Solomon breathed. I held the phone with my shoulder and head cocked to one side while I undid the wire under my dress and pulled it out. I wound it up and put it in its little pouch.

"He was nice," I said finally. "You heard everything he asked me. Very attentive, interested, polite. The perfect gentleman. Almost too perfect."

"How did he compare to Lord Camberwell?"

"Both definitely extracted enough information from me to make some kind of judgment on whether I was a good target. Justin was a bit pushier. Ben held back a little, I think. I doubt it was due to lack of confidence. Something else, maybe, but I can't put my finger on it. He left me with a good impression. A better one than Justin."

"If you were leaning towards one as a suspect, whom would you choose?"

"Neither right now. It's too early." Damn it. I was going to have to date both of them some more. Life could be so hard sometimes. "If the thief wanted to get my confidence, I'd say Ben won that one. If he wanted information, it's a tie."

"I'll let you know if the team agrees," said Solomon. He paused and I waited, wondering what was on his mind. "How was the kiss?" he asked.

I thought long and hard about that. Actually, it was short and quick because I didn't want to dwell on it. It was nice. Delicate. It made my heart race. I might even want another shot just to see if I really liked it, but would I tell Solomon that? No way. "Goodnight, Solomon," I said. "Let me know about my next date."

"Talk tomorrow," was all Solomon said, and I let him have the satisfaction of hanging up on me.

~

After such a nice evening, even if it was a job, the thought of going straight home to my empty apartment and empty bed was too depressing. The image of my new, and now ex-neighbor's, packing boxes would just make me obsess on the thrilling task of packing up my home in preparation for homelessness. So, I did what I always did in moments like this. I want to my happy place: the bungalow halfway between Harbridge and my apartment.

I liked going there to imagine what my life would be like if I lived there, and this evening was no different. Pulling up a short distance down the street, I parked and gazed at the pretty, little house, softly lit by the moon. The silvery glow cast shadows across the lawn down to the white fence and over the For Sale by Owner sign.

I blinked. The For Sale sign.

"Holy guacamole!" I rubbed my eyes, blinked my vision back into play and looked again. Yep, still there.

My dream house was for sale! All at once, I knew how Barbie felt. Except I didn't have a Ken, but, you know, whatever. Can't have everything, I reasoned.

I instantly wanted to get a closer look. I wanted to sit right outside the bungalow and gaze at it, pretending that I just bought it. I wanted to make believe that this was the home I was returning to after a hard day being wined and dined at fancy restaurants. "What a chore," I mumbled to myself, fully aware that my excitement made me babble. At least, no one could see me. Firing up the engine, and with a quick look around to make sure no curtains twitched at my late evening surveillance, I rolled the car forward until I was outside. I killed the engine, positioned my elbow on the door rest and cupped my chin. I also smooshed my nose against the window, but that was an accident. I sighed.

I don't know how long I sat there, staring in a mix of wonder and hope at my dream home, but my eyes were starting to glaze with daydreaming about furnishings, dinner parties, and a family by the time the front door opened and an older lady stepped out. She appeared to look my way. I lurched down in my seat and froze. Shoot. What if she thought I was casing the joint? Or that I was some weirdo? Of course, she could just be taking out the trash.

A sharp rap sounded against the Ferrari's driver-side window and I looked up sheepishly.

"Hello, dear," said the older lady, shouting a little even though the vehicle's windows weren't all that thick. She made a motion for me to roll down the window. I switched on the electrics and rolled it down. "Hello," she said again.

"Um, hi."

She leaned forwards a fraction and peered at me. "Do you have back trouble?"

"Um, no." I shuffled upright.

"Do you like my house?"

I held my hands up. "I swear I am not casing your house."

"I didn't for a minute think you were. That is, you come once a week and just sit here. My husband and I often look forward to seeing you. This is nice. Did you sell your VW?"

Huh? "Oh? No, it's at home. I borrowed this one for work."

"It's for sale you know. The house."

"I, uh, see."

"Why don't you come in and look around?"

"Are you sure? I mean, I'd love to. Can I? Please?" Step inside my dream house? Add to the fantasy... build myself up for a massive disappointment... oh, what the heck. I took a deep breath, ready to decline. Instead, I said, "Yes, please, I'd love to look around your home."

The lady smiled. "Figured you would." I smiled up at her. I couldn't help it. She was so nice and I so wanted to look inside. Besides, she didn't look strong enough to murder me unless she really caught me off guard. All the same... "I'll just text my best friend and let her know I'll be home a little later."

"Come in when you're ready. I'll leave the door open. I'm Anthea Schubert." The lady shuffled off. My ninja-fast texting skills ensured I bounded along the path like an over-excited Labrador thirty seconds later. I may have even slobbered a little in my eagerness to catch up with her.

As I stepped onto the porch, a high-pitched whine pierced the air and the old lady winced with a heavy sigh. The whine cut out and I poked my left ear. Just as I was sure my hearing wasn't permanently damaged, the whine started up again, this time the sound of a dog barking joined it. The lady took a deep breath, her eyes flitting to the neighbor's property and back to me. She smiled and beckoned me in. I took one last look at her hands for weapons — paranoia was better than dead —

and decided I was sure there was nothing concealed in her slacks and blouse. Then I did what my mother always told me never to do: I went into a stranger's house. At least, no one had to bribe me with candy. I'm not sure what that said about me.

The bungalow was everything I hoped it would be. Light, airy, not too large and not too small. Polished hardwood floors gleaming under the diffused light provided by carefully placed lamps. The furniture was a little dated for my taste, but I wasn't interested in that. All I could imagine was coming home and stepping over the threshold into the neat, little living room. I saw myself cooking, well, microwaving, in the penny-tiled kitchen and eating at the breakfast bar, perched on a tall stool. My bedroom furniture, what little there was, would be perfect in the rear bedroom and there was a guest room too. The bathroom was new and freshly scrubbed until it sparkled.

Mrs. Schubert chatted as we walked around, telling me about the two daughters she raised here, how she and her husband were moving to be near their elder girl who had young children. She asked where I lived and about my family, finding our last name familiar, which wasn't all that surprising, given how many Graves were planted in Montgomery, alive and dead. In a couple more generations, we'll probably take over.

"Your home is beautiful," I breathed, checking out the original crown molding.

Mrs. Schubert smiled. "Thank you. For sale, too," she reminded me, as if that thought could possibly escape me.

"I want to live here," I told her, practically tripping over my own tongue in my urgency to get the words out. "I want to buy your house and make it my home."

"I thought you might. We turned down an offer just yesterday, you know."

My heart skipped a beat. "Oh?"

"Only because the man wanted to tear the house down and build some monstrosity on the plot. Said this," she waved her arm around the cozy living room, "was old fashioned."

"I think it's perfect."

"Why don't I give you the flyer we printed and let you think about it some more? Come for tea tomorrow, if you like. I could show you the garden when it's light."

"I'll still want it tomorrow." I waited while Mrs. Schubert pulled a flyer from a writing desk in the corner of the living room and handed it to me. Without looking at it, I folded it in two and tucked it into my purse. I really didn't need my bubble bursting by seeing the price. There would be plenty of time to freak out over that later. I mean, I'd already made an offer. Sort of. It wasn't accepted. And I hadn't thought it through. Much less, knew if I had the money, or even how much it cost.

What the hell. Some decisions just worked out right and you didn't have to bust a gut thinking about how to make them work.

Mrs. Schubert escorted me to the door "Then come to tea and we'll talk."

"I will. Thanks for showing me around."

"It was about time, don't you think?" Mrs. Schubert paused to wink before she closed the door.

I stood on the porch for a moment, breathing in the soft evening air, admiring the quiet, tree-lined street and the neat rows of homes from my new vantage point. Yes, this was exactly where I wanted to be. So what if I would be living alone? Lily wasn't far away. I was only a few minutes further away from family. It was time for a change anyway.

I practically danced to my borrowed car. As I fired up the engine, a howl sounded from somewhere nearby, followed by manic barking; but it was nothing compared to the singing inside my head. I found my new home. Before I took off, I slipped the flyer from my purse and unfolded it. The price stood out boldly even in the small print.

"Holy crapola!" I took a deep breath and stuffed the page back into my purse. "Someone's got to buy you," I told the house. "Why not me?"

I should have gone home and celebrated, maybe opened a bottle of wine. Wasn't that the right thing to do after you put in an offer on your dream home? But when I thought about it, the right thing to do was leave the Ferrari in the agency's parking garage, take my VW, and go back to the apartment that seemed less and less like a home, pull on my ducky pajamas and hyperventilate about how to get a mortgage.

CHAPTER TEN

Lily knocked on my door in the morning. Fortunately, I'd already completed the basics of human hygiene so she didn't have to see my teeth unbrushed and a serious case of bed-head. Even so, she wrinkled her nose at my duck pajamas as she stumbled in, her arms clutching a pile of collapsed cardboard boxes.

"What's all that for?" I asked as she edged past me, the boxes exploding out of her arms into a heap on the floor upon entering my living room.

"For packing. Duh! I came by to see if you wanted them last night, but you weren't home yet. Work? Or did it end up as... pleasure?" Lily gave me a hopeful look. And a really big wink.

"Work, but fun work. Then I accidentally bought a house."

"Oh!" Lily blinked, then shrugged. "You know it's easier to return shoes, right?"

"I didn't actually buy it. I just said I wanted to buy it."

"That's great. I'm glad you found somewhere. I was worried. You definitely need these boxes now."

"You don't have to worry about me." I poked her stomach. "You have enough to worry about. You have a family to take care of now."

"You're my family, Lexi." Lily nudged me and smiled and I poked her stomach again. How the baby would manage to expand her gym-hard six-pack was a mystery.

"Officially," I told her. "I totally forgive my brother for having sex with you."

"You wouldn't if I told you what he suggested last night."

"Please don't ever tell me. Our friendship has to evolve to less telling any more secrets now. I think it's safer that way." I really didn't want to have a heart attack. Well, that is, it sounded like a great way to go if I were the one getting over excited, but I didn't want the last words I heard to be the kinky stuff my best friend and brother got up to.

"Who am I going to tell this stuff to now?"

"A therapist?"

"There isn't enough money in all the world to pay for that."

"Plus, the therapist would probably sue you for therapy."

"Jord better get that promotion. My bar better take off."

"How's that going?"

"Good. Really good. We'll open in a month. I want everything to be up and running long before the baby gets here. Jord finds out about his exams in two weeks."

"Do you know what you're going to do when the baby comes? Will you take maternity leave?"

"Yep. I'm going to be all over this baby, but Ruby is going to manage the bar in the evening, and I'll work days. I won't be behind the bar much, but I'll run it behind the scenes."

"You sure about hiring Ruby?" Our friend Ruby

Kalouza was somewhat a Jill-of-all-trades. I first met her on a case when she worked in an adults-only club that had a definite "less is more" dress policy. Lily was working the door of the club at the same time and, as it turned out, they knew each other for awhile. I bumped into Ruby on a regular basis and she was a good source of information, at times. She didn't mind helping out because she thought my job was cool. Sometimes it was, so I didn't burst her bubble by telling her about the times I surveyed someone so long, I thought I'd never make it to the bathroom in time, or when a lead went bad. I figured sticking with the cool angle made her more willing to help me. That, and the cash I slipped her when I could.

"Totally. She's really sharp. I trust her."

"That's good. And you know the family will rally around if you need anyone. Everyone will help."

"I feel so lucky, you know. I have everything I want. The guy I adore, a family, a best friend, a new house, the bar. How did my life get so perfect?" Lily slid past me and walked into the kitchen, testing the back of her hand against the coffee pot. I knew she would find it hot. I'd only just made my morning cup. I waited while she prepared herself a mug and thought on what she said. Our lives did seem to be pulling together. Hers a little faster than mine, but I'd never begrudge her that. Best friends always wanted the best for each other. That should be law.

"On the downside," I decided, continuing, "not that I want to rain on our parade, but we are thirty soon."

"Pfft. Like that matters. We got our lives together by thirty. That's an achievement. That's a major life thingy. Like, a moment. Some people never make that. We should celebrate."

I gave her a skeptical look. "You think my life's together?"

Lily shrugged. "More than it's ever been. Great job..."

"Don't push it."

"A job you want," she corrected, "hot guys everywhere you turn."

I counted off on my fingers. "Ex-boyfriend, boss, desperate single dating-agency guys, and the targets of my investigation."

"I don't see your point. Plus, you bought a house. Wait. What house? Where?"

"I just told you."

"No, you did not. Tell me everything. Tell me now. Wait until I make my coffee," Lily added as she poked her head inside the fridge. "Where's your two percent? Why don't you keep it in the door like a normal person?"

"It keeps cold better on the shelf."

"It's a refrigerator. Everything stays cold. Whatever." She emerged with the milk, holding the carton aloft like a trophy. She sniffed the opening. "Still good. Unlike ours."

"Is that the only reason you came up? To get coffee because your milk was sour?"

"Nooooo. I brought packing boxes for you. Coffee is like a thank you. From you... to me." She held her mug aloft and smiled benevolently. "Thaaaaank yoooouuu."

I pulled a face and wrinkled my nose, hoping I didn't look like a Pug. "You made it yourself."

"I thank myself." She reached her hand over her shoulder and patted her back too. "Now tell me everything. Where is it? What does it look like? How many bedrooms? Are the neighbors hot? Did you get a deal? When can I house crash?"

"Um..." I began to count questions on my fingers. "Not far from here. It's the buttercup yellow bungalow. Two bedrooms. I don't know. Maybe. Sure!"

"Omigod! The ochre ranch?"

"Yellow bungalow," I corrected.

"Ranch."

"Bungalow. Bungalow. Bungalow."

"Okay, don't have a heart attack. Call it whatever you like. I'm so pleased. This atones for all the times you made me sit outside there with you like a creepy stalker. You are on the only person I know who stalks homes. Except my mom. And the stalking totally paid off. High five!" Lily high-fived me, which was awesome because I deserved it. Also: high-fiving was the only kind of five I would be able to afford once the mortgage was in place. Not that I actually tried getting one, but Serena, who doubled as my accountant, thought I would be able to get one when I called her. The idea of home ownership seemed both near and far, amazing and stomach-churning. "When are we going for a second viewing?"

Just as I was about to suggest a trip, there and then, my cell phone rang, Ben Rafferty's number flashed on the screen. I put a finger to my lips. "Work," I told Lily, before hitting answer. "Hi, Ben."

"Hi, Lexi," Ben's voice came down the line, deep and delicious. "I'm outside your house. I thought you might like to go to brunch?"

My voice came out like a squeak. "You're outside my house?" I dashed past Lily to the window and looked outside. No cars idling at the curb. I closed my eyes and sighed at my forgetfulness. Of course, he wasn't outside "my house." He was outside what he thought was my house.

"I, um..."

"Oh, you're busy?" He sounded disappointed.

"No, that is, I, um, I'm not there. I'm, um..." I flapped my hand at Lily. What should I say? Lily pulled a face, then grinned. She started running on the spot with big exaggerated arm movements. "I'm out running," I told Ben, and Lily gave me the thumbs up. I puffed into the phone for effect. "I'm a little ways away. I'd love to go to brunch, but I'll need to run home first. Why don't I meet you somewhere?"

"I could pick you up in half an hour?"

"Sounds great. See you then! Gotta run!" I clicked off, then looked at the phone. Gah! What had I done? Set up a date with suspect number three and now I had thirty minutes to get dressed and across town. Even worse, what if Ben waited outside? How could I show up in my car when Ben thought I was running? "Can you give me a ride?" I asked Lily.

"I would, but some jerk drove into my car last night and the taillight is busted. I don't want to get a ticket."

"Is the jerk the wall across the street? The same one that got you last time?"

Lily pouted. "I don't want to talk about it."

I could call any member of my family, but they would want to know the details and the chances of any of them driving fast enough was close to zero. Unless Jord turned on the sirens. "Is Jord in a car today?"

"Nope. He's playing Officer Good Cop at some school."

"Poor kids." That left only one other option. "Solomon, can you give me a ride?" I asked when my boss picked up the phone.

"What's wrong with your car?"

"Nothing. It's fine. I have to get to the Chilton house in thirty minutes and I can't be seen in my VW."

"Where's the Ferrari?"

"In the agency garage. I drove my car home last night." I explained my predicament and Solomon promised to pick me up in ten minutes. He didn't explain where he was, but I'd long given up asking. Maybe he was out to brunch too. With her. Maybe Maddox was out to brunch with Detective Blake. I wondered what they were all eating and my stomach rumbled. "I need to get dressed," I told Lily. "What should I wear?"

"Sweats. You're out running." She checked my hair. "At least you won't have to brush your hair."

"I brushed my hair already!" I yelled over my

shoulder as I steamed past her on the way to my bedroom. Pushing the door until it was only open a little so we could still talk, I rummaged through my closet until I found tight running pants and a pink short-sleeved top. I dressed and wound my hair into a low, messy ponytail, reasoning that I could shower and change at the Chilton house.

"Who's the guy?" Lily called.

"Suspect number three. Hot. Sexy."

"Cuff him!" she replied.

"He might not be the one."

"The One one or the suspect one?"

"The thief," I clarified. "He might just be a hot, rich guy."

"I don't know what attracts you to him." Lily snorted. "Is the dating fun?"

"Kind of. I mean, I've had worse jobs than to go out for dinner and talk, and Ben's really cute."

"Are you gonna sleep with him?"

"No! He kissed me, but I can't get too interested because..." Because what? Because I was sad about breaking up with Maddox, even though it was my idea to split, and sadder that I didn't — and possibly wouldn't — ever know the truth about what happened with Detective Blake? Or because I didn't know what the situation was between Solomon and me? Did I want to get back together with Maddox and could I ever trust him, now doubt was in my mind? Or did I want to pursue something with my boss? My head began to hurt just thinking about it.

"When you catch the suspect, you can date this Ben guy for real."

"Yeah, I'm sure he'll be thrilled to find out he was in our suspect pool. He'll find me really attractive then. Besides," I paused, a thought occurring to me. "If he's the genuine article, he's rich and he's looking for a rich woman; and that, I definitely am not."

"Only in spirit, honey."

"Better than nothing. How do I look?"

"Sweaty and you haven't even gone anywhere."

"Great!" Grabbing my purse and keys, I hustled Lily downstairs, arriving on the sidewalk just as Solomon pulled over.

"Do you often run with your purse?" he asked as I slid into the passenger seat.

"Only when there's a sale on in front of me, or a mugger behind me." I dropped it on my feet and folded my lightweight running jacket over my knees. "I didn't think. I was flustered."

He scanned me before pulling onto the street, hauling a U-turn and heading back the way he came. "You look flustered."

"You don't." He didn't. He looked damn delicious and he smelled as if he just got out of the shower. I wanted to lean over and sniff him, but I was pretty certain there was a rule about that in the employee handbook; and if there wasn't... someone should write one. Or maybe Solomon would put smell-care alongside our basic healthcare?

"I'm never flustered."

"I didn't notice. I have fifteen minutes to get to Chilton. Do you think we can make it?"

"No problem." Solomon got us there in ten. Though "there" seemed to have a different meaning to him as he pulled over several blocks away. He nodded towards the door and smiled.

"You lost me," I said, looking from the sidewalk to him.

"You're out running. Run 'home'," he said, adding air quotes with his index fingers. He looked like he was making bunny shadow puppets. I bet he would make a great daddy one day.

Whoa.

What the...?

I scrambled out of the car like it was on fire, then leaned back in to grab my purse, but Solomon got there first. "You're running, remember? I'll take this to the house."

"I need keys. And my cell phone." He handed me the purse and I extracted my necessities. After a moment, I withdrew a ten dollar bill, just in case. In case of what? I didn't know, but I felt weird not carrying money. I stuffed everything into my jacket's zip pocket. "What if Ben is waiting outside? How are you going to explain why you have my purse?"

"I'll think of something."

"Great. And the car?"

"Make something up. Lexi?"

"Yeah?"

"Are you going to let go of the door?"

"Uh, yeah, sure. Which way? That way?" I pointed ahead and Solomon nodded. He gave me brief directions as I wasn't overly familiar with Chilton, not my neighborhood while growing up, or well, ever after, and his instructions matched up with the way I guessed. "Thanks for the ride."

"It's all part of the job." Solomon nodded, leaning over and tugging the door closed. I watched him speed away, then started after him, albeit a heck of a lot slower. And, come to think of it, really put out. Not that I minded exercise. I pushed myself at the gym frequently, though, come to think of that too, a lot less frequently now Lily was taking it easier, thanks to her pregnancy. The thing about the gym was that it was warm and nice and... inside. It didn't spit with rain. I went when I wanted to. I really didn't want to take a run right now, but I had to. Otherwise, Ben would wonder why I wasn't doing what I said I was and I couldn't risk rousing the suspicions of any of our suspects. With a heaving breath, I lifted my feet a little faster and began to run towards my faux-home.

By the time I rounded the corner, Ben was leaning against a black Mercedes, his arms folded, looking just as gorgeous as he had the previous evening. Now dressed down in slacks and a gray, V-neck sweater, the collar of a white t-shirt just peeked above the neckline. Even casually styled, he still had model-worthy looks.

I, on the other hand, just jogged six blocks and was starting to feel out of breath. A bead of sweat made its way down through my cleavage, and a strand of stray hair clung to my cheek. At least, I looked authentic for my running ruse. Plus: exercise. Bonus!

"How do you run and look so beautiful?" said Ben, stepping forward and kissing my cheek.

"Ha-ha. I'm a mess. I ran miles," I lied.

"That explains why you have such a great figure."

"Absolutely."

Ben's eyes skimmed my running clothes. "I guess you want to change before brunch?"

"Absolutely, again. Why don't you come inside and wait?" I pulled the house key from my pocket and made towards the steps. Just as I placed my foot on the first step, the door to Solomon's house opened and the beautiful, young woman I'd seen and spent too much time wondering about, stepped out. She saw me and waved, then held aloft my purse.

"Lexi!" she exclaimed as though we'd known each other years. "Thanks so much for loaning me your purse." She held it out to me and I leaned over to catch it.

"Anytime," I answered, hoping I didn't look too puzzled. So this was Solomon's idea? Get his new girlfriend to sneak me my bag? I wondered what he told her about the ruse; if she even knew his job.

"Friends *and* neighbors," commented Ben. "You are fortunate indeed."

"Uh, yeah, um, this is..." I trailed off. Shoot. I didn't know her name.

"Anastasia," said the woman with a casual flick of her long, glossy hair. "Lexi told me she was heading out for brunch after her run, but she didn't mention her date was so handsome."

I sighed. Great. Not only did she have my boss, but now she was probably going to bewitch my date-suspect too with her perfect, straight teeth, lithe figure, and unbelievably symmetrical face. Sometimes life just isn't fair. She might as well take my job, break my case, and let me go home and back to bed. If that didn't mean ruining my life, it would sound more appealing. As it was, I hoped Anastasia would go away. Pronto. Not that I was jealous. Obviously.

"Lexi is very kind," Ben replied, smiling at me, and seeming barely to notice the opposition... I mean, my neighbor. "And far too generous in her praise."

Anastasia smiled at both of us, raised her hand and waggled her fingers as she turned away. Over her shoulder, she cooed, "Stop by for coffee later, honey. Enjoy brunch!"

"Later, honey," I cooed in return, like the good buds we weren't. "Come on in, Ben. Can I make you coffee while you wait? I just need to shower and change so I'll be a few minutes."

"Just a water," said Ben as I unlocked the door and pushed it open. We stepped inside and Ben shut the door behind us.

"Coming up. Why don't you sit in the living room? Feel free to look around." What I meant was feel free to be light-fingered, or at least check around the place while my back was turned. Of course, I knew full well that Solomon, or one of the team would be monitoring the secret cameras and watching Ben's every move the moment he entered. Otherwise, I probably wouldn't have invited a virtual stranger into my "home" while I stripped upstairs.

I resolved to lock the bathroom door, just in case,

though I was pretty certain Solomon would smash his way through the wall separating the houses rather than let me come to any harm. Even if he did just want to be friends.

I got Ben's glass of water and returned to the living room, only to find him browsing the bookshelves. "Art fan?" he asked.

"Oh yes, and you?"

"I'm sorry to say I don't know much about art."

"Me neither."

"Hence the books?" Ben asked.

"Exactly." I smiled, most pleased with myself that I'd circumvented any difficult art questions. I took a quick look at the bookshelf he pointed out. Yep, lots of art books. Good call.

He took the water from me, sipped it and licked his lips. "Thanks."

"So... um, don't break anything," I laughed, keeping the mood light, but also because I didn't want him to break anything I might have to pay for. I added, "and I'll be right back."

Fortunately, Solomon told me several days earlier to leave a few clothes stashed in the master bedroom just in case of events like this. The dark blue jeans, white blouse and Serena's black blazer I selected would do for brunch. Plus, my purse matched nicely. Shower first. I took the clothes into the attached bathroom, shut the door and flipped the lock. I tugged my cell phone from my pants pocket and speed-dialed Solomon.

"What's Ben doing?" I asked, when he answered two rings later. I saw his car parked so I guessed he arrived home. "Is he stealing anything?"

"No. He walked around a little. Checked out the shelving. Now, he's sitting on the couch, flipping through a travel magazine."

"Oh."

"He hasn't broken anything." There was a small

cough that sounded like Solomon was covering up a laugh.

"Good to know. Solomon?"

"Yes?"

"Are there any cameras in the bathroom?"

"Which bathroom are you in?"

"Hah. That answered my question. If there were cameras, you'd know the answer to that."

"Very quickly deduced, PI Graves. Are you naked?"

"If you had cameras, you'd know the answer to that, too," I replied smartly and hung up. I pulled a face at my phone. What kind of question was that? I was fairly certain Anastasia might have a complaint if she overheard. Also: why did Solomon care whether I was naked or not?

Seconds later a text pinged. Solomon. "Suspect four date this evening. Details to follow," was all it said. Nothing flirty at all. I deleted it.

Men were so confusing.

Thirty seconds later, I was naked and under the shower, a hot stream of water rushing over me. I unscrewed the tops of a few bottles before I found a super nice smelling shower gel and helped myself to it liberally. I figured Solomon probably inventoried everything in the house prior to letting me stay, and I was similarly certain that every single thing would be exactly as the actual owners left it, including the volume of shower gel.

As I scrubbed my skin under the dramatic rainfall fixture, I wondered if I could install something like this in the bungalow, if I could even get used to something as luxurious as my current surroundings... and I was only in the bathroom. The rest of the house was amazing. Which reminded me, I hadn't seen the inside of Solomon's house in a while, since he was still decorating when I did. I wondered what he'd done to the place and if it looked as amazing as this house. I concluded it probably did. It was certainly a cut above my place in West Montgomery, or Maddox's co-op building in Harbridge, or any of the rentals I checked out, but I wasn't going to be jealous or envious. This was a borrowed house, and once I caught the culprit, I'd have to give it back.

Strangely enough, I had no problem with that. I didn't want to be rich and draped in jewels or able to buy expensive art at a whim like David -- not that I would turn it down if the cash were handed to me -- I was content with my life as it was. Pretty much. I had a job, a new house, family, friends. Really, what else did I need?

Probably new shoes.

I gave my hair a quick wash, rinsed and, with a sigh, shut the water off. Toweling dry, I wondered if Ben was still behaving himself downstairs... if Solomon still watched his every move. I wondered what Justin was doing and if he missed home. Then I thought about my date with the fourth suspect this evening, and thanked every deity I could think of that there were only four suspects, and one had already been eliminated in a baptism of fire. I wondered just how I would get rid of two more so I could hand the thief over to the cops and allow my life to return to normal. Although... looking around the luxurious bathroom, maybe I could get used to this kind of normal... so long as I didn't have to live next door to Solomon and the supermodel.

By the time I was dressed, hair blown dry, and downstairs, Ben looked bored. "Ready?" he asked, smiling at me. "Of course, you are. You look gorgeous."

"Same. You that is. You look really handsome."

"And we'll make a charming couple at brunch. I've found a place I'd like to try on the road to Boston. It's a little drive, but I think we'll enjoy it. I hope you're hungry."

"Starving."

"Then let's go eat."

Ben was right. The drive was beautiful, especially when the top of the Mercedes came down and he handed me a pair of sunglasses to match his own. If it weren't for Delgado and Fletcher tag-teaming our tail all the way, I'd have had a fabulous time. As it was, I settled for merely great as brunch turned into a picnic lunch and afternoon at Fairmount Park.

I even forgot about my cell phone in my purse until Solomon walked past, purposefully bumping into me at the park. "Excuse me," he said, stepping around us and walking on. Only after he left and Ben went to get us take-out coffee did I get to read the note Solomon slipped into my hand. "Leave," it read, "date at seven. Emailed details." All too soon, I had to make my excuses and leave Ben and our impromptu, day-long date behind. The only thing that boosted me was the hope that maybe the next guy would slip up and Ben would be off the hook as a suspect. If only I were that lucky.

CHAPTER ELEVEN

Once upon a time, Marty Tookey was cute. Unfortunately, that was fifty pounds and a receding hairline ago. Right now, his face was a little doughy, his cheeks too pink, and his nose a little too squashed. But he had potential. If he were real estate, he would have been a fixer-upper. I don't know if he dressed himself or hired someone with style, but the slacks and sweater, with shirt lapels neatly folded over the sweater's collar, were crisp and stylish, though the extra belly didn't complement the outfit. I wasn't sure how old his photographs in the agency file were, but they definitely weren't recent. Shame. He once was attractive, albeit a good several years younger.

"I have a stylist," he told me, when he saw me eyeballing his clothing. "Do you?"

"No, I'm naturally stylish."

"Oh. That's very honest of you. Your dress is pretty and I like your bag. Claire loved bags."

"Claire?" I prompted. Not that I didn't want to hear how good I looked — I told myself a bunch of times

126

already that I looked great in my ankle-length pants and sweet collar blouse, changed into with only minutes to spare, and I wasn't even being vain — but dropping a female name within a minute of our date's introduction was a really bad start.

"My ex," said Marty.

Yep, bad start. While waiting for him to get uncomfortable with the silence before breaking it, I checked out his hair. A full head, thinning, but no bald spots. Also receding, but not too obviously. No visible hair products. A good sign. All the same, I edged the candle on our table away. One could never be too careful.

"She's so beautiful," he continued. "One in a million. Very stylish. Like you."

"Um... thank you. I think." Way to go on the compliments, Marty. Here was a guy who knew how to make a woman feel like a million bucks. I checked out my reflection in the restaurant's curiously mirrored wall. Heck, who needs Marty? I could inflate my own ego just fine. I gave my hair a quick smooth and blew myself a little kiss.

"We broke up six months ago. That's when I joined the agency," Marty explained, never noticing me fluttering my eyelashes at myself. "Claire wouldn't approve. She thinks dating agencies are too artificial. She thinks everyone should meet naturally. Fate. We met in a park. We were both admiring the roses. She gardens, you know."

"How lov..."

"She can grow anything. Do you have a garden?"

"I..."

"Claire thinks everyone should grow something."

I wondered if she thought Marty should grow a backbone, but I didn't say it. One of us had to be the polite date. It was like good cop, bad cop, except we were good date, crap date. I discreetly yawned and fanned the menu, wondering if it was impolite to eat and run. Maybe Solomon or Flaherty could take over for dessert? Then I could go home and become a nun, if this was the quality of the agency's offerings. The one good learning experience that came out of this case for me, was the knowledge that I couldn't settle with a man just for his money. No, it didn't matter how many millions Marty won, he was definitely not the man for me. Not that I was actually looking for a man. It was just a happy coincidence that I met Ben Rafferty and Lord Justin Camberwell on the case, and that both were dashing, handsome and rich... oh yeah, and potential thieves. Crap.

"Wine?" Marty asked.

"No, you aren't whining at all," I murmured.

Marty looked up. "Pardon?"

"You pick the wine." I smiled and Marty gave me a little frown before returning his gaze to the wine list.

"Red," he decided, after a few quiet moments. "It'll go great with our steaks."

"Our steaks?"

"Claire and I ordered steak the first time we came here. It was amazing. I'm sure you'll like it. Actually, this is our place."

Oh, bravo, Marty, I thought, heaving a sigh. Take your newest date to "your" place. Nice. "I was actually thinking about the chicken."

"Oh no. Oh no, no, no. You must have the steak. Claire raves about it."

I had to wonder where the hell Claire was if she liked the steak so much. "Where is Claire?"

"We split up. She's my ex. You know, I'd really rather not talk about my ex. We are on a date, Lexi, you and I," Marty chastised, narrowing his eyes at my apparent rudeness, which made me wonder if he were just plain ignorant, stupid, rude, or all three. What a trio!

On the plus side, at least he noticed we were on a

date. I was starting to wonder if he thought I was a therapist. I was also quickly learning why his file said he didn't have many second dates, despite attracting plenty of first dates. Frankly, it was a wonder the mystery ex lasted long enough to have "their" place. Maybe Marty was amazing in the sack. As soon as I thought that, my stomach flipped, and I really wished I hadn't. It was the kind of image I didn't want in my head. It reminded me of the time I followed my mother into a lingerie store and found her buying sexy undergarments. Some things should just remain far out of my mind. Like, light years away.

"Are you ready to order?" asked our waiter, approaching so quietly that I jumped when he appeared at the table.

Without, looking up, Marty ordered the wine, then our starters of scallops. "Then we'll have the steak, rare." He looked over to me. "A salad for the lady and fries for me."

"I'd rather have fries and my steak well done. Actually," I turned to the waiter, "I'd also like my steak to turn into chicken."

"I insist you try the steak. Rare is the way to have it." Marty snipped the menu from my hand and handed it to the waiter. "The chef knows how I like it," he added, waving his hand dismissively at the waiter. Noticing the waiter's eyes narrowing slightly, I knew how he felt. What a bossy asshole! The waiter caught my eye, and we both lifted our gaze to the ceiling. For the briefest of moments, I thought about edging the candle back across the table.

Marty, amazingly enough, was an insufferable bore. Between the scallops and steaks — my chicken never materializing — I tried to imagine him in dark clothing, with a mask over his pudgy head, sneaking into the homes of unsuspecting women and cracking open their house safes to steal valuables.

By the time my steak appeared in front of me, it practically mooed, it was so rare. While I couldn't figure out if Marty had the guts for breaking and entering, I was pretty certain he would bypass the safe, waking up the women so he could start telling them all about Claire. I also wondered what he talked to Claire about, seeing as every conversation centered on her. Maybe they just talked about her. But despite my misgivings, I had to persevere. Along with finding out whether Marty had the potential to be my top suspect, I kind of wanted to know if he killed Claire, and maybe stuffed her, like she was a prize specimen for taxidermy, and kept her in a chair in his home so he could talk to her. It was a creepy thought, but as I looked at Marty, fastidiously cutting his steak into equal, little cubes, not altogether an unreal one.

I shuffled my steak around the plate, hiding a lump of it under the heap of salad, and continued to smile at Marty as he whined on and on.

When he paused and looked up at me, I tried to meet his eyes without punching him square between them. "You're such a good listener," he told me.

"Tell me about it," I muttered.

"But you don't talk much. How do you get second dates?" He laughed heartily, like he cracked the funniest joke ever.

Ugh.

"I'm rich and gorgeous," I told him with a shrug. I imagined Solomon laughing at the other end of the wire. It wasn't like my statement was wholly untrue. Unlike many women, I chose to celebrate my attributes rather than whine about my flaws. I got so good at it over the years, I forgot about the flaws altogether, or turned them into positives. That was the Lexi Graves School of Thinking and I graduated at the top of my class of one. It wasn't complete vanity. It was the result of having four older siblings who got all the attention by sheer loudness and size. That made me give myself plenty of pep talks.

"Me too," said Marty, and, get this, cracked a smile. "I have all my own teeth."

"So we *do* have something in common." I smiled back.

Marty continued to smile, but his face started to crumple and a teary droplet filled his lower lid. "I miss my Claire," he muttered, his chin wobbling.

I couldn't resist. "I'm sorry, but who's Claire? Have you mentioned her before?"

"The love of my life," Marty wailed. Pushing his plate aside, he dropped his head on the table, unbridled sobs and snuffles emanating from him. After a minute or two, when it didn't subside, I reached over and patted his head as I would a sick dog. The wailing got louder. I cringed, patting harder.

"Excuse me, I have to go to the bathroom," I muttered, tossing my napkin on the table as I stood. I just couldn't bear it anymore. People were starting to look.

"Don't leave me like Claaaaaaaire," Marty wailed.

"I swear I'll be right back," I squeaked, edging away from the couple shooting daggers at me from the next table. I removed the steak knife from his grip and dropped it onto my plate. "Don't, um, hurt yourself."

"I can't live without my baaaaabbbyyyyy," Marty moaned, then hiccupped.

"Try for five minutes!" I snapped, hurrying away, the eyes of other diners landing upon me. Ugh. They would no doubt think I did this to him! How embarrassing. I put ten virtual bucks on this tale of "The Sobbing Man and the Cold-hearted Hottie" being the dinner conversation at the next family hour of every diner in the place.

The bathroom was empty. I spent a minute gingerly pushing open the stall doors to check I was alone before speaking into my mic. "Solomon, I think we can rule

Marty out," I told the mirror and, somewhere not far away, my boss. "And, in case you didn't guess, this date sucks."

"Your date too, huh?" said a woman's voice behind me. I jumped and whirled around to see my acquaintance, Ruby Kalouza, entering the restroom.

"Yes, dreadful."

"I saw. What a baby."

"Babies are better behaved."

"Amen to that, sister." Ruby edged past me, checked each stall, then stopped and stared at the window. She reached over, opened the catch and pushed it open. "Well, what do you know? No burglar bars! Here, hold my purse a moment."

I took the purse and waited while Ruby hitched her skirt into her undergarments and pulled herself onto the ledge. "What are you doing?"

"Escaping. There's no hope for my date. I hate to stick him with the bill, but I'll commit a random act of kindness every day next week to make up for it."

"I like your thinking."

Ruby swung one leg over, then the other before dropping. For a moment, I grimly wondered if she was okay, until her head popped up into the open space. "Thanks for the distraction, by the way. My date thinks you're both nuts. Hey, you want to come?" she asked.

"Big time," I told her, but I knew I couldn't. One: it was unprofessional to ditch a suspect, even if I'd all but ruled him out. Two: and more importantly, my borrowed jacket was still in the cloakroom, and Serena would kill me if I left it. "But I left my jacket. Here's your purse."

"Good luck, and tell Lily I'll come by the bar tomorrow."

"I will." Ruby grinned, waved, and disappeared. I reached over and pulled the window shut, securing the catch.

"Ruby Kalouza just left the building," I told the mic while I reached into my purse for emergency lip gloss. "I want bonus points for not joining her. I also want a bonus for completing this date against my better judgment."

My cell phone rang and I fumbled in my purse to find it. "Any other demands?" Solomon asked.

"A helicopter, one million dollars in untraceable bills, and a tube of Pringles."

"Or what?"

"I thump Marty unconscious, and you bail me out of jail."

"Date not going well?" Solomon deadpanned.

"Never better."

"Try and get him talking about his other dates," Solomon suggested. "Maybe he'll say something incriminating."

"Yeah, right. He's just a wet blanket and you know it. He couldn't pull off a pity date as the last man on earth. He's only interested in Claire. Can you find out who Claire is?"

"I've got Lucas working on it."

"Ten minutes, John," I told my boss in my sternest don't-mess-with-me voice, "and I'm out of here. I'm telling you now, Marty Tookey is not our guy."

"Enjoy dessert," said Solomon before hanging up.

I tried to get Marty to talk about his other dates, just in case he did have the smarts to rob them, but all I got was Claire this and Claire that, and how wonderful Claire was. I thought Claire sucked, but didn't dare say in case Marty murdered me at the table. On the plus side, I did enjoy the salted caramel and chocolate dessert — Marty feeling too depressed to order for me by that point — but not as much as I enjoyed making my excuses and calling a taxi to go home. Alone. It may have been a terrible date, but I came to some certain conclusions. One: Marty was definitely not our guy.

Two: Claire was a smart woman for dumping him.
Three: I wasn't desperate enough to date just anyone,
and single seemed a really good option if there were
guys like Marty on the market. Four: since Marty would
set the alarm bells ringing of every woman he dated, he
wouldn't get any information from them. That narrowed
our suspect pool from three to two. Trouble was, who
was the thief? Ben Rafferty or Lord Justin Camberwell?

CHAPTER TWELVE

"I swear I'm never dating again." Lily and I were sitting in her shell of a bar while she leafed through catalogs. Page after page of wine glasses, tumblers, and things I didn't know a bar needed flipped past. She tossed the latest discard onto the foot-high stack and opened a brochure of bar furniture. I hoped she would pick some soon, because right now, sitting on the floor, with only flattened cardboard boxes between my pink-jeaned butt and the concrete, was anything but comfortable.

Lily paused mid-flick and looked up, her face skeptical. "Are you sure? There's a lot of guys out there and you have a lot of spare time."

"Meh. I've dated four guys in the past few days. Two yesterday. Started off great, ended up..."

"Oh, please! Don't say you set another one on fire!"

"No!" I rested my head on my knee while I had a mini breakdown. When I looked up, Lily was waiting expectantly. "Suspect number four, also known as yesterday's date number two, spent the whole night talking about his ex-girlfriend. When he started crying, I had to run out on him. I saw Ruby, by the way. She'll come by the bar today."

"She called this morning, but she didn't say she saw you. Why was your date crying? What did you say to him?"

"Nothing! I couldn't get a word in. Besides, he was a big baby."

"Sounds like a suave thief to me." Lily snorted.

"I know, right? My report for Solomon starts with 'ha-ha no way' and ends with 'just no'. I'm pretty sure Marty's not our guy. No one who cries that much can be a jewel thief."

"Maybe he's a genius. Maybe he played you. Did you check to see if you still had your purse on the way out?"

"Yep, I did and it was there. He's really not the one. He's not even number one million. He was a moron, Lily. When did men get like that?"

"I blame Oprah."

"Uh, why?"

"Jerry Springer gets blamed for everything else. I figure it's Oprah's turn."

"What about Ricki Lake?"

"Too cute."

"Chelsea Handler?"

"Scary, but don't you just want to go out for the night with her? I bet she drinks shots and dances on tables." Lily paused to circle a photo of a leather barstool with red pen.

I contemplated it. "Now I want to go out with her."

"Wait until my bar opens. You can dance on the tables all you want."

"This is why you're my best friend."

"That, and you can't get rid of me."

"Hand on heart, I would never try. Also, do I get free drinks?"

"You get a substantial discount."

"One hundred percent?"

"On your first drink," Lily agreed. I loved my negotiating skills. They really were top class. "So, what happens now? You date Hottie and Lord Hottie while Detective Hottie and Boss Hottie watch. You could totally write a novel about that. It'd be really dirty. You could call it The Four Hotties. Make it really dirty, Lexi. Porno dirty."

"I'll make a note of it for my future career file if snooping doesn't work out."

"What else is on the list?"

"Supermodel, fashion designer, actress, foot model."

"All achievable," agreed Lily.

"Especially the last one. I have great feet."

"You could sell photos of them. Some creep would buy them."

"That's pretty much the job description of a foot model. Do you like my shoes?" I waggled my sky blue pumps at her.

"Covet. You're very pastel today. I'm in shades of dust."

"You're totally working it though. Why couldn't we do this at home?" I asked as a workman walked past, carrying something that looked like a collection of two-by-fours and a very large hammer. I wondered if he needed any of them, or just wanted to look down Lily's top again.

"I need to *feel* the place. I need to get the vibe," Lily told me.

"There's no vibe. There's nothing here."

"In my head, it looks awesome."

"How soon will what's in your head transfer to things other people can see?"

"Very soon. We open in a month. Can you bring some of your new hot, rich friends?"

"I'll try," I promised. "So long as none of them are in jail."

Lily looked up and grinned. That was usually a bad sign. "If you can arrest them at the opening party, the bar will get more publicity."

"I think Solomon and the client want this wrapped up faster than a month."

"So what's the plan, Batman?"

"Keep on dating the last two suspects until one of them confesses, or I catch them in the act; then see if Serena will let me keep any of her clothes; then go on vacation. First, though, I need to pay a visit to my bungalow. I want to take some measurements and make the purchase official. How do I buy a house anyway?"

Lily shrugged. "I don't know."

"You're buying one! And you bought this place!"

"I guess 'I don't know' was a lie then. I'll email you my lawyer's details. She's co-ordinating everything. Also, did you go to the bank?"

"I did and they like me. Thanks in advance for the lawyer." I stood and brushed dust from my jeans, watching another workman carry some more stuff across the room. There were some head scratching and "umming" and "ahhing" noises as they clearly debated something. Probably lunch.

"Not so fast, missy. I'm coming too. I want to see the ranch."

"Bungalow!"

"Whatever. You're driving."

"Don't you want to get a bit more vibe?"

"Nope. I'm done vibing. I want to see your new place. Can we childproof it?"

I frowned. "I don't have kids."

"You might one day. Do you think you'll have Solomon's babies or Maddox's?"

My breath caught in my throat and I'm sure I heard the sound of my left ovary twang. I tried to say something, but it came out as "Begerbegerbe - grrrr." Funnily enough, that was the same sound in my brain.

Lily giggled and tucked her arm through mine, pointing at her belly. "For this baby. We will be visiting all the time. You don't have to have a baby with Solomon or Maddox; you can share this one. Do I get my own key?"

"Sure. I'll be here having free drinks anyway."

"Match made in heaven. Let's go!"

~

The sound emanating from the Schuberts' neighbor was horrendous. Machinery emitted a long, loud whine, occasionally punctuated by the sound of a dog joining in. It was already in progress for some time before we arrived, judging by the tired look on Mrs. Schubert's face.

"Does that happen often?" I yelled.

Mrs. Schubert and Mr. Schubert, a little older, taller, and thicker around the waist than his wife, exchanged glances. Both turned to me at the same time and said "Yes."

"Well..." started Mrs. Schubert, her voice rising so we could hear her.

"Yes, yes we hear it a lot," said Mr. Schubert with a sigh. "Sometimes it doesn't happen for days, then it starts all over again."

"What's happening over there? Are the neighbors renovating?" I stood on tiptoes to try and see from the porch into the rear yard, but I observed no evidence of any kind of work activity. No wood or bricks or tools lying around. The house looked neatly kept, the garden plain, but well manicured. The house's windows were shielded with blinds so I couldn't get a look inside. The noise told us that someone was working hard at something in there.

"No," said Mr. Schubert. "We don't know what he's doing." Another look was exchanged.

"He?" asked Lily, nudging me. What was with her? I hoped she wasn't even thinking of perhaps fixing me up with someone she hadn't even seen, and a loud someone at that. I ignored her.

"So far as we know," agreed Mr. Schubert, like he wasn't all that sure. He continued, "Keeps to himself. Single, I think. We used to say hello and wave, but he just ignored us."

"Not so friendly," agreed Mrs. Schubert. "Everyone here is so nice. Except him. Maybe he's from a city where they don't speak to anyone."

"Maybe," I agreed. "He has a dog?"

"A big one, kind of yellow-colored. A Labrador, I think."

"A very loud Labrador. We knocked on the door a while, when he first moved here, to ask him to keep the dog a little quieter, but he just ignored us. We're not mean, you know, we don't mind hearing noise, but not constantly. Not like this," Mr. Schubert explained, finishing just as the dog started barking again. Simultaneously, we glanced over in time to see a delivery guy knocking at the door, a parcel in hand. The door must have opened because the parcel was handed over, while an electronic signing machine was held forwards. I saw a white hand return it, but the occupant was concealed from our view. The deliveryman returned to his truck and shot off, leaving us in silence at last. When nothing else sounded, Mr. Schubert mentioned something about reading his paper before ambling away.

The quiet seemed to cheer his wife up as she invited us inside. Just as the door shut, the machinery whined again, and even with the door tightly shut, it didn't stop the pervasive noise from vibrating through our bones. Mrs. Schubert's shoulders slumped.

"I have to be honest with you," Mrs. Schubert started, hesitantly looking at her husband who made himself comfortable on the couch. He gave her a half-hearted shrug. "This noise happens a lot. It's not why we're moving though, it really isn't. But I don't want to be the kind of person who dupes a person into buying a house they can't live in because of... well," she pointed next door, "that. We understand if you don't want to buy the place. We don't want to put you in any..." Another look was exchanged between the pair, and it didn't take a genius to work out they were worried about something besides the noise.

"What is it?" I prompted.

"We don't want to put you in any danger," said Mr. Schubert. He took off his glasses, folding them atop his newspaper.

Lily gasped and her eyes widened. "Lexi loves danger. This place is perfect! It's cute, it doesn't need renovating, it's a nice neighborhood and it's exciting."

"Hold on," I told her, giving her a little poke in the ribs before turning to the Schuberts. "What do you mean... danger? What's going on next door?"

"Well... we think our neighbor might be killing people. Maybe eating them."

Funnily enough, that didn't put me off as much as it should. I *really* liked the bungalow. Now I was also curious about what was going on next door. Noise I couldn't deal with; danger, on the other hand... "Are you sure?" I asked. "Killing people? What makes you think that?"

"Strange noises, loud music and the dog always yap, yap, yapping. The young man keeps such odd hours, always staying to himself. We never see anyone there, but sometimes we hear shouting. He leaves in the evening sometimes with huge boxes in his truck. We think that's how he disposes of them."

"Have you told the police?"

"Oh no! We don't have any evidence. We've been watching, but he's very careful and we don't want to get too close in case..."

"He kills you?" I asked.

"And eats you," Lily added helpfully.

The Schuberts both nodded with equally depressed expressions on their faces. I didn't notice until then how tired they both looked. They must have had some sleepless nights just worrying.

"Why do you think he eats them?" I asked because I couldn't help it.

"Isn't that what serial killers do?" asked Mrs. Schubert.

Really, it wasn't exactly an implausible answer, though I had to think about it for a few minutes. I couldn't think of many serial killers who ate their victims; but then, I didn't know many serial killers, period.

"Statistically, I think it's unlikely your neighbor is killing and eating people," I told them.

"Maybe he just kills them," suggested Mr. Schubert. "We watch a lot of *Criminal Minds* and we might have overactive imaginations."

"*Might*," agreed Mrs. Schubert.

"There's a small chance they're right," Lily whispered.

"You don't have to whisper, dear," Mrs. Schubert told her, before giving me a pointed look. I didn't know if she was hopeful that her neighbor was a monster, or just pleased that Lily thought cannibalism a possibility too.

"I'm sure there's an explanation," I decided; and before I could think why I said it, I blurted out, "Why don't I look into it?"

"Lexi is a private investigator for the Solomon Agency," Lily told them. "She can solve anything. Killers, thieves, saboteurs... and she always looks really good while she's doing it."

"Aww, thanks, Lily."

"No problem."

"Well, I don't know if we can afford to hire you," said Mrs. Schubert hesitantly. The worried looks were back again, but the noise abated, thankfully.

I waved my hands. I didn't want their money. "Don't worry about that. All I ask is, if I find out what's going on, and you still want to sell, you give me right of first refusal."

Mr. Schubert stuck out his hand and I placed mine in his. "Deal," he said. "But please don't put yourself in harm's way. We could never forgive ourselves if you got eaten."

"I won't," I promised, thinking about what Ruby said to me as she hopped out of the window. "But I will find out what's going on next door. Call it a random act of kindness."

"Me too," said Lily, "I'm going to help Lexi and I don't even want to buy your house. I just want to catch a serial killer. This is going to be so much fun!"

Privately, I disagreed. Loudly.

~

Lily and I staked out the street that evening. It worked well for me. First, it wasn't a date with a loser. Win! Second, I got to hang out with Lily. For the past few days, I had an uncomfortable and burgeoning feeling that with her new business shortly to open, along with her impending motherhood, she was leaving me behind. Third, Lily brought snacks and I was really hungry.

"You think if we ordered pizza, we could get one delivered to the car?" I asked as we waited for something, anything, to happen.

"Yep, but then the VW will smell of cheese."

"Hmm. Maybe not. What about Chinese?"

"Duh. Then it'll smell Chinese. Have a cookie?"

I chewed on the cookie while staring at the house next to the yellow bungalow. We parked a little further down the street, almost on the bend, under a large, old tree of some variety. I didn't know what kind. No one ever asked me to investigate a tree. However, in the hour that we sat here, nothing happened. No noise. No movement. Definitely no bodies.

"I wonder how he cooks them," Lily murmured, reaching into the back for a packet of chips from the grocery bag we stashed there. "Do you think he's all *Silence of the Lambs*?"

"Never seen it."

"We should watch it sometime."

"No thanks."

"Scaredy-cat."

"I won't confirm or deny it. Do you think it's a nice house?"

"I think the whole street is nice. I hope you can live here peacefully without waking up one day to find your neighbor gnawing on your leg."

"That would be a really bad wake-up call. Worse than my alarm clock."

"Bright side, you could compete in the Paralympics."

"I don't think I'll be any faster with one leg."

We fell into silence while we surveyed the house. It was nice, a little on the small side, but with two floors to the bungalow's one — if we ignored the mansard windows — and a well kept garden. From driving past, I knew there was a garage on the far side, concealed from us, and there was a neat, but plain, fenced-in yard to the rear, with a small patio adjoining the house. No noise came from the house, not even the sound of the dog barking, and it was at least fifteen minutes since another vehicle drove past.

"Maybe he's taking a nap. What's his name again?"

I picked up the paperwork I had the Schuberts fill in for me. It was on letterhead Solomon stationery, but I crossed that out. I toyed with writing The Graves Agency on the top, but decided not to, just in case someone found it and laughed. It seemed presumptive, plus, it was only one itty, bitty, pro-bono case. "Aidan Marsh. Thirty-two. Occupation, unknown. Family, unknown. Previous address, unknown. Dog name, unknown."

"We don't know a lot," Lily pointed out as she reached into her bra and gleefully retrieved a cookie crumb.

"Not yet."

I slid the paperwork into the side pocket of the door just as another car drew up behind us. That seemed suspicious in itself, and my heart did a little thump-thump as the driver got out, taking his time to stretch his arms over his head, while revealing a few inches of taut stomach. He strode over.

"Don't look now, but the cops are here," I murmured.

Lily shot a glance over her shoulder and turned back. "Cop. And he doesn't count."

"He still has a badge."

"Yep, and I know what he's done with you and his handcuffs, so I'm not scared. Perturbed, but not scared."

We waited for Maddox to crouch down next to the window. I turned on the engine and hit the button for the electric window to roll down. "Hello, Detective," I said, flashing him a cheery smile and trying to not look suspicious.

"Lexi." Maddox leaned over. "Lily." He nodded to Lily.

"Can we help you?" I asked.

Maddox took his time looking around. "What are you doing?" he asked at last.

"Sightseeing."

"No one sightsees in Montgomery."

"Taking a break." I faked a yawn and covered my mouth. "Must not drive tired." Lily yawned too. So hard, in fact, I thought she might dislocate her jaw.

"What are you really doing?"

"Hanging out with my homegirl? Taking the evening air? What's with the twenty questions?"

"We got a report from a homeowner that a suspicious looking vehicle was parked out here a while and inside,

145

two women were making out." Maddox grinned. "Imagine my surprise when I heard it was your car. I thought, why waste a uniform when I could check it out on my way home?"

"We were not making out," Lily protested.

"Definitely not," I agreed. I turned to my best friend. "Although we did hug at one point."

"But there wasn't any groping," Lily pointed out. She leaned around me to look at Maddox. "Plus, I'm pregnant and it was definitely put there by a man. No turkey basters involved. I can draw you a diagram."

"Please don't."

"I just wanted to make the point that we couldn't be making out if I'm pregnant with a baby put there by a man. Though if I were going to make out with a woman, I'd totally make out with Lexi."

I high-fived her. "Thanks, sweetie."

"Anytime. Though, not, you know, anytime. Still straight and hot for your brother."

"Me too, to the first bit. Vom to the second."

"Glad we got all that cleared up," said Maddox. "Congratulations again on the natural pregnancy, Lily. I'll inform the homeowner you're having some car trouble and not casing the place. Just out of curiosity, which house are you casing?"

"The white one," said Lily.

"Lily!" I squeaked.

"Sorry, it's the pressure! I cracked."

"Why?" asked Maddox.

"You're a scary cop," replied Lily.

"No, Lily." Maddox sighed. "I meant why are you casing the white house? Not why did you crack. And why aren't you working on the other case? You know. The Big One," he emphasized. "Why am I bothering with the secrecy? You know what I'm talking about, don't you, Lily?"

Lily nodded. "Best. Job. Ever."

I wasn't sure I agreed, but it was more interesting than staking out what might be an empty house. I turned to Maddox, telling him, "I still am, but I had to take a night off from dating suspects. It's hard work, you know, being constantly hot and desirable. I'm doing a favor for someone. It's nothing illegal, I promise." I was fairly certain it was nothing illegal. That is, we'd only been here an hour, so it couldn't count as stalking yet, and we hadn't broken in, and no one had been hurt. I hoped my vague explanation would satisfy his curiosity.

"Is this a case for Solomon?" Maddox's eyes darkened, only briefly, at that.

"Nope."

"Call me if you need help."

"You're on the list."

Maddox nodded and stood, leaving me with another nice view of his midriff, where his shirt untucked from his pants. He smoothed the shirt back into place, patted the roof of the VW and strode away.

"Damn, he's one good looking man. Are you sure you don't want to get friendly with him again?" said Lily. "I saw you checking him out."

"I have no idea. I don't know if I can trust him."

"And you don't know that you can't," Lily pointed out. "Maybe he told you the truth. Maybe he was just playing a part and things got out of hand. Maybe he was faithful to you. Oh! Check out his ass. Great ass."

We checked it out as he reached his car, our heads whipping to face front when he turned. Of course, this was nothing I hadn't thought of before. The same words — can't trust, can trust, got it wrong, lies, truth — were going around and around in my head. Thing was, I would never know for certain. Part of me believed Maddox was an honest man, that he wouldn't treat me badly. Part of me was suspicious; some of the things he said about his last undercover case just didn't tally up. I knew he wanted me back. However, I slept with

Solomon not long after discovering Maddox's suspected infidelity, and that was my choice, and therein lay the dilemma: if Maddox wasn't cheating, did that make me the cheater? Or, at the very least, the bad guy for running into the arms of another man? And if he was cheating, then I would be pretty stupid to go back to him.

Either way, I wasn't sure we could ever have what we had before. The trust was gone. Plus, I definitely did have (great!) sex with Solomon, regardless of what Maddox may or may not have done with Blake.

Right now, I didn't want to think about it anymore or my head would explode. "Maddox had a point about asking for help," I told Lily as the window closed. "I'm gonna call Garrett. Maybe he can run a background check on this Marsh guy."

"Cool. You think you can get some stuff from Lucas at the agency to bug his house?"

"Yes, but he'd want to know why, and I don't want to tell him; plus, it's not agency business so I'd feel bad using their resources." I thought about the Schuberts' suspicions, even though they were off the probability scale. "Plus, I don't want to go inside the house," I added. "Just in case."

"I would rescue you."

"Would you?"

"Nope! I'm not stupid, but I would call someone else to do it. Like, Maddox. Or maybe Solomon." Lily peered at me. "Whom do you prefer?"

"Since I'm categorically not going inside, it really doesn't matter," I decided, dodging the elephant of a query.

"So, how are we going to find out what's going on?"

"Good question." I grabbed my cell phone from my purse and dialed Garrett. "I need a favor," I told him.

"I need babysitting," he rebounded, quick as a whip.

"Weekend babysitting or weeknight?"

"How much of a favor do you need?"

"This probably counts as a weeknight favor." I really couldn't think what counted as a weekend night favor, but it would certainly have to be super illegal, and I would have to be really desperate to give up a prime time evening.

"I'll take what I can get. Shoot."

"Can you do a background check on someone for me?"

Garrett sighed. "At least it's nothing highly illegal. What's the name?"

"Aidan Marsh."

"He someone you're dating? Can't you stalk him on Facebook?"

"Gar', no. He's sort of a case."

"Sort of?"

"Um... Not strictly a case. Well, it is a case, but not an agency case, it's more of a..."

"Whatever," Garrett cut in. "I got a dead body in Harbridge to get to. Some old guy died and no one noticed for two years. He's practically a mummy. Date of birth?"

"Don't know. I have an address." I reeled it off.

"That's a start. What do you wanna know about this guy?"

"The usual. Criminal history. Any murders. Prison record."

There was a long pause. "Murders?"

"Or, you know... burglary? Anything iffy." I hoped that was better. I don't know why Garrett sounded so worried. It wasn't like I hadn't met murderers before and survived every damn time. I was shit hot when it came to murderers. Now burglars... they creeped me out.

Garrett sighed again. "I'll get back to you. And, Lexi?"

"Uh-huh?"

"I want Thursday, two weeks time. It's Traci's birthday. I want to make it special."

"You got it." I hung up and made the entry on my phone's calendar. A night babysitting Garrett and Tracey's three terrors wouldn't be so bad. I was pretty certain I knew every prank they could play on me; after all, I taught them most of them. "Garrett's on the case," I told Lily.

"Hurrah. So, what do you wanna do? Sit here a while longer and stare at the house? Or go get pizza and come back tomorrow?"

I thought about it. It had been quiet for some time and I didn't want the neighbors getting antsy again. Plus, I was hungry, and pizza sounded really good and I wouldn't even have to wear a fancy dress. I gasped.

"What's wrong?"

"I just decided sitting at home with a fresh pizza and eating it while wearing sweats sounded way better than dressing up for a fancy dinner."

Lily lay the back of her hand against my forehead. "I don't think you have a fever, but I'm not sure. Do you have a thermometer?"

"Oh yeah, never without one." Lily waited. I raised my eyebrows.

"Oh," she laughed. "Ha-ha. I'm calling Monty's now. I'm going to ask him to burn your half."

"That's mean. I want extra cheese."

"Okay. I'm getting anchovies, bacon and capers on my side."

"Wow. You really are pregnant."

"Tell me about it. I think it happened while we were..."

I clapped my hands over my ears. "La la la la laaah!" Lily giggled. A half hour later found us safely ensconced on her couch, the mouth-watering scent of hot pizza filling the air, and a huge bowl of salad between Jord and us. When they started getting overly snuggly, which made me start feeling sick, I grabbed the last slice of pizza and hightailed it out of there.

~

The next morning, for the first time in the case, Solomon gathered us all at the agency. Instead of the boardroom, which was just about big enough for our own staff, this time, we sat at our desks, while Helen Callery, Maddox and Blake joined us in front of the large whiteboards Solomon set up across one wall.

"Let's compare notes," said Solomon, "and catch this guy."

"How close are you?" asked Helen. She was ensconced in Solomon's office along with Maddox when I arrived, and now she perched on the edge of my desk, clad in a navy pantsuit, bright red lipstick expertly in place and her hair coiffed to the point of not moving.

"Lexi has narrowed our suspects from four to two. Lexi?"

Everyone turned to me and I felt my cheeks heating up. I hated being stared at, unless it was because I looked particularly amazing. If I knew I would be on show today, I would have dressed up, but as it was, I wore skinny blue jeans and a sleeveless white blouse. Thankfully, I added red suede heels. I call the look "casually awesome." Even so, it didn't quite compare with Callery's power dressing suit, or Blake's casual/smart work attire. It was just different. Best of all, it was me. I really didn't know what I was worrying about. I stood, rolling back my chair.

"David Markham is off the table," I recapped for the team. "He's alibied for the time another theft took place. I can also rule out Marty Tookey. He doesn't have the ba... uh, smarts to commit this kind of theft."

"We persuaded Markham that there's no merit to pressing charges," said Maddox, to my relief.

"There's no evidence Tookey has ever left the state," Lucas continued, picking up where I left off. "He's no traveling thief. I found the girlfriend, Claire Archibald. Flaherty made contact discreetly, and apparently, she misses the guy. Nothing else doing there."

I nodded, even though I couldn't imagine anyone missing the douchebag. "That leaves us with Lord Justin and Ben Rafferty. Both are well traveled, as well as charming and affable. I see no problem with either gaining their dates' confidence to access their goods. However..." I paused. This was where I could look stupid, but I had a valid point to make. I pressed on. Better to look stupid than to stupidly leave something important out. "I don't see any motive for either of them to steal."

Solomon nodded, like he agreed, which was reassuring; and after a moment, so did Maddox. "Lucas has been checking into their backgrounds," Solomon told us. "Lucas?"

"There's not a lot to find on either of these guys which appears suspicious," Lucas explained, appearing distinctly uncomfortable in front of a crowd. "Lord Justin was easier to follow. There's a lot of images on line, small mentions in the media, European mostly. Ben Rafferty is more of an enigma. I haven't found anything online about him."

"Is that unusual?" asked Helen Callery.

Lucas shrugged. "Not really. A lot of people don't show up online for whatever reasons. He could just be a very private person. Neither participate in social media, except for Lord Justin's Wikipedia page, but many society figures have those. It doesn't mean he participates in it. I can't access any bank records, and neither is registered to drive here. Lord Justin rents a place, while Ben Rafferty has a suite at The Montgomery. I haven't found the relatives he mentioned in Boston, but maybe they have a different name."

"Ben definitely drives," I interrupted. "He has a Mercedes, but I've also seen him in a town car." I paused while Lucas made a note. "I haven't seen Lord Justin drive, but maybe he just doesn't like driving here. He showed me a photo of his car in England."

"Maddox, what have you and Blake put together?"

"We're still coordinating with other jurisdictions at this point, sending out feelers for where else this guy might have been. So far, we can't connect either the lord or Rafferty with any of the areas. We got some good surveillance footage and photos to work with now ,so we're distributing the pictures in the hopes of getting a hit. It's a small possibility. This guy's a chameleon."

Blake stepped forward, straightening up. "Perhaps Lexi can find out if either of these guys have any distinguishing features, like scars or tattoos, that we can run through our databases," she suggested.

Everyone looked at me. Again.

"Nuh-uh." I shook my head. "I'm not getting their clothes off and asking them to hold still for a photo."

"She's right," agreed Solomon, his voice growing cold. "I'm not putting Lexi in that position. This is a strictly hands-off case."

"Blake wasn't implying that Lexi screws the guys!" said Maddox.

Solomon turned slowly from the whiteboard he was perusing. In a low, angry voice, he said, "You think I'd let my employees screw a target?"

"No, of course not. I was saying Blake didn't mean..."

I held up a hand. "Just for the record, I am not screwing anybody." I pointed at myself, making a circular motion with my hand. "Closed for business here."

"If you happen to see anything unusual. Any birthmarks, scars, that sort of thing, make a note," said Blake, appealing to me directly. It was a good call, I decided, not that I would tell her that. Instead, I simply nodded.

"No," said Solomon. "Lexi, do not put yourself in any situation that makes you uncomfortable, got it? Detective Blake, you want to get their clothes off, do it yourself."

"Hey, whoa!" Maddox stepped in, but Blake put a hand on his forearm and stopped him. The familiarity hit me like a soccer ball in the stomach, washing away the brief moment I felt sorry for her landing in the middle of a Solomon and Maddox pissing contest.

"I apologize if I caused offense," she said. "I wouldn't expect Lexi to do anything unsafe. Just if one of the guys happens to suggest taking his shirt off in the park, all I'm saying is... encourage him. That's all. No impropriety. There's someone watching your back at all times you're with these guys, and we'll get the photos."

"What will you do with the photos?" asked Helen, looking slightly more interested.

Blake smiled. "We'll have to take a really good look at them." I couldn't help smiling too. No harm in seeing a hot guy minus his shirt, then perusing the photos later. After all, it was in the course of putting away a bad guy. It would be a public service! I loved my job.

"Any news on the jewelry theft? Anyone trying to get rid of the items?" Solomon asked, moving on. I guess he wasn't so keen on checking out the photos.

"No." Maddox shook his head. "Blake?"

"We've canvassed all the local pawn shops, and jewelers, to see if anyone's been approached. They all say no, but that doesn't mean they haven't. My gut says the guy is lying low and not attempting to shift them. He probably stashes them until he's ready to move on. Or he might even smelt the gold, remove the jewels, and sell the pieces individually to reset them."

"Can he do that?" Solomon asked.

She shrugged. "It depends on his skill level. We don't know for a fact he can't, so it's an angle we're working. I suspect it's too time-consuming, so I think he'll just sell them when he hits the next town. He's patient, and not desperate for cash."

"So, what now? He's already done a big number on

one of my clients," said Helen. "What could he be planning next?"

"Good question," said Solomon. "Anyone? What's the M.O. suggest, Maddox?"

"Could be anything. This guy changes how he operates every time. The only thing we can anticipate is..."

"He's getting ready to leave," I finished. "We've been on the case for two weeks and he already pulled off a big heist."

"And I came to you six weeks ago," added Helen, nodding to Solomon.

"We've worked on this four weeks," said Maddox.

Solomon said what we all knew, what we were all awaiting to be confirmed. "He'll be out of Montgomery in two weeks, max."

"What's the next step, boss?" asked Fletcher, who sat there quietly the whole time, just taking everything in.

"I want full time tails on the lord and Rafferty. Every movement, we'll know about. Lexi, Helen is throwing a ball for her clients. You're on the list. She'll tell you what you need to know. Get information out of the suspects. We'll go over their files again and talk later on what you can get out of them. Maddox, Blake, you got anything else to put in play?"

"No. We'll keep working our angles and the theft leads. If we don't get this guy within a week, I hate to say it, but I think we should turn this over to the FBI. I spoke to my contact. They're interested," said Maddox.

Solomon clapped his hands together. "Let's catch this guy first. Go to work, people."

The group dispersed as Solomon made his goodbyes to Helen Callery, who promised to call me later with the ball's details, then the detectives. Meanwhile, I lingered in his office, waiting for him to brief me on just how to catch the targets in a lie, or even better, a truth.

"You okay?" Solomon asked me, shutting the door to

the office, and drowning out the general phone noises and chatter of my colleagues getting to work.

"Never better."

"You're not gonna do anything dumb per Blake's idea?" he continued, eyeing me suspiciously. At least, I thought it was suspiciously. Jealously could have worked too, if it weren't such a puzzling idea.

"No. Definitely not. I do not sleep with guys who might steal my stuff. Though there was that one time..." Solomon waited for me to finish, but I cringed, and shut up. "I have better taste now. Sometimes. So, how do you suggest I trap this guy?" I asked as my cell phone started to vibrate. I pulled it out, seeing Justin's name appear on the screen.

"It's Lord Justin," I told him, "What do I do?"

"Take it. Find out what he wants."

I counted to three, put on my best phone voice, and answered. "Justin, what a surprise! An exhibition... I'd love to. Yes. Yes. Sounds wonderful. All right then. I'll see you in an hour." I hung up. "I have a date."

"Exhibition? In an hour?" Solomon asked.

"Oh, good listening. Yes, there's a visiting exhibition at the town museum. He was just walking past and says he recalled I liked art and might want to see it, then have a coffee."

"Do it."

"I will!" I looked at my jeans. "Is this okay for a date to a museum?"

Solomon took a very long look. "You always look perfect," he told me. My heart skipped a beat and butterflies moved into my belly. "Head over there now. I'll send pointers to your phone."

I stood, reaching for the door handle, already checking through my mental list of things I could ensnare Justin with when Solomon said my name softly. "Yes?" I turned to him.

"Clothes on," said Solomon, and I laughed.

"You got it, boss."

~

I got to the town museum, a big, old building, complete with pillars and wide stone steps, before Justin. Built over a hundred years ago, the place gave the illusion of grandeur and was our cultural hub. They hosted all kinds of traveling exhibits, talks, and the occasional concert, though I couldn't remember the last time I visited.

Taking advantage of the warm afternoon, I parked myself on the steps and enjoyed the sun and people-watching while I waited. I wasn't all that sure what I would ask him, how I could trap him in a lie, but I was sure that Fletcher was parked somewhere nearby, ready to listen to everything we said before it got analyzed later.

They say it's about first impressions, but for me, it was usually the second date that confirmed things. While I was giddy about dating a lord on our first date, and bowled over by his handsome face, the second date didn't go so well.

Justin was, in a word, boring. He droned on about places he'd been, name-dropping frequently, but where Ben made even the most mundane thing sound interesting, exciting or funny, Justin couldn't have flipped the switch harder in the other direction. An hour in, and I found myself struggling just to feign interest.

"Tell me, Lexi," he said, offering me a seat on the padded bench under a long window overlooking the rear lawn. "Would you marry a man like me?"

"I, uh, what now?"

"Not now, of course, darling. We've only known each other ten minutes, but perhaps in the future? It used to be done all the time, you know."

"What? Marriage? It's definitely still done," I replied, confused by the sudden turn in conversation.

Justin laughed. "No, you rich, young things popping

over to England and wedding a title," he told me. "We could be quite the dashing couple. You'd look good on my arm."

I was once engaged for, oh, half a minute, but the proposal was a lot more romantic than this. As far as I knew, my ex never wanted to marry me for my money. Though it could be that, like Justin, he thought of me as some kind of trophy wife. Not that it mattered much since I was broke back then, and my ex did a runner, leaving me heartbroken before I decided to enlist with the army. Neither the engagement or the army were my brightest ideas.

"I don't believe in pre-nups either," Justin continued, oblivious to what could only be a look of horror on my face. "What's mine is yours and vice versa. If we ever divorced, and I'm sure we wouldn't, especially with four children..."

"Four?" I coughed.

"Two boys, two girls," said Justin, sounding delighted as if I just agreed. "What was I saying? Oh yes, you'd have a claim on everything that was mine. Gosh, if we married here in the States, you might even get the castle."

"Castle?"

Justin whipped out his wallet, flipping it open to reveal a small, plastic photograph case. "There it is. Not actually a castle," he explained, showing me the magnificent house. It looked familiar, like something I'd seen on postcards or advertisements for gorgeous, stately homes. "That's a family joke. Would you like to live there?"

"Oh, erm, well..."

"Of course you would. The servants would look after you. You'd never have to lift a finger."

"You have servants?"

"Just a small staff of twenty, plus the gardeners and couple of chaps to look after the horses. Racing is a family passion. Anyway, what do you say? Shall we aim for you becoming the old ball and chain?"

"Oh, look at the time," I said, checking my wrist even though I wasn't wearing a watch. "I'm late for an appointment. Must go. Great seeing you!" I staggered backwards, completely terrified at the idea of becoming Justin's ball and chain. I couldn't imagine leaving my family, not to mention the bungalow I just bought, to live in the admittedly gorgeous house... with servants... being waited on... I paused. No! I couldn't even contemplate it. I'd have to live with Justin, who probably only did it in the missionary position with his face screwed up as he thought of England, and racing horses.

Meanwhile I'd be popping out little blonde kid after little blonde kid. "Bye!" I turned and power-walked as fast as my heels could carry me, not even pausing when he called my name, with no stops until I was in the safe confines of the Ferrari.

After catching my breath and before heading home to call Helen Callery about the ball, I checked my cell phone, and found a text from my sister asking me to call. Thinking that maybe it was about my niece, or her ex-husband doing another dumb-ass thing, I called back right away. "Lexi, hey, I was in Alessandro's today, having lunch with some friends."

"That's nice. I was there a few days ago."

"Yes, that's what I was calling you about. Marco, the maitre d' told me your friend's card bounced."

"What?"

"Yeah, Marco said the card was no good, but your friend left before they could ask him to pay another way. It was kind of embarrassing actually, Lexi. I'm sure it wasn't deliberate, but could you ask your friend to settle up with Marco? Normally, they contact the police with something like this, but because he knows me, he didn't. Your friend is really lucky."

"Yeah, I'll let him know. Thanks, Serena."

"No problem. Catch up with you soon. I'm going to dinner with Antonio tonight. He says he has a gift for me. Do you know what it is?"

"He hasn't told me a thing."

"Oh, okay. He's really sweet. I'm so lucky." Serena hesitated. "You'll find the right guy too, you know. Hope you're not worrying about those guys."

"I'm not," I lied, "Not one bit."

As soon as we hung up, I did contact them both, telling them about Justin's bizarre marriage proposal and what Serena told me. It was suspicious. That Justin's payment didn't go through was one thing, an error maybe, but coupled with walking out and leaving his card behind, not to mention his eagerness to lure a rich wife without a pre-nup, smelled like a rat. As Justin pointed out, I could end up filthy rich; what he didn't point out was, that worked two ways... he could claim from me too. Maybe Justin wasn't quite as rich as he made out, and if that were true, maybe he was looking for a way to make a quick buck without a pre-nup?

CHAPTER THIRTEEN

I was glad I had a quiet evening alone with Lily — minus stakeouts and dating disasters — because the next night was all kinds of fancy, and something of a treat. Although Helen Callery set me up with a ticket, and Solomon promised to come through on suitable attire, Ben called earlier that day to see if I were attending. When he found out I was, he insisted on collecting me from the Chilton house at nine sharp. He looked thoroughly gorgeous in his tuxedo, and even better with me on his arm. That I was now sure of his innocence in the face of Lord Justin's bizarre behavior to rid me of my fake riches only added to his allure.

I, of course, looked equally divine in a stunning, fitted, floor-length black gown Solomon managed to procure from somewhere. I even had a diamond pendant and diamond studs to complete the look. I didn't dare ask how much they cost, though Solomon did take the time to mention there would be eyes on me all night. Or more precisely, on the jewels.

"Does anything strike your fancy?" Ben asked,

leaning closer to whisper into my ear. Or bosom. It was hard to tell and, frankly, the lightest touch of his breath on either was welcome. We paused in the corner of the room, the music from a harpist washing over us, and all I wanted to do was ask Ben to whisper again. It was a nice change from beating myself up over Solomon and Maddox.

I looked up at him and smiled. "Oh, yes."

"And how about the silent auction?" he quipped, winking as if he could read my mind.

"Still browsing," I told him. The ball, I learned, was Million Matches' idea of a mixer. Get all the rich folk in one room, encourage them to spend a bunch of money in the name of charity, and hope that some of them get it on with each other, and live to tell all their rich friends about their successful endeavor. Some of the attendees arrived in pairs, like Ben and me; others came alone. I'd already counted hundreds of thousands, if not millions, in jewels, and spotted some haute couture that made my heart race. The women really did go to town when flashing their wealth. The men, meanwhile, were more subtle in uniforms of ebony tuxedos, the occasional flash of a Rolex, or a pair of diamond-studded cufflinks, serving as discreet calling cards for the size of their wallets. Not that any of them needed it. I knew the ticket alone cost a thousand bucks, and the agency vetted everyone to prevent the poor proletariat from gaining entry. What surprised me most was how many lonely millionaires there were in Montgomery.

"Don't look now, but there's a man in a turban staring at us," whispered Ben. He plucked two champagne flutes from a passing waiter's tray and handed me one as I tried a discreet glance over my shoulder. I flinched. The man staring in our direction wasn't wearing a turban. It was a bandage, white fabric folds woven into a thick wrap around his head. His expression was less of a stare and more of a glower. On the plus side, David

Markham was still definitely alive. We both survived our date, although the way he looked at me right now, made me wonder if I would survive this evening. "Do you know him?" Ben asked.

I blinked. "Hmm?"

"The guy in the turban. Do you know him? He doesn't look very happy."

I mumbled something vague, and took a sip of champagne. I was saved from further explanation by a woman in her mid-forties bearing down on us. She all but edged me out of the way as she leaned in to air-kiss Ben an inch from both cheeks. In that close proximity, I spotted telltale traces of a scar just near her ears, and revised my age estimate upwards by fifteen years.

"Darling," she gushed. "How wonderful to see you aren't off the market yet." She gave me a casual sideways glance and moved left, forcing me to step out of her way.

Ben smiled. "You look stunning, Claudia." His gaze flitted towards the large emerald-studded choker around her neck. Each one looked perfect to my untrained eye. She wore a ruby ring on her left hand and an emerald-and-ruby bracelet on her left wrist. They were a little over the top for my taste, but I wouldn't say no. They made my borrowed diamonds look like children's costume jewelry.

"I bid on the Caribbean villa," Claudia continued. "One week for two in paradise. Away from the pressures of Hollywood. I'm an actress, darling," she sneered at me before giving him a pointed look. It was all I could do not to roll my eyes. She totally had the hottie hots for my date! Not only that, but she thought he might want to join her at the villa, and I bet she wasn't planning to pack a Scrabble board. As she gazed at him, a sinking feeling hit my stomach. Claudia was so sure of herself because she'd already been there with Ben. Eww.

"I'm sure your daughter will love some bonding time

with you," said Ben, acting purposefully dense and not rising to the bait. He took a sip of champagne and scanned the room, finally meeting my eyes and smiling.

"She's busy that week. College." Claudia shrugged. She followed Ben's gaze and gave me a casual once-over. If she were impressed or threatened or bored, it was impossible to tell; Botox kept her face frozen. All the same, she gave me a weak smile and returned her gaze to Ben. "I'll call you... lover." With a saucy smile, she drifted away, waving to someone else in the crowd.

Ben leaned in and took my hand as he said, "Subtlety is not Claudia's strong point."

"You're joking?" I murmured and he laughed.

"No, and neither is honesty. As you might have guessed, we dated a couple of times, but her profile claimed she was thirty-eight. The rest of her body, however, doesn't stand up to the claim."

"Ooh. Bitchy." I thought about the rest of her standing up to the claim and sighed. Ben and Claudia?

"It's not bitchy if it's true. As for calling me her lover..." Ben glanced at me and raised his eyebrows, "that's a no. Anyway, she's hounded me ever since."

"I can't see why," I told him, brightening inside as Ben dispelled Claudia's attempt to psyche me out. "It's not like you're gorgeous, handsome, and rich."

He gave a nonchalant shrug. "It's hard to be an Average Joe."

"Yeah, you look like you're really suffering."

Ben raised my hand to his heart and smiled. "Whatever will you do to cheer me up?"

"Give you an alibi for the week in the Caribbean?"

"I'll take that... and..." He was moving us towards the dance floor, my hand still on his heart. "For now, I'll take a dance."

"Don't you want to bid on anything?" I nodded towards the auction tables across the shortest length of the room. Details of the objects to be bid upon were displayed alongside bidding sheets the size of ballot papers, and neat, leather voting boxes, their frames edged with studs, and slit in the top to receive the secret bids.

"I'll bid on anything you choose," he told me. "Just say the word."

We danced for the remainder of the song, then the next and the next. Ben was a wonderful dancer; light on his feet, confident. I left my hand in his, with his other hand resting on my hip. We twirled and whirled, for a while, seemingly like we were the only ones in the room. If I didn't keep reminding myself that I was on a case, and there was still a fifty percent chance Ben was a top thief, I might have let myself fall into the moment, and enjoy the sensation of being in the arms of a handsome man with whom I had no history and no expectations. But I couldn't do that. I had to be professional. I had to remember that even if this was a pleasant case to work on, I was simply dressed in finery, rather than being hidden in a bush, wearing jeans and a sweater. It was still work and I still had a job to do. I still had to engineer a conversation with Justin; and I still had to keep my eye on Ben.

So, after a while, I resisted getting carried away and began to observe my surroundings and the people within. I spotted David Markham again, this time sulking in the corner; and I also saw the wet blanket, Marty Tookey walking around, talking to people and smiling until they politely edged away and he moved onto the next group.

I also spotted Lord Justin perusing the bidding tables before standing alone to one side, observing the room. He caught my glance and raised his glass. I nodded to him and smiled, before Ben whirled me around, dancing us across the floor. All the myriad jewels, their colors, sizes, and shapes made my head spin. Millions of dollars worn on necks, wrists, earlobes, and fingers, plus tens of thousands being bid on lots, as if they had cash to burn. Solomon was right: this was a great night to stake out potential victims. There were dozens of them, just ripe for picking.

"Would you excuse me a moment?" said Ben.

"Of course." I didn't ask where he was going. Besides, I saw him heading in the direction of the hallway where the restrooms were situated. I figured all the champagne was running through him too. Speaking of which, there was no time like the present for a bathroom break of my own, especially with Marty Tookey bearing down on me.

Sidestepping past a couple in deep conversation, their crucial words being "Harry Winston" and "when?" I followed in Ben's footsteps, nodding to Delgado, who pulled security duty at the door, as I passed by. The only reaction I got was a slight flare of his nostrils.

The bathroom was staffed by a surly looking woman with shoulder-length, black hair and more products than were stocked in my hair salon. Nice perfumes, hand lotion, body sprays, and the fluffiest white hand towels surrounded a little white dish that the attendant had her eyes locked on.

Three other women reached the bathroom before me and formed a short queue for the stalls. I joined them, deliberately eavesdropping.

"Then he showed me the photo of his estate," exclaimed the shorter of the two blondes. "I've always wanted to live on an estate. Imagine! In England."

Uh-oh. Leaning in quite imperceptibly, I hoped.

She continued, "He said he could imagine me living there, strolling around the grounds. He even said we'd probably meet the queen!"

Her two friends made enthusiastic cooing noises, but I wasn't sure which element grabbed them most: the estate, the title, or the queen.

"That's funny," said the brunette, "He told me that he

went on a boys night out with the princes, and Kate would love to have a friend like me."

"He. Did. Not," replied the short blonde.

"Did too. He said we'd take the yacht out with them this summer."

"What yacht?" asked the taller blonde. "He has a yacht?"

"I think it belongs to some sheik friend of his. It's moored in France," said Shorty.

"Monaco, Candice," snapped Brunette. "Besides, he was just being nice. I have a date with Lord Justin tomorrow night."

"I'm having afternoon tea with him on Saturday," said Candice, flicking her blonde bob.

"Uh-oh," said the tall blonde, and they both turned to her.

"Uh-oh what?" said Candice.

"I didn't know we were talking about Justin. I slept with him last night."

Last night? After our little museum trip? How rude. All the same, I didn't throw my lot into the increasingly hostile atmosphere. It was three on one, and if they were friends and about to fight, they'd almost certainly turn on me. So, I kept my mouth shut and texted a short version of the conversation to Solomon. He sent back "!" which I thought summed it up nicely. Now Justin wasn't only my top suspect, he was also an ass.

Taking the time it took for them to get more distracted by their argument, I slipped past to use the toilet. By the time I returned to wash my hands, the three were still bickering.

"Great ball, huh?" I chipped in. "Did you bid on anything?"

"The Chopard ring," said Candice.

"The Barbados villa," said Brunette.

"I don't remember," said the tall blonde, "Daddy will let me know."

"Hey, did you meet the English guy yet?" I asked. "Totally cute. I knew I saw him somewhere before. I was just driving the Ferrari past the sexual health clinic on Rosemount Avenue a couple days ago, and he was standing there with a piece of paper, looking really miserable."

The tall blonde's face fell. "He was what?" she asked, looking stricken.

I flapped a towel in the air, then dried my hands. "Oh, it was probably nothing. Those English guys have such a healthy complexions don't they? Have a great night!" I tossed the towel in the basket and made a quick exit as the tall blonde started to wail. Her two no-longer bickering friends crowded her, looking both thrilled and aghast at the same time.

Okay, it was mean, but I probably just saved them, or their daddies, a ton of insurance paperwork, and they'd probably thank me later. Not.

~

I was just texting "No, not really" in reply to Solomon's "?" when I returned to the ballroom, pausing to look for Ben.

"On your right," hissed Delgado behind me. I wiggled my fingers at him in a quiet thanks before striding towards my date.

Ben looked up from the man he was speaking to as I approached, and took hold of my hand. The man greeted me politely and scooted off, leaving us alone, which was just fine by me, although not so thrilling for Claudia, who glared at me. We ignored her, Ben smiling happily at me, while behind him, Helen Callery, clad in a floor-skimming, red gown, climbed onto the stage and stood behind the lectern. To her rear, the auction boxes were assembled, their lids now unlocked and lying open. In her hands were several envelopes, the final bids. I didn't need to worry. I already knew I wouldn't win because I only bid a dollar on a couple of items, but I wondered if Ben would win his bid. He gave me a reassuring smile and squeezed my fingers.

Helen tapped the microphone. "Ladies and gentleman, thank you for joining us this evening to aid local schools. We're delighted to..." Her voice faded away as the room plunged into darkness, every single light snapping off.

Blinking hard, I still couldn't see a thing through the darkness. Ben's fingers slipped from mine. "Ben?" I whispered.

"Right here," he replied.

"What happened?"

"I think there was some kind of blackout."

"Great." Last time I was in a blackout, wearing an altogether different kind of get-up, a man got stabbed. So whatever happened now could only be better than that.

"Took the word right out of my mouth," said Ben. "Shoot. I think someone just fainted. Lemme check."

"Okay." I stood still. Not so much because I didn't want to help, but because I didn't want to fall over someone and make matters worse, if someone really had fainted. As I waited for Ben to take my hand, I listened to whispers rippling through the crowd. Annoyance, sighing, a couple squabbling, someone near me mentioning a fainting woman and then I was bumped. I dropped my clutch bag in surprise. "Oh no," I murmured.

"You dropped your bag," said Ben, his voice suddenly next to my ear. He pressed the little clutch into my hand and I wrapped my fingers around it. He stood so close to my back, my whole rear was pressed against him. Well, not, you know, my rear end, but the rear side of me; though come to think of it, was that *his* hand on my rear? Was it wrong to have a little wiggle?

"Someone bumped me," I murmured. "How is the

woman who fainted?"

"False alarm."

"Good of you to offer help. Medical training?"

Ben chuckled. "First aid only. I do, however, have a fantastic bedside manner."

The flush that heated my cheeks had only just disappeared by the time the lights flickered back on. I had to shield my eyes with my hand, turning to press my face against Ben's strong, manly, yummy chest. Sometimes, my work life was really hard. Today, it was just Ben's chest that was hard, oh… and my struggle to keep my thoughts from going truly blue.

As I became accustomed to the light, blinking into focus like everyone else, I pressed both hands against his chest. Trying not to dribble or breathe too hard, I pushed myself away. Ben caught me before I put any space between us. Staring down at me, his eyes gleamed with anticipation. His head lowered, and his lips parted. I rose onto tiptoes, licked my lips and...

"My emeralds!" came a shriek from across the room. "They're gone! I've been robbed! Stop! Thief!"

Cries went up and my heels went down. The moment was lost. "Thief?" I said, my forehead wrinkling due to my lack of Botox.

Ben looked around. "I don't see any thief."

"But I do see Claudia raising a stink. We should find out if she's okay." Claudia moved a little further away, her hands clasping her throat.

"If we must," said Ben. "I'd rather hide."

We exchanged smiles. Personally, I agreed with him. I really wasn't too interested in Claudia, but I was interested in her suddenly missing jewels. And if what she shrieked were true, the thief was in this room, right now, and I was closer to cracking the case, and getting my miniscule bonus, than I'd ever been.

Claudia was sobbing, or, more precisely, hyperventilating and shrieking while wiping her tearless eyes as we approached. "Oh, Ben, darling!" She threw herself at him, giving me a fraction of a second to leap out of the way before catching me with a bony elbow and doing who knows what kind of damage? "I could have been killed! Murdered! He could have slit my throat!"

Ben gave me a look that I could only interpret as hopeful, but patted Claudia on the back. "Are you sure?" he asked. "Maybe your necklace snapped?"

"No, I felt a hand on my neck. It was so cold! Like a ghost! And then my necklace slipped away. He would have strangled me, I'm sure!"

"He?" I asked, wondering what method of murder she'd pick next.

Claudia wrinkled her nose. "Bigger hands than a woman. Shorter nails."

"So probably human and not a ghost," I told her, watching her eyes narrow. "And you seem okay."

"Physically. I might faint. Ben, catch me!" Claudia's eyes rolled back and she slumped into Ben's arms. Damn it. I should have tried that the moment the lights went out. I might have gotten that kiss then. As it was, it didn't look like Ben had any plans to lock lips with Claudia anytime soon. He looked rather bemused, although increasingly uncomfortable as he maneuvered her to a chaise by the wood-paneled wall, where he lay her down. I saw her fingers tightening their grip on his jacket. Pah. So much for fainting.

I leaned in closer. "She's in a dead faint," I said loudly. "Hold still, Ben, while I throw this pitcher of water over her. It may be the only thing to rouse her."

Claudia's eyes flashed open, her hand went to her forehead and she groaned loudly, probably at the realization she wouldn't be getting any mouth-to-mouth action from my date. "What happened?" she murmured. "Did I faint? Oh, Ben, you darling, you rescued me."

"Anytime, Claudia." Ben extracted himself, not

without difficulty as she clung to his cuff, and stood upright. We were at the front of a small crowd that assembled to watch Claudia's performance, I mean, to check up on her and find out if the theft was true. I might have some reservations about her acting skills, but I could definitely confirm her throat was stripped of the showy jewels.

"Are you okay?" Ben asked me as I took a deep breath.

"Fine," I assured him. "Not shaken, not stirred." That wasn't strictly true; the theft happened on my watch. This was on my head... and I didn't see a thing. Not that I could blame myself for the blackout.

Ben smiled.

"Will you excuse me for a moment? I want to check in with Helen. She looks a little pale," I told him. Helen was being helped down from the small platform, all the color gone from her face.

"Of course."

I took another look at Claudia. She was trying to catch the hem of Ben's jacket, but only succeeded in looking like she had pincers instead of hands. "Try not to get eaten by Claudia while I'm gone."

"Hurry back." Ben glanced over his shoulder to where Claudia was reclining while she retold the story of the theft. He moved another step backwards. One thing she seemed to have forgotten was that the thief was still in the room, but I didn't forget and I was fairly certain Solomon was jumping to attention somewhere closeby. Not *that* kind of attention. My heart raced all the same. I grabbed a fan from the vase on a console and fanned myself as I crossed over to Helen.

"Excuse me, Helen," I interrupted when I found Helen standing in the corner with her assistant, Madeleine. Both women looked pale, but Helen's game face was rapidly coming into play. Madeleine was starting to look bored. "Can we speak a moment?"

"Yes, of course. Lexi, isn't it? Madeleine, check on Claudia, would you, dear?"

"Of course, Helen." Madeleine flashed me a smile as she walked past me. I wondered if Claudia would treat her to a performance too. Probably. Soon everyone in Montgomery would be hearing the heavily dramatized version. Unfortunately, the version everyone would hear about me would probably be that the one, non-serving Graves in MPD let a thief get away. Not if I had anything to do with it! He might have outsmarted me temporarily, but I would catch him anyway I could.

It would be better if my resolve were matched up with a brilliant action plan, but I was pretty much all out of them.

"Solomon should be here any moment," I told her quietly. "Until then, we need to secure the area. I don't want any of the guests to leave. I hate to say it, but they'll need to be searched. The thief can't have taken the necklace out of the building. Not yet."

Helen nodded and made a sweeping motion towards the two doormen who stood by the double doors. They nodded and I saw one tap his ear and speak. As I glanced across the room, I saw the opposite doors close, leaving only one exit. The doormen took up positions in the middle, their hands crossed in front of their groins. They were either ready to leap to action or really excited. I was too far away to tell. So far, I seemed to be the only one who noticed that the exits were blocked. I just hoped Solomon and the team arrived before the crowd tired of Claudia and got antsy. Also, where was Delgado when you needed him?

"Did you see who did it?" Helen asked me. "It was pitch-black. I couldn't see a thing. I only knew something happened when Claudia started to scream. He could have picked someone quieter." She trailed off and sighed.

"I'm sorry, I was as blind as everyone else. Has

Claudia dated anyone in our suspect pool?" I asked.

Helen unexpectedly laughed. "Claudia's dated everyone. Does it matter?" Helen gestured around the room with a sweep of her hand and I caught her point. No, it didn't matter one bit. This was hardly a complexly organized break-and-enter. This theft had more of a smash-and-grab feel to it.

"No, it doesn't. Does Solomon have a list of all the guests?"

"Yes, I emailed it earlier."

"And do you see anyone here not on the list?"

Claudia shook her head. "No, but there's around five people who haven't turned up."

"I'll need those names so we can discount them." I made a note on my cell phone as Helen reeled off the names from memory. Three men, two women: all with something better to do than become suspects, or mingle with the local rich list.

"What should we do now?" Helen asked as I finished making my notes.

I was saved from answering when Solomon appeared between the doormen. They didn't seem to notice him. I kind of wanted Solomon to karate chop them both in the neck just to see what happened, and also to see if he was a secret ninja. On reflection, that probably wasn't a great idea. As I watched Solomon, his eyes sliding from the man on the right to the one on the left, I had to wonder if he was thinking the same thing. He scanned the room until he found me, nodded, and put his fingers to his luscious... lips.

Lips.

Just lips.

Not luscious anythings.

I flushed, nodded, and Solomon slipped away.

"Solomon's here. Just act normal," I told Helen.

"What will he do?"

"He's going to take care of things," I said, sounding

far more assured than I felt. As I spoke, my phone vibrated and I raised it, checking the screen.

"Searching guests on natural exit," it read. "Nobody left yet."

Well, that was succinct. And not very exciting... but a good plan, especially as I quietly had the same one. Damn it. I should have sent a text and gotten in there first! I got the idea though. Searching guests on exit would allow them to leave at their own pace, instead of being shepherded out en masse into the waiting arms of MPD. It was quiet, discreet, and not likely to cause huge embarrassment to the guests or the agency. Plus, I had to hope the chances of the thief ditching the jewels already would be pretty low. In evening dress, there weren't that many places to hide such a chunky piece, but I couldn't see the thief leaving the necklace to retrieve later.

According to Solomon, if nobody left the room yet — and I had to assume the doormen confirmed that — and if the necklace wasn't on someone's person, then it had to be hidden in this room. I looked around. There were vases of flowers, tables, chairs, chaises, sweeping curtains and wood paneling covering every wall of the vast room. There were plenty of hiding places, but every single one was a risky option. Staff would clear away all the fancy decor hired for the evening, and cleaners would follow them. Somewhere along the way, Solomon's team would sweep the room, leaving no corner unchecked, no vase unturned.

No, I decided, it had to be on someone's person, but whose?

CHAPTER FOURTEEN

Helen Callery was a consummate professional. It probably had a lot to do with the sinking ship her dating agency would become if her clients realized they were all suspects. Even worse, if they all realized they were actually targets. So, as soon as Claudia was placated and escorted from the room by a couple of handsome waiters, the hubbub died down, and the auction resumed.

I noticed Helen's assistant, Madeleine, moving around, ensuring drinks were flowing freely, and prompting the applause every time a winner was announced. She was a one-woman cheer team: making small talk, laughing, showing everyone what a wonderful time everyone else was having, and allowing her infectiously pretty smile to turn worried faces into happy, forgetful ones. Most of all, I think the guests were relieved they weren't robbed, which certainly encouraged them to be a little more forgiving. Plus, each and every one had an exciting story to tell about the time a dramatic jewel theft occurred. From what I gathered, everyone was no more than a few feet away from Claudia.

"I guess I didn't win," said Ben with a disappointed shrug as the last lot winner was called.

"Me neither."

"Let's commiserate together?" Ben raised his eyebrows and if I didn't know better, I might have thought he was being suggestive. Oh wait, he totally was. Awesome!

"Do you have something in mind?" I replied, flirtatiously swirling a lock of hair with my forefinger.

"A nightcap? Somewhere quiet... somewhere sexy..."

"Well, I, uh..." I wanted to say yes. I wanted to say, "Hello, okay, right now? Yippee yay. Let's go." But I had a job to do, which involved tracking down a thief, not enjoying a sexy nightcap with one of the top suspects. On the other hand, what better way to get a frisk search completed? Uh, on him. Not me. I hadn't stolen anything.

My phone vibrated and I opened my purse just enough to glance down. Somehow, I forgot the phone was there. "Go," was the single word on the screen.

Oh, well, fine, if my boss insisted, I guess I would just have to take one for the team.

"Sure," I said, "Let's get our coats."

There was no queue at the cloakroom, but before we got there, the two of us were pulled to one side.

"If you'll just come with us one moment, sir," said my colleague, Fletcher, nodding to me politely as if we were strangers.

"What's going on?" asked Ben.

"Just a routine search in light of this evening's events," Fletcher explained.

Ben held his hands up. "Search away."

"If you'll just come into this room, sir. We'd like to be discreet."

"Ma'am, if you'll follow me." Delgado stepped in

front of me. I hoped he didn't have plans to search me. After all, I was pretty certain he recently played strip search with my sister... and some other games I wanted absolutely no knowledge of. Ever.

"Yes, of course," I agreed. "See you in a moment, Ben."

Ben simply nodded and followed Fletcher into a side room where the door closed behind them.

Delgado inclined his head to me and I followed him to the small room opposite, smiling when I saw Solomon waiting inside, his arms folded as he leaned against the wall. We weren't in a closet, but some kind of utility room or office. A table and a couple of chairs were against one wall, but otherwise, it was bare. Delgado shut the door and I leaned against the wall.

"Where were you?" I asked, raising my eyebrows at Delgado. I figured I'd ask first, before I got twenty questions.

"Bathroom," he said, with a shrug.

"Peeing in the dark. Awkward." Delgado cracked a smile. "So what happens now?" I asked.

Solomon spoke quickly. "We're searching every guest as they leave so they don't return to the ball and inadvertently alert the thief. Claudia is giving a statement to the police. Fortunately, she has a paste replica of the jewels at her home so she'll be able to show exactly what they look like, and her insurance is paid up. She's not happy, or at least, she won't be when she sobers up."

I blinked. "She's got a paste set?"

"Yeah. Apparently, some women get replicas made for less fancy occasions." Solomon glanced to the door. "Helen Callery seems to be taking it well."

I shook my head. "She's freaking out."

"She's okay," insisted Delgado.

"No, she's not. She's doing that false 'everything's great—lalala' thing my mother does when she's worried that everything is falling apart. I can see it on her face," I told them. "Duh. Do you two not know women at all?" I asked when they both gave me skeptical expressions.

Solomon and Delgado eyed each other, then me. Both mumbled something about knowing women just fine before shutting up.

"Anyway, that's not it. I mean, she, Claudia, has a paste set!" I continued, ignoring them. Again, Solomon and Delgado exchanged glances before turning to stare at me. If I weren't used to it, I would have been uncomfortable. "Don't you see? That's how you can squash any rumors from this evening. If you can ask Claudia to get us the paste replicas, we can show the guests before they leave, and say it was all part of the evening. A staged robbery with Claudia as the amazing actress. She's an actress, darling," I mimicked.

"It could work, Boss," said Delgado, one side of his mouth lifting into a smile, like he couldn't decide if he were happy with the idea or not. "No one's left yet, 'cept these two."

"Who's going to act as the thief?" asked Solomon

"Tip one of the waiters a hundred bucks to pretend he was the thief. Oh, and get him to sign a nondisclosure too. There has to be an out-of-work actor among them. They're all too good looking not to be."

"You were checking out the waiters?" asked Solomon, his face returning to its stony setting.

"Hell, no. Me? No!"

Solomon rested his chin in the gap between thumb and forefinger and stroked his jaw. "Okay," he said, nodding. "It could work. You and Ben are the first to leave. If Helen agrees and Claudia complies, we'll encourage everyone else to stay with the promise of a big finale."

"Exactly," I added, excitement urging my mind and mouth to race. "Make the guests feel like they're part of it. Search them, conduct mini interviews, do everything you need to for a real investigation, but, at the end, tell them it's all show. A big charade for their benefit. Like one of those murder mystery evenings."

"Helen will like it," Solomon decided. "It'll appeal to her flair for the dramatic. Delgado, I'll find Helen and you get a waiter."

"But don't terrify him," I interrupted, mostly to Delgado, who looked like he might take a waiter to one side and knock him down. "Find out how many of them are out-of-work actors. Get the one who can put on the best show. And if Claudia doesn't seem interested, you might want to point out the Hollywood producer on the guest list."

Solomon checked his watch. "Time for you to go. You can only get frisked for so long," he said, his voice velvet smooth.

A blush rose on my face and I turned away before Solomon or Delgado could see it, not that it mattered because Solomon's cell phone beeped.

"Ben's clean," said Solomon. I glanced over and saw him studying the screen before slipping the cell phone into his pocket. "Let us know where you go. I have to stay here a while. I don't want to have to search Montgomery for you if you get out of range."

Something told me he would though. "Okay. Hey, Lord Justin was standing real close to Claudia before the lights went out. I think he was a little further away when the lights came back on; and you heard what happened with the women in the restroom. He's playing them, as well as me."

"I heard. We've been watching and he's been very busy with the ladies this evening. Delgado will frisk him," said Solomon. Delgado cracked his knuckles. Somehow, I didn't think Lord Justin would be enjoying the rest of the evening.

"Justin definitely needs to be searched thoroughly. My money is on him. I don't think he's the man he pretends he is. Something about his story doesn't sit right," I told them and they both nodded, but made no move to do otherwise. "Okay, so I'll check in soon," I told them, waiting for Solomon's nod before I slipped out, closing the door behind me.

Ben was waiting at the cloakroom. He clearly got there a minute or two before me because he already had his coat on, and mine folded over his arms. "Let me take those," he said, relieving me of my purse and phone before I had a chance to protest. He lay them on the counter and held my coat up. I spun around to slip my arms into the sleeves, adjusting the lapels as I turned. Ben picked up my purse and phone and handed them to me. I tucked my cell phone into my pocket and slid my arm through his, smiling up at him as we left the building, and a performance the likes of which Montgomery had never known.

~

Ben's idea of moving on somewhere else, turned out to be a bar across town, only a couple of blocks from where Lily's bar was. I felt a little over-dressed in my glamorous gown, but Ben didn't seem at all bothered by the sideways glances many women shot at him, and one or two guys too. All he did was settle us in a suddenly free booth — these things just seemed to happen for him – and order us drinks, as he loosened his bow tie, letting it hang limply about his neck. He also tweaked open the top button of his shirt. There was something devilishly handsome about him, more so in the low light of the bar.

"Champagne cocktails. Bar Raphael. Mr. Rafferty, you do know how to show a girl a good time," I told him, leaning in so I didn't have to yell. Really, yelling couldn't be any further from unsexy, and I was doing my best. Also, I had to throw in the bar name just to tell my sanctioned stalkers-slash-colleagues where I was, in the event they were roaming around looking for me.

Honestly, it was like knowing my dad was waiting outside, ready to leap in the moment our kissing moved beyond the peck on the cheek stage. I tried to recall if that ever happened. Maybe two uncles, several cousins, my brother, Daniel, and one time, Grandma O'Shaughnessy, when she visited — shudder — but never my dad. He just wasn't fast enough to catch me.

"Yes, I do," Ben agreed, with a sexy wink.

"Do you think they caught the guy yet?" I asked, toying with the stem of my glass.

"The guy?"

"The thief?" I reminded him. How could he forget?

Ben shrugged. "Who knows? Maybe it was Claudia all along." He smiled and raised his eyebrows with a suggestive flicker.

"Oh really? You think she masterminded the whole thing?" I was feigning interest. Not that it was hard; any perspective on how the thief could get away with a theft like that in a crowded room was intriguing.

"I wouldn't be surprised."

"I think we'll have to disagree. I think it was a criminal mastermind." I sipped my drink. Delicious. I would miss cocktails with Lily for the forthcoming months. Perhaps Ben would... no, I couldn't think like that. Even if Ben were off the hook, I still couldn't date him. Everything about me was a lie, designed to lure him. Once he knew the truth, it would be over. Besides, a third man in my confused mind? No.

"In Montgomery? Do criminal masterminds take the time to come out here?"

I thought about all the cases I worked so far, ever since the day I slipped in the blood of my dead boss's corpse. "You'd be surprised," I told him, "at what happens in Montgomery."

Ben leaned in, close enough that I could smell his shower gel. "Now you sound like a woman with secrets."

I pressed a finger to the center of my chest, coincidentally tapping the top of my cleavage. Ben's gaze drifted down and lingered. I bet that was a coincidence too. "Woman of mystery."

"Maybe I should be suspicious. Perhaps you are the great jewel thief of the night," Ben teased. He took a sip of his cocktail and placed his glass on the table. A bead of liquid lingered on his lower lip and I concentrated hard, restraining myself from leaning over to lick it off.

Then I leaned in and pressed my lips to his.

What? Willpower isn't my strong point. It's not even in my top five strong points.

Before I could pull away, Ben's palm rested against the back of my head and he pulled me closer. I slid further around the velvet banquet table until our thighs bumped together. His other arm encircled me. My hands brushed over his shoulders and around his neck and my tongue meshed with his. His hand stroked the back of my neck, grazing the clasp of my necklace, which, unfortunately, reminded me why I was here. This wasn't a date. This was all a ruse. Ben might be a millionaire, but I was not the heiress he thought I was. No matter how attractive and charming, he was still a suspect until someone said otherwise. No matter how good he kissed, or that he lit a fire in my belly, this was going nowhere.

I pulled away, gently. His hand remained on the back of my neck as his eyes burned into mine.

Maybe I should just have one more little kiss?

Just to make sure.

I blinked. No. I had to be professional. I had to... Oops! Was Ben kissing me again? Damn, no one could blame me for this one!

"Mmm," I murmured as we drifted apart one million fantastic minutes later. Ben's thumb stroked the nape of my neck, playing with the catch of my necklace...

My necklace.

Where was Ben when Claudia's necklace was stolen

from her throat?

I was certain that he was standing next to me, but now when I thought about it... I just couldn't be sure. We weren't holding hands, or standing with linked arms. In the dark and distraction caused by the bubble of panic, he could easily have slipped away, and returned just as the lights came back on.

Yes, Ben had ample opportunity to steal Claudia's jewels. At least, he had as much opportunity as Lord Justin, or anyone else in the room who was near her.

What if I'd gotten it wrong? What if I sent Solomon and Delgado after the wrong guy while I played tongue tickle with the real thief?

Thing was, I couldn't possibly work out how Ben could've gotten the necklace out of the venue? He'd been searched, and I had to assume thoroughly by Fletcher, though he didn't appear to be violated in anyway. Eww, I didn't want to pursue that thought. Maybe if Ben was the culprit, he stashed the jewels somewhere, ready to retrieve later. But where? And how?

"Something on your mind?" asked Ben.

"Just my hair," I said, stroking a stray lock behind my ear. Ben laughed, but the tension I felt didn't disappear. Instead of feeling relaxed, I was on high alert; like on the verge of breaking the case. It felt like it was within fingertip's reach and I could grasp it at any moment.

"You seem tense."

"I guess I'm a little tense after the theft. The thief must have real temerity to snatch those jewels from amongst all those people." I shook my head as if to show my real dismay.

"Worried it could have been you?" Ben's finger moved from my clasp, under the slim chain and lifted the pendant. "Pretty little thing," he murmured, but I don't know if he was talking about the necklace or me.

"Isn't everyone worried?" I countered. "Aren't you?"

Ben dropped my pendant and lifted the edge of his

sleeve, flashing a Rolex and a bright pair of gold cufflinks. "I'm good."

"I see that. Speaking of which, did you see anything that happened? Anything at all?"

Ben shook his head. "Nothing. It was too dark. Maybe I should eat more carrots," he joked.

"Maybe." I took a sip of my drink, taking my time, before adding casually, "I thought you were closer to Claudia than I." Ben arched his eyebrow and I backtracked, scrambling for the right words. "I mean, closer geographically, not closer physically. Not that I'm implying you got close to Claudia physically at all."

"She would eat me alive." Ben laughed, politely ignoring my fluster. "I really didn't see a thing. I was next to you the whole time the lights were out. Weren't we holding hands? And I think you were closer to Claudia, but I don't really remember."

"I don't think so..." Actually, I was almost certain we weren't holding hands. I'd just dropped my purse and Ben stooped to pick it up off the floor. I had my wine glass in my other hand.

"Huh. I wonder whose hand I was holding!" Ben laughed at his own joke and I stashed my concern away to address later. If I probed any further, Ben would think I was suspicious, and that would just spoil the evening.

I set my suspicions to one side by the time I caught a movement from the corner of my eye. The shape was too familiar for me to ignore, unlike the many other people who passed our table in the hour or so since we arrived. Casually tossing my hair, I looked around, pretending to be interested in the crowd, until I found him.

Solomon.

He sat a few tables away, side on to us, his back to the wall. I knew he would have surveyed the room already, and I knew he would be looking at us, even if his face pointed to his companion. Opposite him sat Delgado, looking a little uneasy at being in a bar, though a lot suaver since he lost his jacket and tie and simply wore an open necked shirt. Perhaps he wasn't the party type. Solomon, meanwhile, seemed to look at home wherever he was. He had that kind of presence.

With a hint of annoyance, I saw *he* hadn't gone unnoticed. A group of women at the next table were each checking him out. Not that he seemed at all interested, he didn't even seem to see them. He barely even noticed when one stupendously long-legged woman rose from her chair, sashayed towards him, and "accidentally" bumped his chair, pretending to be flustered and apologetic, probably saying that she wasn't watching where she was going or something equally inane. Solomon gave her a disinterested smile, said something, and turned away, dismissing her.

I watched the woman wrinkle her nose in surprise before turning to her friends, and giving them a little shrug. Insensitively, I wondered if she planned to literally throw herself over him on the way back from wherever she was going. The bathroom, I suspected, when she walked past the bar, slipping from view behind a boxy pillar.

I turned my attention back to Solomon, wondering what he said to Delgado, who nodded, turned his head, turned back, and nodded again. I searched the crowd to see their newest source of fascination and found... Oh... What? Maddox. Great. What was he doing here?

The pretty, but annoying, Detective Blake wasn't with him, so I thanked my sweet blessings that it was just the annoying men in my life who seemed to be following me, rather than waiting out in their cars somewhere for me to flip the safe word before charging in to rescue me. The only thing worse would be if my three brothers amazingly decided that tonight Bar Raphael was their new drinking joint. Somehow, I felt safe; between their respective wives, and Lily, and the MPD drinking hole of choice, O'Grady's, I didn't think

Bar Raphael stood a chance.

I started to rise. "Will you excuse me a moment? I have to powder my nose."

Ben got to his feet like the perfect gentleman. "Shall I order more drinks?"

"Please."

His eyes lingered on me for a moment before he turned to get the cocktail waitress's attention. He raised one finger, then slid back into the booth. I walked purposefully towards the bar, turning to look at Ben just as I passed Solomon. Ben's eyes were on me, and he flashed me a confident smile, as he turned to the approaching waitress. I took a right at the bar and headed towards the small corridor leading to the restrooms. Instead of entering, I waited, and a moment later, Solomon was beside me.

"What are you doing in here?" I asked. "You'll blow my cover."

"Rafferty has never seen me, and I doubt he'll recognize Delgado. We're good."

"You don't know that for sure." Solomon gave me an offhand shrug that said he already weighed the situation and thought it was fine. I guess I had to bow to his superior judgment, though a knee in the nuts would have been more satisfying. "Okay, shoot. Why *are* you here?"

"Keeping an eye on my employee," Solomon told me without a trace of interest in my luscious female wiles. Instead, he made it sound difficult to keep his employee "property" safe from harm.

"You could do that outside," I told him.

"Easier inside."

"Why aren't you frisking people back at the ball?"

"Fletcher is, with a couple of my other guys."

"Who? Lucas? I don't think Lucas likes people so much." Aside from his girlfriend, I didn't think Lucas had much interest in people at all. I never saw him outside the office. I suspected he slept there occasionally so he either had a very understanding girlfriend or a very cross one.

"Not Lucas. We expanded the staff."

"We did?" Color me surprised. I knew Solomon had expanded the agency and taken over the floor above, but not that we had any new hires.

"Yep. Fletcher said Lord Justin left ten minutes ago. He was clean."

"Really?" I blinked with surprise. That was annoying. Unless Justin was dumber than he appeared, he didn't steal the jewels and attempt to smuggle them outside on his person. That still didn't mean he didn't do it, I reminded myself, but I wasn't sure if that was because I wanted the thief to be him... or just not to be Ben.

Solomon nodded, but if he were disappointed, he didn't show it. "I'm not convinced. The man was on edge about something. All I know is, so far, we haven't found the jewels and I don't think we will. I stuck a tail on him."

I smiled at the thought of Justin wearing a tail. "That sucks. Did the ruse play out?"

This time, Solomon smiled. "Claudia came through with the paste jewels. She got a big round of applause. That was good thinking."

"She gonna sue?"

"Nope. The dating agency worked something out with her."

"Good."

Solomon nodded his head towards the bar area. "What's your take on Ben Rafferty now?"

I sighed. "I think he might be responsible for the theft. At least, I can't rule him out."

"Fletcher searched him and he was clean," Solomon countered.

"I know, but he could have ditched the necklace somewhere." I didn't dare say Fletcher missed them on

Ben's person. "I just don't think we should rule him out just yet. Nor Justin. Speaking of Ben, I have to get back."

"Don't stay too long. Make your excuses and leave. Tomorrow morning. Ten a.m. My office."

"No problem, Boss." Solomon's eyes narrowed, but I ignored him. Well, I ignored him right after noticing him. Beside the point. "One other thing, why is Maddox here?"

"He wanted to eyeball Rafferty. This is the only opportunity he could get, apparently." Solomon's lack of expression gave nothing away; if he didn't believe Maddox, I couldn't tell.

I didn't ask why Maddox decided to take a closer look on tonight of all nights. I just gave a little sigh. I was pretty certain Maddox could eyeball him from afar. I was also pretty certain Solomon could too. Something told me Ben's devilish good looks had a whole lot to do with them both crashing my date much more than the idea that Ben was a suspect. After all, Solomon's man cleared him, even if my intuition gave me the annoying, niggling feeling otherwise. I wanted to rule Ben out, but I couldn't. It was frustrating.

"I hope he enjoys his eyeballing. I'm heading back for another cocktail." I made to move past Solomon, but he caught my arm, holding me still. For a moment, he said nothing, just smoldered in the sexiest way possible. He probably didn't even know he was doing it; I think it just came naturally to him. "Remember," he said, leaning down towards me as someone pushed past, "remember this guy is a suspect."

"I'm all over him... it," I assured him, but somehow, the way Solomon narrowed his eyes again, and the way the vein at his temple throbbed, I wasn't sure I picked the right words. He looked like he wanted to say something else, but then the moment passed and I moved away.

Ben had a fresh cocktail waiting at the table for me

along with an array of witty observations about the people around us. We talked and laughed, and flirted for close to another hour before I fake-yawned. I told him I had to head home for my beauty sleep and to deposit the diamonds in the safe.

"Do you have plans tomorrow?" he asked me.

I gave a noncommittal shrug. "A few things to do. Maybe I could call you?" I added.

Ben nodded. "I'll wait by the phone."

"The phone that sits in your pocket?" I teased.

"Oh, you got me. The very same phone that I just called my driver on. C'mon, Cinderella, I'll take you home before you turn into a pumpkin."

Funny thing was, he didn't know just how close to the truth his fairy tale analogy really was. So, I might not turn into a pumpkin, but the prince was definitely depositing me at a castle that wasn't mine, and my jewels and clothes would be returned, leaving me in... well, a really nice pair of jeans, actually. I certainly wasn't reduced to rags just yet. I wondered if and when I returned the jewelry to Solomon... would that make him my fairy godmother? The thought made me chuckle to myself.

"Thank you, Prince Ben," I said, linking my arm in his as we made our way towards his waiting car. "Whatever would I do without you?"

"Kiss frogs?" Ben quipped and we laughed.

We were silent on the way "home," and I caught a glimpse of Delgado once, in his car, just as we exited our car, and Ben walked me to "my" door. He left the car idling at the curb as he stooped to kiss me goodnight and it was the kind of kiss girls dream of. Full lips, gentle nibbles, just the right amount of tongue, and the warmest hands slipping inside my coat to caress my back through my thin gown. Then he was gone, leaving me light-headed and breathless on the porch.

How I stumbled inside, I didn't know.

Fifteen minutes later, and I was changed into Cinderella's true clothes; the borrowed ones neatly folded and left on the couch, along with the jewelry. I figured Solomon would see them on the cameras and collect them later. Meanwhile, I planned to go home to my own bed, my head still spinning with the evening, the theft, and the kisses.

Unfortunately, when I opened the door, my purse and keys in hand, I walked straight into Maddox. He caught me, his hands pausing on my upper arms for the briefest of moments.

"Hey," I started, then stopped, uncertain of myself.

"I came to check on you."

Oh, really? Suddenly, I was number one priority? "I'm fine. Heading home."

"Back to reality, huh?"

"Looks that way to me."

"You want me to give you a ride?"

"No, I'm good. Thanks, anyway."

"This Ben guy..."

"Gone home," I told Maddox and he nodded.

"Where's your boss?" he asked.

I nodded towards the soft light coming from Solomon's house as we walked down the steps and onto the sidewalk. "Home?" I guessed, but I couldn't be sure. Maybe it was his lady friend waiting for him? I looked around for Solomon's car, and spotted it parking on the street. It wasn't there when I arrived. Maybe he was home after all. Delgado was definitely gone, probably following Ben. "So... it's been a long night, Maddox. I need to head home to sleep. I'm meeting Solomon tomorrow at the agency."

"I heard. I'll be there."

I beeped open my car and reached down for the door handle. The light pinged on inside. "Good night, Adam," I called, as I climbed inside.

He raised a hand, his palm flat, and the street lamp

illuminated him like he was a ghost. "'Night, Lexi."

I noticed Maddox's vehicle behind me all the way home. He waited until I entered my building, even idling at the curb before he pulled a U-turn and left. A part of me thought it was nice that he made sure I got home safely; another part of me wondered why he didn't just leave me to get on with it, like Solomon. Another part of me wondered what I liked best: having my independence trampled on, or just expected. And another part of me, a much more pressing part, wondered why I was devoting anymore brain time to the utter confusion that was Maddox, Solomon... and my suspect, Ben Rafferty. Hottie, damn good kisser, and back on the list as potential jewel thief.

Wow, that made him sound really interesting; far more so than the word "millionaire" implied. No wonder good girls went for bad boys.

CHAPTER FIFTEEN

"You wanna go on a stakeout?" I asked Lily when she answered her door. I didn't really expect her to say yes. Lily met with suppliers all of yesterday, according to her late night text, then had dinner with Jord so hers was a later night than mine. But I knew she loved a stakeout, and I knew she'd want to know why she missed it, which was the only reason I waited on her welcome mat with two travel cups in my hands.

She yawned wide, clamped a hand over her mouth and ran one hand through her untidy pile of hair. Clearly, I'd just gotten her out of bed. Oops. I checked my watch. Six-fifteen. Double oops. Lily was never a morning person. On the other hand, waking her up early was good preparation for motherhood. I deserved a medal.

"Right now?" she yawned.

"Yeah. Mrs. Schubert called and said the weird noises started at five a.m. and she swears this time, she heard a woman screaming."

"Yikes."

"Pull on your Action Woman panties and let's go."

"I hate the word 'panties'."

I gave her a sympathetic nod. "I hate the word 'moist'."

Lily shuddered. "I don't even want to go into why those two words belong together."

"I have absolutely no idea what you mean," I lied, holding a travel mug out to her.

"You made me coffee?" The hope in Lily's voice seared through me. It must have been a very long time since she had any caffeine. At least a couple of months since her health kick started. I hated to burst her bubble.

"Nope. It's a healthy, veggie shake. Vitamins and... stuff."

"Thank you. So sweet." Lily brightened when she saw the second cup I held. "You're having a health shake too?"

"Shut. Up!" I recoiled. "I got coffee. That shake reeks. Now, are you coming or what? Do I have to stake out this psycho on my own?"

"I'm coming."

"Cool. I'll tell you about my latest dating disaster on the way."

"Oh, thank God. I was afraid you'd given up on all that. Give me ten minutes. Do not leave without me," Lily demanded before shutting the door.

Lily didn't seem her usual self on our drive over to my dream house-slash-neighborhood-serial-killer-stakeout, but I figured she was tired. So I talked away, telling her about my suspicions surrounding Ben, and how I thought he might be the thief. It was disappointing because it actually made him the least date-able of the undate-ables. Dating anyone was hard enough when it was a charade, but having two former lovers watching over me was unendurable.

"Imagine if you humped Ben," chipped in Lily, playing with the recline function on the passenger seat, "it would have been like a triple whammy in one room."

"I don't think I could deal with that. I think that's just asking for trouble."

Lily snorted. "Yeah. You *never* do that." She yawned again. "Sorry. Didn't get a lot of sleep."

"Jord? I asked, trying not to wince.

"No. I didn't feel well."

"Catching a psycho will make you feel better. Here we are," I said, her last comment sliding past as I pulled up several houses away from Aidan Marsh's home. This time, we were at the other end of the road from where we staked out previously. The last thing we needed was an early morning surprise from Maddox. Although, come to think of it, I used to enjoy them. If I really thought about it when I took the call from the Schuberts, I would have suggested taking Lily's car to make sure we weren't recognized. Now I thought about it, and as I looked over, Lily appeared kind of green and hadn't touched her shake. "Are you okay?" I asked.

"Just tired and kind of queasy. I think I ate something bad last night. Jord and I went out to dinner at that Japanese place. The one you don't like."

"What did you eat?"

"A lot of seafood. It was good, but this morning, I'm re-evaluating that."

"Do you think you have food poisoning?"

"Maybe. I don't feel like I'm going to be sick, just... queasy." She wrapped her arms around her stomach and leaned back, setting her face stoically.

"Want me to take you home?"

"No, let's watch for this guy,. It'll take my mind off feeling crappy."

We waited quietly for twenty minutes before I saw the front door open. A man exited with a large, brown Labrador at his side. "That's our guy," I told Lily.

"The one walking towards us?"

"Yep. Um, look busy." We both tried to find

195

something to do.

"If you were a guy, we could make out," suggested Lily.

"Why am I the guy? Anyway, I wouldn't make out with someone who looks as green as you. Besides, it's too early in the morning for the make-out ruse. Plus, we could be gay. We could make out anyway. Not that I want to," I added.

"Me neither."

"Hey, not that it matters now," I told her just as Aidan Marsh passed by the car without giving us a second look. The dog didn't either. Our intense conversation about what we could be doing ended up being the perfect cover, which was a stroke of luck. I wasn't sure it would fly, however, when he came back. I mean, what the hell could we be talking about so long, and so early?

"Are we going to follow him?"

"Too obvious in the car, and it's too quiet to follow him on foot."

"Oh, good," said Lily, reclining the seat a little further back. She exhaled deeply and closed her eyes.

I watched her for a few seconds. Lily was rarely unwell, and it always showed when she was. "Are you sure you're okay?" I asked again. "I could take you home. I don't mind. Maybe you need to go back to bed."

"No, really, I'm fine."

"Okay." I drummed my fingers on the wheel, wondering how I could speed up the stakeout. There wasn't a lot we could do while Aidan walked his dog and left his house empty. At least... we thought it was empty. "Do you think you can keep an eye out for a few minutes in case Marsh comes back?"

Lily opened one eye. "Sure. Where will you be?"

"Snooping around his yard and peeking in his windows."

"Subtle."

"I try. No point pretending it's something it's not. Call me on my cell phone the minute you see him. I'll be as fast as I can."

"Okay. Hey, Lexi?"

"What?"

"Good job he's not walking a Chihuahua. You might have time enough to find his victim while he walks that slobbering mutt."

I forgot a victim might be inside. It seemed a huge oversight on my part. "I thought the dog was cute," I said.

"I bet it would eat you as soon as lick you. He probably bred it to dispose of his victims. Labradors eat anything. I saw it on Animal Planet."

With the charming thoughts of my imminent death and body disposal, I pulled a face, stuck my tongue out at Lily, and exited the car, patting my rear pocket to make sure my cell phone was snugly against my butt. Taking a quick look around, I shut the door quietly, There was no one else on the street. I guessed we were a little too early for the school and work crowd, but they would soon appear, giving us some extra cover.

Hightailing it over to the house, I walked quickly along the path to the door. The half moon window over the door was too high for me to see through, even on tiptoes. The wooden blinds hung closed at what I assumed were the living room windows, so I ignored them and walked around the side. I was just beyond the fence of the yellow bungalow. The six-foot high fence blocked my way to the backyard. I tried the door in the middle, but it was locked with a padlock as thick and unwieldy as the frame. Ugh. What was it with potential suspects? Why couldn't they make anything easy? I mean, we didn't catch a thief last night, and this morning, I couldn't even get into this guy's yard. You would have thought he might like to catch someone entering, especially with people becoming ever savvier at evading murderers today.

I stood back and wished for life to cut me a break. Then I spied a large planter sitting at a right angle to the house and fence, a half-dead palm inside. I stood on the lip and grabbed the top of the fence until I could see over. Not that there was much to see. A couple of ragged dog toys, a patch of neat lawn, patio, and beyond a thick tree, some kind of outbuilding. Not a garage, but perhaps, a studio.

Before I could think better of it, I pulled hard on the top of the fence and launched myself upwards, my feet scrabbling against the panel until I could swing a leg over. For a moment, perched on the top, I was thinking it was an awful long way down. Then I slung my other leg over and dropped, landing in a crouch, and glad I was wearing old jeans and a fitted jersey jacket. I was so impressed with myself, I kind of wished someone filmed my *Nikita* moment.

Walking around the corner of the house cautiously, I found the garden as empty as I expected. The lawn was neat and boxy without any suspicious, newly-dug or raised "flower beds," although the patio appeared new. I looked in the kitchen window and saw relatively clean countertops with the usual appliances: toaster and coffee pot, as well as a pile of dirty dishes in the sink. So far, a very single man home. Two dog bowls were on the floor next to the dishwasher and a bag of doggie treats sat on the countertop. There was probably enough to last a Chihuahua its entire life, but I figured the Labrador probably ate that much in a week. I tried the door handle. Locked.

Moving along the side of the house, I came to French doors that opened onto the patio. These were drapeless too, and inside was a dining room: just four chairs and a table, beside several bookcases, heaving with books. No stereo or TV. The decor may have been minimal, but the quality of the furniture was outstanding, the kinds of things my sister would like. High-end rustic, if there were such a thing. Definitely not the black leather and chrome one would expect of a single man, though come to think of it, that wasn't Maddox's or Solomon's style either. Maybe single men were getting better at the furnishings thing? I paid mental homage to *Queer Eye for the Straight Guy* and all the reruns that must have inspired him. Turning away from the house, I started towards the building at the end of the garden.

Studio or garage? Both had plenty of places for hiding victims, especially as I didn't see any hint of a basement. No outside stairs or entry, and absent any windows, I wasn't certain there was one at all.

I jogged across the lawn and pressed my face against the single window to the studio. Disappointingly, instead of finding a tied-up victim, it turned out to be less torture studio and more storage cabin. Tables, chairs, bookcases, and side tables all jostled for space. Some were covered with dust cloths, while others were not. I wondered why he needed so much furniture, or if he inherited it and didn't know where else to put it. Also, I couldn't smell anything gross, so I was pretty certain nothing was decomposing inside. I didn't relish the moment that I'd have to ask Garrett exactly how soon a dead body starts to stink.

That left the attached garage. I gave my phone a quick check - nothing - and jogged back to the house, all the while checking to see if I left any footprints in the dry grass. None. Wow, I really was a ninja! Rounding the house, away from where I entered, I walked quickly towards the garage. It was connected to the house and I guessed there must be an internal door. There wasn't a door leading from the garage to the garden, but there was a picture window that spanned the width of the wall. It was, mercifully, uncovered, allowing me to peek inside.

The garage was set up as a workshop. One wall

displayed tools, everything from hammers to screwdrivers to saws, while the floor held various other mechanical equipment. Vises, electric saws... a throne-like chair with thick leather restraints to secure the arms and the neck. I dropped my eyes. The same restraints were positioned for the ankles too.

Holy guacamole.

I gulped and pressed a hand to my mouth, my stomach doing a little flip at the sight. Pooling at the base of the chair was something ominously dark that stained the concrete floor.

When my phone started to vibrate in my back pocket, I leapt higher than an Olympic pole-vaulter. Well, my stomach did anyway. I checked the screen, just in case it was my mom being inopportune, but it was Lily. There was only one reason she would call: our target was nearing home and I had to get out of there.

I started to make for the way I came in, but a noise at the gate stopped me. Hearing the sound of the padlock snapping undone, I spun around and jogged back to the garage, looking for an escape route. No plant pots here, just the thick tube of rain guttering. Grasping it, I stuck my toe onto the thicker edge of the first join and lifted myself, scrambling up the eight feet onto the flat roof, before rolling onto my back just as a dog barked below.

With my heart pounding, I flipped onto my hands and knees, staying low, and crawled to the front of the garage. I prayed to anything that could hear me not to let me fall through the roof and be the next restrained victim of that chair. At the roof edge, I inched forward and looked down at the sheer drop onto the driveway. I had no other choice. Swinging one leg over, then the other, I rolled onto my stomach, pushed with my arms, and launched myself off the garage roof.

Two minutes later, I was back in the driver's seat. Of my car, that is, certainly not of my life. I wasn't even sure I had a license for that.

"You should have seen yourself," said Lily. "That was so cool."

"I think I grazed my elbow," I moaned, twisting my arm to take a look. Sure enough, a small rip in the fabric proved a scrape was evident. It was covered in dust and dirt, "But it was cool," I conceded.

"What did you find? Anything?" Lily wanted to know.

I sucked in a breath. "A big problem. I think the Schuberts are right. Something weird is going on in there. There was a huge chair that looked like a throne with scary-looking restraints; and I think I saw blood on the floor!"

"Ohmigod! You could have been killed!"

"Only if he caught me, which he didn't. Thanks for the thirty-second warning."

Lily ignored my sarcasm. "So... what now? Are you going to call the police?"

"Not without a body, and I definitely didn't see one. I don't think they'll raid the place just because of that scary chair."

"Yep, if that were the case, there would be the bad furnishing police," agreed Lily. She pressed a hand to her stomach and closed her eyes again. "Half the town would be in trouble."

"No more stakeout today," I decided. Then, sounding suspiciously like my mother, I added, "You're going home to bed and I'm going to the office. I have a thief to catch before I take out this killer so I can buy my house."

"There you go, taking charge. Lexi Graves, super PI." Lily buckled her seatbelt and gave me a weak smile, but didn't talk the rest of the way home. That was more worrying than the waxy pallor of her skin.

~

I made sure Lily went to bed, and took the time to text message Jord, even though Lily insisted there was no need. Then I headed upstairs to shower, change into something clean, and get ready for work.

With just our team present and Maddox, we reconvened in the boardroom, rather than using the whole office. I would have liked to appear more professional and arrive to work early, but as it happened, I had a wardrobe crisis and arrived last. I was just in time to snag the last sugar donut and a lukewarm cup of coffee.

Solomon perused an opened file in front of him; Delgado and Fletcher were checking through a stack of photographs; and Lucas was reading a comic. None seemed at all perturbed at how unprofessional they looked. All of a sudden, my clothing choice seemed like a really important decision, and I was glad I took the time to search out the powder blue, cowl neck top I wore today, along with indigo skinny jeans and super-high heels. No one could say I wasn't professional. By the way Maddox looked at me, he could say a lot of things, but nothing that I was ready to hear. I wasn't sure when, or if, that date would ever happen, a thought which filled me with sadness.

"So, where are we now?" I asked, taking the chair between Delgado and Lucas. I contemplated plucking the comic from Lucas's hands and tossing it in the trash, but I worried he would hack my Facebook in retaliation.

"Square one," said Solomon, without looking up.

"Better than zero," I quipped, but Solomon didn't laugh. Clearly, someone got out of the wrong side of bed this morning. Maybe his company blocked his path. I kept my face even, but gave him a Botox death stare. Yep, one that no one else could see. I settled down to munch my donut sullenly while waiting for the meeting to begin. Just as I began to mentally sing "I know a song that will get on your nerves," Solomon looked up at last, casting a glance around the room as I pretended not to notice his bulging bicep in his short-sleeved t-shirt.

"Every guest was searched last night and they all

came up clean," he informed us. It didn't surprise me. They would have been celebrating if they found Claudia's necklace. "I sent a cleaning crew, but we didn't find the necklace in the building, so we have to assume it got out some other way. There are several windows from where it could have been thrown and retrieved later."

"Risky," said Delgado. "Lots of groping in the dark for an itty, bitty necklace."

Solomon nodded. "I agree. Any other suggestions?"

We looked at each other. Nope. Some detectives we were.

"I don't agree. It was a huge piece. Maybe someone was waiting. An accomplice could have caught it," I suggested, surreptitiously licking my fingers because a waste of sugar was a damn waste.

Solomon gave a slow nod. "Possible. Delgado, go with Lucas, and see what cameras are around the building. Lucas, see if you can access their feeds and identify anyone. Check out any vehicles in the area. I want to know whom they belong to."

"You want me to go outside?" asked Lucas. He folded the comic, appearing worried.

"You've done it before," deadpanned Solomon.

"I don't like it. I like my computer."

Solomon pointed to the door. "Go."

Delgado got up, trying to hide a laugh behind a cough, and Lucas slunk after him. He still had the comic.

"Hold up," I said and they paused, waiting for Solomon's response to me. "Maybe we're going about this all wrong. Instead of trying to figure out how the necklace got out, maybe we should set up another opportunity for the thief. After all, if it's gone, it's gone."

Solomon inclined his head towards the chairs and Lucas hurried back to his, clearly relieved he would not to be heading into the big, wide world. I wasn't sure what his problem was. He had to get to and from the office somehow. Though now that I thought about it, perhaps I should check the basement for tunnels. Also: it must be really frustrating to be his girlfriend, unless she was agoraphobic.

I continued, "We're down to two suspects: Ben and Justin. It could be either one of them, and we're wasting time searching camera feeds and dumpster diving. Let's set them up instead. Let's set them up with a job so tempting, they can't possibly resist it. Last night's theft could have just been a crime of opportunity. This one won't be. So far, the thefts have been jewels. The thief will want this. One of them will turn up and we'll be waiting, then blam!"

"I like her idea better," said Lucas.

Solomon leaned back in his chair, his face thoughtful. "It's another shot in the dark," he said finally. "But it's as good a shot as searching camera feeds and dumpster diving."

"It might be the only shot we get," I told him. "We don't know how long the thief is going to stay around. He could be gone tomorrow. I've dated both these guys, and I can't get a definitive take on which one it is. Justin is hinky for sure, but I can't count Ben out."

"What does your gut tell you?" asked Delgado, turning from me to Solomon. "Boss?"

"Ben. He's too good to be true," I said, with a sinking feeling, at the same time Solomon answered, "Justin. Sleaze."

I threw my hands upwards. "See my point?"

Solomon smiled and shook his head. "Yeah, I do. Okay, people, heads together. I still want you and Lucas to check the area," he told Delgado, ignoring Lucas's frustrated sigh as he rose again. "But we'll run with Lexi's idea too. The rest of you have got one hour to come up with the best damn ruse you can, one that will make this thief really eager. One he can't resist."

CHAPTER SIXTEEN

As it turned out, setting up the suspects was easy. Once we fine-tuned the details of the ruse, placing jewels as the thief's primary interest this time around, it was simply a case of making a couple of calls.

While Solomon and company listened in, I talked to Ben first, then Justin; each time exclaiming how excited I was at the jeweler's visit to my home that day. "I just can't decide," I twittered, catching myself twirling a lock of hair around my finger, and quickly releasing it, "between the diamond ring or the pendant. There are some rings I like too. Maybe I should get them all? Anyway, the jeweler knows I love his pieces, and as a valued customer, he's letting me keep all of them overnight! He said the safe in the living room is fine, so long as I'm careful. I mean, duh! Of course, I'll be careful with five million dollars in diamonds! I'm just going to try them on, play princess, and then go out with my girlfriends."

"So?" I asked Solomon after hanging up on an overexcited-sounding Justin. "How'd I do?"

He relaxed in his chair. "Great. You did great."

"They didn't seem all that interested in the jewels. Ben definitely was not; Justin got a little excited, but maybe he just likes shopping?"

"They wouldn't want to set off any alarm bells. Notice how they just let you prattle on until the subject changed. One of them knows everything required to pull off a robbery. The value, the pieces, where to find them, and your scheduled movements. They also know there's a time limit on stealing them, since they'll be gone tomorrow. It's a big haul."

It sure was. The real question, however, remained, was it good enough to work? Or too risky? I guessed it depended on other factors we couldn't determine: how smart the thief was, and whether he had the *cojones* to pull off the opportune job.

"I liked the bit about the unset diamonds," Solomon added. "Nice touch."

"Thank you."

"If our guy is getting jumpy, or getting ready to put his exit strategy in play, this could be his big ticket out of town," said Delgado. He toyed with the headset before dropping it onto the table. I wondered if he enjoyed listening in. Maybe he was getting some tips for my sister's upcoming birthday? Somehow, I doubted he could afford the prices we were talking, but I got the impression he had good taste and liked bringing her gifts. There was no time like the present - no pun intended - to meddle. I mean, find out.

"Do you know it's my sister's birthday soon?" I whispered to him as Solomon and Lucas huddled their heads together, conferring on something about the digital files database. Yawn.

"Yeah. We're taking Victoria to a cabin at Lake Pearce. Serena wants to go hiking and have a picnic."

My mouth dropped open. "Say what?"

"Cabin, hiking, picnic," replied Delgado, more

succinctly.

"Yeah, I got that. I just don't get the bit about my sister doing all that." Serena thought "roughing it" was a lower thread count than eight hundred on the sheets of her hotel suite's queen size bed.

Delgado shrugged. "It was her idea. And Victoria will be exposed to nature."

"Nature?" I mumbled, still taken aback.

"What's wrong with you today?"

"Nothing. I just... Cabin? Hiking? You *have met* Serena?"

"Yep. I was going to drive them to the city, stay in a hotel, and take in a gallery; but she said she had plenty of the fancy stuff with her jerk of an ex-husband, and wanted to play it low-key. We booked the cabin a month ago, and went shopping for one of those papoose things to carry Victoria." Delgado's eyes took on a dreamy, glazed expression. I never expected him to be the kind of guy to fantasize about having a family, but it was definitely heart-warming to see.

My one big worry about camping and hiking was that serial killers could be lurking behind any tree - well, you never know, right? But I figured if there was anyone I'd feel safe hiking with, it would be Delgado. He could carry my niece in the papoose, along with a picnic basket, and, using his free hand, shoot any threat before it ever manifested. Also: I thought it was kind of awesome that he was taking such a family-style vacation with my sister and her daughter. He seemed to absolutely adore them both, which was more than I could say for her ex-husband, who visited Victoria exactly twice since the divorce. As a result, for the next five minutes, Delgado would be my number one colleague, mostly because Serena was a ton less annoying ever since she got divorced and started boinking my scariest co-worker.

"You two done talking vacations?" asked Solomon.

"You're just jealous. You don't vacation," I told him. Delgado picked up a file, ignoring our boss.

"I do. I just don't talk about it at work."

"Since when do we have rules on what subjects we can talk about at work?"

"Since when do you talk back to the boss?"

"Since when did you think that question wasn't stupid?" I shot back. Delgado snorted. I added an extra minute of time for him. "Where do you vacation anyway?"

Rolling his eyes, Solomon shook his head, and fortunately for him, gave up. "Let's gather our thoughts and get the surveillance in place. Lucas, you can set up at my house to monitor the video feeds in Lexi's 'home'," he said, adding air quotation marks. That was probably so Lucas didn't try to set up the video in my actual apartment. If he did, I would have to kill him, and I didn't want to make a mess. "Lexi, it's better if you're not in the house while we wait to see if the suspect turns up."

"I want to be there at the bust," I told them. "I'm not missing out. It was my idea!"

"You'll be doing surveillance down the street," Solomon continued. "You take the front. Fletcher can take the back."

"Why? Shouldn't I take the back? Ben and Justin both know me."

"The rear of the house has poor lighting, and Fletcher has plenty of experience in all things that go boom with the CIA. It makes sense to put him in the dangerous spot, and you in the one that's least so."

"Works for me," I decided, rather than arguing I was in the army and thus, ready for anything. While that was kind of accurate, it wasn't exactly the full truth. The army thing lasted a few weeks, but it did earn me kudos around the office, so long as I didn't reveal any of the details. Most of all, getting stabbed or chloroformed would totally ruin my day, and I wasn't sure my insurance would pay out any more. Fletcher no doubt relished the opportunity to take out a bad dude. It would probably make his day. Some people had an odd sense of fun. But I didn't actually want to fight Ben or Justin. I just wanted to cuff one of them and hand them over to MPD. Then maybe rub Maddox's nose in it a little bit, before celebrating.

"Great," said Solomon. I ignored the sarcasm in his voice and waved him on to continue.

"Lexi, you take the first four-hour shift, seven to eleven. Delgado, you take eleven to three. Flaherty will relieve Fletcher for the second shift. I'll get a couple of the new guys to work shifts too. We'll have the front and back covered at all times. Hopefully, we'll be done by morning."

"Where will you be?" I asked.

"Everywhere," said Solomon, giving me a little shiver of something I probably shouldn't have gotten a thrill about. "Go home and get some rest. Lexi, you need to be seen in the Chilton house today, so maybe you want to rest up there before you start your shift."

"Sure thing, I'll grab a couple of items from my apartment and head over there now. Hey, what if he comes in early to hide there before I supposedly go out?" I froze where I stood and watched the others eyeing each other. Clearly, that idea didn't occur to anyone. "I'm not taking a snooze if someone is hiding in the closet," I told them. "That's how urban legends start."

Solomon picked up the desk phone and punched in a number. "Send someone to sweep the Chilton house," he told the person on the other line. "Yes, now. My team is due over soon. Get a guy on the front and one on the back until I relieve them." He put the phone down. I waited, keeping my face expressionless so he couldn't see if I were impressed, or riveted with curiosity over whom he just called. The guys upstairs? So much for snoozing, I'd definitely be looking outside just to see if I could catch a glimpse of them.

Solomon dismissed me with a hand wave. It made me think perhaps he wasn't too impressed with my casual little wave when I was about to leave before. Seeing I didn't move, Solomon looked up. "Go," he said.

"On it, Boss." I nodded to my colleagues and hightailed it out. It wasn't until I got to the parking lot that I realized Solomon not only eradicated the danger by placing me on watch at the front of the house, but also assigned me with the least risky shift of all. I didn't know if it were because I was the newest team member, and therefore kept in all low-risk assignments, or because Solomon was overly protective. Maybe it was both. I couldn't decide if it was sweet or insulting, so instead, I focused on catching the thief and being home in time for a movie and ice cream; or if it was really late, cocktails and dancing on tables.

~

By the time I got to the Chilton house, Solomon had sent a short text: "Sweep complete. Safe." Not exactly chatty, but it confirmed the most important things... or did it?

"Check under beds?" I texted.

"Yes. Thief sleeping," came the next message.

"Thrilled," I replied.

"7 PM. Don't oversleep. Eat," instructed Solomon.

"Yes, Boss," I said to the phone. I parked my car several houses away, ready for the stakeout later, and went inside, casually looking around just in case any PI-type men were lurking there. None. The street was empty. Damn. I looked up at Solomon's living room window as I took the first step to mine, and saw a woman move across the room. The mystery guest. Great, now I could think about her while trying to chill out next door.

The house was quiet as I stepped inside, no obvious

signs of anyone else having been here. All the same, it gave me goose bumps to walk around it, knowing someone was almost certainly figuring out how to break into it later, not to mention the people watching over it outside. Speaking of whom... I went upstairs and first peeked out the front, then the rear windows. Nothing. I repeated this several times and only once saw something I actually wanted to see: the guy from Not Wong Chinese arriving with my dinner. Handing him his money, I took another look around from the doorstep and retreated inside. I ate my meal at the bar in the kitchen, while my curiosity gnawed at me. I took another look from the living room window. Where were Solomon's men hiding?

The ringing of my cell phone made me jump so high, I nearly threw my egg roll into the light fixture. "Boss?" I said upon answering.

"Stay away from the windows," he commanded. "No one looks out windows that much. My guys complained."

"I was looking for the takeout guy."

"For three hours?"

"I was really hungry."

"You only placed the call half an hour ago."

I looked up at the discreet camera hidden on the living room bookshelf. Of course, Lucas was probably already next door, monitoring the feed. "Okay, you got me. Where are these guys hiding?"

Solomon paused, and I pictured him smiling. "Obviously, in really good places," he said. "Get some rest. I don't want you falling asleep on the job."

"Do I ever?" I started to ask, but he was gone, so I took his advice. I finished dinner, washed my knife and fork, and threw the cartons in the kitchen trash, though finding the trash was actually quite a feat. Solomon texted me and told me it was in a concealed panel, after Lucas probably watched me scour the kitchen for it.

Then I had a nap on the incredibly comfortable couch in the living room. I didn't check for the guys again, but I didn't intend to fall asleep either. When I woke up, I felt utterly refreshed.

After stretching, using the bathroom, and filling my plastic bottle with tap water, I locked up the house and strolled to my car. No one was around, and the street was quiet. I pushed the driver's seat back, and settled in for a long wait, calling Solomon. "I'm here," I told him.

"You're in the VW?"

"Of course. It would be stupid to stake out my fake house in my fake car."

Solomon laughed. "I see you. Keep your head down. If anyone complains about you, you'll have to sweet talk your way out of it. Shouldn't be too hard."

I snorted. "Do you know how many cops I'm related to?"

"Yep. I'm heading out back with Fletcher," he said, catching me off guard, although I didn't know why. I should have expected him to be home. I wondered if they both ate dinner with the mystery woman. Then I wondered why I was so bothered. "Call if you see either suspect."

"Ten-four."

"Do you even know what that means?"

"Duh!" I said, hanging up, although I thought Solomon might have been teasing. Instead of wearing out the car battery, I stuck my earphone jack into my cell phone and set it to play my music. It beat doing nothing. I couldn't read a magazine or a book, in case I missed Ben or Justin, or much else. Surveillance was never sexy. It was really just waiting it out. Beside me, for insurance, was my camera, retrieved from the trunk with a fresh digital card inside, so I could record any suspicious activity. Somehow, I didn't expect much to occur with the early shift. Why would a thief break in during daylight hours? When people might see him? Surely, he would act under cover of darkness, when everyone was asleep.

An hour into my surveillance, I was yawning and craving a coffee. Thirty minutes later, after several frustrating games of Solitaire on my phone, I contemplated downloading a bunch of apps I didn't need. A man walked past, wearing a baseball cap and a leather jacket, holding a bunch of flowers, and I was ready to accuse him of anything just to save me from boredom.

Two hours in, and I waved to Jord, who cruised by in a patrol car. I called my mother and agreed to have dinner on the weekend, then texted several friends, and prank-called Lucas once. I had a really good sulk when I saw Solomon leaving his house, his arm wrapped around the Anastasia's waist as he led her towards his car. From my position, I even saw him lean over to buckle her in before they sped off. Well, I conceded, at least my replacement was hot. If I had to be replaced by someone, it was a damned nice compliment that she was practically a supermodel. All the same, kind of unfair that he dodged his shift, not that I would even ask where he was going. I was not a jealous ex. Or even an ex.

By the time Lily called, I was ready to beat my head against the steering wall from boredom.

"Hey," she said weakly. "I don't feel good."

"Food poisoning hitting hard?"

"I don't think it's that... I think it's..." Sobbing sounded in my ear and Lily sniffed. "My stomach hurts and I don't feel well."

"What's going on?"

"I think it's the baby. Something's not right. I've been in pain since yesterday. I thought maybe it was food poisoning, but I don't think it is. It got worse all day. I tried calling Jord, but he isn't picking up."

"I saw him fifteen minutes ago. He's in a squad car.

He might not have his cell phone with him," I told her.

"I figured. Lexi, I think I need to go to the hospital. I know you're working, but can you come get me?"

I didn't have to think about it. I didn't have to hesitate. In the case of best friend versus job, there could only be one winner. "Yes," I said. "I'll come now." Lily started to cry again. "Sweetie, I'll be right there. Don't panic. It's probably nothing. Alice went to the hospital three times when she was pregnant with Rachel, and everything was fine."

"Do you think so?" she said, her voice edging towards a whimper. Lily rarely got upset, and when she did, there had to be a really good reason.

"Absolutely," I assured her, even though my heart was pounding. "Let me make a couple calls and I'll be right there. Okay? Sit tight until I get there."

"Okay," she murmured before hanging up.

I took a moment to catch my breath and calm myself before calling Delgado. He picked up on the second ring with a gruff, "Hey."

"Hey, Delgado, I'm at the Chilton house and I have a family emergency. I need to leave. Can you take over now?"

"I'm at your sister's place. I'm leaving now anyway, but it'll take me thirty minutes to get there. There was an accident on Century and traffic is backed up. Hold on." There was muffled talking, and I could just about hear my sister asking questions before Delgado came back on. "Serena wants to know what kind of emergency."

"Lily isn't well. I'm going to take her to the hospital."

"Okay. I'll be there soon as I can."

"Thanks, I appreciate it." I called Solomon next, but his phone rang out. I tried twice more, but voicemail didn't click in. For the next few minutes, I tapped my feet on the floor with my hands on the wheel, growing increasingly agitated as I waited. Solomon didn't return my call, leaving me with a problem. I was caught in a crisis of ethics. My friend needed me, but I couldn't leave my post until I was relieved. The moment Lily told me she was in trouble, my interest in catching the thief ended. I wanted to leave now. Also, it was Solomon's own damn fault for not picking up, and the traffic issues on Century weren't my problem either.

I felt torn over what to do, and watched a couple of pedestrians walk past, one of them holding the leash of the tiniest dog I'd ever seen. Leather jacket man came along right after them, and I lifted my camera to get a better look as he paused outside the house. Unfortunately, I could only see the back of his head. There was something familiar about it though. Maybe he was one of the street's residents. The bouquet he held was pretty. He looked like he was getting the courage to give the flowers to someone, which explained why he passed by twice.

I jumped as my cell phone trilled again, and Lily's name flashed onto the screen. Dropping the camera onto the passenger seat, I answered.

"Did you leave yet?" she asked.

"No," I admitted. "But I will. Very soon."

"I think I saw some blood. Lexi, I'm so scared. I tried Jord again, but I got voicemail and my parents are in Brazil. Or Guatemala. I don't know. I thought about calling your mom, but I don't want to upset her..." Lily's voice trailed into a heaving sob.

That was it. I started up the engine and checked the dashboard clock. Twenty minutes until Delgado got here. For the last three and a half hours, barely a single person entered the street, either on foot or in a car. "I'm leaving now," I told her. "Stay on the line, okay? You're going to be okay." I wasn't sure whom I was trying to assure as I pulled onto the quiet street, driving past Solomon's house, then my fake home. I noticed the lamp in the living room was left on. Funny, I thought I switched it off, but it was irrelevant now.

Lily needed me and that was all that mattered.

CHAPTER SEVENTEEN

"Where the hell have you been?" yelled Solomon from across the office the moment I stepped through the agency door, albeit late in the morning. I yawned, narrowing my eyes, and wondering why the hell he wasn't telepathic, and how that could possibly be my fault, before shutting the door.

He waited at the office door, arms folded, as I walked towards him. Clearly, he got a better night's sleep than I because he was wearing black pants, a striped, black-on-black, open-neck shirt and he looked damn good to my tired eyes. I thought about wrapping my arms around him and resting my head on his shoulder, but I was pretty certain he wouldn't call that appropriate employee conduct. We just weren't that huggy an agency. "My office," he said, his voice straining with obvious frustration, while tilting his head inside. Like I couldn't guess.

I stepped through and Solomon banged the door shut behind me. "I called you ten times. Didn't you get my messages? You left your post," he said, moving around me to sit behind his desk, without making any indication for me to sit, but I did anyway.

"I'm sorry." I didn't even think of checking my phone before crawling into bed, or after; but even if I did, I'd probably have ignored the messages.

He raised his eyebrows. "Sorry? Great. Just great. The plan worked, by the way. The house got hit. Unfortunately, no one saw a damn thing!" Solomon leaned back, his jaw set in a firm line. I don't think I ever saw him so angry, or so ready to raise his voice.

"I had an emergency."

"Emergencies don't count when you're on the job!"

"I called Delgado and told him I had to go. I also tried calling you. Where were you? You left, too."

"That was different."

Huh. Well, isn't everything different when a guy is involved? Sure, I was being unfair, but it seemed really unfair to blame me for the job going south when he deserted his post too. At least, I tried to call him. I guess he was just too busy with Anastasia. "This was important. Didn't Delgado tell you where I went? I called him."

"No, we were too busy finding out how the hell we missed our guy. What the hell kind of emergency did you have anyway?"

The fatigue and sadness caught up with me and fat tears prickled the corners of my eyes. In the quiet of the room, I said the words I didn't want to voice. "Lily lost her baby."

Solomon stared at me for a long moment before running his large hand over his short crop of hair. His face softened, the hard lines of anger disappearing. "Shit. She okay?"

I shook my head. "No, not at all. I took her to the hospital and stayed all night. Jord got there at midnight, but I couldn't leave her. We took her home this morning. My mom is with her now."

"You should have called," Solomon said at last; and I came this close to snapping. Didn't he pay attention when I said I tried calling? Didn't he see the missed calls?

"I did. Several times last night. Then, your cell phone wouldn't go through to voicemail. Didn't you see this morning?"

Solomon reached into his pocket. He tossed the phone onto his desk in annoyance. "Fuck! Battery is dead." He rummaged in his desk drawer, pulled out a charger and plugged the phone in to recharge. "Damn it. Obviously our calls missed each other."

I would normally take some satisfaction in my boss screwing up, but today wasn't the day. All the same, it was a relief to know he wasn't infallible. "Yeah, so that was my emergency. I'm really sorry I screwed up," I said, in all sincerity. I wouldn't change a thing though. I'd leave my post again and again. On the plus side, I knew who and what were important to me.

Solomon waved a dismissive hand. "No matter. Lily's more important."

"Yeah." We were both silent for a moment, just breathing while the tension dissipated. I wondered what Solomon thought about it. I remembered Lily was crying when I left her, and I thought I might cry too. "So, what happened at the house?" I asked. "You said the thief took the bait."

"We think he came in through the rear of the house, so you're off the hook on that one. Lucas noticed there was something wrong with the cameras, which must have coincided with Delgado arriving, so he sent Delgado to investigate. He entered, got hit over the head, and while he was down, the thief escaped through the front."

"Oh God. Is he okay?"

"Yeah, he went to the Emergency Room to get checked over and he's fine. No concussion. Man's got the thickest skull I've ever seen, and I mean that as a compliment."

"Did he go for the safe?" I asked. "The thief, that is."

"Looks that way, from what I could see, but he didn't get a chance to open it. Not that he would find anything. We screwed up."

"Not really. We know either Ben or Justin fell for the ruse, and whoever it was, he screwed up too."

"Yeah, but there's a good chance they know now that it *was* a ruse. Your cover's probably blown," Solomon pointed out. "This case is done."

"We don't know that for sure."

"All the same, don't make any contact with either suspect. If they contact you, we'll discuss what to do. Right now, I don't want to take any risks. I'm one man down and I don't want to risk you getting hurt too."

"I'm glad Delgado's okay."

"Me too. He was the last person I expected to see in the ER last night. Your sister took him home to her house."

That was news to me. It was nice of Serena to pick him up. I made a mental note to check in on them both later. "Wait... you were at the ER too?"

"I had to take my sister there. She tripped on the stairs. Sprained her wrist and broke a finger."

"Your sister?" I frowned. "I saw you leave with Anastasia."

"Anastasia *is* my sister."

Holy. Guacamole.

"Anastasia is your sister," I repeated slowly, like a moron.

"You catch on quick," said Solomon. "I'm glad I hired you."

"Your sister. Huh. I thought..."

"You thought what?"

I looked up to see Solomon's quizzical expression. Oh, how embarrassing. I was jealous of not the new woman in Solomon's life but his sister. "Nothing, I didn't realize she was your sister, is all." I shrugged like it didn't matter, but it did. It mattered, although I wasn't sure how, and I resisted being so selfish as to think about me right now.

"My sister is staying for a few weeks until she gets an apartment in the city. She got a job already and she starts soon, so I insisted she stay with me. She was going to help out in the office for a couple weeks, but now she's injured, I told her to rest up."

"That makes sense," I agreed, remembering Solomon had taken care of his sister and brother when their parents passed. Now that she was injured I felt worse for my less than charitable thoughts towards her. "It must hurt."

"She took two painkillers, but said it isn't too bad. Her finger is in a splint and she has an ice pack on her ankle. I'm gonna check in on her soon. You need some time off? You want to take the day off?"

"No, thanks, but I want to keep busy. There isn't much I can do for Lily and she's got Jord and my mom. I don't want to get in the way."

"If you need to leave, tell me. Sometimes family is more important than career," Solomon said, displaying the kind of wisdom I never associated with him before.

"Thanks, but if we don't get this guy, we may never get another chance," I reminded Solomon. Not that he needed reminding; I was pretty certain it was forefront on his mind. "I know this case is important to you."

"It would be good to have MPD owe us a favor. Combining the agency business with local law enforcement would be great for the agency, especially if they tell other districts. I told you from the start, this case isn't about the money. It's about building a network of contacts. Montgomery's a big town, but not that big. The higher value clientele will come from elsewhere. We'll take point here."

"Is that who's paying for the new floor?" I asked, indicating the ceiling.

Solomon deliberately ignored me, which I thought rude because I really wanted to know what was going on up there. The construction work seemed over, judging by the quiet, and I saw several guys and one woman entering the floor. What was going on, however, remained a mystery. "Write up your report for the file, Lexi. And let me know if you get a call."

"How do you know one of them hasn't left town already?"

"I put a tail on both of them this morning."

"Didn't you already have a tail on them?" I asked.

Solomon's shoulders dropped. "Would you believe that both of them gave the guys the slip last night? I've had men all over town looking for them."

"How many slip-ups have we had on this case?" I asked aloud, even though I didn't mean to. I was just thinking it.

"Too freaking many," sighed Solomon. "But not any more. Ben Rafferty and the lord aren't escaping this town without my leave."

"Yes, Boss."

~

I set up office in the boardroom, or the bored room, as I called it today. With my laptop and cell phone sitting idly on the table, all I could do was drum my fingers and hope I hadn't been made. While I waited, Lucas buzzed around like a high-tech worker bee, waiting for the moment my phone rang so he could kick in with his recording equipment.

"Lucas, tell me what's going on upstairs," I said, fixing him with a stare and my straightest, no-nonsense approach.

Lucas halted like a bunny in headlights. "I. Don't. Know."

"Yes, you do!"

"I don't!"

"Oh, come on! I know you do. Solomon and I already had an argument about you leaving to go upstairs to the mystery control room."

Lucas pretended to pout. "I don't like it when Mommy and Daddy fight."

"Then tell me everything." I fixed him with my tell-me-everything stare; the kind that said if he didn't spill all the beans, I would make his life a living hell for the next two weeks, minimum. How I would do that, I didn't know, but neither did he, which was what counted. At that moment, however, when Lucas looked like he might just break under my bluff, my cell phone trilled.

"Thank God," muttered Lucas. We both leaned over to look at the screen.

"More like, thank Ben," I interjected. "Guess my cover isn't blown with him."

"Don't count on it. Give me a second before you answer." Lucas reached for his headphones and hit "Record" on his device. I waited for him to nod, then picked up the phone, hitting "Answer."

"Hey," I cooed down the line, my heart beating fast. Was he calling to say hey, or just to boast how he foiled our plans?

"Hey, sweetheart," said Ben, sounding at ease with the world and not at all like someone who had just committed a crime. "How are you fixed for this evening?"

"No plans. I thought I'd just take it easy after..." I trailed off, remembering that if Ben were the thief, he would know all about the events of the night before. It would be odd if I didn't mention the break-in. It wasn't like I could have missed it. And if he didn't know...

"What's wrong?" Ben asked, his voice turning concerned. "Did something happen?"

Too right, buster, I thought, but maybe it was

nothing to do with him. I felt a little better at that. I said, "Someone broke into my house last night."

"You're kidding me. Are you hurt? Are you okay?" Ben asked, anxiously.

"I'm fine, I was out of the house, so I only found out when I got a call from..." I paused and Lucas mouthed three letters slowly. Right. "MPD. Uh, the police department."

"Why didn't you call me? I would have come straight over. I don't like thinking of you alone in that big house especially after someone broke in."

"Oh no, I didn't want to impose. Besides, nothing was taken and I'm fine."

"What were they looking for?"

"I don't know," I lied, continuing smoothly, "but I guess they got disturbed before they could grab anything. The police think it might have been kids. Maybe they were looking for cash, or something easily pawned."

"I'm glad you're okay." Ben paused. "Why don't I buy you dinner later to take your mind off it? That is, if you're not worried about leaving the house empty. Are you staying there? Or do you prefer to check into a hotel?"

Lucas nodded. I nodded. We both waited, then it occurred to me to speak. "Actually, I am staying at my house and dinner would be wonderful."

"Great. I'll pick you up at seven."

"I'll be waiting."

"And if there's any problems, call me right away, okay? Lexi, I mean it. I don't want you to think you can't call me just because we haven't known each other very long. If you call, I'll be there."

"I really appreciate it, Ben, thank you. Dinner will definitely take my mind off it."

"See you later then, Lexi."

"Bye, Ben." We hung up and I gently placed the

phone on the table. I held my palms up to Lucas and shrugged. "I didn't get the impression he knew anything," I said.

"Kind of keen to get you out of the house," remarked Lucas, hitting "Stop" on his recording equipment.

"Maybe he was just trying to be nice."

Lucas arched one eyebrow. Damn it, I wished I knew how to do that. "Since when are people ever purely nice?"

"I'm always nice!"

"Five minutes ago, you were ready to spit in my coffee if I didn't 'fess up to agency secrets."

I leaned in, my elbows on the table. "So there *are* agency secrets. I knew it."

"Why don't you just ask Solomon?"

I grunted. It wasn't ladylike, but it did reveal my feelings. "He won't tell me anything."

"Maybe you should kiss him again."

I gasped and tripped over my words, making noises that sounded like "Burble burble... well... I never... how dare you... what? Burble."

"Knew it," said Lucas, looking smug. "He looks at you like you're the wave he's ready to ride."

Awesome, but... "What kind of metaphor is that?"

"Who cares? It's accurate."

"He does not look at me like that!"

"He looks at your butt like that."

"Everyone looks at my butt like that."

"I don't."

"You're engaged."

"But not blind."

"You want to check out my ass, geek boy? You wanna surf my ass?" I started to stand; but what I really should have done was look over my shoulder before I opened my big mouth. Solomon chose that precise moment to enter the room. He gave me a look that didn't evoke happy thoughts, and I slid back down into my chair, my ass fully hidden from view and certainly not ready to ride like a wave.

"Progress?" Solomon asked, looking sour.

Lucas spoke while I mentally berated myself. "Ben called. He's taking Lexi out at seven. Seemed to want the house empty."

Solomon inclined his head towards me, his face still expressionless. "That your impression?"

"That we're going out, yes. That he wants the house empty, not sure. He seemed surprised when I said the house was broken into last night. He didn't mention the jewels I was supposed to have."

"Could be just good acting." Solomon shrugged. He was turning back to the door as my phone rang again.

Well, what do you know? "Lord Justin," I said, leaning in to see his name flash on my screen.

Solomon glanced over at Lucas. "You getting this on tape?"

"Yes, Boss."

"Let me know." Solomon left the room, shutting the door quietly behind him. He may not have been able to see my ass, but I got a pretty good look at his as he left. It was damn nice. Droolworthy.

"Your cell's still ringing," said Lucas, dragging me back to the task at hand.

I grabbed the cell phone as he hit "Record" and answered, "Hello?"

Lord Justin's smooth accent floated down the line. "Good morning, my dear. How are you today?"

"Very well, thank you," I replied, wondering if everyone in England talked so politely.

"I thought I might take you to afternoon tea," Lord Justin continued. "Show you a little English hospitality."

"Sounds delightful."

Sounds delightful, mouthed Lucas, who raised one pinky as he pretended to drink tea. I stuck my tongue out at him. Then, doing my country proud, I flipped him the finger.

"Shall I pick you up in an hour?"

"Actually, I'd prefer to meet you. I'm out... shopping right now."

"Any pretty baubles?" Lord Justin asked. My alarm bells rang as Lucas and I raised eyebrows at each other. What an odd inquiry, I decided, and curiously appropriate, after the attempted theft.

"I hoped to purchase some new jewels today, but alas, my house was broken into and I returned the jewels without making a, uh, purchase." Yikes. What was I saying?

"Goodness!" Lord Justin gasped. "What a violation! I trust you're not hurt?"

"Not at all. I was out when the house was burgled. Besides, nothing was taken. It was probably just a bunch of kids."

"The little beasts! The rogues! The audacious youth of today!"

"Um, yeah..."

"I'll protect you, my lady, don't you worry your pretty, little head. Diamonds, did you say?"

"Thanks." I made my excuses while taking down the address, and hung up before he offered to get his sword out.

"Have you heard yourself and your weird imitation of an English accent?" asked Lucas. He flapped one hand and squeaked "Alas! My house!"

I grimaced. "I wasn't trying to do it. It just came out!"

"Of your pretty, little head?" teased Lucas and we both rolled our eyes. "What a dick."

"Yeah, but he did mention the jewels. He even said diamonds."

"I have a little gadget for you to take on your hot date and fancy tea," Lucas told me, turning away to reach into his bag. He put a small device on the tabletop and pushed it towards me. I caught it as it skidded to the edge of the table and turned it over.

"What is it?"

"A phone cloner. You have to get Lord Justin's phone and plug in the device. You'll need approximately a minute for it to download, then we'll have full access to everything on his phone. It might just give us the clues we need to determine if he's guilty."

"I thought you'd already broken into his email account and accessed his phone records?"

"Yep, duh, that took minutes. This will give us a better picture. The cloner will copy everything from photos and notes to text messages and more." Lucas pushed a second identical box towards me. "And this one is for Ben. Same deal. Get his phone for sixty seconds and clone it. Bring them both back to me A-S-A-P and I'll extract the data."

"Okay, fine. I gotta shoot if I'm going to make this tea and take a nap." I yawned. I was long past the days when I could stay up all night and work. "What does one wear for afternoon tea? Should I wear a dress?" I mused, not really expecting an answer.

"I don't know. I guess a *Downton Abbey*-type dress is too much for this era."

"You watch *Downton Abbey*?"

"My fiancée makes me. I pretend to enjoy it."

"You totally enjoy it."

"And you totally checked out our boss's ass as he left the room." Lucas tapped his temples. "I'm not just a ridiculously handsome geek, you know. I notice stuff."

"Pffft." I blew a raspberry and left, though I was pretty sure I didn't win that round of teasing. Even worse, if Lucas noticed something was happening between Solomon and me, did the other guys also? My job never felt more precarious as it did now, and it usually felt pretty rocky. My only redeeming factor in their eyes would be for me to catch the bad guy. Even more so now, because of the sheer amount of screw-ups on this case already; and that's exactly what I planned to do. Right after I return to my apartment and put on a nice dress and pumps, because I wanted to look really good while I was doing it. I mean, come on, priorities, people!

CHAPTER EIGHTEEN

Lord Justin waited on the steps of The Belmont, a small hotel tucked away behind the most exclusive part of Chilton. He wore a pink tie with a dark gray suit that had an actual pocket square, the hot pink silk peeking over the crease. He waved when he saw me pull up, and walked slowly down the steps, arriving on the sidewalk just as I handed my keys to the valet. I forlornly watched the Ferrari for a moment as it was driven away. What I wouldn't give for my bonus to be those cute wheels. It was the car my little VW would never be. On the plus side, my VW was all mine and unlikely to be the target of every car thief within a fifty-mile radius of Montgomery, so there was that.

"You look splendid," gushed Justin as he leaned in to air kiss me three inches from both cheeks.

"I know. I mean, thank you, so do you," I gushed in an equally superfluous manner. I was wishing I had a fan to direct some air at the sudden flush of heat on my face. It really wasn't okay to be so vain, but you know, he was right, I decided. I took his proffered arm and caught sight of my reflection in the hotel's shiny, streakless, glass doors. My yellow sundress, nipped in at the waist and flared to the knee, looked super cute, paired with my navy blazer and navy and white striped pumps. Not quite a bee, and not quite a sailor, but somewhere attractively in between. I was getting anxious for my first proper tea with the lord. As if on cue, the little finger of my right hand began edging away from the other fingers, as if ready to partake in a little tea drinking all on its own. It was just a shame that Justin was fifty percent likely to be a felon and one hundred percent likely to be dating a bunch of women.

I don't know if it was because Justin looked so showy, or perhaps, his accent made the wait staff seem extra deferential. Maybe it was because I just looked utterly fabulous on his arm, but his chest seemed to puff out more and more as we went into the hotel. By the time we were seated at our table, next to full-length windows that overlooked a pretty courtyard garden, Justin's chest seemed to have increased in size by at least a half. If he started pumping weights, he'd probably look pretty good, but not as good as... no, I refused to think about him.

"Again, I must say, you look divine," sighed Justin, as he ran his eyes over my top half... where they seemed to linger. Well, men were men no matter where they came from, I decided. Give them a title, and they still looked at your boobs. I shouldn't be surprised. "A true lady," he continued. "Just the type of female who would feel right at home in my family's country seat."

"Do you have a big, er, seat?" I stuttered.

"Enormous." Justin winked. I wondered if we were still talking houses, or if I'd gotten it all wrong and "seat" meant something else to an Englishman. "Acres and acres. We have three full-time gardeners for constant maintenance. The house has staff, too, of course," he added, like it was perfectly natural. I wondered if it was natural to keep mentioning it. Hadn't he tried to lure me in with stories about his wealth already? Not to mention the women I briefly met at the ball.

He reached for my hand and held it in his own, examining my nails before running his thumb over my palm. "These are hands that haven't seen a day's work," he told me.

What?! They'd seen days, nights, and weekends in all kinds of crappy jobs. There wasn't anything these hands hadn't done unfortunately, except, you know, anything illegal. Well, body-trading type of illegal. These hands had definitely done other illegal stuff, and they were about to do one other thing that might be viewed dimly in the eyes of the law. Fortunately, I wasn't too clear on that and pled ignorance as my defense. For most people, ignorance is the world's worst defense, but most people weren't related to a large chunk of MPD, several of whom wanted babysitting. Good babysitters were hard to find. Lucky me.

However, I decided to appear affronted at the assertion that I might have to work. After all, wasn't I an heiress in Justin's eyes? "Of course not," I sniffed. "I'm rich!"

Justin's eyes flashed. "Filthy rich, darling?"

"Rolling in it." Before Justin asked just how much I had to roll in, the waiter approached and we spent a little time looking through the menu. Justin insisted we "partake" in the "traditional" champagne afternoon tea: tiny sandwiches, miniature cakes and all.

While we waited, I reached into my purse for my cell phone before laying it on the table. "I hope you don't mind," I said, "but I'm waiting for a call from my jeweler. I decided I didn't like the ones I had at home when someone broke in, so he's showing me some new pieces. Diamonds," I added, watching his reaction carefully, "big ones."

"Not at all," Justin replied with a shrug as if he didn't care, but something about the way his eyes widened at the suggestion of big diamonds told me he cared a lot. Again, I had the feeling that he wasn't quite as wealthy as he claimed. He was always just a little bit too interested in how much I supposedly had. On the other hand, maybe rich people were all nosy show-offs. I didn't know any personally, so I couldn't be sure. Justin took his cell from inside his breast pocket and laid it on the table. "My money guy said he'd call about some investments this afternoon."

I looked at his phone. He looked at mine. Neither rang. But I did have his phone in the open, and that's exactly what I wanted. Problem was, how could I clone it without him noticing? It wasn't like I could point into the courtyard and shout, "There's an elephant!" to keep him looking for the few minutes it took to copy all his data.

"So," said Justin, raising his eyebrows and blinking. "How do you feel about living in England? Or would you prefer the States after our wedding?"

"I, uh, wha.." I started, almost jumping from my chair in surprise. I flapped my hands as my breath caught, and the next thing I knew, the approaching waiter tripped over my foot, sending the carafe of water he carried in slow motion over the table and onto... Justin's lap.

Bull's eye!

"Argh!" yelled Justin, jumping up as if the water were hot tea. "You damned fool!"

"Sir, I apologize," stuttered the waiter as the commotion drew glances from around the room. "Allow me..." He produced a cloth and made attempts at dabbing Justin's crotch while Justin tried to fend him off. Somehow, neither seemed to be enjoying the "Step-backwards-and-dry, step-forwards-and-flap-hands" dance. Except for me.

"Lexi, I'll return shortly. Out of my way," snapped Justin, giving the waiter enough time to jump sideways as Justin stormed from the room.

"I'm so sorry," said the waiter, with an apologetic look. He gave a nervous glance across the room toward the doors Justin just exited. Beyond it, loomed a suited presence, whom I could only assume was his boss.

I pasted on a bright smile. "Don't worry about it," I told him, remembering my days as the world's most inefficient waitress. They were only a few days. Well, a week, really. Lily and I both got fired at the same time. She got another job the next week while I sulked. "He needed to cool his jets anyway. Would you replace his chair in case it's damp, and perhaps mop up the water?" I asked as pleasantly as I could. The poor guy's nerves were on edge, but he just did me a huge favor, even if he didn't know it. Plus, you could always judge someone by how they treated waiters, and I liked to put myself in a good light.

The waiter heaved a grateful breath. "Of course, Madam," he said, grabbing the chair and racing from the room. As heads returned to their own conversations, I carefully extracted the small cloning device from my purse, reached for Justin's phone, and mated the two. Almost immediately, the red glow appeared, then "1%."

"Come on," I urged it softly. "Let's do this!"

"5%, 10%," the little device carried on. As the waiter changed the chair and a busboy cleared away the damp mess, I held Justin's cell phone in my lap, smiling nicely at anyone who looked my way. With the table put to rights, I focused my attention on the courtyard windows, ideal for checking the reflection of an approaching angry lord.

Uncovering the device, I peeked into my lap. "75%." Nearly there. My heart began to beat faster, and my nerves began to tingle. Surely, Justin would be dry by now? So close. All I needed were a few more minutes.

"85%."

"90%."

I checked the window and saw the reflection of the waiter as he entered with a tiered, cake stand laden with an assortment of goodies. Immediately behind him was Justin, glowering still, but considerably dryer.

"94%."

My heart thudded. I wasn't going to make it.

The waiter stepped forward. Justin stepped forward. They stepped together. Justin narrowed his eyes. The waiter grimaced. They both prepared to step forward again.

"96%."

"Come on, come on," I urged the gadget.

Justin signaled to the waiter to move with an angry cut of his hand, and the waiter slunk forward. He fussed over the presentation of the stand, while a pretty little waitress approached next, adding a champagne bucket and two delicate, long-stemmed flutes. Justin stood behind them, his route blocked. I could not care less. He was rude, slightly stupid, and, I remembered all of a sudden, a bill evader. I wondered if he planned to stick me with this one too; or did he think I didn't know that he slunk out of Alessandro's with a bad card?

"98%."

"Thank you," I murmured, beaming at the servers as they shrank away from Justin. He eyed the champagne bucket suspiciously then dramatically went about testing the chair, presumably so his effort of drying his lap was not in vain. His back was turned to me.

"100%."

I detached the cloning gadget, letting it drop into the folds of my skirt, and returned the phone to the table, moving my hand to pick up a finger sandwich as Justin turned to face me. He sat down with a roll of his eyes as if he were extremely put out.

"Mmm," I smiled. "These look delicious." With my

heart beating faster than normal after my close call and lucky escape, I took a satisfied bite. Another bite, and the tiny, crustless sandwich was gone. Damn, crazy English sandwiches.

I didn't have to talk much over tea. Justin droned on and on about the family estate and how he would take over soon, but only after his father passed. For now, he was content to look after his business dealings here in Montgomery. As to why he picked our large town over other cities not so far away, or what his businesses were, remained a mystery, and Justin evaded those questions like a pro. "Maybe I'm just not cut out for the city," he said eventually with a casual wave of his hand as he reached for a tiny cake. "Just like you," he added, which was a fair point, given our location. "Do you ever see yourself as a country girl?"

"I haven't really thought about it," I admitted, which was true. "I, er, like walks in the country and, um, nature." What else *was* there in the country? "Not bears or coyotes or opossums though."

"We don't have any of those." Justin paused and frowned. "I think. Lots of sheep. And cows. Oh yes, many cows. I'll show you a photo." He picked up his cell phone, pressed a few buttons and turned the screen to face me. I wasn't all that enthusiastic about seeing a photo of cows, but I was pretty amazed by the size of the house in the background of the lovely pastoral scene.

"Lovely cows," I squeaked. What else does one say about cows? Having never been asked to admire any before, I had no idea of the proper protocol for speaking about them. I only got through the section on greetings in the etiquette handbook, and that was complicated enough. "Is that your home?"

"Oh yes, that's our old house," said Justin.

"It looks very old." And by old, I meant enormous. Well, old too. It also looked very familiar. Perhaps I'd seen it in a magazine or on television. It was the type of quintessential country house that would be proudly featured.

"It is. Been in the family for years. All we need now is a new lady at my side when I take over." Justin gave me a knowing look. I looked at the house again. Wowsers. I could live there.

That dream, however, was dashed when I remembered it would involve living with Justin. He just didn't do it for me. I took a third look at the house and sighed. Damn it, he still didn't do it for me. The situation I was in should have been in the urban dictionary under the definition for "tragedy."

Justin sipped the last of his champagne before retrieving the phone just as it rang. He spoke monosyllabically for less than a minute before hanging up. "Must dash," he said, rising. "Crisis with one of my investments needs my immediate attention. I would escort you to your car..."

"Don't worry about me," I assured him. "I need to, uh, dash too. Urgent appointments."

"Of course you do, darling." Justin reached for my hand and drew it to his lips, giving my knuckles a lingering kiss. "Until next time."

"Until then." I fluttered my lashes a little and Justin left, but not before giving the waiter another narrowed-eye look. Behind Justin's back, I smiled at the waiter and he left me alone to finish the last of the delicious, little cakes. As I gathered my things, dropping the cloning device into my purse and pulling on my jacket, the waiter approached. "Shall I clear, Madam?"

"Yes, please. And I'm sorry about my friend being a little touchy."

"Not at all, Madam."

"Thanks anyway." I gave him what I hoped was a reassuring smile as I navigated my way between the tables to the exit. Just as I crossed the lobby, I heard someone calling me in visible distress. Turning, I saw the waiter hurrying towards me. "Madam," he exhaled, waving a slip at me. His nose and cheeks were starting to pink, but not with anger like before. This time it looked more like... embarrassment.

"Yes?" I waited, wondering what on earth I left. My purse was in my hand and I'd already checked my cell phone and wallet were inside.

"The bill, Madam," the waiter said in a low voice.

"Pardon?"

"The bill has not been paid, Madam."

"There must be a mistake." I frowned. "My friend didn't pay?" The waiter colored a deeper pink, giving me my answer. The rat! Justin, not the waiter. How rude. "Of course, I forgot. Silly me. Let me give you my card," I said, rummaging in my purse for my wallet. Finding it, I took the slip and winced. Of all the bills to land me with! And just how much did teeny, weeny sandwiches and itty, bitty cakes cost? Thank God we didn't order full-sized ones! With a thudding, and not particularly full, stomach, I handed my card to the waiter and waited as he processed it. If Solomon didn't consider this a work expense, I couldn't eat for the next month.

"All done, Madam," the waiter assured me, handing me the receipt. "Have a wonderful day."

Not likely, I decided, as I left, giving my ticket to the valet. Climbing into my car, all I could think about was what a jerk Justin was to stiff me with the bill and how I hoped the cloning device snagged some dirt on him for payback. Also, I was really hungry.

~

"You smell like fries," said Solomon when I pulled into the agency parking lot a half hour later and wound down the window. He waited for me by the elevator, just as I asked him to. He didn't give an indication how long he'd been standing there, so it could have been seconds, minutes, or hours.

"Whatever," I snipped, running my tongue over my

teeth.

"I didn't say I didn't like it. You got any leftovers?" He stooped to look through the window, his eyes searching my car for telltale wrappers.

"Nope, sorry."

He sniffed. "I thought you went for afternoon tea?"

"I did. Have you seen how small those sandwiches are? I just ate a Big Mac and large fries. Speaking of which..." I pulled the bill from my purse. "Lord Justin stuck me with the bill. Again."

"Really? Jerk." Solomon looked at the bill. His nose wrinkled ever so slightly with distaste. I wouldn't like to be Justin when Solomon decided he wanted to have words about the bill. "I'll take care of it. Add the fries to your expenses too. You clone his phone?"

"Yep." I dropped the gadget into his outstretched palm. "Hope there's something juicy on it. I know I'm a heiress and all, right now, but seriously, where's this guy's manners?"

"Don't worry about it. Lucas will find out the situation with Justin. You coming in?"

"No, sorry, I have to meet Ben. I'm kind of running late and I need to change."

"Have a shower too. Burgers are fine, but they aren't the best scent on you."

"Thanks a bundle. And you wanted some!"

Solomon gave me a look. It wasn't an "I want a burger look," but he definitely wanted something tasty. Before I started to salivate at the thought of being his "objet de nibble," I stuck my tongue out at him and hit the electric window. "Let me know what you find," I yelled as the window rolled shut. Then I hit the gas, leaving Solomon in the parking garage with the lingering scent of my burger and fries.

~

After the disastrous date with Justin, I was ready for a pleasant evening with Ben. Even better, I couldn't wait until Lucas got back to me with some dirt on Justin. There was something wrong with the lord, but only a real intrusion of his personal life could uncover what. Unfortunately, I hated waiting.

"You look distracted, honey," said Ben, taking my hand as we left the restaurant. The night had fallen, leaving the sky inky black, and a silvery half moon hung over us. All we needed was a shooting star to highlight the evening. That, and maybe to clear Ben of any wrongdoing, and for me to become the person he thought I was. It was a shame we didn't meet in another life. I could have really liked Ben. I did really like Ben. Unfortunately, my world would eventually return to normal soon, and that would be that.

"I'm sorry, I am a little distracted," I admitted, wondering what I could add to that. Happily, Ben beat me to it.

"It must be the burglary. So, no one saw a thing?" he asked, for what was probably the third time. "You didn't even get a glimpse of this guy on security footage?"

I shook my head. "Nothing."

"Was anyone hurt?"

I paused. How could he have possibly known that? Wait, he didn't ask "How was the person who got hurt?" but "if anyone *was* hurt." That was different.

"I don't think so," I said, adding, "Oh, I think someone in the street saw my door wide open and went to investigate. I don't really know what happened."

Ben nodded, as if it were likely that a friendly neighbor would check up on me. "And he didn't see the thief either?"

Again, I got the feeling that his questions were too much, too prying. "He?" I asked. "I don't remember saying the person who got hurt was a he."

"Didn't you? Maybe I just assumed. I guess I thought it was unlikely a woman would investigate. All the same..." He waited.

"No, I don't think so." I shrugged with what I hoped was a blasé look. "I don't know. I guess someone would have told me," I continued in the lie. Of course, Delgado was fine, albeit a few stitches and a day of rest, but I could hardly say that. I struggled again to remember if I identified the gender of my "friendly neighbor." I really didn't think so, but I couldn't be sure. It was possible Ben just assumed. He had as much chance of being right as wrong. Maybe it was nothing. Maybe I was just antsy because I expected someone to call any moment and confirm Justin was our guy.

"You look cold. Here, take my jacket," Ben offered as he slipped his jacket off and tucked it around my shoulders before I could protest. Not that I was planning to. I was a little chilly in the night breeze even though I swapped my pretty dress for navy-colored pants and a sheer pink blouse... I ditched the burger-and-fries scent for a spritz of Calvin Klein. As I pulled the jacket around me, something dropped from the pocket onto the floor and I stooped to pick it up, moments before Ben could, his fingers missing the packet by inches. I turned the thick paper over as I stood. Tickets. Train tickets. For tomorrow.

"Are you going somewhere?" I asked, frowning. He didn't mention a trip all evening.

"No. I'm returning those." Ben plucked them from my hands, folded the tickets in half and pushed them into the rear pocket of his jeans, before rubbing his hands over my upper arms. "Let me warm you," he said, looking down at me with his dreamy eyes.

The uncomfortable, niggling feeling I had about Ben increased the closer I got to him, even though I tried shrugging it off as simple nerves. By the time he leaned in to softly kiss me on the lips, I was a ball of insecurity. He planned to leave without telling me, and he wanted to know too much about the burglary, so could he be the thief? Was he the thief? Had he played me the whole time? Of course, there was the possibility that Lord Justin also played me, but there was something about Ben that just didn't sit right the more I thought about it.

No matter what else was wrong with Justin, he was too much of a bumbling idiot, wasn't he? He didn't play the game at all successfully. He made too many mistakes.

But Ben didn't.

Ben was handsome, smooth, suave and intelligent. He was everything our profile indicated our thief should be, and my gut knew what my heart refused to believe.

He was the thief.

I was sure of it. But how to prove it before he escaped town? In a movie, I'd catch him in the act, like we planned or cleverly tricked him into admitting it. This, however, was real life, and Ben was too smart for that. Ben was the thief who never got caught.

Until now.

Not that I was totally up on my own abilities to catch him, but... someone had to do it, right? Maybe tonight was my night.

"Hey, gorgeous," Ben said, his eyebrows knitting together as he drew back from the kiss I barely returned. "Everything okay?"

I gave him a disinterested half shrug, then remembered I was supposed to be into this. Aiding the charade was Ben's appearance. He looked super hot in black jeans and a white t-shirt, the short sleeves framing his bulging biceps nicely. His chest, straining under the material, was something else. I stared at it the way a really rude guy stares at breasts. One pec popped up, then down again. My mind went blank. What were we talking about? And was that his phone pressing into my hip? Or something else?

Wait.

He was distracting me. He was making me forget what I was just thinking and I couldn't let him.

In a flash, I remembered what I saw the night the Chilton house was hit. There was someone walking along the street. Not once, but twice. But it wasn't any random stranger. It was Ben. I was sure of it. Yes, he was wearing a cap last night but I knew his profile and if I'd paid better attention I would have caught him then. There was only one reason he could have been there.

I stepped back and took a deep breath. Ben watched me, but didn't move any closer.

"It's you! I saw you last night!" I gasped as my mind whirred. Of course, it must have been so easy. He was incredibly handsome, charming, romantic... Really, Ben appeared to be most women's idea of a perfect guy. He would never have trouble convincing any woman to share her secrets, especially those of the shopping variety. Inviting him into their homes would feel natural, just as it did with me; there was nothing about Ben that screamed "unsafe." Or "sleazy" like Justin. He could access anything. As a career felon, he would know exactly what to look for. He could probably case the house in minutes. Come to think of it, it was a good job Ben only wanted to be a thief, because he could have been a successful serial killer. What a comforting thought.

"What am I?" Ben asked slowly.

"You're not looking for love," I continued.

"Uh..."

"You're using the Million Matches agency to find victims to steal from, not a wife!"

"Slow down, Lex..."

"I know it's you. I don't know how you did it, but I know it's you!"

"All this from seeing me outside your house?"

"The same night it got burglarized! That was no coincidence."

"Maybe I brought you flowers that night. Did you think that maybe I had a legitimate reason to visit the

243

beautiful woman I enjoy dating? That maybe I didn't find you home and waited?" Ben's eyes narrowed, his face seeming to darken with annoyance, and he breathed heavily through his nose like an angry bull.

Actually, no. That never occurred to me, but I wasn't going to admit it to Ben. Instead, I wracked my brain. Was he carrying flowers? I couldn't remember. My mind launched into a panic after Lily's call.

I sped on, carried away with the story I knew must be true. Images flickered through my brain as the mini movie of that night replayed for me alone. "You saw I wasn't home, so you broke in. I know you entered from the rear and you must have exited via the front door. You switched on the living room lamp." I ran a hand through my hair, trying to remember the events as best I could. The lamp that I hadn't switched on. The shadow in the room. "But there was nothing for you to steal. It was a set-up."

"You set a trap for me?" Ben stepped back, incredulous.

"You bet we did."

"And you expected to find me... what? Carrying out your TV? Slipping your stereo into my backpack and making off? Was I wearing a striped suit, a mask, and carrying a bag marked 'swag' in this fantasy of yours?" Ben folded his arms and waited, but right at that moment, my cell phone vibrated in my pocket. I held a finger up to him, not a rude one, but to tell him to hold it while I checked the screen for the text message that just came in.

Lucas. "Got him," it read, "Lord Justin an imposter!!! Solomon and Maddox arresting now."

"Oh, shit," I whispered, as I looked from the screen to Ben's stony face.

I had the wrong guy.

I was so convinced that Ben was the thief, I blustered on. How could I have gotten it so wrong? So completely wrong?

"You want to check your wallet and mine right now?" Ben continued, emptying his pants pockets. "Make sure I didn't pickpocket you while you checked your phone."

"I am so sorry," I whispered, staring at the cell phone in my hands. "I got it wrong. I got it really wrong."

"Damn right you did!"

"Please, Ben, I... I'm really..."

"Save it," snapped Ben. "You don't get to accuse me of being a thief and a fraud, then just say sorry and we continue our date. You know I tried to make a real effort for you. I thought you were a great girl while you thought I was playing you the whole time. Here's a newsflash, Lexi, if that's even your real name, I'm not the player, you are! This was a set-up the whole time! You tried to play me and you lost. I'm out of here." Ben stepped backwards and heaved a breath. When I reached for him, he took another step back, brushing my hand off while simply shaking his head. "See you around," he muttered before walking out.

If I were he, I would have done exactly the same thing. Even worse, he was right. I did play him. I pretended to be someone he wanted for the purposes of attracting him just so we could bait him.

Now I didn't have the thief, the guy, or even a date... and Maddox and Solomon both scooped me to the arrest.

Life really sucked.

CHAPTER NINETEEN

I didn't have the heart to go to work and catch the celebration that, no doubt, was now in play at the successful completion of the case. Instead, I dragged my tired and embarrassed self over to the agency's parking garage to swap my conspicuous, cherry red Ferrari for my reliable, unremarkable VW and headed over to the Bonneville Avenue to do a sulky stakeout on the weird neighbor since the Schuberts called to say the strange noises had been on and off all day. Maybe I could complete *this* case without it blowing up in my face.

I checked on Lily before the stakeout and found her lying on the sofa, looking red-eyed and pale. She told me she didn't think she had a single tear left. Freshly stocked with new magazines and snacks, which I brought over, like that made any difference to her grief, I shed a few tears for her after I got back into my car.

Aidan Marsh's car was gone and the house seemed empty when I got there. After the last time, I saw no point in canvassing the house or rear yard again, and certainly not without my look-out-slash-partner in "It's-not-a-crime-if-no-one-sees-you-doing-it."

Retouching my mascara, I checked my reflection in my small pocket mirror, while feeling horribly selfish for not staying with Lily. At least, she wasn't alone; my mother arrived as I left, and Lily's own mother even phoned. Plus, Lily insisted that I find out what the heck this guy was up to and give her all the gory details, without becoming his next victim. And even if I did, she promised not to rest until he was brought to justice, which wasn't too reassuring.

So here I was. Mascara in its rightful place on my lashes, and thumbs twiddling while I waited for a sign that Aidan Marsh was due home. Absent of any other ideas, the only sign I looked for was the dude actually arriving.

Had I really thought about it the last time we were here, I would have stuck a tracker on his car and monitored his movements. However, that would have alerted Solomon, or at the very least, Lucas, to my activities and I didn't want that. Plus, I would have had to investigate every suspicious movement, maybe even go body part-hunting if he went to the woods or the recycling depot. That was something I'd yet to do and really didn't look forward to. Not that I was lazy, it was just that hunting for body parts sounded totally gross.

Thinking about gross reminded me of Lord Justin the Douchebag, and Ben Rafferty. How could I have gotten it so wrong? I knew there was something fishy about Ben, but in reality, the Big Kahuna was Justin. There was only one way I could find out how they caught Justin: by calling the agency. I swallowed what was left of my pride and called Lucas, the one co-worker least likely to laugh at my mammoth mistake. Also, the most likely to know exactly what information we got when I copied Justin's phone.

"Hey, Le..." Lucas started, picking up the phone.

"Don't say my name!" I squeaked, sliding lower in

my seat. After a moment, I straightened up. This wasn't a video call after all. No one could see me. Shame really, since my lashes looked great. Maybe an extra touch of eyeshadow... oh wait... phone call! "Um, that is, I don't want anyone to know I'm calling."

"O-kaaaay. Um, why not?"

"Because I got the wrong guy! I'm such a doofus!"

Lucas made a rude noise. It was hard to tell if he agreed with me or not. "You did not," he said, "you did great cloning Justin's phone. Oh, he's not Justin either. His name is Ken Moody and he's not from England. He's from Nebraska."

"He's not even English?" I gasped.

"Nope. Never been there."

I let out the breath I was holding, asking in disbelief, "So none of his story was true?"

"Not one bit. He made the whole thing up. Bought a title from the Internet. Copied a photo of the *Downton Abbey* house online, claiming it was his family's place..."

"I knew I saw that house somewhere!"

"Yeah. That's how he got the accent too. Watching reruns. Oh, and you want to hear the kicker?"

I straightened up. "There's more?"

"Ken Moody is married. Twice."

"He got married twice? That's not so bad."

"No, he's married *twice*. Two different women, same time. One in Florida, one in Utah. Both now want to kill him."

I let out another gasp of air I didn't know I was holding in. "He's a bigamist?"

"Yep."

"Wow! He really isn't that good looking."

"That's what you're taking away from this?" came Solomon's voice down the line.

"It's an important observation!" I squeaked, sliding down in the seat again. It was. I mean, I wasn't even into my first marriage, and Lord Justin, aka Ken Moody, managed to convince not one woman to marry him, but two. At the same time. There was hope for me yet!

"If you're thinking there's hope for you yet, I'll point out that Ken Moody is a bigamist and that's only one of his many crimes," said Solomon.

Eek! "I was not thinking about marriage. At. All," I protested. "I'm not ready. I have a lot of clothes and can't give up an inch of closet space to a man. Also, I'm very independent, and I am not, I repeat *not*, picking up any man's socks. And I like going out and wearing pajamas with animals on them. Not sexy ones. The pajamas, not the animals. The animals aren't sexy either. Also, I wear different clothes when I'm going out, not pajamas. I'm just not ready for marriage." I clammed up. I wasn't ready to talk either.

"Let me know when you're ready," said Solomon. I heard the sound of the phone exchanging hands before Lucas came back on the line. "Ready for what?" he asked.

"To know what happens next," I said quickly, frowning as I thought about what Solomon said. Let him know when I was ready for what? Living with a man? Was he implying he wanted to marry me? He did have a lot of closet space, now I remembered it. And he wasn't doing his sister, a good thing in anyone's world. Plus, he was unmarried and not a criminal. And unfairly handsome.

And... there were an awful lot of "ands" working in Solomon's favor.

It was too much for now. I had to focus.

"Okay. So, when we realized Lord Justin wasn't whom he said he was, Solomon took the evidence to Detective Maddox and they arrested him. He confessed immediately and he's still being interrogated," Lucas told me

"Did he confess to targeting all those women?" I asked, because that was the clincher.

"That's what Maddox is working on now. He zipped his lip when we charged him, and demanded a lawyer."

"So, he said... nothing?" I paused, waiting.

"As far as I know. Solomon's still in the office and he said nothing to me. Anyway, isn't Maddox your, uh..."

"Ex," I confirmed, like Lucas didn't know.

"Yeah. So... you call him! I have two cases of beer on ice and we're waiting."

"Great idea! Never thought of that," I snipped sarcastically. Maddox and I got on okay, but I wouldn't say we were exactly on best terms, given our break-up. On the scale of whom I wanted to call, he rated after my boss at this point, but since my boss said nothing, and my colleague knew even less, I rethought what my next call would have to be. I just hoped Maddox was so engrossed in the case, he didn't want any small talk, or haggling about our break-up again. That was one thing I didn't want to think about at all. The hurt was too deep, and the confusion even deeper. I didn't know how I could ever truly know if he told the truth about the night I saw him getting cozy with another woman. Until then... well, I couldn't get back together with him while my mind and heart were at odds; but there was another part of me that couldn't let go.

It didn't escape my mind that all of my issues with Maddox were similar to my issues with Solomon. I didn't know what the hell to do about him either. One thing was for sure: Ben Rafferty wouldn't be returning my calls. "Ugh," I grunted. "I'll call Maddox."

"Call me right back," said Lucas. "I want to know what you know."

"What if I know nothing?"

"I want to know that too."

"Don't hold your breath," I told him. "Also, can you tell Solomon that I accused Ben and now my cover is definitely blown?" I hung up before Lucas could say a word and immediately dialed Maddox before I lost my nerve. I rather hoped he would be in the interrogation room, so I could leave a voicemail. I was startled when he answered.

"This is a surprise," he said, like we weren't working the same case. "How've you been?"

"Peachy. Apparently, you got our guy. Has he cracked yet?"

"You got our guy," replied Maddox with a sigh. "I assume this is why you called. Well done on getting the information we needed to make the arrest."

"No problem. So..." I prompted, hurrying him along, even though a little blush of pride crept across my cheeks.

"He's with his lawyer now. One minute he was a Chatty Cathy, now he won't say a word."

"Damn. You think he's behind all this?"

"Looks that way, but I won't know until I get in the room with him again. We're talking strategy right now."

"Huh." I wondered who "we" were. "Will you call me back when you know something?"

"Sure. Can I help you with anything else, Lexi?"

"No, I'm good. That's it."

"Okay then. Maybe we can get a drink when this is wrapped up? Congratulate ourselves."

"Sure, uh, I guess so."

"Later then, Lexi."

"Bye."

I stared at my phone for a moment, my frown deepening. Did I just agree to a date? I sucked in a long breath and grimaced into the rearview mirror. This day was never ending... wait. Was that...?

Aidan Marsh's car pulled into the driveway, halting in front of the garage doors.

Oh, hell. I'd had enough of today. Solomon might want to marry me, Maddox wanted a date, Ben hated me, and Justin, I mean Ken was a fraud... Today seriously sucked. As if accusing the wrong guy weren't bad enough, now I had a date with my ex. On the upside, I assisted MPD in catching a fraudster, and it was only a matter of time before Lord Justin cracked, so Solomon's real objective of networking with local law enforcement was achieved.

I could go home, order a pizza and drink the biggest glass of wine ever just as soon as this day was over. Before I knew it, I was hightailing it out of the car and across the street, only slowing to a jog when the Schuberts' neighbor exited his car and popped the trunk. I skidded to a halt just as he came around the other side. Between us, the trunk opened all the way. I looked at him, and he at me quizzically. We both gazed into the trunk.

No dead bodies. Hurrah! Just a heap of grocery bags.

The man flapped his hands and cocked his head, demanding "What do you want?" tacitly.

"Do you kill people?" I asked. Oh, my mother would be so proud of that one, but it just didn't sit well my saying "Hi" and "how are you?" and all that jazz, when I really only wanted to know one thing. There was something familiar about his hand movements. He repeated them and I frowned.

"Am I being *Punk'd*?" asked the man in a strange accent, scanning over his shoulder for cameras.

My nose wrinkled. "No! It's a genuine question."

"Oh." Aidan Marsh scratched his head.

"You don't need to think about it. It's a pretty easy question."

The man continued to frown and stared at me a long while. "No," he said finally, the syllable sounding slightly off key.

"Okay." I rocked back on my heels and almost stuck my hands in my jacket pockets so they didn't flap around aimlessly. Instead, I refrained just in case he was lying and I had to defend myself right there on the street before being dragged inside and strapped me into the torture chair in the garage. "Are you sure?"

"Yes," he said, very slowly; then, "No."

"Yes or no?"

"Yes, I kill people. I mean, no, I don't!" His shoulders slumped. "And yes, I'm sure. It's my dog."

"Your dog kills people?" I gave him a look. The one I used a lot when I was temping, usually upon discovering the dumb-ass filing systems and foot-high backlogged files of my temporary employers. It was the look I reduced to three letters: WTF?

"No! He's just a nuisance." At that, the dog in question galloped around the car and sat at his owner's feet. He was big and really cute. He looked up, panting, and his tongue rolled out. The dog's, that is. Not Aidan Marsh's tongue. He just looked confused. We both watched the dog. The man scratched the dog between the ears and his ears went up and down. Again, the dog's, not the man's. While they bonded, I took a closer look at the lettering on the dog's vest. It read "Assistance Dog."

"Why's your dog an assistance dog?" I asked. The man ignored me, only scratching the dog's head. I waited. After for-freaking-ever, I coughed. The dog looked at me, then nudged his owner. It was only when the man lifted his head that I noticed the small devices tucked behind his ears. Hearing aids. Sign language. Of course!

"You said something?" he prompted.

"Yeah, but... are you deaf?"

"Dead?" He frowned. "No."

"Deaf."

"Yes, definitely deaf. Mostly. I can hear some loud noises though without my aids."

"Oh." We looked at each other some more. The dog barked. I really didn't know what to say. The situation had me stumped. Sure, we confirmed he wasn't a killer, and neither was the dog, but the hearing situation really threw me. It explained the strange inflections when he spoke though. "So..."

"You don't need to raise your voice," the man said. "It won't make any difference."

"I wasn't going to!"

"So, what do you want? Does this have anything to do with the Schuberts next door?" He raised a hand and waved, and I looked over my shoulder. Sure enough, the Schuberts were standing on the porch. It was no ruse so he could whack my head off and let the dog eat me. What a relief! The Schuberts gave a confused, half-baked wave, more like a flap, in return. "Has Barney been making strange noises again?" Aidan stared down at the dog, then looked over to me. "Oh, jeez, he has, hasn't he? What the hell did he do now?"

"There's been a lot of strange noises coming from your house," I answered, turning to him. I opted to go with the truth because there really wasn't anywhere else to go. "Machinery. Screaming."

"Screaming?" The man seemed genuinely puzzled. I flapped my hands around, then stuck them around my throat and mimed screaming while simultaneously strangling myself. Judging by the bewildered expression on his face, as well as Barney's, my demonstration didn't seem to help matters much. Go figure. "Who are you?" he asked at last.

I stuck my hand out. "Lexi Graves, Private Investigator."

"Aidan Marsh. Confused." All the same, he shook my hand.

"That makes two of us." I looked over my shoulder to where the Schuberts waited patiently. "Four."

"Pardon? You said something."

"Oh, right. It doesn't matter."

"I hate it when hearing people say that. It's really annoying. See how you like missing what people say because they don't bother to turn their head towards you."

"I thought you had hearing aids."

"The batteries are weak."

"You're really grouchy, you know that, right?"

"You would be too if Barney woke you at five a.m. every day, by licking your face."

"Nice." Barney stuck his tongue out and some slobber hit the floor. I wondered if his rough tongue had exfoliating qualities. Somehow, I didn't think Aidan gave two hoots. "So about these strange noises?" I asked, just as Aidan reached into the trunk and pulled out his groceries. He set them on the ground at our feet, then reached in again. This time, he pulled out a brand new and very shiny hammer. The clawed end looked lethal. He set it on top one of the bags and pulled out a couple more tools that seemed threatening. "Maybe later," I said, stepping back.

"Not the serial killer thing again," sighed Aidan, giving me a sideways glance. "I make furniture, okay? I have a workshop in the garage. Sometimes I use power tools."

"And the screaming?"

"You are so fixated on screaming. I don't know. Barney sits on the TV remote a lot. Two nights ago, I found him watching a horror movie. He's really weird. I tried to get him into *Marley and Me*, but he refuses to watch it. That might be a good thing. I tried Disney cartoons too, but he always switches back to the horror channel. If anyone has serial killer tendencies, it's him."

Barney barked and edged forwards in a butt-shuffle. For a mad dog, he sure was cute with his thumping tail and tongue-lolling expression. He stuck his head forward, sniffed my hand and gave it a good, long lick, leaving my hand very wet. I ran it down my skirt, glad we'd shaken hands already, and doubly glad that it was still attached to my arm.

"So what about all the blood in your garage?" I

persisted.

Aidan set the grocery bags on the ground and frowned. "Blood?"

"Yeah, you know, red stuff." I mimed stabbing myself in the heart and spurting blood everywhere.

"You don't have to keep miming. I've seen blood before. I'm deaf, not exsanguinated. Come see the workshop." Leaving the groceries where he set them, Aidan shut the trunk and picked up his shiny new tools. He rounded the car and pulled the keys from his pocket, searching through them until he found the correct one. He stuck it in the lock, then rolled the garage door up and over, revealing what did indeed look like a workshop. Still, with all the neatly assembled tools on the walls, and the throne-like chair, as well as the mysterious red stain on the floor, it did look like a killing workshop. I wondered if Aidan would blame that on Barney too.

Aidan beckoned me closer. I took another look at the Schuberts, craning their necks, and I nodded towards the garage. I figured I was okay. If Aidan didn't let me out, they'd know where to find me. If they tried to rescue me, and he captured them too, I would have company at least. Really, there was a bright side to everything. Maybe if the PI thing didn't work out, I could become a life coach.

I stepped into the cool climes of the garage and looked around, jumping when Aidan nudged my arm and pointed at the floor. "Red paint," he said. He walked over to the chair and ducked behind, its huge frame hiding him completely. When he reappeared, he held a bucket of paint. It was a nice brand; no wonder the color looked so rich. "It's for a fancy club in New York. They want two of these things, painted red, leather buckles, the works."

"Whatever for?"

"Who knows? I prefer not to ask. Some of my clients

are... odd. Here, this is my portfolio. Take a look." Aidan handed me a thick folder and I opened it to page after page of stunning furniture. A master of both wood and ironwork, Aidan did rustic as easily as wildly contemporary. "You made all these?" I asked incredulously.

Aidan nodded. "Every piece. I keep some in the studio in the garden if you want to see?"

Looking up from the collection, my eyes went around the garage, taking in all the power tools. I guess this explained the noise. The Schuberts would be so pleased. I wondered if Aidan would give me a discount. "How are you at making windowseats?" I asked. "I'm buying the house next door."

Aidan grinned. "No problem." His face paled and he glanced outside. "Oh shit! Barney!"

"What?"

"I left him with the groceries."

Aidan pelted out to the front and I followed him. When I got there, Aidan had his hands on his hips, while berating a very satisfied-looking Barney, whom he caught muzzle-deep in a grocery bag. An empty packet that once contained sausages listed on one side. Aidan grabbed him by the collar and dragged him out of the bag. Barney had a steak half hanging from his mouth. I swear if dogs could smile, he did.

"Aidan Marsh, meet your neighbors, Mr. And Mrs. Schubert," I told him, as the older couple approached. Mr. Schubert wielded a wireless house phone; while Mrs. Schubert carried a wooden mallet, not for tenderizing the steak. It appeared that Barney was in no danger of giving it up. "Aidan is a furniture maker. He has a workshop in his garage. And this is Barney. He's just weird."

"Aidan Marsh, the designer?" breathed Mrs. Schubert. "I've just been reading about you in my interior design magazine. They say you're the hottest

257

new talent around. Your furniture sells for a fortune. And you're our neighbor!?"

"Not for long," I reminded them. "Also, he totally doesn't kill people, but I think his dog might need therapy."

"We know a great dog therapist." I raised my eyebrows as Mrs. Schubert hooked her arm through Aidan's. He seemed a little taken aback, but didn't shake her off, mostly because she had him in a vise-like grip and kept beaming up at him.

"Lexi told me you heard things. I'm sorry about all the noise," Aidan said as he scooped up the remains of his groceries with his free hand. "Barney is supposed to tell me if it gets too loud with my tools, but he just turns on the TV and makes it worse."

"Maybe he's lonely," said Mrs. Schubert. "He could come play with us until we move."

Mr. Schubert nodded. "This young lady is buying our house."

"High five," I said, raising my hand. After a tentative pause, Mr. Schubert high-fived me.

"That's the spirit," I told him.

"We'll contact our realtor and tell him we're proceeding with the sale," said Mrs. Schubert. "You still want to, right, dear?"

"Absolutely! Yes, please! Thank you so much!" I turned to Aidan. "I'm really glad you're not a psycho."

"You're welcome?" he said, after a moment.

"And you'll send us a bill for all the surveillance work you did?" Mrs. Schubert asked me, with a nod to Aidan, in a not particularly subtle way. I hoped it wouldn't make the neighbor thing awkward.

"No charge. I'm just happy to solve the mystery," I told them, hoping Aidan was watching.

"You could have just asked," Aidan told Mrs. Schubert as she steered him towards the house. "You really thought I was a serial killer?"

"Oh no, no! Goodness! Not at all!" She pulled a face at me and widened her eyes. Oh great! Now it looked like I suggested he was. Over Mrs. Schubert's head, Aidan grinned. He stuck his tongue out. I stuck mine back out at him and decided I liked him. A wet nose snuffled my palm then licked. That was fine too, mostly because it was Barney and not Aidan.

"Yes," said Mr. Schubert, coming to my rescue. "We thought you were killing all kinds of folk in there. So, you create all this furniture my wife likes? Oh great." He didn't sound thrilled. He sounded like a man who expected a shopping spree in the imminent future. My father had a similar sort of a tone, but I knew he loved buying my mother whatever she wanted. After all, my mother was lucky to get him, but my father was even luckier to get her.

"Come in and have a drink. I just made some oak patio furniture," said Aidan. His baffled expression turned to warm smiles, and he seemed pretty amused by the whole turn of events. Or maybe it was just because the Schuberts were so wowed by having a cool designer and master craftsman as their neighbor. "Lexi?"

"Oh, no, I can't, but you go ahead. I have to get home," I explained, although a little bit of me wanted to take a look in his house. I figured there was plenty of time for that once I moved in next door. Maybe Aidan and I would become friends. Maybe he'd let me take Barney for a walk. Barney sniffed my leg, looked up with a doggy grin, and did a huge doggy burp. Maybe not.

Mrs. Schubert and Aidan prattled on, and I'm pretty certain I heard him ask if I were single, but I didn't hear her answer. At the driveway, Mr. Schubert shook my hand. "Guess, I'd better follow and make sure she doesn't spend anything," he said, with a sigh. "Thank you for your good work, young lady. It's a relief to know he wasn't killing people all this time. We would have struggled with our consciences if we didn't do anything."

"You're welcome. I'm glad to help."

Mr. Schubert leaned in. "Of course, if you never see us again, you remember this is where you last saw us." He leaned out again. And winked.

"You got it." I gave his hand one last pump, glad to see the couple happier than when I first met them. I continued to wave at the happy trio as I walked back to my car. I buckled myself in, and reached for my cell phone.

"You're not going to believe this," I said to Lily when she answered.

"You're not dead?" she asked. "That's great!"

"I know, right?" I happily relayed the results of my investigation as she oohed and ahhed. Finally, she said, "Whoa. This is unreal. So, he's a deaf, blind, animal-loving serial killer? Wow."

"Where did you get blind from?"

"You? Didn't you say that?"

"No!"

"But he is a deaf, serial killer?"

"No. He's just a nice guy with a stupid dog. He's not violent at all. I thought I covered that?"

"I must have missed that bit. Is the dog deaf too?"

"No that would be pointless, wouldn't it? A deaf guy with a deaf assistance dog?"

"I guess. Ooooh! Oh! Oh! Did you two have a moment?"

"Me and the dog?"

"No. You and the deaf guy? Did he look into your eyes and realize that now he's met you, the world is his oyster and he can achieve anything? Is he totally in love with you?"

"No! Jeez, Lily, he's deaf, not stupid. And he's not Helen Keller."

"Of course not. Helen Keller's a woman. And dead."

"I was going more on the blind, deaf, and super intelligent thing."

"And dead. Don't forget that," added Lily. "Is he good looking?"

There was a long pause. "Kind of. He has nice eyes. We didn't have a moment; but Barney licked my hand, so I definitely think *we're* friends."

"Good enough for me," said Lily, "but I admit I'm easily pleased."

"I know. You're with my brother." Lily giggled and blew a raspberry. "I'll be home in a little while. Want to hang out?"

"You know better than to ask that. I'm not going anywhere."

"Do you want me to get you anything? Do you need more pain medicine?"

"No. Just come over and talk and tell me gossip. You can free my mind from its misery for a few hours."

The pang of her pain hit me squarely in the heart. For a moment, being so pleased with myself, I forgot everything in Lily's world wasn't perfect. I felt mean and horrible and selfish. I could do much, much better, and I would. "Done. I'll be there soon. I'm finished with Aidan and the Schuberts for now. I have news from the fraud case too."

"You solved it? Great! Are you still buying the house?"

"For sure."

"I have an IKEA catalog. You want to go through it?"

"Yup." I would have gone through any catalog she liked, just to keep her company and take her mind off her sadness for a few moments.

"See you soon."

"Love you, Lily."

"Love you, too, babe."

CHAPTER TWENTY

The worst thing about the job... No, wait, one of the top ten worst things about this job, when it wasn't awesome, was the waiting. Waiting for cases to come in, waiting for targets to move, waiting, waiting, waiting... This time, I was waiting for Maddox to call with an update on the investigation into Ken Moody, our wanna-be aristocrat. Since my call, there was not a word. In this case, that didn't bode well. Why didn't Moody crack the moment he knew the game was up?

"I gotta get out of here," I told Solomon as I stood up and stretched. The boardroom felt stifling. The hammering on the floor above was starting up again, and we were yelling, though Solomon remained as tight-lipped as ever about who and what he was installing up there. I didn't miss the epiphany that if I were such a great investigator, I could just find out for myself, but I did my best to ignore that. I just solved one itty, bitty case of false assumptions, and was instrumental in a breakthrough on another. The moment Moody confessed, I planned to take off for a few days and spend some more time with Lily. Jord, my mom, and I were keeping Lily company in shifts for a few days. I wanted to help her pack up her home as well as mine, mostly as a ruse to keep her company. It seemed strange to think that our lives had suddenly changed so dramatically. We would go from living in each other's pockets to separate homes in different neighborhoods. Our lives had changed so much in a year. Lily had Jord, and I had a new neighbor with a dog in need of therapy.

"You got any plans?" asked Solomon, without looking up from his paperwork.

"Um... yes?"

This time, he looked up and smiled. The drilling stopped. His eyes rolled upwards then back down, fixing on me. I tried not to think about him drilling.

"Why did you just say 'huurrrrr'?" asked Solomon.

"Did I? I think you misheard. I think I said, hurry up."

"Me?"

"No! Me? Why? What are you in a hurry for?"

Solomon frowned. "Nothing. What's gotten into you?"

Nothing. That was the problem. "I bought a house," I told him, before I started thinking about things I shouldn't think about. "I'm mortgaged for oh, the rest of my life, but I do have a house. I can paint it."

"What color?"

"I don't know. I kind of like it yellow."

"You bought the yellow bungalow on Bonneville Avenue?"

"You know about it?"

"You mentioned it a couple times. Fletcher said he saw you parked up there a few days ago."

"That's the one. Anyway, I have to go sign the paperwork."

"Let me know what to get you for a housewarming gift. You need anything?"

"Not that I can think of, but thank you."

"A vase? Pans?"

"Pans for what?"

"Cooking."

I put my index finger to my chin and blinked. "I've heard of that."

"I'll get you a cookbook."

"I think there's an insult in that," I told him, planting a perky smile across my lips, "but thank you!"

Solomon glanced up again. "Meals for two," he said with a wink. He raised a hand and waved before losing himself in the paperwork again. I rolled my eyes and flipped him the finger as I left. Only I did it behind my other palm, because he recently raised an objection about the number of times he'd seen me flip him off. He should just be grateful I didn't remind him how many times I'd seen him naked. I thought he'd probably like hearing that, so I kept my mouth shut as I exited, grabbing my bag from where it lay on my chair and slipping out.

All the paperwork was set out for me by the time I arrived, so it was just a case of formalities. With my autograph on the dotted line, all at once, I felt thrilled that the Schuberts pushed for a fast sale now that the issue with the neighbor was cleared up. Admittedly, I was slightly sick at the thought of spending more than two decades in debt. What if I lost my job *and* the house? What if the neighborhood totally nosedived and drug dealers moved in? Of course, there was the other "what if"…

What if it were all just perfect?

I left the office with butterflies fluttering in my stomach and my whole body tingling with excitement. I had an awesome job, currently doing nothing but waiting, yet pulling a salary. I had a house, a wonderful family, and a best friend. All I needed now was a romantic involvement who couldn't possibly be a cheat, my boss, or a criminal. Or maybe, I didn't need one at all. "Who needs a prince?" I told myself as I reapplied lip gloss in the car mirror. "I can save myself."

My cell phone vibrated against my leg, which was a pretty rude reminder of what possibly lay in store for me by not waiting for Prince Charming. I rummaged around until I found it in my pale blue leather tote bag. Maddox's name flashed on the screen. He could only be calling for one thing: he had news.

"Hey," I said, "what's happening?"

"Nothing."

"Still?"

"Yeah."

"So... short call?"

Maddox laughed. "What I meant to say is we came up empty on Lord Justin, uh, Ken Moody. He insists he had nothing to do with the thefts and has alibis for the time windows for three of the thefts. We checked them out and they stand up. It's not him, Lexi. He may be a lowlife, but he's not our guy."

I sank back in my seat, wishing I were in my comfy office chair. Or even better, on my couch. "His alibis are rock solid?" I asked in disbelief even though I already knew the answer. Of course, they were. Maddox would have checked, double-checked, and triple-checked.

Maddox confirmed it with a sigh. "Yeah. There's one other thing. We've been calling the dating agency non-stop and no one's picking up."

"That's odd. The receptionist seemed pretty efficient and I'm sure Helen Callery wouldn't tolerate unanswered calls from her big shot clients. You want me to check it out?"

"That's kind of why I was calling. Would you? I can clear it with your boss. I need to call him next."

"No need and no problem." I paused, mulling over my thoughts. "You know, my gut always said Ben Rafferty was the one."

"Then why did you discount him?"

"We cloned Moody's cell phone and it had the evidence we needed for you to arrest him."

"Did you clone Rafferty's?"

"No. I was going to, but I couldn't get it and thought there was no need to when I got the call about Moody."

"So, you don't know for sure he wasn't involved?"

"Well..." I thought about it. What did I have to go on? My gut kept telling me he was the thief. He had just as much opportunity as Moody, and he was damn good looking. He was even more appealing than having a European title. Yet, he seemed so insulted and forlorn when I accused him. Except, what if that were all an act? What if in reality, I alerted him and gave him notice to escape. "Pick Rafferty up," I said.

"You're sure."

"Yes. I was sure right up until the evidence against Moody threw me. Now he's the only one left," I said, my excitement building. Maybe I wasn't wrong after all. "But I blew it. He knows I'm not who I said I was. And I saw train tickets! I think they were for today. Pick him up now, Maddox, but it might be..."

"Too late," finished Maddox. He covered the mouthpiece and I heard some muffled speaking before he came back on the line. "I'm heading to his house now. Blake is putting a BOLO out on him in case we missed him. You get over to the agency and see why no one's answering. I don't like it. I'll call Solomon. I'll be in touch." He hung up before I could even wish him good luck. Not that Montgomery's one-man, crime-fighting machine needed it. Well, Montgomery's one man and the vast majority of my family. Speaking of which, why had no one invited me to dinner? Surely Ken Moody's arrest was enough to warrant a call?

I called my mom while I drove over to the dating agency. It turned out to be a long drive, thanks to a truck jack-knifing somewhere ahead and slowing the traffic to a crawl on Century Street, the most direct route downtown.

"Mommy's sweetie," said my mother on answering.

"Ugh. What's up with you?"

"I just babysat Victoria. I'm broody so I'm going to treat you like a baby for the next ten minutes."

"Please don't. I thought you were looking after Lily?"

"Jord got off his shift and came home and I thought I'd leave them together a while."

"How was Lily?"

"Sad, but very brave." My mother sniffed. "My heart breaks for them."

"Mine too."

"So what's happening, Mommy's precious? Daniel said he heard you helped solve a big crime."

I rolled my eyes at the driver crossing by slowly in the opposite lane. I got an eye roll back. I wondered if she were on the phone to her mother too. "Sort of. We got a guy for something, but not the something we wanted to get him for."

"Smoochie-poos not making any sense. Tell Mommy about it."

"Ugh. Stop it!"

"Sorry. I can't help it."

"You can't get broody. It's wrong. You're..."

"What? Old? I read a story about a woman who had a baby at seventy-two!"

"If you do that, I'm disowning you. You have five kids and we're all grown. Can't you get a dog?"

"I didn't think of that. Would Sophie be a cute name for a dog?"

"I guess. So long as it isn't a Rottweiler."

"Maybe a teacup Rottweiler," mused Mom.

"I don't think they come in teacup size. But you should think about getting a dog or another hobby! Why aren't you taking classes? What happened to sign language? I know someone you can practice on."

"It was too quiet; but if you know someone, maybe I'll pick it up again. It's like a secret handshake on steroids. Anyway, I can't decide between MMA for the over-fifties or embroidery for beginners."

"Tough choice," I agreed. "I see your problem. They're just so similar."

"Pfft," said Mom. "Maybe I could become a PI?"

"Please don't."

"I'd be helpful."

"Maybe Garrett could take you on a ride-a-long?"

"Oh! You think he would? Great! I'll call him." My mother sounded so delighted, I wondered how bored she must be lately. Truth be told, I didn't spend nearly enough time with her in recent weeks. I found myself wondering what I could do to make it up. After all, there were many, many criminals out there to catch, but only one woman who would always be my mother. "So, did you call for anything in particular, honey-bunny?"

"I wondered if you'd like to go for lunch soon? Maybe do some shopping?"

"That sounds just wonderful. Oh, Lexi, I'd like that a lot."

"Great. I'll call when I finish work and we'll pick a day."

"I'm so pleased. It'll be nice to catch up, just you and me. Now, what's this job you're working on? Are you being safe? Are you going to get hurt?"

"Who me? No! When do I ever get hurt?"

"Shot. Nearly thrown off a building. Broken arm. Did I get those in the right order?"

I winced. "Uh, yeah. But not this time! This time, I just get to wear pretty clothes and date creeps."

"That doesn't sound much different from your normal life, honey. How's that nice man of yours? Solomon?"

"He's not mine."

"Maddox?"

268

"Not mine either."

"You know all your brothers and sisters were married by your age."

"Don't remind me. Anyway, Daniel is on his second marriage."

"The first one didn't count!"

"And Serena just got divorced."

"And now she's found a lovely man. You should think about settling down."

"Jord only just got settled."

"He doesn't have perishable eggs, darling."

"Okay, thanks! Listen, I'm at the place I was heading to, so I have to go, but I'll call back later, okay? We'll set lunch up. Great talking to you! Don't get a baby! I bought a house! Bye, Mom!" I hung up. Fifteen minutes later, I arrived at Million Matches.

I parked in one of the designated spots, the spaces marked by a discreet double M symbol. I figured they must have chosen to abbreviate it because no client wanted to advertise having resorted to an agency just to get a date. I really didn't know why. An introduction agency was really no different from being set up by a friend, or a family member, except you filled out a questionnaire before the date, and got a bill, and you both knew you were looking for someone special. Maybe I would try Internet dating. Lily got dozens of emails when she tried, and received hardly any penis photos. What could go wrong? My dating life couldn't get any worse. Come to think of it, I wasn't even sure I had a dating life. After all, didn't that mean actually dating?

Before I got out of my VW, I tried calling Ben. I sighed deeply when the call rang out, not even going to voicemail. Of course, he could be really mad at me for accusing him, but when he didn't answer, I got worried. Shouldn't he want to yell at me or something...? If he were innocent.

I had a bad feeling deep in my gut. It was possible that MPD had picked him up, but Maddox didn't call to notify me, and I was sure he would send a text message, if nothing else. Plus, it was less than an hour after putting out the BOLO. That would be fast even by Maddox's standards. I stuck the phone in my pocket, grabbed my bag and headed over to the agency's building. Just as I entered, my phone beeped. "Be careful," read a text from Solomon, "checking on you in ten minutes."

"You got it, Boss," I said to my phone before sticking it back into my pocket.

The reception desk was manned, and I announced myself, signed in, and headed to the elevator, riding it to the Million Matches floor.

As soon as I entered, I knew something was wrong.

The hairs on the back of my neck stood up and a cold chill ran down my spine. The filing cabinets behind the reception desk were all pulled apart, with files scattered all over the floor. The desk was swept clean and it smelled like someone had tried to start a fire. Yes, the wastebasket, peeking out from under the desk, had a blackened lip. What the hell went on in here?

I stood very still, my hand in my pocket as I clicked the tiny switch on my phone to turn the ringer silent. The last thing I needed was for my phone to ring, alerting an intruder. I waited for what felt like many minutes, but couldn't have been more than thirty seconds. I heard nothing.

No footsteps. No creaks. Wait. There was a muffled sound coming from somewhere down the hallway. Before I took another step, I carefully extracted my phone and texted 911 to Maddox and Solomon. Whatever happened, one of them would be on their way.

Cautiously, I turned away from the disarray and towards the hallway leading to Helen Callery's office.

270

The closer I got, the louder the muffled noise became until I recognized it was sobbing. Continuing to approach the source of the sobbing, my fists clenching and unclenching with nerves, it became very obvious to me that I didn't have a weapon.

I edged past the two doorways leading to the small kitchenette and a bathroom — both clear — and stopped at the doorway to her office. Keeping my back to the wall, I peeped my head around the door. At first, I saw nothing. No criminals rifling the room. Actually, no one at all. Nothing seemed out of place... nothing except the legs sticking out from under the desk. Well, that evoked old memories best forgotten.

Fortunately for me, this pair were wriggling and wearing the most divine Manolo Blahnick pumps. I rushed over and rounded the desk, bending down beside Helen Callery. She had a piece of silver duct tape stuck over her mouth, her hair was a mess, and mascara was smeared on her cheeks. Her left eye was swollen enough that I'd put money on her having a black eye by morning. Her hands were bound behind her back so she couldn't do anything, but wriggle.

"Mmmm, mmm, arrrrf!" she groaned and wriggled some more.

I reached for the tape. "I'm sorry," I said, "I'm going to rip this off on three, okay? One..." I ripped it off.

"What happened to three?" Helen squeaked, her hand darting to her lips. The tape left raw, red marks around her mouth.

"I thought it would be better if you weren't expecting it."

"You thought wrong! It hurt! That bitch!"

I sat back on my heels. "Me?"

"No! Madeleine!"

I looked around. "Where is Madeleine?"

"Damned if I know. She did this to me." Helen rolled her shoulders and I helped her up. Her wrists were bound by tape too, several layers thick.

"Do you know where she might have gone?"

"Long gone I should think," Helen told me while I searched her desk for a pair of scissors. I found them in the top drawer after she told me where to look, and set about cutting through the resistant layers. "I got back from lunch and caught her doing something on my computer. She knows everything we do here is confidential, and no one should have my password, but me. I don't know how she got it. When I demanded to know what was going on, we fought and she knocked me down. She straddled me..." Helen heaved a sob and her chin wobbled.

"Go on," I coaxed.

"She hit me several times before I think I passed out. When I woke up, I was bound and my mouth was taped, and I saw her working at the laptop. I don't know what she was doing." I tore off the last little bit binding her and Helen pulled her hands free. She attempted to tug the remaining tape off her wrists and winced.

"I think we need to soak them off," I advised her. "You sit up here on the desk chair and I'll check what she was doing on your computer."

"She's going to ruin my business! What the hell got into her? Maybe she wants to steal the business."

Somehow, that didn't ring true to me. I couldn't see two millionaire matchmaking businesses competing with each other in Montgomery. I didn't know what Madeleine was up to, but I had a sick feeling she was somehow connected to the thief. Maybe even connected to Ben.

I pulled the chair upright and tugged it over to the desk for Helen, helping her to sit before turning to the open laptop. Madeleine didn't bother to shut it down and it opened to the desktop when I hit the spacebar. I couldn't tell what was tampered with; that was a job for Lucas. All the same, I checked the recycle folder. Empty.

"Did you trash any files recently?" I asked.

Helen frowned. "I guess."

"The recycle folder is empty. I think Madeleine purged it clean, but I can't be sure that's all she did. What kind of information do you keep in here?"

"Everything to do with the business. All client information. Payment records. Photographs. Supplier information. Access to our database."

I pursed my lips as I thought about it. "Where do you keep your client files?"

Helen shuffled the chair over. She reached for the mouse. "Here, they're all here," she said, clicking a folder, and opening a subfolder. "Why?"

"Just a hunch," I told her as I scrolled through. "Just as I thought..."

"What?"

"At least one client file is missing." And wouldn't you just know it? The file I couldn't find belongs to Ben Rafferty. I would have tried to investigate further, as much as my limited technical knowledge allowed, but I heard a footstep in the hall, the barest sound that told me someone had entered the office suite. Fueling our worry, they didn't declare themselves.

"Someone's here," I whispered to Helen and her eyes widened as I dropped into a crouch. She shuffled off her chair and dropped next to me, pressing her back against the desk.

"Madeleine?" she mouthed.

I shook my head. "I don't know. I'm gonna go see." She grabbed my arm and I had to peel her fingers off. They were surprisingly claw-like and she had one hell of a grip. "I'll be right back."

"There's a gun in the lowest drawer," she whispered.

"Why have you got a gun?"

Helen shrugged. "Why not?"

"Could have used it!"

"On Madeleine? I was going to, but she hit me over

the head. I didn't get a chance or I would have put a cap in her head."

"Guess you didn't want to deal with her unemployment paperwork, huh?" Helen gave me a stern look that reminded me a little of both Grandma O'Shaughnessy and my old boot camp sergeant. I shivered, and edged away, reaching for the bottom drawer. Sure enough, a small revolver lay in a box.

"Where are the bullets?" I asked.

"There's a carton at the back of the drawer. I don't keep it loaded."

"No problem." I grabbed the carton, emptied a few bullets into my hand and loaded the gun. I checked the safety was off and listened hard. A creak sounded further down the hallway. I made to creep around the desk, but Helen's claws, sorry, fingers, hooked around my elbow.

"Be careful," she said, giving my elbow a little squeeze. Well, that was nice.

"No problem."

"Also, shoot to kill." Awesome.

"Thanks for the suggestion."

"You're welcome." Helen gave me a tight smile and sniffed, probably a little too loudly. I hoped our intruder didn't hear.

"Dial nine-one-one," I told her. "Be right back." I edged around the desk and a little scrape told me Helen was tugging the phone towards her. I checked quickly that she had it in her hands before running across the room to the door. Standing behind it, I peered through the crack. I had to withdraw quickly when I saw a figure advancing. I counted to five, then checked again. The figure was in shadows, obscured by the diminishing late afternoon light.

Taking a deep breath, I jumped around the door, and raised the gun, aiming right at his chest. Or his heart. Whatever. I was going to hit something! The figure raised his gun and aimed it at me; and for a moment, we were caught in a stalemate.

"Lexi?" he said, stepping forward.

"Oh! It's you! Maddox, I could have shot you!"

"I could have shot you!"

"I could have shot you first!"

"What bit of me were you aiming at?"

I waved my hand at his torso. "That bit," I told him. "And I wouldn't have missed!"

Maddox lowered his gun and looked back towards the reception. "Looks like this place has been turned over."

"Nah. They just have a really poor maintenance staff."

Maddox frowned as he turned back to me. "Really?"

"No, Detective Dumb-ass. The place got turned over by Madeleine, who, by the way, is not just any old receptionist. I've got Helen Callery in her office. She says Madeleine hit her over the head and tied her up. When she awoke, Madeleine was at the computer. I think she was erasing files at the very least."

"Whoa," said Maddox. "Madeleine is in on this? Madeleine? That cute receptionist?"

"Even cute people can commit crimes."

Maddox gave me a look and I shrugged. "Yeah, looks that way."

"Hmm."

"Are you two going to help me or what?" called Helen. "The police are on their way."

"The police are already here," said Maddox, flashing his badge.

"Thank God my taxes pay for something," said Helen. "You're fast."

Maddox huffed what might have been a laugh and looked over at me. "Are you putting the gun down or what?"

"Oh, right, sorry."

As he passed me, he said in a small voice, "I object to Detective Dumb-ass. That's Detective Great-Ass to you."

"I know. I've seen it."

"You've held it."

"Don't remind me." I mean, really, was this not the worst moment or what? Just for old time's sake, I checked out his ass as he passed. It really was a great one.

"Did you get Ben Rafferty yet?" I asked him.

"Not yet."

"Madeleine erased his file from the agency records, so my hunch says they're connected somehow. I didn't find his file in the trash file either. I think forensics needs to check it."

"That will take forever. Can you get Lucas to do it?"

I nodded. "Sure. He can crack anything."

"Tell him not to crack it, but just find and retrieve whatever got erased. I want to know what Madeleine is hiding. You okay there, Ms. Callery?"

"Could be better. My head hurts."

"I'm going to call a paramedic to check you over." Maddox's phone rang and he eyed it, letting it ring as he said, "Lexi, can you sit with her? I gotta take this call."

"Sure."

While Maddox answered his call in the corridor, I helped Helen back into her chair and placed a call of my own. "Lucas, I'm at the dating agency, and I have a laptop that needs your expertise." I quickly explained the problem and Lucas told me to bring it right over, that Solomon told him this case took priority.

"We got him," said Maddox when he returned. "Couple of uniforms spotted Rafferty heading out of town and pulled him over. They're taking him to the station now. I gotta go and take the lead. Stay with Ms. Callery until the paramedics get here; then get that laptop to Lucas. I want to know the minute something turns up."

"You got it. What about Madeleine?"

"Now that the whole of Montgomery can stop looking for Rafferty, they're on the search for Madeleine. We'll get her. She can't have gone far. Crime scene investigators will comb this place for evidence too. Don't touch anything."

I didn't touch a thing as we waited for the paramedics. I didn't even touch my gun when Blake stuck her head around the door and asked Helen a few questions about what happened. By the time Maddox told me it was okay to go, and they were leaving, I was relieved.

Helen was escorted out by two paramedics who treated her scrapes and bruises, as well as a suspected concussion. Right after the investigators arrived to do their thing, Garrett called me. "You owe me babysitting," he said before hanging up.

I looked at the phone for a moment, wondering what the hell I'd done when it rang again, my brother's name again on the screen. I answered, but before I could say anything, he said, "I hate you. I'm the only lieutenant in the history of the world taking his mom on a ride-a-long." He hung up a second time.

"Hmm," I said to a stray cat that strolled past. It paused, looked at me, then peed against the wall. I edged away and called Garrett back. "You made lieutenant," I said, before he could cut me off. "That's great! Why am I baby..."

"Hate was too strong," he cut in, "I apologize, but you still suck. You told Mom to ask me for a ride-a-long and now she wants to be a PI. You're babysitting at eight p.m. next Tuesday while I take my wife out for dinner." He hung up. After a moment, I shrugged and entered the date in my diary. Then I headed back to HQ, the laptop tucked safely in my purse, alongside Helen Callery's gun. Just in case.

CHAPTER TWENTY-ONE

I waited, lounging in my office chair with my feet on the desk, for Lucas to give me some information, and thought about Ben. Mostly, I thought about how disappointed I was that he was our real thief. Despite kicking myself for being wrong, I had felt relieved to hear that Lord Justin, aka Ken Moody, was the culprit. I felt mortified to accuse Ben. That said, Ben really played me. He had me utterly convinced that I was wrong and all along... To think I doubted myself. Next time, I'd listen to my gut instinct all the way. Lesson learned.

I watched Solomon move about his office. He grabbed his jacket, pressed a few keys on his laptop, and closed the lid. As he reached the door, he looked up, and our eyes met through the glass partition. "You okay?" he asked when he shut the door behind him.

"Meh."

"Good 'meh' or bad 'meh'?"

"Meh meh meh."

"Have you thought about going into rap?" That coaxed a smile out of me. "You better not be feeling bad about all this. It just got complicated. Cases do."

"I knew Ben was the one. I should have fought for it."

"We already had Justin, Ken Moody, whatever his name is, under arrest. Your job was to foil a fraud and you did. You did just fine," Solomon assured me.

"We got the wrong guy."

"We've got Ben Rafferty now."

"Not his accomplice."

Solomon shrugged. "Not yet, not today. Maybe tomorrow. We underestimated Ben. It didn't occur to any of us that the scope of this operation involved a partner. You uncovered that."

"Who do you think Madeleine is to him anyway? His wife? Girlfriend?" I mused. Ick. I hoped she wasn't either. I'd feel bad about kissing him if that were the case.

"Could be. Could be a friend or relative, or just someone in it for the money, just like Ben... What is it?"

I stopped listening the moment Solomon mused on who Madeleine really was and my mind reeled. "You know, we could find out if they are related. When I went to Million Matches, the kitchen wasn't cleaned. Maybe Madeleine used a mug or something. There might be DNA. Oh my God! At my house too! I mean the Chilton house. Ben sipped a glass of water and I put it in the kitchen to wash, and you know, I never got around to it. We could have his DNA too. That's better than a fingerprint! Oh! We have fingerprints too! Oh shit! The crime scene investigators got to the agency just as I left."

"How long ago?"

"Maybe an hour." Solomon was on the phone in a flash. "Who're you texting?" I asked.

"Your ex. He needs to preserve that evidence, get it bagged and tagged and sent to the lab."

"Who's the rapper now?"

The corner of Solomon's mouth edged upwards and his chest heaved — not that I was looking — like he wanted to laugh. "Let me know what happens with the laptop," he said.

"Where are you going?"

"I was going to MPD. Now I'm heading to Chilton to get that glass. Fingerprints and DNA could crack Ben Rafferty's real identity. You did good."

I reached for my lip gloss and pocket mirror. "I know."

The time it took for Lucas to investigate the computer gave me more time for contemplation, and not one bit of it was about Solomon's broad, strong chest. Well, those few seconds were all about his physique, but mostly I thought about Ben and all the problems he caused. Money, gems, and other things stolen. Financial loss, shattered memories, and sentimental pain.

I wondered which was worse and concluded the loss of all those stolen items probably meant different things to different people. That got me to thinking about all the other intangible things Ben was messing with. The women he preyed on may have had affection for him, which would have, no doubt, eroded their confidence in themselves, once they knew they had been played. I considered all the emotional fallout from that. Did Ben leave a string of broken hearts across the country? Internationally? Were these women loath to trust another man? I wondered how he slept at night. Considering that he had great skin, no bags under his eyes, and made this his career, I had to conclude, he slept pretty damn well.

Really, I had to consider myself very lucky I didn't lose a single thing to him. Except I liked him, and that bugged me. He was sweet, funny, and charming. Not all of that could have been an act. He was really handsome too; that definitely was no act.

One thing was for certain: I would drive myself mad trying to work Ben Rafferty out, and my energies were better served elsewhere. Like catching other criminals and online shopping. I just hoped he confessed now he was in handcuffs.

All the same, my thoughts drifted back to Ben and the strange familiarity that kept troubling me over and over. I was sure I had seen him somewhere before. Somewhere recently. If only I could figure out where I knew him from, I might get to Madeleine, then we'd get three criminals for the price of one. MPD would love the Solomon Agency for that. Or not... It really depended on their caseload and how much they loved paperwork.

From my drawer I grabbed my pad of paper and pulled a pen from the mug on my desk. I wrote BEN RAFFERTY at the top and followed his name with a big, fat question mark. Where were all the places I might have seen him before? TV? Newspaper? Magazine? I wrote the three on the pad and sub-headed that list "Not in person". I drew a line down the middle of the pad and added another sub-heading to the right side. "In person." So where could I have seen him? The store? Grocery shopping?

After I scrawled a few ideas, I tossed my pen on the pad. It was impossible! If it were somewhere public, that would be no help at all. It wouldn't even necessarily pinpoint an area where I could go look. It was not only a waste of time, but a dead end. I thought about the night I saw him outside the Chilton house. I didn't recognize him straight off then. I could have seen Ben anywhere.

Maybe if I went to MPD and actually looked at him? Something might jog my memory. Only I was stuck, waiting on Lucas...

"Lucas?" I called as I swiveled in my chair. "How's it going?"

"Good. I'm done. This Madeleine is not as tech-savvy as she might think, which is good news for us. She's good, but I retrieved all the files. Want to take a look?"

"You bet."

Lucas turned the laptop towards me as I rounded his

desk. "Here's a list of the deleted files," he told me.

"You have the files too?" Lucas gave me the "Are you stupid?" look and clicked another button, opening a folder. There were only a dozen files, including Ben's, although that one I knew about. There were several women, with a couple of names I recognized, so I figured the rest must be on the agency's books too. There was a file with my fake name on it. The last file was named "Madeleine."

"Have you looked through the files?"

"Yeah." Lucas nodded. "They're all intact even though she tried to load a virus to corrupt everything. It was pretty amateur." Lucas pointed at the screen. "Most of these are agency profiles, including details of dates and follow-up notes entered by Helen Callery. That includes yours and Ben's. Madeleine's file is in employment records."

"Do we have their photos?"

"No. I figure they didn't scan them."

"That's probably why Madeleine went through the office files. I wondered why she would start a fire. Maybe it was too risky to take them. I bet when we audit them, we'll find that it's only these files that are missing." I made a circular movement with my hand while pointing at the digital icons.

"I wouldn't be surprised if Madeleine made copies of every file in this laptop before she tried corrupting it," said Lucas. "It would make sense if they wanted to spend more time targeting clients."

"That's not good news. She might keep that information to use in the future."

"I'll be able to tell you soon enough if she copied them."

"Can you tell me while I'm on the move? I have my cell."

Lucas glanced up and shrugged. "No problem. Where are you going?"

"MPD. I want to take another look at Ben. I know him from somewhere, I just don't know where."

"Are you sure?"

"Not a hundred percent, but close as."

"Do Solomon and Detective Maddox know?"

"Not yet. I've stuffed up enough on this case. When I know something, I'll tell them. Besides, Maddox already has Ben in custody, so I'm not sure it's even all that relevant."

"If you think it's relevant, maybe it is." Lucas turned to the screen, striking keys and losing himself in the familiar "tap tap tap" of his keyboard.

I smiled at the back of his head. "When did you get so wise?"

He looked up. "Fooled ya," he said, grinning.

I pulled up across the street from MPD, turning off the engine just as my cell phone started to ring. I had a mind to ignore it, but good sense told me to answer it. Good sense served me right. Funny, I usually had a good time when I ignored it too.

"Boss," I said, on answering.

"Employee," said Solomon. I held the phone away from my ear and stuck my tongue out at it. "I have the glass. I'm going to take it into MPD. The CSI's collected a few items from the dating agency for comparison."

"It'll take them forever to get DNA and prints."

"They probably already got them when Rafferty got booked," Solomon replied, sounding like he couldn't care less. "This is just backup, assuming his accomplice may have the abilities to hack into MPD's systems."

"You think so? Lucas said the virus Madeleine uploaded was amateur."

"Lucas thinks so. Plus, your definition of amateur compared to Lucas's are worlds apart," he reminded me.

"Isn't Lucas reaching?"

"Maybe, but I'd rather take precautions. I'll take the glass to a friend of mine who works in forensics. I hope

Maddox will give me something from the dating agency, a cup or mug, or whatever they find that I can get tested too."

"You think he'll just give you evidence?"

"Sure. It means he can skip the over-worked queue for their crime lab and get the results faster. Plus, it's just backup information; we have enough samples from what I can guess. My contact has a bonafide lab but whatever Maddox takes to court, he can get from his own lab later. We'll back it up as consulting detectives."

"I'm at MPD now. You want me to run it by him?"

"No. Wait for me there. I'll be there in fifteen."

"Awesome," I said, my voice dry. I really, really didn't enjoy the idea of being stuck in the same room as Maddox and Solomon. Again. The only thing that could make it worse would be stuck in the same room as my ex-boyfriend, ex-lover, and all three of my brothers. The icing on the cake would be if Delgado, my potential future brother-in-law turned up for the floorshow. On that cheery thought, I decided there was no time like the present to hightail it over there and get the whole thing over with.

I managed to bump into Garret on entering the building. "Don't mention babysitting," I told him. "I'm down for it."

"I wasn't going to mention babysitting. I was going to ask what you were doing here. Is Mom with you?" He looked over my shoulder.

"Hah. No. I'm consulting on Maddox's theft and fraud case."

"Ah."

"No smartass comments?"

"None. Too busy. How's Lily?"

"Sad."

"It's too bad that happened to her. She'd have made a great mom."

"She still will someday."

"That's positive thinking, Lexi. I like it. Tell her Traci and I say hi and we'll come by when she's feeling a little better. Sam and Chloe made her a card. Sam wrote 'Get better soon, butt face.' I'm not sure she'll like it."

"She might. I'm sure she'll appreciate the thought." I paused. "Not Sam's thoughts so much."

Garrett smiled. "Okay, so if you're looking for Maddox, I'll take you upstairs."

"You sure you have time?"

"Sure thing."

Lucky me, we picked up my second oldest brother, Daniel, en route. Fortunately, I staved off one uncle and four cousins on the way, or it would have looked like I was arriving at Maddox's desk with an entourage. I figured I was plenty awesome enough on my own.

Maddox glanced up when the three of us crowded in front of his desk.

"Why aren't you interrogating the suspect?" I asked.

"I'm letting him sweat."

"I don't think Ben sweats. He just glistens a little."

"I think the cuffs are helping."

I nearly quipped, "Didn't know you were into that sort of thing," before remembering one time when he definitely was. My brothers did not need to hear about that. It was enough that they glared daggers at Maddox for weeks and already made his life plenty uncomfortable during our break-up. The three of them assured me Maddox was safe for now, and I didn't want to stir things up again.

"Great!" I beamed.

Maddox frowned. "That's scary." Then he got a look that told me he thought the same as I. He smiled to himself.

"He's right," said Daniel, nudging me in the ribs. "You look like you might kill someone and get away with it."

"I'm touched that you think I'd get away with it." I

turned back to Maddox who was waiting patiently for the Three Graves Comedy Show to end. "So... Ben? Whatcha got?"

"It's quite a story." The chair in front of me burst out from under the desk and I just caught a glimpse of Maddox's boot retreating. I took the hint and sat. My brothers took up positions either side of me. When I glanced over, they both stood with their feet shoulder-width apart, hands folded in front of their crotches. They looked like club bouncers. I watched Maddox look from Garrett to Daniel. Garret, his senior, he couldn't do much about. Daniel, his senior's brother, he couldn't do much about either, so he sighed instead. I could have done something about it, but that was no fun, especially once I spied Detective Blake entering the room. She started to approach, stopped, looked at the three Graves looking her way, thought better of it. She switched her route to walk out the other door, past her colleagues who didn't make any effort to talk to her. Maddox made no move to call her over.

Hmmm. So, Blake wasn't exactly popular. I wondered just how hard life had been for her at the station, and struggled to give a shit. I had no fondness for the woman, and a low opinion of her. All I knew was she partnered up with Maddox, which included going undercover as his girlfriend in a sting, a role she really warmed to. How far it went... well, there was no need to go into that again. We'd spoken briefly on occasion, but made no effort otherwise. I was aware she was still a part of Maddox's team after transferring here, but I heard nothing about her one way or the other. Come to think of it, my family had been unusually discreet about not mentioning her, and they knew everyone in law enforcement. My heart warmed a little at their protective natures.

"Go on," I urged Maddox. "Though if you've got coffee..."

Maddox smiled warmly and it made his eyes crinkle in a particularly sexy way. "We've pieced together most of it," he said. "Ben Rafferty is almost certainly an alias. We can't tie him to the crimes yet, but we will."

"Wait! He hasn't confessed? Has he lawyered up?"

Maddox shook his head. "Not yet, but he will. They always do."

"Any sign of Madeleine?"

Again, another shake of the head. "Not yet. We're sure Madeleine is an alias too. We don't have any photos of her as she was never under surveillance, so if you can get one, that would help."

"I'm sorry, I don't think I have anything, but I'll check our files. Maybe one of my colleagues snapped a photo of her."

"Thanks, appreciate that."

"Solomon says he has a forensics guy who can run their prints and DNA." I shut my mouth. Oops. Was I supposed to not mention that? I didn't want to steal Solomon's thunder.

"That would be useful. We ran Ben's prints against our databases and got nothing."

"Nothing?" said we three Graves in unison.

Maddox sucked in a breath and let it out slowly. Yeah, we were exasperating. Whatever. "Nothing," he confirmed. "Local and national."

"I hear Madeleine is good with computers," I dropped in.

Maddox nodded, letting that register. "Then we need to check the prints manually against the crimes we think are linked. That's gonna take time. Time we don't have. The moment Ben asks for a lawyer, he'll be out of here and we'll have nothing to charge him with. All the lawyer needs to do is point out our evidence is circumstantial, and I don't see him desperate to confess."

"Solomon said he'll be here soon. He's got a glass with Ben's prints. We're hoping for DNA."

"Where'd he get it?"

"The Chilton place."

I felt a tap on my shoulder. "Lexi, how are you mixed up in this?" asked Garrett, looking down.

I flapped a hand at him. "Undercover consulting," I explained as succinctly as I could, wanting to get back to the story. "I told you."

"Anyway," Maddox said, looking from Garrett to me, "I spoke to a guy in Charlotte and he said he had suspicions about a female accomplice, but nothing he could readily put a finger on. I asked him for a description and he said there was a blonde hanging around, but he couldn't really describe her beyond 'white and a nice figure'."

"Madeleine has red hair, but she could've dyed it."

Maddox gave a nod of agreement and reached for his desk phone, which started ringing. He answered it, spoke briefly and put the phone down. "That was Blake," he told us. "Ben asked for a lawyer. We can't speak to him anymore until his counsel is here."

"That sucks."

"This is less fascinating than I thought it would be," said Daniel, over my head, to Garrett. "You want to get something to eat?"

"What's the special today?"

"Burgers. With real meat."

"Tasty." Garrett's hand landed on my shoulder and he squeezed it softly, which was a little like being gripped in a vise. "You okay here, Lexi? Or do you want to sample MPD cuisine? See what they make us run on."

I thought they were less interested in feeding me, and more worried about leaving me on my own with Maddox while Blake lurked nearby. All the same, I refused their offer with a simple "No, thanks."

"Good call," said Daniel, squeezing my other shoulder. Ouch.

"I know we can't talk to Ben, but can I take a peek?" I

asked, when my brothers left.

"Huh?"

"You know, an eyeball. A look-see. A..."

"I know what a peek is. Haven't you seen the guy enough?"

"Yeah, but I just wanted another look."

"You and the whole female contingent of MPD," huffed Maddox.

"If it makes you feel better, I'm not going to perve."

Maddox rolled his eyes. It wasn't smart, but appropriate. "I'll see what I can do. Shouldn't be a problem. Let me get this," he said, as his cell phone began to ring. Answering the call, I looked around the room, taking in the whiteboard full of scrawled notes, and the heaped piles of paperwork consuming his fellow detectives' desks. I really didn't know how they could work in such chaos, but I sure as hell wasn't going to offer to file any of it. "There was a possible sighting of Madeleine; she was heading towards Boston," he said, setting the phone down. "Uniforms are tailing her until they can get a decent sighting."

"Why don't they just pull her over?"

"They don't want to spook her."

"If it's really her, she'll notice. She's not stupid."

"I don't think she's even stupid enough to get spotted," said Maddox, "but you never know. This Rafferty guy did. Excuse me again." This time, he grabbed the desk phone and spoke into it. "What?"

"You have an excellent phone manner," I told him when he hung up.

Maddox laughed. "Ben's lawyer just got here. You'll have to wait on that peek while they talk privately."

"No problem."

"Coffee?"

"Please," said Solomon, making me jump.

"When did you get here?" I asked, twisting to find him looming over me.

"You'll never know," he said before turning to Maddox. "How's it going?"

"Lexi and I will fill you in while we get that coffee. Follow me. I hope you like coffee that tastes of nothing, but keeps you awake long enough to get the shakes." He didn't even wait to hear the answer, instead pushing back his chair and indicating we should follow him. Solomon's eyes roved over the same whiteboards as he waited for me to get up, and I was pretty certain he memorized the whole lot.

The breakroom-slash-kitchen was small, stuffed with old furniture, and a coffee machine that had seen better days. Maddox set about fixing the coffee, which involved hitting the machine hard enough to get it to start, then spending several minutes hunting for filters. While that occupied Maddox, I relayed to Solomon what Maddox already told me, with Maddox occasionally chipping in.

"Your uniforms are tailing the wrong woman," Solomon said when we finished. "Madeleine is long gone. I don't think she's even a redhead anymore. If she was in on this from the beginning with Ben, they must have an exit plan. They know how to move fast, change their looks, and never leave a trace."

"Didn't help Ben," Maddox pointed out.

"He was unlucky, but he knows there's nothing to hold him on until he can be tied to a crime. So far, we've got this one theft we can put him in the vicinity of, and a whole bunch of suspicions. Once his lawyer sees how little we've got, he gets boosted and he's in the wind. He'll put his exit plan into play and that's it. Ben Rafferty ceases to exist." Solomon clapped his hands together as if to say "the end."

For a moment, we stood there looking at each other, then the coffee machine made the most awful gurgling noise and we all looked at it instead. That was the moment Detective Blake stuck her head around the door and we all looked at her next.

"Boss, a moment," she said, pretending not to notice us staring.

Maddox nodded and without looking at me, followed her out of the room.

"You okay?" asked Solomon.

"I wish people would stop asking me that! I am okay, I am totally okay, I am so okay, I'm the okay queen!"

"Just asking," said Solomon, with a slightly bemused look. "You really want this coffee?"

"I'd rather have a donut, but this station isn't nearly clichéd enough."

"We'll get a donut when we're done."

"It's a date." I froze, my mouth clamped shut, and my eyes widened. It was a flippant remark, but our history was too loaded for joking about dates.

"It's a date," said Solomon, softly.

Maddox stepped into the room and paused. He looked from me to Solomon, and for a moment, I wondered if he heard us. Then, he gulped and said, "We've got a problem."

Chapter Twenty-Two

"How the fuck did Ben Rafferty escape the police station?" yelled Maddox at the squad room, now filling with officers, both in uniform and plain clothes. Detective Blake stood to one side, slightly behind Maddox, looking chagrined. Maddox seemed like he was about to combust, the strain of the audacious escape showing. That, and he appeared more pissed than I'd ever seen him. "Since when do we let criminals go? Someone had better come up with an explanation pretty damn fast before I have you all on report!"

Soft murmurs rumbled through the gathered crowd. A few shoulders shrugged and some looked around, waiting for the idiot who let Ben go step forward. Unsurprisingly, no one came forth.

"Where's that lawyer of his?" demanded Maddox. "Who showed him to the interview room?"

"I did," said a young, suited man that I didn't recognize. "And it wasn't a him. A her."

"A her?"

"You know, a female lawyer."

"Damn it, Ray, I know what a 'her' is! Where is she now?"

"Well, sir..."

"Let me guess. You can't find her!"

Ray shook his head and fidgeted on the spot, seemingly unsure whether to fade back into the comfort of his brethren, or face further questioning.

A horrible thought crossed my mind. Surely not? Surely, they wouldn't be so daring? I leaned into Maddox, whispering, "What did she look like?" His eyes showed the comprehension crossing his face as he groaned, slamming a hand to his forehead.

"Ray, what did the lawyer look like?"

"Uh..." Ray scratched his head, leaving a tuft sticking up at the crown. "Caucasian, brunette, real long too, young, like maybe thirty at most, pretty."

"Madeleine," said Solomon, softly.

"Shit," said Maddox.

"I'm kind of impressed," I said. They both glared at me. Detective Blake glared too, but I pretended not to notice her. "Oh, come on! It's pretty bold. Busting Ben out of the station takes some nerve. It's better than a confession!"

"Ray, get me security tapes from the route she took to the interview room. I want to see for certain." Maddox looked around as Ray scurried from the room, grateful for anything to do besides getting berated. "Which one of you idiots was supposed to be watching Ben?"

"That would be me," said Blake softly.

"You're an idiot," said Maddox, not bothering to drop his voice She colored, her cheeks blooming pink. "How did they get past you?"

"I went to the bathroom. I didn't feel well."

"Why didn't you get someone to cover?"

"I did!" Blake protested, her cheeks pinking with anger and embarrassment. "Callaghan was supposed to stand outside until I returned."

"Callaghan!" Maddox yelled.

The man I assumed to be Callaghan stepped forward. He looked familiar and I had to think hard before I recognized him as a guy Jord once shared an apartment with. I was sure he'd been to my parents' house for dinner once or twice, but that was years ago now. He nodded to me and gave me a tight, little smile of recognition. I nodded in return.

"You know this guy?" Solomon asked softly, his lips inches from my ear. "Could he be compromised?"

"Old friend of one of my brothers," I told him. "Nice guy. Not the smartest, but good at his job."

"Captain Almond waved me over. I talked to him, but I swear I had my eye on the door the whole time," explained Callaghan, no doubt realizing that he was knee-deep in doo-doo. I wondered just what Maddox would do to the poor guy. But what could be worse than everyone knowing he let such a big fish walk out of the building, undisturbed? He made a rookie error by stepping away from the door and they all knew it.

"It only takes a few seconds to slip out of there and into the next corridor. Next time, do your job, Callaghan, or you won't have one. You too, Blake. Ray, you got the video?" Maddox asked as Ray paused in the doorway.

Ray gave an eager nod. "The tapes are ready to view in the AV room."

"Let's go. Solomon, Graves, you're with me. Blake, get out there and find them. They can't have gone far!" Maddox stormed from the room, ahead of us.

I turned to follow them, but stopped as Blake put her hand on my arm. She leaned forwards and whispered in my ear. It wasn't an appropriate time, and I didn't quite know what to make of it, but she was gone before I could reply.

I hurried to catch up to Maddox and Solomon as they rounded the end of the corridor, my heels making loud clicks on the floor, complementing Solomon's heavy, solid footfalls. True to his word, Ray had the video feed on the door to what I assumed was the interview room where Ben was held. He hit "Play" and we watched as a woman, her back to us, entered the room, carrying a large bag. Callaghan shut the door behind them and nodded to Ray who retreated out of shot. Callaghan fidgeted outside for a moment before we saw Captain Almond walk past and go out of shot. Seconds later, Callaghan looked in his direction, said something, and nodded. He glanced at the door and moved out of shot, just as he said, leaving the door unguarded.

It took only moments for the door to open. The woman stepped out first. I got a good view of her suited body and exceptionally nice pumps, but her hair concealed her face. All the same, I would swear it was Madeleine's jaw line. She pushed a sweep of hair behind her ear and inclined her head. For a fraction of a second, I saw her. Madeleine. Great wig! It was too long to be her own. I wondered where she got it, and if the red was a wig too.

Then Ben stepped out, his head down. He wore a pale suit, shirt and tie, looking every inch a smart civilian. As we watched the jacket came off and he pulled a sweater over his shirt, changing his look in an instant. He kept his head tucked down as they moved into the corridor. Someone bumped into Ben, a young uniformed woman, hurrying past with a stack of files in her arms. Ben simply looked away, down, then up, and straight into the camera. For a fraction of a second, I thought he smiled as he pulled on a baseball cap.

Like the proverbial ton of bricks, it hit me where I saw Ben before. It wasn't at a coffee shop, or the mall, or through a bored glance at the next checkout in the grocery store. It was a random meeting. I knew I'd never have worked it out, because it just didn't seem like a place I'd ever see him. It was on a stairwell in a dank apartment building in the midst of rundown

Frederickstown, and he looked very different in jeans and a ball cap than in the beautifully tailored suit he wore on the video.

"Madeleine," sighed Maddox. "We should have anticipated this."

"They are formidable opponents," said Solomon, shaking his head. "I'd hire them, if I didn't think they wouldn't rip me off that same day."

"I gotta go," I said, staring at the video showing Callaghan taking up his post again, none the wiser that he was guarding an empty room. "I'll be right back," I said, edging backwards.

"Replay the video," Maddox said, and no one paid me any attention as I left the room. Except Solomon, who just frowned, but didn't try to stop me.

I floored it to Frederickstown, arriving ten minutes faster than I should, thanks to my knowledge of the back streets and skill at avoiding every traffic camera. I parked unevenly outside the building.

Yep, this was where I saw Ben Rafferty. I was sure of it. Just as sure as the realtor telling me the whole building was already rented. What I wasn't sure about was why Ben would come back here? Or if he would come back here? But no one else except me knew to look for him here. With the whole of Montgomery searching for him, and Maddox on the warpath, he needed a safe place to hide. Safe from everyone but me. I grabbed Helen's gun from where I stowed it in the trunk during my station visit and tucked it into my waistband.

As luck would have it, the front door lock was broken, and all I had to do was tug on it to gain entry. No doorman here, no concierge, just an easy pass across the spartan lobby to reach the stairs. I took them two at a time, heading up to the top floor. As I reached the third floor, I heard sounds coming from inside the tiny apartment I saw before. Amazingly enough, it was rented out. I passed by without stopping. The fourth and final floor had a matching layout to the other floors. One door on the left, one on the right. The left apartment that looked over the street was partially open. The other muffled the sound of a baby crying.

I turned to the left, stepped forward and pushed the door open while reaching for Helen gun. Now I extracted it, and stepped inside.

Whoever was here didn't make any effort to decorate it. Sparse. A bed with a chocolate brown comforter, neatly made. A couch. No TV. Cautiously, I checked the doors. Tiny bathroom - empty. Closet - empty of clothing. Kitchenette - but no evidence of anyone cooking here. I checked the cupboards and found a couple of dinner plates, mugs, and glasses.

Returning to the living room, I looked around, confident now that I was alone. A small desk was in the corner. Something, or somethings, were tacked to the wall recently and there were tears where the tape was ripped off. I checked the wastebasket even though I knew Ben Rafferty wouldn't be stupid enough to leave anything behind. Same with the drawers - empty.

I stared out the window, wondering where he could be. It didn't look like he was coming back. As I pondered his next move, I saw Ben standing on the sidewalk across the street. Almost immediately, my cell phone rang.

"Unbelievable," I said, as I saw the name flash up. "Hello, Ben," I said into the phone.

"Hello, Lexi." Ben's voice was smooth. He lifted a hand and waved. I thought about flipping him the finger, but instead, I raised a hand too, dropping it quickly. "You found my home away from home," he said.

"It's not much of a vacation retreat," I told him. "You could do better."

"Sometimes, you just need somewhere to lay your head. You know, I thought you would recognize me sooner."

"Soon enough."

"Yet... not," said Ben, and I thought I saw him smile.

"So you recognized me from that day in the stairwell?" I asked.

"I never forget a pretty face. I remembered you from that day, but couldn't work out why a rich girl like you was in Frederickstown. Then it all changed on our last date. Tell me, Lexi, who are you?"

"Shouldn't I be asking you that?"

"You could, but you wouldn't get an answer. You, though..." Ben put a finger to his chin as he gazed up at me, "I don't think you're a cop, so I guess that makes you some other kind of law enforcement?"

"Ben Rafferty... stumped for an answer? Who knew?" I was teasing, but stalling for time too. There was no way to let Solomon or Maddox know where I was, or that I was currently talking to our chief suspect.

"That's not the question you should be asking."

"Oh? What is?"

"You should be asking how long it took me to make you. I didn't at first, I'll grant you that, but after a while... I got suspicious. You were just too pretty, and lovely, and rich, to be at that dating agency. A woman like you? Unable to get a date? it didn't sit right."

I wasn't sure if that was a compliment; if so, it was a backhanded one. "Thank you?"

"You're welcome. I thoroughly enjoyed dating you, by the way. Excellent company."

"You're not so bad for a criminal either."

"My turn to say thanks?" Across the street, Ben's smile broadened.

"You're not exactly welcome."

"Spoilsport."

"Just out of curiosity... When did you make me?" I asked.

"Ah! At the ball."

"The ball?"

"You didn't work it out? How I got the jewels out of there? They were in your purse, my sweet Lexi. You didn't get searched, confirming my suspicions."

Memories of that night flooded back. Dropping my purse, Ben handing it to me, the two of us separated for the search, then Ben taking my purse from me when he helped me into my coat. He had a fast hand!

"I see you figured it out. Listen, gorgeous, Lexi, I'd love to stay and chat, but my sister and I want out of Montgomery. I sense we overstayed our welcome. She didn't want to hang around but I just had to know who you were and what you were up to. Nearly got caught this time. What a rush!"

"Your sister?" Ben was silent for a moment, and I got the feeling he didn't mean to let that slip. "You and Madeleine are in a whole world of trouble, Ben."

"Only if you catch us."

"You can count on it."

"Bye, Lexi."

"One last thing!"

"Yes?"

"Was anything you said real?"

"You tell me." Ben blew me a kiss, sending it soaring towards me with a gesture of his open palm. "Until we meet again." He hung up, and I watched as he dropped the cell phone in the trash, turned, and walked away. Seconds later, he was lost from view around the corner. Whether those were his parting words, or just a feeling deep in the pit of my belly, I knew I hadn't seen the last of Ben Rafferty. And considering I was on the side of the good guys, a little bit of me felt pleased.

I hit speed-dial. "Hey," I said. "I found Rafferty's hiding place in Montgomery, but you may as well not bother. He's already gone."

"Are you sure?" asked Solomon.

"Yeah, I'm standing in the apartment. It's empty."

"Secure it and send the address to me."

"No problem. I'm going home; and John, I'm taking a few days off. I've got a house to pack up, a best friend to look after, and a whole lot of clothes to return."

"Take it easy," was all he said.

I secured the apartment by slamming the door shut and allowing the lock to click, certain that there was nothing worth securing, and jogged lightly down the stairs. The baby ceased crying, and cooking smells were drifting through the central stairwell, making my stomach rumble. After sending the address to Solomon, I turned the VW around and headed for home, glad I had one.

~

"So you let him get away, just like that?" Lily snapped her fingers and gave me The Look.

I shrugged and reached for another slice of pizza. We were eating out of the box because my idiot brother decided, in his wisdom, to pack the plates without labeling the box. "I figured I was never going to get down the stairs, out the door, and across the street to knock him out and sit on him until MPD got there."

"True. You gonna tell Maddox?"

"Hell, no. Let him keep on thinking they lost him."

Lily raised her glass. "I'll drink to that. The morons."

"Did I tell you Rebecca Blake spoke to me?"

"As in Detective Blake? That Detective Blake? What's the bitch got to say for herself? Why did you even listen? Of all the nerve!"

"It was okay. She apologized actually. Told me nothing happened between Maddox and her. That she would have liked it if something did, but he was always clear that he had a girlfriend and wasn't interested."

"Oh, really?" Lily's eyes widened and her hand scrabbled around the box, looking for the last slice. She fixed on it and brought it to her mouth, her eyes never leaving my face. I absently swatted at my mouth, just in case there was a stray string of cheese that fascinated her. "You believe that?" she asked. "You want to eat salad tomorrow?"

I sighed. "I don't know. I guess. Yes to the salad."

"Why? She's a scheming boyfriend stealer!"

"Maybe not."

"Again," Lily paused, "do you believe her?"

"She has nothing to gain from telling me. Maddox could've lied in the hope of keeping us together, but Blake? From her perspective, it looks like she loses if she says nothing happened. She doesn't get Maddox and she doesn't keep me away."

"Or, things with her and Maddox have ended, and she's trying to get on his good side by getting you two back together. She did screw up the case."

"I didn't think of that, but somehow, I don't think so. I'd never try getting an ex back with his ex. There're some guys I dated that I'd like to dump back on their exes... but this? I don't know. All I can think is Blake had nothing to gain from telling me nothing happened. So, yes. I believe her. I believe nothing happened."

"So, let's say, we believe her," said Lily, ignoring my epiphany. "What now?"

"Honestly, I don't know. It would be easier to keep on hating Maddox for cheating, but he always told me he didn't, and it got blown out of proportion. Now I just look like a jerk for not trusting him."

Lily's slightly greasy palm landed on the back of my hand. "No, you don't. You saw something going on that could have been something going on, but instead, it was something going on that might just have been undercover goings on."

"I'm going to take a moment to process that." I flopped back on the couch and Lily did the same.

"When you're done being a human computer, what are you going to do about Maddox now? He's still in love with you, right?"

"Yeah, but I don't know. I think the bad feelings went on too long and then all that stuff with Solomon..."

"All the awesome sex?"

"Ummm, yeah, that stuff..." That, and all the feelings, the good and the bad, the jealousy, and the upset, the not knowing whether to believe my own eyes, or what Maddox told me, all that and... Solomon. It was a helluva lot to process. I wriggled uncomfortably on the couch. "Where are the pillows?"

"In an unnamed box somewhere over there." Lily waved a hand towards the window. "Jord's been really great with taking over the packing, but he doesn't label anything. I think he packed my toothbrush."

"How's he bearing up?"

"Okay. He's sad. We both are, but we can't change it. This baby wasn't meant to be for us, but that doesn't mean we won't love the memory of what could have been."

"Will you try again?"

"I don't know. Maybe." Lily smiled sadly. "In a while. After we settle into the new house and the bar is running okay. Ruby's been great, you know. She's babysitting the bar between her shifts and she got the builders to agree to take fifteen percent off the whole bill if they run over the deadline. I'm glad I hired her. So, baby making is a future thing, for now."

"I'll be there when you're ready. Well, not for, you know, the conception. I'd rather be out of town for that."

"I'll give you notice."

"Please don't."

"Your parents still have sex, you know."

I gaped at her. "They do not! You take that back!"

"I wonder if Jord and I will still be doing it at that age?"

"I'm hoping you'll stop pretty soon." I squeezed her hand. "Could have picked worse guys, I guess."

"I have, but I returned my membership card for

Gross Guys by the Dozen," said Lily, and for the first time in a really long time, she laughed. She gave my hand one last squeeze, got up, and headed into the kitchen. She returned with a bottle of champagne and two straws. "Remember this?" she said and I cringed.

"No glasses?" I asked as she wrested the cork from the neck, sending it popping to the ceiling. Lily raised an eyebrow. "Silly question," I agreed. "What are we toasting?"

"The end of an era? Not catching a criminal, but having fun trying? Maddox not being a cheating dick? New homes."

"I'm still in shock and awe that Rafferty got away."

"Only because you kind of let him. That's shock and awesome, in one."

"Don't ever tell anyone," I said and she crossed her heart. "So which do we toast? All of the above?"

Lily nodded and dropped the straws into the neck, wedging herself next to me before offering me one. "Works for me, but you know who we're missing? Who we haven't talked about yet?"

"Solomon," we both said at the same time.

"Yep. How do you feel about him?"

"I've felt really confused for a long time, and now Blake has given me closure about Maddox and I... I'm okay. I feel sad because I don't know what could have been with him."

"That's not what I asked, Lexi. How do you feel about Solomon?"

I took a deep breath. "I think I love him."

Lily nodded. "Thought so," she said, and we both put the straws to our lips and took a long draw of champagne.

~

I left Lily's at nine and stumbled up the stairs to my apartment, fondly remembering all the times over the years I'd staggered up there. The end of an era indeed.

303

With Lily moving out in just a couple of weeks, and me a few days after, there would be very little opportunity for partying in the meantime. On the plus side, Lily was already planning the big opening night for her bar, and once I got the keys for the bungalow, I'd barely have to trip in my heels at the front door to land in bed.

Almost as soon as I put my key in the door, the buzzer rang. I stumbled in, and pressed "Answer" for the entry phone. "Hello?"

"It's Maddox. I know it's late. Can I come up?"

I paused. What the hell? "Sure."

I waited for Maddox at the threshold, smiling when he joined me. Something got damaged between us, something deep within, but something was also repaired through Blake's startling confession. For the first time in a really long time, I didn't feel unhappy to see him, or angry. Rather, I felt confused, unsure, and a little bit happy too. Maybe we couldn't have a romantic relationship, right now, or at all – truly, I didn't know — but maybe we could be friends instead. It was a warming thought.

"I wasn't sure if you'd be home," he said.

"I planned on going to Serena's to return the clothes I borrowed, but there was an accident with a bottle of champagne at Lily's..."

"Let me guess," Maddox laughed. "You two drank it."

"Yup."

"You're not planning on driving at all this evening?"

"No, officer. I'm taking a short walk to bed without breaking a single law."

"Glad to hear it." Maddox shuffled from one foot to another.

"So, what can I do for you?"

"I came by to see if you needed help with the big move. You need any boxes, or labor? I can take a couple days off if you need my help."

"That's really nice of you, Adam."

"So...?"

"Let me think on it, okay? But I really appreciate it."

"Okay, well, let me know." Maddox turned to leave.

"Hey, Blake talked to me today."

Maddox paused. "She did?"

"Yeah. She told me nothing happened between you guys."

"I told you that too, more than once." He held a hand up. "I know. You don't have to say anything. I didn't put her up to it... I want you to know that."

"I know."

"So, what now?"

"Maybe we can be friends?"

Maddox seemed to think about that, then he nodded, gave me a sad smile, and nodded again. "We always were, Lexi. I just don't want to give up on the idea that you've given up on me. Not yet." He stepped backwards and half turned. "Call me soon if you need help with the move. I'm in the queue behind your brothers, cousins, uncles, your sister's scary boyfriend, and your dad." I waited for him to mention Solomon, but he didn't. That spoke volumes. Maddox knew something went on between us, but he didn't know what the situation was now: nothing, just my heart racing fast whenever my boss was round — the way it once did around Maddox — and my admission to Lily.

"There's always room for another," I told him, "'Night, Adam."

"'Night, Lexi. Sweet dreams." He gave me a wave, and a happier smile, before clattering down the stairs. After hearing the front door shut, I stepped inside and closed mine. I kicked off my shoes, hung my jacket on the rack, strolled into the living room, and screamed.

"Didn't mean to scare you," said Solomon, rising from my couch.

"Great job not doing that! What the hell are you doing in my living room?"

"You mean besides listening to you make friends with the ex?"

"Besides that."

Solomon held his hands out, palms up. "Waiting for you."

Well, duh, I guessed that. There was no other reason to break in. Speaking of which... "You broke in!"

"Actually I didn't. The door was open. So I figured I would wait."

"Huh? Oh." Did I really not close the door when I got home? Well, I guess with the upstairs neighbor gone, leaving just Lily and me in the building, I must have forgotten to flip the lock on my way downstairs. But that still left... "How'd you get through the front door?" I demanded.

Solomon grinned and my heart almost stopped. He was beautiful. "Magic."

"Okay, Mr. Magician. You waited long enough for me, not to mention impolitely listening in on a private conversation... so what can I help you with before I kick your ass out on the street?" Solomon produced an envelope and a small box and passed them both to me. "What's this?" I asked, sliding a thumb under the flap.

"Your bonus check."

Oohhhh! Nice! I took a look at the figure. It was new furniture-nice. Maybe not Chilton-expensive, but I was definitely going to IKEA. "Kind of early. The case only just got wrapped up, and, I hate to add, we didn't even catch the guy." I opened the small box. A single donut. I smiled.

"Actually, we did. Our job was done the moment Ben Rafferty was taken into police custody. His escape proves it was him beyond doubt and we have plenty more evidence for MPD to talk across jurisdictions. We may not have Rafferty, but this is the biggest break in the case since he started operating."

"So, MPD are happy?"

"Not thrilled exactly, but they got a pat on the back when the case was turned over to the feds. They'll take it from here. All eyes are looking for Rafferty and Madeleine. We've got photographs, fingerprints, and DNA. It's only a matter of time before they get caught."

"How did Helen Callery take the news?"

"With her usual panache." Solomon laughed. "That woman is hell on wheels, but she's happy. Her business isn't ruined. Life goes on as normal." He stepped closer to me, the soft, dusky moonlight washing over him as it swept in through the windows. I found myself moving towards him, my feet carrying me on their own accord. We both stopped, inches from each other and Solomon gazed down at me. I wish I knew what was going on in his head, but if pushed into a guess, I'd say lust. I couldn't blame him; I looked super hot. "You and me," said Solomon, "where are we? Besides me being jealous as hell each time you went on a date."

"My living room?" My heart beat faster as Solomon's head dipped lower.

"I want to take you to your bedroom."

Funnily, my brain couldn't put anything else together other than, 'Huuuuuh.'

"I want to make love to you. All. Night. That's a promise. Then tomorrow, I want to take you to brunch. It's time we started dating. Properly. Like a couple."

HUUUUUH, went my brain again.

"I want you, I can't stop thinking about you. If it works out, and we both know it will, I'd like to spend every night making love to you."

"Who's going to work nights?" I asked, almost kicking myself for such a question. I mean, really, who cared?

"Who cares?" said Solomon softly.

"You do."

"True, I do, but stop deflecting. Throw me out, or take me to bed."

I did the best thing I could. The only thing I wanted to do. I took John Solomon to bed and he kept his promise. All. Night. Long.

Lexi Graves returns in

WEAPONS OF MASS DISTRACTION

Out now in paperback and ebook!

When a client drops dead during Lexi's spin class, she's not too surprised. After all, it's a tough class. But within days, another death occurs, this time, on the treadmill. Then, when her running partner bites the dust, it becomes personal.

Sent undercover, Lexi takes a job as Montgomery's newest gym instructor in a bid to find the killer. With her professional and personal lives headed on a collision course, Lexi is glad to take the case. Now she only has to convince her boss, and new boyfriend, Solomon, that she's ready to solve her own case after she learns a disturbing connection between the victims. Faced with complex and dangerous circumstances, Lexi needs all of her past experience in order to catch the killer before another person falls victim.

To make matters even more challenging, Lexi's best friend, Lily, is planning for better or worse with Lexi's brother. Just one problem: all the local wedding boutiques have been repeatedly targeted by a highly organized gang of thieves. Roped into surveillance, rather than taking any chances and losing her best friend's dress, which would ruin the wedding, Lexi risks having too much to handle. The only thing she has to do is put a killer behind bars, save the dress, and save the day... Piece of cake!

ABOUT THE AUTHOR

Author and journalist Camilla Chafer writes for newspapers, magazines and websites throughout the world. Along with the Lexi Graves Mysteries, she is the author of the Stella Mayweather urban fantasy series as well as author/ editor of several non-fiction books. She lives in London, UK.

Visit Camilla online at www.camillachafer.com to sign up to her newsletter, find out more about her, plus news on upcoming books and fun stuff including an exclusive short story, deleted scenes and giveaways.

You can also find Camilla on
Twitter @camillawrites
and join her on Facebook at
http://www.facebook.com/CamillaChafer.

Made in the USA
San Bernardino, CA
27 August 2016